MY MOTHER

Jemma Wallace

First published in Great Britain in 2020 by Trapeze
an imprint of The Orion Publishing Group Ltd
Carmelite House, 50 Victoria Embankment
London EC4Y 0DZ

An Hachette UK Company

1 3 5 7 9 10 8 6 4 2

A CIP catalogue record for this book is
available from the British Library.

ISBN (Mass Market Paperback) 978 1 4091 7356 4
ISBN (eBook) 978 1 4091 7357 1

Typeset by Born Group
Printed and bound in Great Britain by Clays Ltd, Elcograf S.p.A.

www.orionbooks.co.uk

Foreword

We are the 1 in 4!

One weekend, single mum Emma took her young daughter to the local cinema. When requesting a family ticket, the assistant responded "but you're not a real family". Upset and angry, Emma left the cinema and contacted Gingerbread, the national charity for single parent families. Together we went on national TV to highlight Emma's experiences and the stigma still attached to single parent families today.

Inspired by Emma, Gingerbread launched a new campaign, *We are the 1 in 4*, to challenge the discrimination often faced by the UK's one in four families headed by single parents. We asked supporters to share examples on social media to demonstrate how widespread this problem is; but also to challenge those perceptions and show real, positive images of life in a single parent family.

We had an overwhelming response, especially on Twitter. It was clear we'd started a really important conversation, with lots of followers sharing their experiences. Within a month of launching, we reached over 105K impressions on Twitter. The campaign caught the attention of Sam Eades, Publishing Director of Trapeze Books, an imprint of Orion Publishing Group. Touched by the campaign's message, Sam contacted Gingerbread to learn more about the organisation and understand how we could work together to raise the voices of single parent families.

We launched the "One in Four new writer competition" in September 2017 to find a debut writer with first-hand experience of life in a single parent family. Whether they had grown up in a single parent household or were a single parent themselves, we wanted to find a new talent to write a novel celebrating the brilliance of single parent families. Too often, diverse families are under-represented in story-telling or portrayed negatively – we wanted to change this. We wanted to shine a light on the brilliant work single parents do.

A publishing contract with Trapeze was on offer to the winner! The prize was to be awarded to the most original and exciting proposal for a contemporary novel. We promoted the competition far and wide, calling on aspiring writers to submit the first 5,000 words of a novel, a 500-word synopsis, plus a short bio about their experience of single parent family life.

We received a whopping 250 entries. Eight individuals were shortlisted and, in early 2018, joined Trapeze Books at a mentoring session to take part in writing workshops and seminars supporting them to learn new writing skills and techniques. This was a fantastic runner up prize.

Following the mentoring session, Gingerbread worked alongside author Tilly Bagshawe, journalist Marisa Bates, agent Rowan Lawton, and Sam Eades, Mireille Harper and Katie Brown from Trapeze to judge the eight short-listed entrants. The standard of writing and storytelling was fantastic, but we knew there was one clear winner.

Single mum Jemma's submission *The Truth About My Mother* was brilliant. A multi-generational novel following two women from the same family as they each embark on their own journeys through single parenthood in 1958 and 2012, Jemma's story explored changing perceptions of single parenthood. It was inspired by Jemma's own family experiences of her grandmother raising her mother alone in the 1950s. We knew we had an outstanding writer and inspirational story – we were delighted to give Jemma the opportunity to develop her book and awarded her the prize.

In 2018, Gingerbread celebrated 100 years of delivering change for single parent families. Today, our mission is to champion and enable single parent families to live secure, happy and fulfilling lives. One way we achieve this is to challenge the stigma that still remains for the close to two million single parent families in the UK today, and to celebrate the value that diverse families bring to our society. We are immensely excited that Jemma's novel will play an important part in helping us to achieve that. As with all single parents, there is a unique and inspiring story to tell, and it's time those one in four voices are heard. Well done, Jemma!

Victoria Benson
Chief Executive Officer, Gingerbread

Jemma Wallace is a writer from Edinburgh, where she also works part-time as a web editor for the University of Edinburgh. She has one son, Archie, and the novel was inspired partly by her own experience of single parenthood and her grandmother's experience of being a single mother in the 1950s. *The Truth About My Mother* is Jemma's debut novel, for which she won the Trapeze and Gingerbread 'One in Four' writing competition.

For Archie

Prologue

Silly old fool. Jeannette stares up at the kitchen ceiling and through slightly blurred vision notices a long deep crack running from one spotlight to another. From where she is lying she cannot see the clock on the wall and the loud tick-tock of time passing is becoming increasingly muffled. The sound has been joined in her ears by the steady beat of her pulse, as her heart continues trying to push the blood around her body, perhaps unaware that there is a leak; a slowly seeping wound that trickles through the back of her hair. Every bone and muscle in her body is protesting, aching against the cold granite tiles and her head throbs in rhythm with the other beats, from the spot where it hit the floor with a sickening thud.

In her mind she had fallen in slow motion; one foot whipping up, caught unawares by an invisible spillage, the other foot following closely behind, her hand trying to reach out for something to grab hold of. Lying here now, it occurs to Jeannette that this could be the beginning of her end. Eighty-nine-year-olds don't fall like this and survive. And if the fall doesn't finish her off soon, then the hospital diseases surely will. Another tear trickles down the side of her head.

Her granddaughter Amy had warned her to take it easy, to stop trying to do everything for herself and to wait for the home help, Shona, who popped in once a day to scuttle around, tidying sporadically while heating up some

I

god-awful frozen ready meal. Amy also insisted she keep the damn mobile phone in her cardigan pocket, so that if anything did happen, she could call for help.

The phone is ringing loudly now and vibrating, rattling its way across the small table beside her armchair in the next room, merrily singing out the tune her great-grandson Brodie helped her select. What was it called again? Something beginning with an 's' . . . silver, solarium . . . she can't quite remember. She supposes it doesn't matter now anyway and buoys her hopes by the thought that if she isn't answering her phone, whoever is calling will start to worry. Unless it's just those PPI buggers again.

Jeannette closes her eyes, trying desperately to take her mind somewhere else, somewhere far away. She is on the beach in North Berwick, sitting on a woollen rug next to her best friend Morag, their shoulders touching as they watch the children play near the water. Her daughter Judith, only three years old, is kneeling next to one of Morag's older girls, who fills a bucket with wet sand before turning it over and patting it sharply. The wind whips at all the children's hair, obscuring their faces from view. Jeannette's heart tugs as the memory pulls away, twisting into another. She is in the registry office watching Judith stand at the front of the room, holding hands with Tony. Her daughter is smiling euphorically, gazing at her soon-to-be husband, her hand placed protectively on the small bump swelling underneath the makeshift wedding dress. Jeannette feels herself trying to stand, she wants to get up, to tell her daughter that she's being foolish, that she has her whole life ahead of her; that this man, this boy standing next to her, doesn't deserve her love.

*

2

When she opens her eyes again slowly, the crack is still there, deep and black against the bright white of the kitchen ceiling. Jeannette knows, as she has for years, that there was not one person in the world that could have stopped Judith walking into that registry office on a Friday in the spring of 1975. Seventeen years old and swept along by a handsome young man; the brooding type that seemed to have all the girls craving a boy who would treat them badly.

Jeannette's dislike for Tony began the moment they met. He couldn't look her in the eye. Her own mother had been adamant; if someone couldn't look you in the eye, they were not to be trusted. Seventeen years of protecting, nurturing and loving Judith, stolen away by the boy who lacked the ability to cherish even himself. Judith lost that first baby at twenty-one weeks. She called him Jonathan and let the hospital keep his remains for medical science. Jeannette suggested they have some kind of memorial service for the lost baby, but Judith said she didn't want to think about it ever again, that she was sure Jeannette was happy Tony's baby was dead, and despite Jeannette's protestations, the void between them widened. When her great-grandson Brodie was born, they had shared a moment of reconciliation; the event bringing out an unexpected sentimentality in them both. They had even held hands outside the delivery room while they waited for Amy to be checked over. If only they could have made it last.

Jeannette groans loudly as another sharp pain shoots up through her left leg and hip and more tears spill down the side of her face, the liquid collecting in her ear, deafening her further. She'd thought about her life decisions so many times and been certain she had made the right ones, but suddenly the image of her own childhood projects in her mind, starkly contrasted against her memories of Morag's family home;

bustling and full of happiness and life. Something splits. A door to a room she has never wanted to explore creaks open and Jeannette begins to understand why Judith felt as though she had missed out on something growing up. They only ever had each other, just the two of them. She understands now because she had felt it too as a child, she was feeling it now; the loneliness was overwhelming.

There had been suggestions made throughout Jeannette's pregnancy of adoption; it was the only option available to so many unmarried mothers, but one she had vied strongly against, despite the difficulties she would inevitably face. But lying here, Jeannette begins to wonder for the first time if Judith would have been happier being adopted into a big family; if she would have thrived among brothers and sisters and family pets and, most importantly, if she would have been happier to grow up in a home where there was a mother *and* a father. They would never know now. The long-ago decision weighed more heavily than it ever had. If she died here today, she wouldn't be able to apologise to her daughter; to let her know that she thought she had done the right thing at the time, but that she might have been wrong.

Jeannette feels something trembling and thinks the mobile phone might be vibrating in the next room again. Perhaps it is Amy or Ben. Thinking of her grandchildren lifts her spirits a little. If Judith had been adopted, then Amy and Ben may never have existed and she couldn't imagine the world without them, or Brodie, all of whom fill her home and her heart with love and laughter whenever they visit.

A fresh wave of tiredness crashes over her, bringing with it the strongest desire to close her heavy eyelids, even just for a few seconds. At least she doesn't feel as cold anymore, in fact she doesn't feel anything much at all, which is a relief from the pain. Her body is light, as though she might float away like one of those helium balloons all the children get for their birthdays these days, and she thinks that perhaps she will try to move in a minute. Just a little rest and then she will have the energy to push herself over and maybe even crawl to the phone. It might still be ringing for all she knows; she can't hear a thing except the sound of water in her ears ebbing in and out, swooshing back and forth, and then she is back on the beach in North Berwick again and Judith is running towards her, smiling, her face visible, with her arms outstretched . . .

I

Edinburgh, 2018

Ben Aitken was finishing his third gruelling nightshift when the trolley trundled by, carrying another unfortunate victim of mishap towards one of the curtained cubicles. He briefly wondered if he should lend a hand before heading home, they were short-staffed as always, but one of his colleagues slapped him lightly on the arm.

'I've got this,' he said. 'You get off.'

Relieved, Ben was about to turn away, his thoughts drifting to the heavy feather quilt at home; he would get a few hours of blissful rest beneath its cocooning warmth, then eat dinner with his pregnant wife, before showering and returning for his fourth and final nightshift that week. It was only by chance, one last backwards glance, that he spotted the familiar slippers: dark-blue velvet embroidered with a thistle on the front of each. A vague memory of his grandmother sitting in her favourite armchair, peeling back the Christmas wrapping paper, exclaiming at how lovely they were, pushed to the front of his tired mind. He hadn't chosen the gift, but knew the minute he saw them, that when his gaze travelled up the trolley past the white blankets and thick black straps keeping the patient secure, it would be his grandmother's face he would see.

He had rubbed his eyes, exhaustion causing him to doubt

his own mind, but as he listened the paramedic confirmed the worst to his colleague. 'This is Jeannette Aitken, eighty-nine years old; slipped at home; blunt force trauma to the back of the head; possible fracture to the right elbow; consciousness inconsistent . . .'

'That's my grandmother,' he announced to no one in particular, and his colleague pointed him in the direction of the staffroom with an instruction to try and get some rest, he would come and find him as soon as there was any news.

Ben lay on one of the nightshift beds and dialled his sister's number over and over, listening each time to the voicemail for a moment before hanging up and trying again. He didn't want to leave a message but she would be at work by now. He knew her boss had a strict rule about mobile phones, but he kept on dialling, kept on trying, his eyelids growing heavier and sleep within reach despite the knot of anxiety twisting in his gut.

She should've been dead.

Her brother's words echoed through Amy's mind as she abandoned the car on the grass verge of the overcrowded hospital car park. She'd missed eleven calls that morning before managing to sneak off to the toilet at work.

'It's an absolute miracle she's still alive.' Ben had yawned loudly at the other end of the line.

'But will she be OK, is she awake?' Amy was locked in one of the cubicles, her voice low in case her boss, Christine, had followed her from the office. It wasn't unknown.

'She's been conscious but she's sleeping again now. When can you get here?'

*

Amy held on to her son's sticky little hand as they searched the maze of hospital corridors, following the signs according to Ben's instructions. Brodie spotted his uncle first, yanking his hand from his mother's and racing ahead.

'Hey, big guy.' Ben grabbed the little boy, swinging him up towards the ceiling before pulling him in for a hug. 'How're you doing?'

'Good,' Brodie replied. 'I've just had chocolate for my tea. In the car.'

'Lucky you.' Brodie slid down to the floor. 'Can you see that machine over there?' Ben pointed and Brodie turned; his gaze following the direction of his uncle's finger.

'Yes.'

'Well, it sells chocolate. And I quite fancy having some for my dinner too.' He reached into his trouser pocket and took out some change. 'Could you do me a favour and go choose some for me please? At least three things, I haven't eaten all day.'

Brodie nodded quickly and ran over, his fingers and nose pressed against the glass as he studied the vending machine's contents closely.

Amy pulled Ben into a quick hug. 'How is she?'

Her brother scratched at the light stubble forming on his jawline; he looked far more tired than she'd ever seen him, the dark circles weighing heavily under his eyes.

'I can't believe I'm saying this, but they've just sat her up in bed.' He gave a gentle laugh and shook his head. 'She was complaining about the view of the ceiling. Apparently she had enough of that this morning.'

Amy smiled. 'Sounds like Grandma. Do you know what happened?'

'She just slipped. Shona found her. She must've been down there a while though.'

8

'How long?' The thought caused Amy to shudder.

'They think a couple of hours at least. Shona feels terrible. She was running later than usual. The guy she visits before had some kind of faecal incident she had to clean up.'

Amy wrinkled her nose. 'But will she be OK? There's no lasting damage?'

'They're still running a few more tests but nothing bad has shown up so far. Euan thinks she should stay with someone for a while when she does get out though, or have someone stay with her.' Ben indicated another doctor standing at the reception desk, laughing with one of the nurses. 'I'd offer but Natalie's having a hard time sleeping and I think it might be too much for her just now.'

'No, you can't ask her to do that, not with the baby about to arrive. It's OK, Grandma can stay with us. Brodie will just have to bunk in with me for a while.'

Ben looked sceptical. 'You sure? I thought you had enough on your plate at the moment?'

'Well, Mum's isn't an option.' Amy sighed. 'Do you know she's actually living in that studio place now? I honestly think she's gone mad this time. Anyway, I'm assuming we can still get Shona to pop in and help out at mine, and I'm only in the office three days a week, so I should be around enough to make sure she's OK.'

'As long as you think you can manage.' Ben looked at his watch. 'I'll help out as much as I can, but I've been in this place for over forty hours this week already. It's been non-stop.'

Amy touched her brother's arm gently.

'I hate to break it to you, but it's not going to be any better at home soon. Babies don't tend to let you have much sleep for the first wee while.'

Ben yawned widely. 'Oh God, Amy, what have I let myself in for?'

They were laughing as Brodie reappeared at Ben's side.

'I got you Maltesers,' he announced, holding up three identical packets.

'Just Maltesers?' Ben raised an eyebrow. 'Was there nothing else to choose?'

Brodie grinned, revealing the dark gap where his latest tooth had fallen out.

'I like Maltesers,' he said, holding the packets tightly to his chest.

'Oh, I see. So, I'm not getting any, am I?'

'No silly-billy. It's one for you, one for Mummy and one for me.'

'What about Great-Grandma?' Amy asked. Brodie blinked slowly.

'Does she like chocolate?' He squeezed the packets more tightly, the paper crinkling in protest.

'Yes, she does. And she's here because she's fallen over and bumped her head, so some chocolate might really cheer her up.'

Amy watched this information seep into her son's mind. A deep conflict played across his features before he looked up, glancing between them both.

'I suppose, because she's not feeling well, she could have mine.' Brodie closed his eyes, his hand shooting out, offering the packets to either one of them as though they should remove them from his possession immediately, before he changed his mind.

'How about you give them to her yourself, big guy?' Ben took Brodie's other hand in his own. 'Come on, let's see how she's doing.'

'Oh no.' Jeannette wagged her index finger at Amy. 'No, no,' she said again, shaking her head. 'I am not being a burden to any of you. I will go home, to my own house, and I will just stop making myself cups of tea.'

Amy wished Ben hadn't left to get on with his next nightshift. Their grandmother would be far more amenable to any suggestions he made.

Jeannette set her mouth in a firm line and nodded once, resolutely. She was sitting up in the hospital bed, her tiny frame sunken into the giant white pillows behind. On the tray table in front of her was a rapidly cooling cup of tea and some toast, which she'd reported was 'very dry' but would eat anyway because she didn't want to make a fuss.

'You've been incredibly lucky, Mrs Aitken.' A male nurse stood at the bottom of the bed, scribbling notes on Jeannette's chart and flipping between pages. 'But the doctor really would prefer you to stay with someone for a while. Just so you can get a wee bit extra help with things.' He flashed Amy a smile. The blush began rising from her neck upwards almost immediately. She turned away and perched on the edge of the bed, taking hold of her grandmother's hand. There didn't seem to be any flesh between the papery layer of liver-spotted skin and the bones beneath.

'I want you to stay with us, Grandma. Please? Brodie will love having you there, won't you, Brodie?' Her son looked up from the mobile phone she'd used as a sit-down-and-stop-touching-everything bribe.

Jeannette tutted loudly. 'I don't want to be a bother to the wee fella, or to you, dear. I wish I'd just waited for Shona to arrive and then none of this would be happening.'

'Look, how about you come and stay with us for a couple of days and see how you get on. I'm not going to hold you prisoner, I promise.' Amy crossed her heart and smiled. 'Just for a while, until you're better.' She squeezed Jeannette's hand lightly.

'Sounds like a good idea, Mrs Aitken.' The nurse unclicked the top of his pen and slid it into his pocket. 'A day or two more in here first though. We need to keep an eye on you for a bit and then we'll get you home.'

Jeannette gave another loud tut and bit heavily down on a piece of the dry toast. It didn't look as though she had much choice.

2

'Hey kiddo.'

Amy let Brodie clamber up and wrap himself around her in their morning ritual hug. She'd noticed recently that he was getting heavier, almost too big to lift, which only made her more determined to keep these habits going while they still could, even if it did run the risk of back injury. She had watched Brodie blow out the six candles on his birthday cake the month before and experienced a flash of realisation that her baby was morphing into a boy all too rapidly.

She placed her son's usual breakfast cereal down on the kitchen table and gave his back a light rub as he clambered up onto his favourite chair. He crunched happily away for a few seconds before the first request of the day came in.

'Mummy. Can I have an iPad?'

Amy was beginning to realise that parenting was a series of negotiations and that six-year-olds were just obsessed with getting 'stuff'. Admittedly in the last year the type of 'stuff' had gone from pocket-money toys (plastic dinosaurs and small Lego sets) to much pricier items, such as Xboxes and PlayStations. She supposed it had only been a matter of time until it was the turn of the iPad.

'I thought you'd gone off the idea of having an iPad?' Diversion into a conversation rather than a straight answer was becoming her preferred evasion method.

Brodie looked thoughtful for a moment, batting his long, fair eyelashes.

'Nope. I still want one,' he said finally, before stuffing another spoonful of cereal into his mouth.

'Let's talk about it when we get home this evening, shall we? I'm just going to check on Grandma. Eat your cereal and watch a cartoon.'

She flicked on the small television set on the corner of the kitchen worktop; a guilty pleasure and sometimes all too necessary distraction tool.

The door brushed against the carpet making a low swooshing sound as she pushed it open and popped her head around into Brodie's bedroom. They had tried to clear as many of Brodie's things out as possible so her grandmother would feel comfortable, but there was nothing she could do about the dinosaur wallpaper and matching curtains. Jeannette didn't seem to mind. Ben had been to her house and picked up a few things to make her feel more at home: a lamp, her quilt, the jewellery box that Amy had been allowed to riffle through as a child to try on the various necklaces and bracelets she kept for special occasions. Jeannette was still sound asleep on Brodie's single bed and looked peaceful enough; lying on her back, eyes closed, her breathing only just perceptible by the slight rise and fall of the quilt. Amy closed the door again softly.

She hadn't realised how much she would enjoy having her grandmother come to stay with them. In the four weeks since she'd arrived, they'd fallen easily into a routine; Jeannette preferring to sleep late into the morning so she would have the energy to stay awake a little longer in the evenings.

'I spent my whole working life getting up at the crack of dawn. I think I deserve a lie-in these days,' she'd argued.

Originally this was so she could watch her programmes; the soaps, the dramas, sometimes the news, which she would inevitably grumble at, declaring the state of the world a terrible thing. More recently though, Amy and Jeannette would spend their evenings talking. Amy suspected she was enjoying the company more than her grandmother was, who was perfectly used to spending the evening by herself and had often expressed her contentment at living alone. It was something that Amy missed, however, being a single parent; not having someone to come home to, someone to talk to in the evening. Especially once Brodie was in bed.

The thing about their evening conversations Amy was enjoying the most, apart from the lessening guilt now she had someone to share a bottle of wine with occasionally, was hearing the stories about her mother, Judith.

Judith wasn't the type of person that shared information generally and certainly not stories about her relationship with her own mother. Amy had witnessed the rift between them over the years, but as Jeannette told tales of her daughter, her eyes would fill with so much love and happiness that Amy couldn't understand how things had gone so wrong between them or how they seemed to have reached a point of no return.

'OK, clothes and shoes on – they're on the couch.' Brodie, still at the kitchen table, had found his mother's phone, his eyes glued to the screen. He didn't respond.

'Brodie,' Amy said again, more loudly this time, gently removing the phone from his grasp. 'Clothes and shoes on now, please.' She pointed in the direction of the living room. The little boy muttered something inaudible but slid down off the chair and went to do as he was told.

By the time they got in the car that morning, Brodie had apparently forgotten all about the iPad. They drove up Easter Road, sailing through the series of traffic lights that on a bad day could double the journey time, passed the early-morning shoppers and workers scuttling along, everyone in a hurry to get somewhere. Brodie's school was near the nursery he'd gone to when he was only nine months old. Amy could still remember the tugging feeling in her stomach as she handed her baby over to a stranger, how she had stupidly never imagined life beyond maternity leave, but that all too quickly she realised she had to take hold of the needle that would burst the bubble they'd been living in. Of course, it got easier with time, as everything does. The girls looking after him at the nursery were lovely and Brodie thrived. Amy began to enjoy being at the office and relearned how to have a conversation that didn't always revolve around weaning and nappies. She had been dropping him off for his first day at school, in what seemed like the blink of an eye.

They found a parking space not too far from the school, a blessing which always made her feel as though the day had started favourably, then walked to the breakfast club Brodie attended most mornings, held in an annexe behind the main school building.

'Have a good day, sweetheart.' She bent down to kiss the top of her son's head. He grinned up at her, his blue-grey eyes catching the early-morning sunlight.

'Have a think about the iPad, Mummy,' he said, before dashing through the entrance, his schoolbag and jacket already scraping the floor as he shrugged them off.

Amy shook her head and smiled. Of course he hadn't forgotten, he was just playing the long game with her. He would use the drip-drip of suggestion until she could work out a way to fulfil his wants. He was a clever boy and the tactic had admittedly worked for him many times in the past.

What he didn't realise was that an iPad was currently behind a whole list of other things on her priority list including new brake pads for the car and a boiler service. It was how they'd lived for the last five years though, sometimes robbing Peter to pay Paul, as her grandmother would say. Juggling money and making things last was the norm, but she knew they were lucky really, that they didn't struggle nearly as much as some people did, even those families with more than one income.

The walk from Brodie's school to her office only took ten minutes. Christine wasn't a woman worth challenging on timekeeping and it was always a good feeling to know she wasn't going to be late, that she wouldn't have to run into the office already apologising for her existence before the working day had even begun.

When she first went back to work, her manager had been the lovely Sheila. With three kids of her own, albeit grown-up by then, she was sympathetic and understood that Amy's mind may not always be fully on the job for the first few months. Sheila helped her ease gently back into the working world and Amy was entirely grateful. Nick had only just left their lives at that point. Amy felt able to tell Sheila what had happened, about everything she'd been through and in turn Sheila made work something Amy didn't have to worry about, among all her other worries at the time.

When Sheila announced she was leaving, to partly retire and to do a bit of consultancy work, Amy had been happy for her. She never imagined her new boss would lack even the tiniest amount of empathy towards others. Even Christine's glossy black hair didn't dare go a strand out of place under her watch. It became quickly apparent that Christine counted minutes and micromanaged everyone's tasks and if things weren't done the way Christine would do them, there would be a protracted explanation as to why her way was the best way. Amy had Christine to thank for their military morning routine. The consequences of being late, even by a few minutes, just weren't worth it.

Amy was thinking about the day ahead as she walked towards the office. A luxury-holiday brochure required proof-reading and she was quite looking forward to the prospect of daydreaming about exotic foreign escapes while making sure the correct spelling of *exclusive* has been used throughout.

What she didn't expect, and which took her completely by surprise, was to be within twenty metres of the front doors of the building and spot an entirely recognisable silhouette standing facing the wall, a mobile phone raised to one ear. At first she told herself, *Don't be silly, it can't be him*, and tried to push the rising panic down. But as the figure slowly turned, still talking into the phone, and she watched his familiar profile appear, there was no denying it: it was him. He stopped as he caught sight of her and fixed his eyes on hers. His mouth curled up into a smile as he raised his free hand and waved and Amy felt bile rising, burning her throat. Fight or flight. She was always usually one to back away from confrontation, but something was pinning her to the spot. Her body began to shake but her legs were filled with cement; heavy and unable to move, she stayed rooted to the spot.

He walked towards her, ending his call, slotting the phone into the top pocket of his suit jacket. He hadn't changed a bit. His dark hair was a little longer but still styled in the same way, slicked over to one side. His smile was just as bright and unnerving, especially as Amy was completely unsure what her own facial expression was doing at that moment. She didn't want to be making as much eye contact with him, but her gaze would not leave his. She was seeing a ghost: terrified and transfixed. He was a metre away when he stopped.

'Amy,' he said simply, his eyes soft, searching her face.

She wasn't sure if her voice would work. What came out at first was more of a croak. She coughed, clearing her throat, felt the saliva building in her cheeks but forced herself to speak.

'Nick,' she managed to reply, before throwing up, narrowly missing his perfectly polished shiny black brogues.

For a reason she was unsure of herself, Amy agreed to meet her ex-partner at lunchtime that day.

'Somewhere public,' Nick had said, as if reading her mind. 'I'm so sorry for surprising you like this,' he'd gone on. 'I can see it was a bad idea now.' Although physically unchanged, there was an unfamiliar bashfulness in his manner, which Amy found unnerving. He was the same but different all at once. He offered her his silk handkerchief and led her to sit on one of the benches next to the entrance to her office. A few of her colleagues gave her quizzical stares as they passed. Some of them probably recognised him but weren't sure where from.

Amy thought she may have been in shock because despite vomiting, she hadn't felt entirely uncomfortable sitting next to him, just a little numb. She supposed that was why she'd agreed to meet him. He wanted to talk. Perhaps she wanted to hear what he had to say. He said he needed to explain a few things, no pressure and nothing heavy.

It occurred to her that the whole situation was entirely heavy, and it was just like Nick to trivialise things, but she didn't say; the power of speech having temporarily abandoned her as her brain tried to compute what had just happened. She managed to nod agreement to lunch, to the time and place and then walked (she must have walked but didn't remember doing it) into the office at 9.15 a.m. and watched Christine's mouth recite the same lecture she saved for all latecomers, hearing not a word of it.

Nick was already sitting at a table in the café when Amy pushed through the heavy glass door, a small buzzer going off somewhere behind the counter. It was just after twelve and the place was bustling with the early lunchtime crowd. It hadn't occurred to Amy that Nick wouldn't be alone. In the seat next to him was a stunningly beautiful woman with caramel skin and a long sheet of glossy golden hair cascading down over her left shoulder. The woman was concentrating intently on her mobile phone, tapping away using a manicured finger. She was exactly the type of woman Amy had imagined Nick would want to be with when she'd first met him; exactly the type of woman Amy wasn't.

Nick was focused on a folded-over newspaper, leaning back in his chair, shirtsleeves rolled up, an empty espresso cup on the table in front of him. Amy stood awkwardly for a moment before he noticed her, at which point he sprang up, looking nervously from her to the other woman.

'Amy, this is Vanessa,' he blurted. His head was pivoting between them like a tennis spectator. Amy had never seen him as jittery as this; certainly not in public.

Vanessa looked up from her phone, her eyes travelling slowly down the full length of Amy and back up again. 'Hello,' she said, unsmiling.

Nick indicated the chair opposite his. Amy sat without removing her coat.

'Tea?' he guessed, signalling the waitress. Amy nodded. Vanessa placed her mobile phone face down on the table in front of her and fixed her gaze upon Amy.

'Would you like something to eat?' Nick went on. 'They've got sandwiches and . . .'

'No, thank you.' Amy could feel the black crow in her stomach unfurl its wings. Sitting across from her ex-boyfriend and his new girlfriend was causing the bird that had haunted her since childhood to express discomfort. Her grandmother had likened the feeling to butterflies once but Amy had been allowed to watch Hitchcock's movie when she was far too young and butterflies seemed too innocent to be the cause of the feeling that would churn in her gut.

'So?' Nick leant forward, trying to make eye contact. 'How are you?'

Amy raised an eyebrow. She'd been planning on keeping calm but could feel the irritation creeping up through her chest, feel her neck beginning to flush. She pushed her nails into the palms of her hands, her fists clenched. When she didn't answer straight away, Nick realised. He placed his hands together in front of his face and sighed.

'I'm sorry.' He shook his head, chastising himself. 'How's Brodie?'

Amy glanced again at Vanessa whose stare was still fixed.

'What's going on, Nick?' Her voice felt as though it wasn't quite coming from within, as though she was listening to someone else speaking. 'Why are we here?'

'Look, I know.' Nick raised his hands up in the air, letting them land on his thighs with a slap. 'I am so sorry, Amy. That's the first reason I'm here: to apologise. I should never have run away like that from you, or from my son.'

Amy flinched; a long-forgotten ember of guilt sparked.

'I was all over the place back then, you know that.' Nick took hold of Vanessa's hand. 'I've been facing up to things recently, talking.' He delivered one of his dazzling grins to his girlfriend. Vanessa returned an almost identical facial

21

expression, then looked back again at Amy, the smile slipping from her face like melting ice cream.

'I'm pregnant,' Vanessa said. The announcement landed on the surface of the table with the delicacy of a dropped brick.

Nick flustered. 'We weren't . . .' he glanced at Vanessa, a flicker of agitation crossing his features before he turned back to Amy. 'Vanessa wanted to meet you so we could tell you the news. She thinks . . . sorry, we think, it's important that I reconnect with you and Brodie, now I'm going to be a father again.'

Amy tried to swallow but her mouth was dry. It was all too much to take in, but then Nick had always been a bit too much. She looked again at Vanessa, who seemed to be challenging her to say something. In the end she plumped for the obvious.

'Congratulations,' Amy tried.

Vanessa remained completely unreadable; her features fixed. 'Thanks'.

'We're really happy,' Nick continued, squeezing Vanessa's hand before she pulled it away and began tapping on her phone again.

Amy thanked the waitress for the tea and took a small sachet of sugar from the middle of the table. She poured it into the steaming mug and stirred, watching the brown liquid swirl.

'How *is* Brodie?' Nick asked again.

'He's really well.' Amy kept her eyes down, staring at the cup. Why had she agreed to meet? She wanted to get up and leave, to get away from Nick and Vanessa and from their announcement.

'He's in Primary 2, isn't he?' Nick slid his hand across the table towards Amy. For an awful moment she thought he was going to try and touch her, then remembered Vanessa was there.

'He is. Like I said, he's doing great.' Amy glanced up. 'You're looking well.'

She wasn't sure why she said it other than a diversion felt necessary. It was also true though. It was why he'd always managed to get jobs in television. He was clever too, a really talented journalist, the camera loved him, and his charm meant he was never short of offers of work.

Vanessa stopped tapping on her phone but didn't look up.

'That's really kind of you to say, thank you.' Nick looked pleased, hopeful even. 'I'm so sorry, Amy, so sorry for everything we went through. I've told Vanessa about it all, about everything that happened between us.'

Amy wondered which version of events he'd given her; she was sure it couldn't be the full, uncensored story. Nick was never any good at painting himself in his true light.

Vanessa put her mobile phone down again and crossed her arms. Her stomach was completely flat; Amy assumed it must be very early on in her pregnancy.

'Our children are going to be related. I suppose that's why I wanted to come and see you.' This unprompted explanation caused another fluttering in Amy's gut. She wasn't sure how much longer she could do this. She simply nodded and took a sip of tea.

'Have you got a picture of him you can show us? A recent one maybe?' Nick asked.

Amy hesitated. She felt uneasy at the thought of showing Nick a picture of Brodie, now that he was virtually a stranger. The last time he saw her son – she'd stop thinking of Brodie as 'theirs' a long time ago – he was ten months old; he didn't know the boy the baby had grown into. What would he think when he saw how very like Amy Brodie had become, how he didn't have Nick's olive skin or dark hair?

Amy reluctantly dipped into her handbag to find her phone. There were photos of Brodie on it from a recent trip to Edinburgh Zoo. Brodie posing like a meerkat; Brodie doing a monkey impression; Brodie walking towards the camera like a penguin, his hands straight down by his sides, face cracking with a huge grin. She handed Nick the phone, showing a photo of her son sitting at a picnic bench, a huge ice cream cone in one hand, his other one giving the camera a thumbs up.

'Oh wow . . . can I just . . .' Nick took the phone and studied the picture closely. He stared for a long time; his eyes flicking over every detail. 'Is he tall?' he asked eventually. Amy felt a sudden flash of fear; a long-forgotten Pavlovian response to Nick's areas of sensitivity. His height, or lack of it, had always been an issue; she had built up quite a collection of flat shoes throughout their relationship.

'He's quite tall, yes.' Amy reached forward for the phone, unnerved that Nick looked as though he might be about to cry.

She had witnessed him crying on numerous occasions before. At the beginning she had thought it was endearing; a man who was comfortable enough to show his emotions. In time though his tears were often of regret or self-pity, the memory of which was making her feel increasingly uncomfortable now. Nick sniffed and ran a hand through his hair as he passed the phone back, quickly plastering a smile onto his face.

'Would you mind sending me some photos?' he asked. 'I know it's cheeky, and I know we've got masses to talk about, but I've really missed him.'

Amy didn't know what to say. It was incredibly difficult to reconcile the man sitting across from her, with his mild manners and emotional response to a photograph, with the man from years before who'd thrown a full bottle of baby milk directly at her chest at 3 a.m. one morning when Brodie was only a few weeks old. Amy wondered fleetingly if he'd mentioned that incident to Vanessa.

'I need some time, Nick. It's been so long and so much has happened. This' – she spread her hands wide – 'is a lot to take in. I know we need to talk about things, about Brodie, but I just need a bit of space to think about all this first, if that's OK.'

Nick smiled. One of his television smiles.

'Of course, of course! I know you need time. I just want a chance to prove to you that I've changed. I want you to know you can trust me. I *need* you to know you can trust me.' He put his arm around Vanessa's shoulders. 'And I'm so glad our news hasn't freaked you out too much.'

Amy swallowed another mouthful of tea, trying to push down a response along with all the memories of Nick that were flooding through her mind, some bad but others good. Because there were good memories too, enough of them to have made her doubt the worst ones at times. For some reason, the most prominent recollection she was having trouble squashing down was of the time when they had been lying in bed, Brodie in between them, Nick saying how amazing it was that they'd created this little person together, how it proved their love for each other was so strong, strong enough to have produced this perfect little human being.

She shook her head of the thought and stood, picking her bag up from the floor. The café had become too hot; the air thick and humid from the constant hissing of the coffee machine.

'Like I said. I need some time.'

'Absolutely, there's no pressure. Can we keep in touch a bit and maybe meet again? Perhaps I could see Brodie, once we've had a chance to talk, I mean?'

She nodded. 'I'll be in touch. I better get back to work.'

Christine would be watching how long she was away for lunch, making sure she made up time for her lateness that morning.

Nick pushed back his chair, but Vanessa remained seated. She glanced up and gave Amy a small, insincere smile, then went back to her phone.

'You're looking great too by the way.' Nick reached out and gently touched the side of her arm, his eyes fixed on hers momentarily until Amy couldn't bear it a second longer and looked away. 'You look really well; really happy.'

'I am,' she replied, nodding once and turning to leave. The crow was now beating its wings, threatening to launch into full flight.

By the time she'd finished work, picked Brodie up from after-school club and put her key in the front door, Amy thought she may be about to collapse. Jeannette was sitting in the squishy beige corduroy armchair she'd adopted as her preferred position in the living room, watching the end of one of her favourite soaps, the volume turned up so high it was making Amy's head thump.

'My wee scone, how was school?'

Brodie was already beside Jeannette, unzipping his school bag and dragging out a huge piece of paper covered in various patches of bright felt-tip pen.

'Look at this Gee-Gee,' he said, unfurling the paper. 'I did a picture of everyone in our family tree. See, there's you at the top.' He pointed at a stick figure wearing a purple dress.

Amy stabbed at the minus volume button on the remote control.

'And there's Nana, and my mum. Miss Swinton says we've to do the other bits at home.' Amy caught Jeannette's eye. 'I told them I don't have a dad, but Rory says I have to have a dad because everyone does. I don't have a dad though, do I, Mum?'

Amy wondered if the universe was conspiring against her, or if she had just buried the truth for so long that it had all built to a bursting point, which happened to be today. It wasn't the first time Brodie had asked about his dad and she supposed she'd told him that a dad was someone that was around and who took care of his children. Brodie had obviously taken this literally to mean he didn't have a father at all.

Jeannette and Brodie were both watching her expectantly.

'Well, it does take a man and a woman to have a baby.' She paused, trying to gather her thoughts. Why hadn't she prepared properly for this. 'So, there was a man who gave me something to help me make you.' Brodie's brow furrowed with confusion. Jeannette raised an eyebrow at her granddaughter.

'What did he give you to make me with?'

Amy looked furtively around the room. She could feel small pools of sweat beginning to gather under the creases of her arms. She noticed the spider plant dangling down over the windowsill.

'A seed. Someone gave me a seed to make you with.'

'Who?'

'It was . . .' Amy stuttered, pleading with Jeannette silently for some assistance.

'It was a very kind someone and we'll have to try and find out for you, OK, Brodie? Now go and wash your hands while Mum and I get the tea on.' Jeannette patted Brodie on the back, who followed her instructions with the newly developed obedience he saved only for his great-grandmother: she only had to ask once.

As they listened to the water running in the bathroom, Amy slumped down on the sofa. Closing her eyes and letting her head roll back, she let out a long, slow sigh.

'Thank you,' she said eventually.

'He's going to want to know more, you know. You're going to have to come up with some real answers very soon for that little boy.'

'I know, I know. I just don't have a clue what to say. Where do I start? He's still too little to understand.' An image of Nick sitting at the café table that afternoon flashed through her mind. 'He turned up today, this morning. At my work.'

'Who did?'

'Nick. He's got a new girlfriend. I met them at lunchtime. She's pregnant.'

Jeannette pursed her lips. 'Oh my. So, he wants to be back in touch with Brodie to prove he can be a father?'

'I don't know if that's it. I think he might've grown up a bit. Changed maybe. He seemed different, calmer somehow.'

'He'd have to change quite a bit from what I remember if he was going to make up for the way he behaved before.'

'Brodie needs a father.'

'Does he?' Jeannette left the question hanging between them as Brodie ran back into the room and jumped onto the sofa next to Amy. She pulled him down towards her into a hug.

'Fish fingers OK for tea?' she asked.

When Friday night finally arrived, Amy had successfully managed to avoid any more 'Dad' questions by hiding Brodie's family tree picture behind the sideboard in the living room. She knew this was weak-willed and wouldn't last forever but she needed some time to think about what she was going to do. Nick had been in touch earlier in the day – just a text to ask if it might be possible for them to meet up again but the response weighed heavily on her mind. He was keen to meet Brodie but understood if that would take more time.

With Brodie tucked up on one side of her double bed, Amy kissed him goodnight.

'I'll check on you in five minutes.'

'Promise?' Brodie's eyelids were already heavy. Amy knew that in five minutes he would be sound asleep.

'Promise,' she replied, kissing his forehead one more time. 'Sweet dreams,' she whispered as she pulled the bedroom door to, leaving it slightly ajar to let in a slither of light from the hallway.

In the kitchen, Amy opened the fridge and poured herself a large glass of white wine, condensation immediately forming on the outside of the glass. In a smaller glass she poured some sherry for Jeannette. Lifting it to her nose, she sniffed and was reminded, as she always was, of her dislike for the sweet liquor.

'Are you sure you don't want some white?' Amy asked, handing over the drink.

'No dear, this is lovely, thank you.' Jeannette took the glass and tapped it lightly on Amy's.

'Cheers,' they said simultaneously.

Amy sat down in the corner of the sofa, curling her legs underneath herself and savoured the first mouthful of cool liquid.

'I needed this.'

Jeannette took a sip of her own drink. 'It's certainly been a busy few weeks.'

For once, the television or radio wasn't on and Amy was glad of the silence. Jeannette had been attempting the puzzles in her weekly magazine, but Amy could see that even through her thick glasses, her grandmother was struggling to read the clues.

'What am I going to do, Grandma?' Amy felt the recent events beginning to overwhelm her. She wiped quickly at a tear that rolled down her cheek, struggling to hold back the torrent that threatened to follow if she were to let it.

'That depends. Do you think it would be a good idea for Nick to be involved in Brodie's life, or yours for that matter? Do you trust him?'

Amy drank some more wine. Nick and trust were two things she hadn't married together for such a long time.

'It feels like he's a complete a stranger now. I've been thinking about what I said about Brodie needing a dad. I wasn't thinking straight. It would be great for him to have a dad, but he has to be a positive thing in his life. I'm just not sure whether to believe Nick, whether he's changed. Oh, I don't know, it's all too confusing.'

Jeannette took another small sip of her sherry.

'I do have some experience of being a single parent, remember? I know how hard it can be, believe me. When I was bringing up your mother, there was very little sympathy for someone in my situation.'

'But it must've been easier, being able to tell people you were a widow? Even now people would judge me less if Brodie's father had died rather than just ran away.'

'What made you think I was a widow, dear?'

Amy frowned, trying to think back.

'Emmm . . . you told me I think, when we lived at Morag's. You told me my grandfather had died a long time ago.'

'I suppose he was your grandfather, but I find it difficult to think of him as that because we were never married.'

30

'I don't understand. Did he die before you had a chance to get married?'

Jeannette laughed lightly, shaking her head.

'No, dear. George couldn't have married me because he was married to someone else.'

Amy sat up straight, pulling her legs out from underneath her and leant forward, cradling her wine glass in both hands.

'Wait a minute. Are you saying you had an affair? Grandma! Why have you never told me this? Does Mum know?'

'Och wheesht, lassie. Your mum probably knows as much as you do now, and that's because she's never taken an interest in asking me any questions as a grown-up. I couldn't have told her the truth when she was little and by the time she was a teenager . . . well, you've seen how she is with me.'

'Why is it that you and Mum have never been able to make up? Surely when she left my dad, it should've got better?'

'Oh, lots of reasons probably. Some of which I most likely don't even know. But I told her not to marry your dad and I think that remains the main cause . . . among other things perhaps.' Jeannette took a deep breath as though transporting herself back to that moment in her mind. 'She was seventeen and completely full of herself and when I met your dad I could tell it was a disaster waiting to happen. But she did it anyway. And then, when she was pregnant with your brother and your father was carrying on with his nonsense, she arrived at my door one night and asked to come home.'

Amy had never heard this story before. She leant further forward, listening intently.

'I told her she'd made her bed and she could lie in it. She's never forgiven me for that. I'm not sure I've ever forgiven myself.'

'What was my dad doing that was so bad?'

'Nothing to your mum, really. I suppose that's why I didn't let her come home. I thought Tony wouldn't hurt her. Not physically anyway. He was full of anger, but he always had the good grace to take it out on the largest man in the pub. I don't suppose it made for a very happy home though.'

Amy thought about her dad these days; she couldn't imagine him complaining in a restaurant let alone starting a fight in a pub. He was married to Muriel now and they went to church every Sunday.

'And you've never had a conversation with her, about her own father?'

Jeannette shook her head gently. 'I suppose that's why I'm wondering what's the best thing for you to do about Brodie's father. I wouldn't want you to make a mistake or have to hide the past from your son.'

Amy swallowed another large mouthful of wine. 'I really don't know what the best thing to do would be. It was much easier being able to ignore it.'

'Not easier for Brodie though, dear.' Jeannette looked at her granddaughter over the top of her glasses.

'I know, I know,' Amy conceded. 'Anyway, I'll work out something soon. I just need to think about what's best. But in the meantime, I am genuinely shocked at your behaviour.' Amy laughed. Jeannette scowled. 'Sorry, it's just – you had an affair! Pretty bold for back then I'd imagine. Did you love him or was it just a fling?'

'Oh goodness, Amy, it certainly wasn't a fling. I loved George deeply. He was the love of my life. Unfortunately, I didn't seem to be the love of his, in the end.'

'And what happened to him then?'

Jeannette closed her eyes. She could instantly conjure him in her imagination, even after all these years: his smile, his long fingers that tapered elegantly, the trilby hat he wore and the dark silk scarfs he would drape around his neck. If she tried hard enough, she could smell his cologne and feel the touch of his lips against her own.

'Perhaps it's better if I start at the beginning,' Jeannette said. 'I think we might need another couple of these though.' She raised her empty sherry glass. Amy jumped off the sofa.

'Coming right up.'

3

Edinburgh, 1956

Jeannette had been working as Annie Forrest's secretary for just over a month when her boss's husband, George, strode into the office one lunchtime and, still wearing his hat, stuck his hand out for Jeannette to shake. She stood up from behind her desk, a little taken aback by the force of the man, and shook his hand. Their eyes had locked for longer than she would have liked as he flashed her a hint of an amused smile that seemed to travel all the way up his face and into his bright blue eyes.

Annie leant out of her office door.

'I'll be another ten minutes,' she said to her husband. And to Jeannette, 'Be a darling, Jean, and make this tired husband of mine a coffee.'

Jeannette nodded. 'Milk and sugar?'

'Just black.' George removed his hat and leather gloves. 'Allow me to help,' he began following her across the office floor.

'There's no need, I can—'

'I insist,' he said, cutting her off.

They stood a few feet apart in the tiny staff kitchen as she struck one of the long Cook's matches and lit the gas stove.

'Jean,' he tried her name. 'I'm not sure you look like a Jean.'

34

'It's Jeannette actually. Two *n*'s, two *t*'s. The French spelling.' Jeannette had heard her mother say this on so many occasions during her childhood that it was almost an automatic response to anyone who asked about her name. 'People always want to shorten it.'

'Ah, well that makes more sense. Jeannette is much prettier. And I agree, a pretty name should never be shortened.' He smiled.

She felt her face beginning to grow warm under his gaze and busied herself with the kettle, which seemed determined to prove the old adage.

'What is it that you do, Mr Forrest, for a living? Only if you don't mind me asking, of course.' Despite her discomfort at their proximity, her mother had always insisted on educating Jeannette in the advantages of polite conversation.

'Call me *George*, please. And no, I don't mind at all. I'm a lawyer. Obviously not here.' She could still feel his eyes upon her.

'Have you ever worked with Annie's father?' Jeannette gave up on the kettle ever fully boiling and poured some of the hot water over the granules of instant coffee.

'That was the plan.' He thanked her as she passed him the cup and placed it on the countertop. 'I was meant to cut my teeth elsewhere then come and work for Annie's father but, between you and me,' he lowered his voice and leant towards her conspiringly, 'the salary was always much better at the other place.' His smile seemed to be setting off something in Jeannette that was making the room feel too small and too warm for them to both occupy.

Annie appeared in the doorway to the kitchen.

'There you are. I thought you were lost. Come on, George, we'll be late for the Hammersmiths.' Annie glanced between them. Jeannette busied herself turning off the gas flame which was still burning brightly.

'Good God, we couldn't possibly be late for the Hammersmiths.' George placed his hat back on his head. 'Sorry, no time for the coffee after all, I'm afraid – I hope it won't go to waste.' He turned back just before leaving the room. 'It was very nice to meet you, Jeannette,' he said. And then he was gone.

Jeannette spent the rest of the afternoon typing then retyping letters as instructed by Annie. She couldn't quite understand why she felt so shaken by the meeting but was sure that it had stirred something within her, something she hadn't felt before. She wasn't entirely sure what it was and couldn't quite decide if it was pleasant or not.

Until the moment she met George Forrest, Jeannette's spinster status had been of little concern to her. She envied none of her contemporaries their relationships, least of all her cousin Jane, who had developed a facial tic within a week of marrying the dutiful Derek; a man whose compulsion for cleanliness required Jane to bleach their entire three-bedroom semi-detached house twice a day, once in the morning and once before bed. On meeting George, however – or Mr Forrest, as all the others in the office referred to him – the possibility had occurred to her that perhaps she was missing out; that the movies she went to see each week at the Cameo cinema were not all based entirely on fiction. Real love, she had decided, may actually exist. He walked through her mind constantly from that day. The notion of talking to him again, of being in his company, monopolised her thoughts. She began to know what people meant when they said they were drawn to someone; she had a desire to know more about him. It felt to Jeannette as though the moment in the kitchen was just the beginning of their story.

Jeannette was twenty-eight years old on the day she met George. All of the other girls she'd gone to school with were married by then. Her father had once attempted to orchestrate a union between Jeannette and a man named Norman, shortly after her twenty-first birthday. Norman, with his brown woollen suit and rapidly receding hairline, worked with her father and would visit them (invited, of course) on a Saturday morning as he walked back from seeing his elderly mother who happened to live on the street behind theirs. It was an occasion that she would be forced to join, the teapot going cold alongside plates of untouched digestive biscuits as she became increasingly unable to sit still and listen to Norman describing the complex plans that would finance his retirement.

Her mother, never one to suffer fools (although she suffered her husband for long enough), would make an excuse to avoid these meetings, something muttered about an arrangement with a friend, or a forgotten item from the shopping list, as she hurriedly took her jacket from the stand in the dimly lit hallway and quietly slipped out through the front door.

Jeannette couldn't remember on which visit it was, the fourth or fifth perhaps, that she finally lost all patience with Norman's monotonous tone.

'I really don't think this is a good idea,' she blurted as Norman sipped at his tea, the bristles of his well-trimmed moustache twitching slightly as he did so.

Jeannette dared a glance at her father who was predictably clenching his jaw, his stare warning her to stop right at that minute. She didn't care. She would happily accept the wrath of her father in place of the agitated ache she felt when being forced to sit in a room with Norman for any length of time.

Norman forced a tight laugh.

'Well, of course it's a good idea,' he nodded to her father for confirmation. 'Financial planning for the future is a necessity . . .'

Jeannette raised a hand. She couldn't bear to hear another word.

'Not the pension, Norman. I mean us.' Jeannette gestured between them. 'I don't think you and I are a good idea. I'm very sorry.'

Norman leapt from his seat as though electrocuted, spilling tea on the good sitting-room rug, flustering and apologising repeatedly. Jeannette felt a pang of guilt. He wasn't a bad man, just dreadfully dull. She'd embarrassed him. Her father barked at Norman to sit down but Norman was not for staying a moment longer and continued to apologise, gathering his overcoat and scarf, unable to make eye contact with either of them before he ran from the house, leaving the front door wide open so the neighbours could hear the commotion that followed between father and daughter.

Her father never attempted to introduce her to anyone after that and she had been glad of his eventual accept-ance that she would find her own partner, despite the ever decreasing possibility of this happening.

It had been over a month before she encountered George again. He arrived at the firm another few times to collect Annie after that. They would be on their way to lunch or to a gala dinner; Annie emerging from her office in a long gown she must have kept for such occasions in the tall cupboard behind her desk.

George always dressed smartly, his tall frame providing the perfect hanger for the expensively tailored suits he wore.

Jeannette had begun to think of herself as obsessed as a silly schoolgirl when, one evening, as she walked along Princes Street towards home, he suddenly appeared in her eye line, striding purposefully towards her. His face broke into such an enormous grin that Jeannette couldn't help but mirror his expression and she knew instantly that she hadn't just imagined something between them.

'Jeannette,' he tipped his hat as they stopped opposite one another. 'I see you've escaped the office.'

'I have,' she laughed. 'They do let us go home on occasion.'

She reached her hand to the side of her head, smoothing down her hair. Why hadn't she taken more time to fix it that morning?

'And is that where you're headed now, home?' he asked. Jeannette gave a small nod.

'I don't suppose I could interest you in a small libation instead, could I?' George tilted his head. 'Annie has the Women's Guild round tonight and I'm avoiding going home until all trace of embroidery has vanished from my home.'

Jeannette hesitated. 'I'm not sure I—'

'My treat,' he said forcefully, the flecks of blue and grey in his eyes dancing.

Ten minutes later, they were sitting across from one another in the refreshments room of the Princes Street train station, the air thick with cigarette smoke. Jeannette wasn't sure why she had agreed to join him, other than the fact that she had wanted to be near him. And she supposed he had also made her feel as though it was the most natural thing in the world for them to go and have a drink together. As she sat down in a booth in the back corner of the restaurant however, she immediately thought of Annie and tried to imagine what possible reason she could give for being here with another woman's husband. Guilt threatened on the

39

edge of her consciousness, but she pushed back against it; she had no intention of doing anything other than drinking a drink with this man.

The refreshments room was bustling, people coming and going in a constant game of musical chairs as they watched the train arrivals and departures boards. The waitress barely noticed them as she took their order.

'I'll have a single malt, double, thanks, and a . . .?'

'Just a small sherry for me, please.' Jeannette wasn't sure if it was the right thing to order but it was the only alcoholic drink she'd ever tasted; always a sherry at Christmas with her mother.

George clasped his hands together in front of him on the glossy red tabletop and leant towards her. 'So, Jeannette,' his mouth moved slowly over her name. 'What is your story? Where are you from? Who are you?'

'That's a lot of questions, Mr Forrest, is there one you would you like me to answer first?'

'*George*, please.' He nodded his thanks to the waitress as she placed the large glass of amber liquid in front of him. 'There's something very interesting about you, Jeannette. I don't think I've met many women like you before.'

'Of course you have.' Jeannette thanked the waitress for the sherry and then paused until she was far enough away not to be listening. 'There are hundreds of women like me, everywhere you look.' She gestured around the room.

'Not like you. I think you're a bold woman. I don't think you're like these other women at all. I don't think you would accept any nonsense from anyone.'

'Annie is a bold woman.' Jeannette took a sip of her sherry, the sweetness glossing over her lips.

'She is indeed. But her boldness comes from a private education and a father that championed success in all of his children, even his daughter. Your boldness seems more natural to me.'

'Does Annie have siblings? She's never mentioned any other family.'

'She wouldn't. If sibling rivalry were to have originated in the twentieth century, it would have come directly from Annie and her brothers. Each one determined to be more successful than the other. Do you have any siblings, Jeannette?'

She felt another flush of pleasure as her name rolled from his lips.

'No, just me. My mother was from a family of nine girls, so I have plenty of aunts and cousins scattered around the country, but no brothers or sisters myself. My father was an only child too, which perhaps explains his constant desire for solitude.'

'And do you have a desire for solitude, being an only child? I see you're not married' – George glanced down at her left hand – 'but is there a significant other, someone in hot pursuit of your affections?'

She knew he was teasing, and it struck her that if anyone else had asked that question she may have felt a prickle of annoyance. For George, she was simply keen to answer.

'Unfortunately not,' Jeannette smiled, looking up at him from beneath her eyelashes. 'I am a dusty, old, left-on-the-shelf spinster, I'm afraid.'

George let free a loud laugh and lightly slapped the table. 'Well, we must get a cloth immediately and dust you off! The shelf is no place for someone with a name as pretty as Jeannette.' They both laughed and Jeannette thought the sherry may be going to her head; she was feeling warm and a little fuzzy around the edges. It also occurred to her that she hadn't eaten since breakfast.

George waved the waitress over and ordered another two drinks. Jeannette began to protest.

'Nonsense, another one won't hurt. You don't have anyone waiting for you at home, do you?' Jeannette thought of her father. If he hadn't gone straight to the pub after work then there was a chance he would notice she wasn't there, but only because his tea wouldn't be on the table.

'No. No one at home,' she lied.

'Tell me about your mother. One of nine? Is she Catholic?'

Jeannette smiled. 'Not a Catholic, no. I think she just had a very young and innocent mother and a father with too much energy. I suppose you would've said she was a bold woman too. It must have been where I got it from.'

'She *was* a bold woman?' George placed his glass down on the table, wrapping his long fingers around it.

'She passed away,' Jeannette looked up towards the ceiling, counting the passage of time in her mind. 'Oh, it must be coming up three years ago now. Three years in September, that's right.'

'I'm sorry. It's never easy losing anyone but losing your mother, the person that brought you into the world. I think it's the hardest one, don't you? Were you close?'

Jeannette considered the question. She meant it when she said her mother had been bold. She took no nonsense from Jeannette's father, which was probably the only reason their marriage had lasted. Her own relationship with her mother had been tempered by the tension in the household, by the atmosphere that would buzz between her mother and father, the source of which was often a mystery to Jeannette until after she had gone.

It was then she had discovered her mother's secret; that there had been a baby, during the first war. The father was a soldier who never returned to make an honest woman of her. The baby, Lily, was almost two years old when she became ill and eventually died of pneumonia. All that remained of that part of her mother's life were the birth and death certificates and a photograph of the little girl sitting upright on a plump cushion, dressed in a beautiful white gown with a locket around her neck containing a picture of the soldier. Jeannette discovered the photograph and the certificates as she cleared her mother's belongings in the bleak days that followed the funeral. From his reaction, her father had known about his wife's past but was unwilling, as always, to discuss something that had clearly been buried deeply. Jeannette rescued the photo and the certificates (*illegitimate* written in bold script) from the dustbin outside the back door that evening, tucking them among the pages of a novel next to her bed.

'I think we were as close as we could be,' Jeannette decided finally. 'She taught me how to face the world and how to get up and on with things, even when times are hard. I don't suppose she could've given me a better gift than that.'

George lifted his glass. 'To mothers,' he toasted. Jeannette clinked her glass against his and noticed that his eyes were glistening a little. *Perhaps it's just the whisky,* she thought.

They finished their drinks and agreed it was probably time to get on with their respective evenings. George was sure the Women's Guild would have cleared out by the time he got home, while Jeannette had decided she would catch a late film at the Cameo; an idea that seemed spurred by the sherry, alongside a desire to avoid the cold, silent stone walls of home. She would hopefully be at the cinema long enough to miss her father stomping and staggering his way up the stairs to bed. Once his head hit the pillow, he was impossible to wake. The fire brigade had arrived in their street in the middle of the night once to put out a blaze caused by Mr Donoghue's pipe two houses down, but despite several attempts to rouse him, her father had simply grunted and rolled over, muttering expletives at the very idea of consciousness.

They parted at the top of Lothian Road. George was heading south towards Morningside, a leafy part of the city where the gentry spent their hard-earned money on huge stone houses with sprawling gardens and ornate cornicing in each room. The Cameo cinema, with its films written in lights and diamond-chequered entrance, was just a few feet away.

'Thank you for a lovely evening,' he said. 'It really was a pleasure.'

Jeannette nodded. 'I had a lovely time. Thank you.' They smiled at one another, their eyes lingering, neither ready to look away.

The cinema doors opened suddenly and a crowd of chattering people pushed out onto the street. George dipped his hat and turned to walk away. He glanced back once and gave her a small wave. Jeannette remained rooted to the spot, watching him disappear into the distance until he was finally gone from sight. She instantly felt as though the last two hours had perhaps been a dream.

The man at the booth repeated the ticket price to her three times before she handed over her money. She never could remember what film she sat through, alone, that night.

4

Edinburgh, 1958

If she had known how very alone she would have felt in that moment, Jeannette may have done things differently. Looking down at the tiny bundle, her baby girl tightly swaddled by one of the nurses in a white hospital blanket, an almost overwhelming feeling swept through her entire body, nestling down inside her. It was love, she was sure of that, but not a love she had experienced before. She had loved her parents in a way, her mother more than her father, whose own capacity for love was questionable. She was in love with George, her baby's father, but the love she felt for him was a passionate kind that lit her up inside, sometimes burning so brightly she wondered if it might fully ignite and ultimately destroy her. This love though, the love she felt as she watched her daughter's lightly fluttering eyelashes, dark like her father's, was something attached to her core: solid and sure.

They had met again, after the drinks in the smoky back corner of the train station refreshments room. The next time, it had been planned. George sent a telegram to the office containing only the name of a café and a day and time, an act that she felt was a little too daring given the proximity of his wife's office door to her own desk. She read the telegram, memorising the content before tearing it into the tiniest pieces she could manage.

45

She arrived for their second meeting unsure once again why she was going along with George's suggestion but with a deep desire to be near him all the same. They sat for hours, talking and laughing. It was a Sunday. Annie was at church with her family. George wasn't a religious man and had refused to step foot in a church other than on his wedding day, and only then under pressure from Annie's family.

'It wasn't long after the wedding that I realised we were more like best friends than lovers.' He'd taken a sip of his coffee and Jeannette jolted; she didn't think she'd ever heard anyone use the term *lovers* in real life before; it seemed awfully grown-up. She felt a sudden embarrassment at her own immaturity.

'We haven't slept in the same bed since David was born,' he went on to explain. Jeannette was strangely comforted by the thought, but unsure why.

'But why didn't it work? What happened to the love you had when you got married?'

George looked thoughtful for a moment. 'You know, I have no idea. Perhaps we both mistook fondness for love. All I do know is that it wasn't anyone's fault; not mine and certainly not Annie's. It was just one of those things.'

He had reached across the table and touched her hand at that moment and she felt something rush through every nerve in her body and she had a sudden urge to lean back across the table and kiss him. But she didn't, of course.

'Another thing I know is that I have never felt anything like this with anyone.' His eyes searched hers and a second wave of desire swept through her and she knew exactly what he was talking about; she had never experienced anything like it before either, but she was almost certain that it really was love.

*

Jeannette tried to convince even herself for quite a while that they were just good friends. It was how she managed the early days of their affair, how she managed to continue to work for Annie, how she could look her employer in the eye.

Then came the trip to York. He was going for a meeting, staying overnight, and he wanted her to accompany him. They travelled by train and checked into the bed and breakfast as Mr and Mrs Forrest, then had dinner in a small restaurant with red-and-white-checked tablecloths. Afterwards, they walked together along the cobbled streets, holding hands as though they were a real couple. George stopped just before they arrived back at the bed and breakfast and placed his hands on either side of Jeannette's face. He was staring so intently, she felt as though he might be able to see into her soul. 'You know how much I love you, don't you?' he asked, and Jeannette had nodded once.

After York, she could no longer convince herself they were just good friends.

The problem with being pregnant, she had found, was the bump. There was only so long that loose clothing could conceal the swelling belly beneath and, at a point, around six months, the situation had become undeniable. Her slight frame coped with the first three months as though she was just eating a little extra; too many biscuits with cups of tea at the office, putting on a little weight around her hips. She was fortunate enough that there was no morning sickness and, apart from feeling a little more tired than usual, she was able to carry on as normal, getting up each day and going to work with the woman whose husband was responsible for her burgeoning belly.

George had been relatively calm when she stuttered her fear to him through uncontrollable tears. She didn't have to worry. He would sort things out. He just needed time. She mustn't say anything to Annie until he'd had a chance to deal with things first.

'But she's going to notice, soon.' Jeannette had stroked her stomach. They were in their usual café, sitting beside one another in a booth near the back.

'And she'll congratulate you.'

'Only because she won't know who the father is. She'll be expecting me to hand in my notice.'

'It won't get to that stage. I'm just waiting for the right time to talk to her. I don't want it to come as a shock.'

'I'm not sure it's going to come as anything but a shock, George.'

Jeannette wasn't sure if it was because she was pregnant, or just very tired in general, but she had started to feel a little impatient towards him. He kept insisting he would deal with it, but time was passing, and he always had an excuse why he couldn't quite tell his wife about the pickle they were in.

And then, without warning, the day came. Jeannette had thought she'd known exactly how the conversation would unravel when she was called into Annie's office early one Tuesday morning.

'You're with child?' Annie eyed the bump as though challenging Jeannette to deny it.

Jeannette nodded, unable to meet the other woman's eyes. Instead, she focused on Annie's hand on the mahogany desk, her fingers tapping lightly, the heavy diamond ring she wore on her left hand clunking occasionally on the deeply polished wood.

'No one can know,' Annie said, finally breaking the silence.

Jeannette glanced up. 'I think it's becoming a bit too obvious,' she replied, looking down again at the blouse so tightly stretched across her abdomen, the threads in the fabric were beginning to separate.

Annie rolled her eyes heavenwards. 'I mean about the father, silly girl.'

Jeannette smarted. There were fifteen years between them. Annie, in her mid-forties, carried herself with the certainty of someone who knew how to handle anything, or anyone for that matter, exuding a confidence that didn't exist among the type of people Jeannette had grown up with. She felt entirely inferior.

The sun outside the window dipped behind a cloud, shifting the light in the room. Jeannette felt the blood rushing from her head, her whole body was beginning to tremble. Was Annie saying what she thought she was saying?

'You've been seen together. A number of times actually. I haven't mentioned it to George yet, I was waiting for him to have the gumption to tell me himself, but once again he's proven what a coward he is.' Annie reached across the desk and opened the silver cigarette box, not offering one to Jeannette. 'He's always been fairly good at ending these things before it all gets too complicated.' Her laugh was humourless. 'Not this time.' Annie flicked the heavy silver lighter and inhaled deeply on the cigarette, pausing momentarily before blowing a thin trail of smoke up into the air above her head.

Jeannette's head began to spin. Had he done this before? She could distinctly remember a conversation in which he'd told her he had never been unfaithful any time during his marriage. She was special; they were special. In fact, he'd been increasingly adamant, as the pregnancy progressed, that he would find a way to leave Annie, for them to be together. They'd even talked about having more children.

'What I don't understand, and hopefully you can explain to me, is why you thought you could work here while pregnant with my husband's illegitimate child?' Annie pursed her lips, folding her arms across her ample chest. She leant back in the chair and raised an eyebrow, waiting. The cigarette burned in the ashtray.

Jeannette was unable to stop herself from crying. Shame burned her cheeks and she bent as far over her bump as she could, holding her head in her hands as the tears turned to sobbing and her breath became shallow and she felt like she couldn't breathe, like she would never catch her breath again.

She heard Annie push her chair back, then moments later felt her hand rest on her back. 'Come now,' she said, her voice softening, 'it's not good for your baby for you to be this upset. Take a breath.' She crossed the room and picked up the heavy crystal decanter, the glass clinking as she pulled out the stopper and carefully poured a measure of the amber liquid into a glass.

Jeannette followed the instruction to take a sip of the brandy and then blew her nose on the handkerchief that was offered, the kindness in Annie's voice intensifying her own guilt. When Jeannette had finally managed to control the tears, so they only fell silently, Annie sat back down behind her desk, clasping her hands together and leant forward. She stayed like this for what seemed to Jeannette like a painfully long time. Eventually she spoke.

'It's not an ideal situation, Jean. I was disappointed when I found out it was you. I've always liked you.' Annie paused and let out another long sigh. 'I assume you've guessed by now that you're not the first?'

Jeannette felt a fresh wave of nausea crash over her. She didn't want to know if it was true. The thought that she could have mistaken what she and George had together clawed at her heart.

'My husband has a wandering eye, always has,' Annie continued, 'And men have desires. You probably know that we live very separate lives in that sense, but we are very much a team and there is no possibility of him ever leaving or, heaven forbid, divorcing me, to be with you. But I do understand that he has a responsibility.' She paused. 'That *we* have a responsibility.'

The sun reappeared outside the window, casting a beam of light across the room, dust particles dancing in the air. Jeannette felt the heat instantly building, along with a feeling that she had just lost control over her situation, that she would now have to come face to face with the reality: she was having a baby, she wasn't married, she had no way of doing this without help from someone and that Annie seemed to be hinting that she was about to be that very person. Jeannette looked at Annie properly for the first time that day, noticing the redness in her eyes.

'I'm sorry. So sorry,' she managed to say.

'Well, it's a bit late for that now, but thank you.' Annie nodded, rapping her knuckles sharply on the desk. 'I think it's best if you go home for now, take the rest of the week off.'

Jeannette began to protest, Annie interrupted.

'Don't worry, I'll make sure you're paid. Come back next week and we can work something out. I need some time to think about things.' Annie rubbed her temples. Jeannette felt her guilt grow a little more. How could she have thought that her love for George was worth the pain this would cause?

'Annie, I really am sorry,' she said again before leaving the room, set in the knowledge that no apology would ever be enough to remedy what she had done.

She had very nearly not survived the whole ordeal of giving birth. Amidst the bright lights and searing pain, Jeannette could recall very little, waking days after her daughter was born to an unfamiliar man, repeatedly asking if she knew what day it was. She tried to raise an arm and wave him away, the urge to sleep too intense. Her body was dreadfully heavy, as though each limb was lead-filled, pinning her to the damp mattress beneath. The man, a doctor it transpired, was persistent, however; his bristly moustache twitching, reminding her of Norman, as he asked again if she knew what day it was. Jeannette responded by retching, an action that propelled the doctor backwards. He was swiftly replaced by a nurse who held a stainless-steel container at arm's length and commented that it was 'better out than in'.

Jeannette had no idea what day it was. She had been peeling potatoes at Morag's kitchen sink when she first felt the pain, no worse than her monthlies to begin with. It could very well have been days or even weeks since Morag had told her to get into the Land Rover, she would drive her to town. She simply had no idea how long ago that had been. But despite this, Jeannette became almost instantly aware of the absence of the little creature that had been slowly swelling her stomach for the last nine months and cried out in an uncharacteristically dramatic fashion for her baby.

The last two months of her pregnancy had been spent living with her best friend Morag and her husband Tom on their farm in East Lothian. Her father, on discovering his daughter's situation, had tried to temper his anger, until one Saturday, after a particularly lengthy session in the local pub, he'd been unable to control himself; his shame had apparently grown in proportion to her rapidly increasing belly. He had dragged her by the arm, out onto the street and then retreated back inside his home, slamming the front door behind him. She was thankful that her coin purse had been in the pocket of the apron she was wearing, otherwise she would have had to beg someone for money to make the phone call to the farmhouse.

Morag and Jeannette had been best friends since primary school, living around the corner from one another for most of their lives. Unlike Jeannette, Morag had four brothers and a sister, all of whom she fought with constantly, seeking solace as often as she could in Jeannette's smaller, much quieter home. Jeannette much preferred the hustle and bustle of Morag's house, where there was always laughter, even among the shouting and arguing. It provided a stark contrast to her own father's unpredictable moods and explosive outbursts, borne from his apparent disappointment with life in general. If Jeannette wanted anything from a relationship, it was to have the exact opposite from what her mother and father displayed as a marriage. She wanted Morag's parents' easy way with each other, she wanted a house full of fun; noisy birthday parties with games and cake and too many people trying to squeeze into the front room. Morag had exactly this now. She had married a boy her brother knew from working one summer on a farm and had become a farmer's wife. Her transformation from city to country girl taking only a matter of weeks, as she mastered keeping a farmhouse ticking along with constant baking, cooking and mending. She even managed to survive wringing a chicken's neck in the first week as Tom's wife, although Jeannette suspected Morag carried more guilt for this act than she would ever be willing to admit.

*

It had taken a while to muster enough strength to sit upright in the bed and to hold her baby that first day. George arrived at visiting hour and they sat together, staring in wonder at their tiny creation, who was so like her father it was impossible to deny his involvement.

They had stumbled through Annie's discovery of their affair. George continued to promise Jeannette that she was the only one, that Annie was just bitter and trying to drive a wedge between them and Jeannette wanted to believe him, needed to; he was all the hope she had.

Her father had been given the news of his granddaughter's arrival but there had been no response; not that she had expected one, but it stung like a thorn all the same.

Despite Morag's hectic schedule, which included organising the lives of her five children ('I've become my mother, haven't I?') she had driven her rickety Land Rover into Edinburgh and visited Jeannette in hospital as often as possible, bringing home-made pastries and doorstop sandwiches, none of which Jeannette could manage to eat, yet she was touched by the gesture. Morag picked at her own food as she chatted about the farm or read articles out loud from the newspaper, much to the annoyance of the lady in the adjacent bed who made audible tutting noises. Morag would simply raise her own voice in response. Jeannette had been invited to stay with Morag and Tom again on the farm, as soon as she was fit enough to leave hospital. At first, she had refused, she didn't want to burden her dearest friend, yet, in truth, she could think of no better place to be. She knew George would arrange something if she asked him to, he'd already expressed his concern at her apparent homelessness, but she also knew the only thing he could manage wouldn't include himself. The thought of being alone somewhere, silence wrapping around both her and the baby, filled her with a haunted sensation of fear she had never experienced before. No, Jeannette needed to be swallowed up into Morag's bustling home and family for a while, needed to be surrounded by distracting chatter from the children and warmth from the huge stove in the slightly disorganised kitchen.

When the day arrived to leave hospital and take her baby home, Jeannette wrote Morag's address on the discharge form and signed her name as *Mrs Jeannette Aitken*, her usually neat handwriting jagged, as though an errant spider had stepped in a puddle of ink and staggered across the page.

George had arranged to pick them both up at noon and drive them to Morag's farm.

'You have to let me do something,' he had complained. He had also sent a package of gifts for his daughter earlier that week: clothing and soft toys and a sturdy carrycot that he assured her had a base and a set of wheels that turned it into a pram. It was the latest model, apparently. Jeannette didn't doubt it; he was never a man to scrimp. At twenty five minutes past twelve he arrived; his cheeks flushed pink. He'd had trouble with his car. He kissed Jeannette swiftly on one cheek, then bent down over the baby, landing his lips gently on her forehead. Jeannette saw two nurses glancing over and then at each other, eyes knowing. The glances during her time on the ward had taken on something of a theatrical production for Jeannette. The staff had assisted in registering her daughter's birth, an act that sent the rumour mill among them into quite a spin due to Annie's insistence that George be omitted from the birth certificate. Jeannette could understand the desire to withhold from publicising his involvement on a legal document, Annie's family were lawyers after all, and they would be advising in order to protect their integrity as well as their wealth. The rationale didn't make it sting any less though and although the word didn't appear on the certificate, the suggestion of *illegitimate* still burned brightly when the father was *unknown*.

Jeannette watched George gather the bags. He was preoccupied, she could tell. No point in asking him what with though, he wouldn't want to trouble her, and she knew if she asked him, his answer would be *Nothing*.

'I'll take these to the car and come back for you both,' he smiled. Jeannette felt a familiar push and pull within; a part of her wanted him near but another part fought strongly against his presence in her life. She had to stop herself from telling him just to leave.

He returned five minutes later as Jeannette was placing their daughter in the carrycot. The baby slept soundly, her rosebud mouth puckered, her tiny brow furrowed slightly.

George placed his hand on Jeannette's shoulder, squeezing gently. 'All set?'

She gave a small nod, feeling suddenly light-headed at the prospect of leaving the safety of the hospital for the unknown reality that lay beyond its walls. One of the nurses looked up from stripping the sheets from the bed Jeannette had only just vacated.

'You off?' she asked, waddling over to them, her rubber shoes squeaking on the linoleum floor. 'Let me have one last look at baby. She's been one of our longest guests for a while, think a few of us have fallen in love a little bit.' The nurse, one of the kinder ones, less guilty of the glancing and whispering, bent down to stroke the baby's cheek, her starched uniform crunching with the effort. 'Bye bye, Judy,' she said.

George and Jeannette shared a look, both smiling. 'It's Judith,' they said in unison.

When Judith was two months old, George picked Jeannette up from the farmhouse and drove her into Edinburgh, just the two of them. He had a surprise. They were standing in the stairwell of a tenement building in Edinburgh's New Town, George behind Jeannette, their bodies slightly touching as he held his hands over her eyes. He had covered them all the way as he led her up two flights of stairs, making her promise to keep her eyes closed and not to peek.

'Ready?' he whispered.

Every nerve ending still tingled when he was close. She nodded. He let his hands slip down, resting them on the sides of her arms. Jeannette opened her eyes slowly, adjusting to the bright light that was flooding in through the wide bay window. She looked around the unfamiliar space, noticing at first the small green velvet sofa and comfy floral armchair opposite one another in front of a cast-iron fireplace. A beautiful bouquet of deep red roses sat on top of a polished round table in the corner of the room. Jeannette walked towards the window where a rocking horse was positioned, looking out over the Edinburgh skyline. She let her hand fall to stroke the soft grey mane, the fine silky strands slipping through her fingers.

'For Judith,' George placed one hand on the rocking horse.

He draped an arm over her shoulder as they both looked at the view from the second-floor window across the city. The top of Calton Hill was just visible in the distance. Edinburgh's disgrace, the unfinished monument meant to commemorate the Scottish soldiers and sailors who lost their lives in the Napoleonic wars, silhouetted against the overcast grey sky. They had walked up Calton Hill together once, she remembered, before the baby. It had been a sunny but blustery day and George's hat had blown off and they had chased it down the hill together, laughing as the wind teased them, letting it drop to the ground until they were within grabbing distance, only to pick it back up again and whip it further away. That seemed to Jeannette like a lifetime ago.

'It's yours,' George said. 'The flat that is. For you both.'

'How much is the rent?' Jeannette was certain that she couldn't afford to live here on the type of wages she was used to earning.

He smiled. 'I mean it's really yours. I bought it for you. It's all above board, the deeds are in your name. I want you to make this your home.'

'And you?' Jeannette asked.

She didn't want to turn her head to look at him. She had known since their baby was born that the chances he would ever leave his wife were diminishing by the day. His expression was often pained; a man torn between two obligations, the more historic of which was pulling with greater strength. He turned Jeannette to face him, holding her at arm's length.

'For now, just the two of you. Annie knows; I couldn't exactly hide this type of spend from her – not that I would want to. She's suggested you might take your old job back, you know. She won't be there; she's thinking of doing some charitable work and there's a new woman in charge of all the girls.' George sighed, pulling her into his arms, resting his chin on the top of her head. 'Anyway, she wanted to give you the option of taking your job back. She's not a bad woman you know. She just can't bear the thought of a divorce.'

'I know,' she said, wanting to deter him from further explanation. Jeannette had heard this so many times before. George and Annie's son, David, was fourteen and being prepped for law school, he was their priority; their families

58

were entwined, mostly in business, but there were deeper ties there too. Jeannette had always known she couldn't compete with their union, yet for some reason held on to a tireless hope, a hope that some miracle would occur, enabling them to be together.

George let his arms drop from around her and stepped away, running his hand along the mantelpiece. 'I'll give you money, towards everything.' He gestured around the room, 'Other than this, I mean.'

Jeannette felt a flicker of irritation. 'Why would I need more? I can work, Judith can go to the council nursery. We'll survive.'

'You must let me help,' George pleaded.

'We can talk about it another time, let's not worry about it for now.'

She looked once again around the room and wondered fleetingly if Annie had chosen the furniture. It didn't really matter, she supposed. It was a home for her and Judith. She'd overstayed her welcome with Morag, although her best friend would never admit it. Jeannette needed to begin her life again, to be back in Edinburgh where she belonged. It was her home, her city. She was unsure about Annie's job offer but it might be her only choice; at least the girls in the office already knew her predicament. If she went to work anywhere else, she would have to keep up the pretence. She twisted her mother's wedding ring on her left index finger, a habit she was growing increasingly conscious of. It fitted better now that the pregnancy swelling had gone down. For his sake, she mustered all the enthusiasm she could.

'It's fantastic, George, really lovely. Thank you.'

She pushed up on her toes to give him a kiss on the cheek. The tension in his face immediately drained away.

'I'm so glad you like it. Let me show you the other rooms.'

He took her hand and led her around the rest of the flat and she smiled when she should and exclaimed at how large the rooms were and how wonderful the light was and how high the ceilings were, all the time feeling the familiar knot of disappointment in her stomach pull a little tighter.

The drive back to the farm took just under an hour, most of which they spent in silence. George tried to coax Jeannette into conversation, but her answers were monosyllabic, and she rested her eyes, blaming the baby and the sleepless nights for her quietness. The car rumbled along, grey tenement buildings giving way to houses set back from the road, before the sea was rolling by the windows to the left.

In a scene so distinct from the city they had departed an hour earlier, Morag was feeding the chickens in the yard next to the imposing granite farmhouse when they returned. She gave George a polite nod as he opened the car door for Jeannette, who shooed away his offer of assistance.

'Baby's sleeping,' Morag said, glancing again at George and taking her friend by the arm. 'You look tired. Let's get you inside for a seat and a cup of something.'

'I should probably be getting back.' Both women turned. Jeannette gently broke free from her friend and walked back towards George.

'I'm so sorry, this tiredness is making me forget my manners. Thank you for today. Thank you for everything. Can we talk later about it all?'

'Of course.' George smiled, kissing her cheek swiftly. 'I'll be in touch. Give Judith a cuddle from me.'

Jeannette nodded, watching him fold his long legs into the car and pull the door shut with a loud clunk. The tyres spat gravel as the car pulled away.

'Come on, Jeannie,' said Morag, as they walked around the side of the house to go in through the back kitchen door. 'You look like you've got something to tell me.'

'A house?' Morag put a plate in front of Jeannette, on which sat an enormously fat scone, fresh from the oven and split in half, two pats of butter slowly melting into pools of golden yellow. Jeannette's mouth began to water, she realised she hadn't eaten at all that day.

'Not a house, a flat,' Jeannette corrected, picking up a piece of scone.

'Are you going to accept it?'

Jeannette hadn't considered the alternative.

'Do you think I shouldn't?'

Morag pulled another tray of baking from the enormous stove. 'It's not that I don't think he owes you something. I'm just a bit put out that he's chosen the place. Why didn't he ask where you wanted to live? It just all feels a bit . . .' She paused. 'Controlling, I suppose.'

Jeannette took another large bite of the soft buttery scone and chewed slowly. Her friend was a magnificent baker. She really was going to miss the endless supply of home-made treats all the inhabitants of the farmhouse were accustomed to.

'Does Annie know about it?' Morag continued.

Jeannette closed her eyes, nodding. She swallowed the last piece, washing it down with a long drink of the slightly warm milk Morag had poured. The sound of a tractor revving in a nearby field floated in through the window, mixed with the shouts from a couple of the farmhands working nearby. They would be descending on Morag soon for some afternoon sustenance.

'I think she probably had a hand in choosing it,' Jeannette admitted, rubbing her temples. The fact the flat was on the second floor hadn't escaped her notice. It wasn't ideal to have to lug a baby up and down two flights of stairs, but she had accepted this was perhaps a penance, a small twist of a completely deserved knife from Annie.

'Oh, Jeannie.' Morag slid the chair out next to her friend at the table and sat, taking one of her delicate small hands into her own plump cushiony one. 'I know you should take it, it's a home for Judith. I'm just worried about you, that's all.'

Jeannette mustered a smile. 'It's fine. You honestly don't have to worry about me. Besides, I can sell it and buy somewhere else if we're not happy there. He says the deeds are all in my name. There's something else too.'

Morag raised an eyebrow.

'Annie says I can have my job back.'

Morag thought for a moment. 'What's that saying, the one about friends and enemies?'

'Keep your friends close and your enemies closer?'

'That's it. Well, you, Jeannie my love' – Morag waggled a finger at her friend and smiled – 'are in the latter category.'

They both laughed.

'Seriously though, do you think it's a good idea to go back and work for that family?'

Jeannette sighed. 'I suppose it seems like it's my only option at the moment. I won't have to explain my situation to them. Or worry about anyone finding out. I'm not sure how easy it would be to get another job anyway, certainly not if I admitted the truth.'

'Firstly, you would be able to get another job, I hope you know that, but you are right about one thing; you won't have to worry about your other obligations if you go back.'

'And secondly?'

'Oh. I don't actually have a secondly.' Morag smiled reassuringly.

The sound of the baby crying drifted down from upstairs. 'I'll go.' Morag stood. Jeannette began to protest but Morag shushed her. 'Here.' She placed another scone in front of her friend, along with a pot of sticky home-made blackberry jam. 'Eat this. There won't be any left once my lot get back from school and you're getting far too thin.'

They moved in on a Saturday afternoon when the rain was bouncing off the pavements and great torrents of water rushed down the gutters of Edinburgh's city-centre streets. It was the end of July and their arrival back into the rain-soaked capital was in stark contrast to the sunny, carefree days they'd spent surrounded by fields and open space on the farm. Morag's husband, Tom, lugged their suitcases and all the baby paraphernalia Jeannette had accumulated since arriving at her friend's house out to the Land Rover and took his eldest son with him into Edinburgh to deliver their possessions. Jeannette was travelling with Judith into town by train, arriving at Waverley station on the 11.05, where George had promised to pick them both up and take them to their new home. She couldn't imagine calling it home somehow, though she imagined that would be something remedied by time. She also couldn't quite keep herself from thinking about all the furniture that wasn't hers, about the colours on the walls or the long, heavy floral curtains that hung in each room, none of which she'd chosen. The rocking horse had probably belonged to David, George's son. The green velvet sofa, with its delicately carved wooden feet, certainly wasn't a piece of furniture she could imagine George, or any man for that matter, selecting. She had to keep putting it out of her mind. She was grateful and felt shamed by the whole thing simultaneously, having thought previously of herself as independent, always earning her keep and at times had even been the breadwinner, when her father couldn't work because he'd found himself spiralling into a bottle of whisky.

The alternative to the generosity that was being extended by George, and Annie, didn't bear thinking about. She knew of women, like herself, who had found themselves in a similar situation but didn't have any support, and least of all from the man who had been partially responsible for their position in the first place. Adoption. The thought horrified Jeannette. How could anyone survive their core being torn out as they handed their baby over to strangers? She knew she was lucky not to be forced into something she couldn't imagine ever being able to do. She knew that someone providing a safe place for them to live was beyond fortunate. But she also knew that she was now in a situation that she had never wanted to be, and that George had made promises, said things to her all the way along that had made her think he would look after her, morally as well as practically. She wasn't the type of woman to give herself away easily; she had never given anyone else what she'd given George, and perhaps she never would have, if she'd known that his words would never be anything more than just that.

5

Edinburgh, 1960

George insisted on taking them Christmas shopping to Jenners department store on Princes Street. Jeannette stood at the window of the flat watching for him long before he was due to arrive. She didn't recognise the car when he pulled up outside. She'd been expecting his blue Austin to swing around the corner but instead a shiny dark green car appeared, from which George emerged in his long black winter coat, his face obscured by the trilby he always wore. Judith was playing with her doll on the floor, pretending to feed the baby then tucking her up in bed under a blanket, all the while crooning a vaguely recognisable lullaby. Jeannette wanted to be down at the car before he had a chance to come up the two flights of stairs. They always had such little time together and she'd hoped they could finish the Christmas shopping and still have time for him to come back to the flat before he needed to go away again. She was hurrying to put on her coat just as she heard George slip his key into the lock. He was in the living room, sweeping Judith up into his arms before Jeannette had a chance to fasten the buttons.

'How's my girl?' he said, holding the toddler high in the air above his head before bringing her in against himself for a hug. Judith squealed with delight, placing her pudgy hands on his clean-shaven cheeks. 'And my other girl, how's she?' He turned and smiled, not quite catching Jeannette's eye, keeping his attention on Judith.

Jeannette felt the muscles in her shoulders tense. 'I'm fine. Can we get going? I was hoping to be back in time to have some tea. Morag's sent a parcel of baking and it's far too much for just us.'

'Ah, now that might be tricky.'

Her heart sank immediately, the response to such disappointment had become sadly automatic. 'Don't worry. You've got other commitments. I understand. Shall we go?' she said.

'Jeannette . . .' George put Judith down on the rug. The little girl stretched her hands up towards her father. 'Don't be like that.'

'Like what?' Jeannette snapped

'Like this. Please, don't. David's playing his bagpipes in a school thing at four, I said I would watch him. I promised.'

It was just after midday. Jeannette felt the familiar tug of wanting to tell him not to bother with them, to just leave, but it was fighting against the desire to spend even just a short amount of time in his company. She knew he couldn't ignore his son, knew, even if they were together one day and Annie became his ex-wife, the tie would always remain. He would forever be drawn in opposing directions.

'We better get off then,' she said, placing her hand on his arm and conjuring up something of a lukewarm smile.

They parked the car on Princes Street, near the entrance to the department store. Its opulence was apparent from the exterior of the building; ornately carved sandstone sweeping round the entire corner of Princes Street and up into South St David Street. The Scott Monument loomed over them from the other side of the road.

'Have you ever been up?' Jeannette asked, indicating the tall tower.

George shook his head. 'Not great with heights,' he admitted.

'Oh. I didn't know that,' Jeannette said, surprised. She supposed there were quite a few things she didn't know about George, having never spent enough time in each other's company to perhaps share the more pedestrian aspects of themselves. Their time together these days tended to focus on Judith; George eager to know all that he'd missed in his daughter's life between visits. Before Judith, they had talked mostly about their imaginary future together, the barriers to which were also a common theme of conversation.

George carried Judith into the store, Jeannette walked a few steps behind, watching him point out the lights and decorations to their daughter. She loved seeing them together, loved the way they were both so at ease in each other's company despite George's somewhat erratic existence in their lives. They made their way through the other shoppers, weaving in and out, through the perfumery with all its floral and spiced scents mixing into an overwhelming headiness, and passed the men's suits, which hung against polished wood, lights angled to highlight the expensive Italian wool. In the toy department, George let his little girl point at anything she desired, instructing the sales assistant to package it all for collection later. Jeannette was carried away with the extravagance. To an onlooker they must have seemed like any other family, albeit quite a wealthy one, but it wasn't the grand gestures and ridiculous number of presents that she wanted, it was just him, and Judith. She could almost believe in that moment that this was her reality, that the three of them were a family, like any other. A couple of hours later, when George pulled up in the car outside the tenement, however, she came back down to earth with an enormous crash. He wasn't coming inside, he had to get off. He apologised again. Jeannette and Judith waved as his car pulled away.

George arrived again on Christmas Eve just before Judith's bedtime. He insisted on making her hot milk and had brought home-made biscuits for her to lay out for Father Christmas. Jeannette thought fleetingly that Annie must have made them but didn't want to ruin their time together by saying it. Judith was too young to know what was happening but was clearly enjoying the fuss he was making of her. He put her to bed, Jeannette listening from just outside the bedroom door as he told her all about the man that would bring presents down the chimney that night and how she must go to sleep or she would wake up to a lump of coal.

Jeannette poured a whisky from the bottle he'd insisted she keep for him there, a single malt from Islay, where Annie's family owned a holiday home. George sat on the green velvet sofa. Leaning back, he stretched out his legs, laid his head back and closed his eyes. His face was drawn, more tired than usual. Jeannette sat down next to him and put her hand on his. He curled his fingers around hers.

'Will you come over tomorrow at some point?' She had been rehearsing the question all evening in her head, terrified of the answer.

George opened his eyes, rubbing one with his free hand.

'I'm planning on it, yes,' he said. 'It'll have to be sometime between brunch and the Queen's speech, I think. Would just after noon be all right?'

'We'll be here.' Jeannette hadn't told him that she had refused Morag's repeated invites to the farm for Christmas Day, just in case he could spare them some time.

'I won't be able to stay for long, I'm afraid. And don't worry about Christmas dinner for me. I won't want to eat one here then stomach another one at home.'

Jeannette smarted at the reference to home. She had wanted this to be his home. Had dreamt of them going to sleep and waking up together every day. It had happened occasionally, when Annie had been out of town visiting relatives mostly. It was never enough.

George squeezed her hand and, sensing her disappointment, gathered himself.

'Let's sort out these presents then, shall we?' He smiled and kissed her on the lips.

By midnight they had wrapped all the gifts for Judith, the pile under the Christmas tree enough for three children and an obscene amount for just one. They cleared the paper cuttings and stray bits of string and tape, standing to admire the tree with its lights and tinsel.

'I suppose it's Christmas Day now,' George said, pointing at the small gold carriage clock on the mantelpiece. 'Let's see if Father Christmas arrived for anyone other than Judith, shall we?'

He leant down at the side of the tree, picking up a package that was wrapped differently from all the others, indicating for her to sit before handing her the small box.

She pulled at the pale cream ribbon. Inside, there was a delicate gold watch, which sparkled in the light from the fire.

'Oh George, it's beautiful.'

He took the box from her and placed the watch on her wrist, fastening the catch.

'Beautiful and practical,' he said, smiling.

Jeannette laughed. 'I hope you don't mean to compare me to a watch.'

'You do have a very practical side to you, Miss Aitken,' he teased. 'Do you like it?'

'I love it.' Jeannette touched the watch face; it was almost half past midnight. 'Thank you.'

She leant forward and kissed him on the lips. Holding his face in her hands, she pulled back just enough to look in his eyes.

'I love you,' she said, unable to stop the words from tumbling out.

'I love you too, Jeannette,' he replied, kissing her again, more passionately this time, pulling her closely to him.

They made love in the bed that she slept in alone most nights, and held each other afterwards until George said, 'It's time for me to go,' and Jeannette watched him from under the covers as he dressed. She could see that his thoughts had already left her, that his mind was now occupied with his other life, even before he had tied his shoelaces.

Judith woke early on Christmas morning, climbing into her mother's bed before she had fully woken. Jeannette hugged her little girl, wishing her a merry Christmas before taking her through to the front room and letting her loose on the mound of presents under the tree. She helped her unwrap all of the gifts her father had bought and wished he could be there to see the sheer delight on Judith's face at the brightly coloured building blocks and the doll with its pretty clothes and the huge teddy bear with its red silk bow tie, which she hugged tightly and called Daddy.

By 9 a.m. they'd eaten breakfast and the thought of the few hours before George's visit was stretching before them, unfilled. Perhaps they should go for a walk. It was a cold day but crisp, no snow but no rain either. They would wrap up warm and walk over to the water of Leith, Judith loved the swooshing sound the river made as it ran past them on its way to another part of the city.

She hadn't meant to wander so close to where her father still lived. Judith had been toddling along and Jeannette had mindlessly followed. The streets were quiet, everyone inside their homes enjoying Christmas Day with their families. She began to feel a sadness creep over her as they stood at the end of the street where she'd grown up. She could see the front door from where they were standing. The small patch of grass in the front garden was overgrown and the fence crooked and broken. She moved towards the house as though there was something pulling her, a force she couldn't resist. They hadn't set eyes on each other since the day he had thrown her out on the same cobbles that she'd played on as a little girl, making up games with Morag to pass the time and their youth.

Jeannette picked Judith up, balancing the toddler on her hip as she stepped over some rubble in the front garden and, in reaching the front door, hovered her knuckles undecided for a moment before giving the door three sharp raps. The sound echoed inside. She tried again, this time using so much force that Judith giggled at the noise.

'Do you like that?' Jeannette whispered. 'Shall we do it again?'

She knocked another three times, more loudly again and they both laughed, Jeannette almost forgetting what they were doing until the front door swung open just as Judith shouted out, 'Mummy!' and Jeannette's father appeared framed in the doorway, unshaven, dressed in dirty clothes and wearing a scowl that would sour milk.

It was the smell rather than the sight of him that took her by surprise. A deep dark stench of alcohol mixed with body odour and perhaps a hint of something lavatorial too.

'Merry Christmas, Dad,' she tried, but he wasn't looking at her, just at Judith for what seemed like an insufferably long time before he turned and walked back into the house, leaving the front door open.

Hesitating a moment before following him in, Jeannette was thankful that the smell seemed to be local to her father, rather than to the house in general, although that wasn't in great condition either. There were newspapers and official-looking letters strewn across the floor, a stack of crumpled clothing piled on the bannister and a trail of empty glass bottles up the stairs.

The door to the front room was open, her father had already sat back down in his usual chair and was rolling tobacco into a cigarette, his head bobbing as though suspended by a piece of elastic, as he tried to focus on the task at hand.

'Dad?' she said. 'It's Christmas Day.'

He didn't look up. Judith was wriggling, innocently curious about the man in the chair. Jeannette let her daughter down and began picking up the papers that were strewn around the room. She'd never seen him this bad. His face was completely grey, unshaven and he clearly hadn't washed for days.

'Are you working, Dad?' She tried to keep her voice light as she picked across the room. He grunted and gave what she took to be a small nod.

Judith was standing only a foot or so away from him now, watching his long fingers attempt to wrap the paper around the tiny strands of brown tobacco, which kept falling onto the rug below.

The little girl looked at her mother and then back at the stranger. Pointing, she said, 'Daddy?'

For the first time, her father looked in Jeannette's direction and their eyes met.

'No, sweetheart,' she said. 'That's your grandfather.'

The old man bristled as though he might be about to object to this description, but his granddaughter stepped a little closer just at that moment and put her hand on his knee and said, 'Granda.' Jeannette knew that even her stubborn, cantankerous father would find it difficult to ignore her little girl, especially as she was now staring up at him with her big brown eyes and long dark eyelashes, smiling and waiting expectantly.

They left, an hour or so later, Jeannette having cleared most of the rubbish from the house and coaxed her father to wash and have a shave so at least he could listen to the Queen's speech later in a semi-respectable fashion. They weren't exactly back on the best of terms, but it was a beginning, perhaps a fresh start. She had watched him watching his granddaughter and knew that the shame he'd felt was melting, being eroded by the innocence that only a child can bring. They would never be close, they never really had been, but she cared for him still and wanted to help her father. With her mother gone, it was her duty after all.

It was just before noon when they finally arrived home. Jeannette half expected to see George's new car parked outside, but there was no sign of him. She took Judith upstairs, unwrapping the layers of clothing that would need to be washed after being in her father's house. The little girl settled down in among her new toys and Jeannette decided she would cook something of a Christmas lunch, even if George wasn't going to eat anything during his visit.

She was quite occupied with the roasting of the small chicken that Morag had sacrificed and donated for the day (despite Jeannette's insistence that she didn't know what to do with it) and not paying too much attention to the time as Judith popped in every few minutes with a new toy to show her mother, to which Jeannette would respond with delight. She'd bought some small sausages from the butcher and wrapped them in bacon, roasting them alongside the increasingly brown chicken and prepared some Brussels sprouts to boil with the carrots and potatoes she had peeled. Jeannette was not a dab hand in the kitchen, never had been, and probably lacked the basic patience required to ever become one, but felt as though she was doing a fairly good job that day. Pouring a second sherry she looked at the clock and went to the front window to see if his car was there. It was quarter past two.

They listened to the Queen's speech, by which time she knew he wasn't coming, then Jeannette fed her daughter some of the roast chicken with mashed-up carrots and watched with amusement as her little face grimaced at the slightest taste of a Brussels sprout.

She didn't feel like eating anything herself. Instead she poured her third sherry, promising herself it was the last and sat on the green velvet sofa, watching Judith build a tower of blocks, before they crashed down, and she clapped her hands and then started all over again.

Darkness had fallen, and the fire was hungry for more coal. Jeannette was about to drop another few lumps on the embers when there was a knock at the door.

Finally, she thought as she brushed the coal dust from her hands, *he's here*. And then, momentarily, she wondered if he had forgotten his key. She felt instantly guilty at how disappointed she was to open her door and see Morag's husband, Tom, standing there. He explained that he'd had an errand to run in the city and Morag had instructed him to come and check if she was fine, and if she was on her own that he was absolutely not to leave her there but bring her back to the farm for Christmas night. Jeannette felt hot tears burn at the back of her eyes but didn't want to burden Tom and so instead she did as she was told and gathered some overnight things for herself and Judith. She thought of her mother and put on a brave face, a favourite instruction of hers, and she talked with Tom all the way in the rickety Land Rover until they arrived at the farm and the door flew open and they were welcomed into the warm kitchen, full of people and chatter and laughter. Jeannette passed Judith to Morag's youngest daughter who loved little girls and then she hugged her very best friend and held on to her for the longest time because she knew, deep down, that this was where she was truly loved.

6

Edinburgh, 2018

'I always just assumed he was your husband.' Amy had finished another glass of wine and was feeling pleasantly light-headed.

'It's not my finest moment, dear. He belonged to another woman. It wasn't something I would've told you when you were a child, and I suppose even now it feels strange telling you. I wouldn't want you to think any less of me.'

Amy laughed. 'I could never think less of you! You're my hero. It's because of you that I knew it would be OK to bring Brodie up alone; because you did it all those years ago. Right enough, I thought you'd been widowed but that doesn't matter. I just want to know more about what happened.'

'Oh, I think that's enough for now. This old woman needs to go to bed before she falls asleep in this chair. Can you give me a hand getting through?'

Amy leapt up, placing her empty wine glass on the mantelpiece. The hour hand on the clock was almost at eleven. 'Of course, sorry, Grandma – I didn't realise how late it was getting. Here, let me help you.'

Amy bent down to let Jeannette put an arm around her shoulders, gently easing her grandmother up from the chair. She was becoming so light and fragile, there was nothing of her. Amy took her time, letting Jeannette shuffle her feet slowly along the carpet and out into the hallway.

'I've been thinking,' Amy said.

'That's dangerous.'

Amy ignored the comment.

'I think we should get Ben round soon to check you over. Or one of the doctors from the surgery, if they'll come out. Just to make sure everything's OK.'

'I'm fine dear, really. No need for a fuss.'

'It wouldn't be a fuss. Just a once-over, make sure you're recovering properly.'

Jeannette tutted. 'Amy, dear, I think I know if I'm doing OK. You must remember, I'm eighty-nine years old. I'm hardly going to be full of the joys of spring all the time.'

'I know. But it would make me feel better.' Amy lowered her grandmother to sit on the edge of Brodie's bed, helping her to unbutton her blouse before passing over the night-gown from the chest of drawers and turning away to give her some privacy. 'I'm just worried about you,' she said.

'No need to worry, dear. There's life in me yet.'

Amy had four missed calls from Ben when she woke at 7 a.m. on Saturday morning. Rubbing her eyes, she sat up and pressed dial.

'It's a girl!' he announced as soon as he picked up. 'I have a daughter!'

'Oh wow! Congratulations! Is everything all right, how's Natalie?'

'She's great, the baby's great. Everything's bloody great.'

'Have you got a name yet? Ben?'

Her brother was talking to someone else at the other end of the phone, thanking them for their congratulations.

'Sorry, Amy, that was a colleague. God, this is so surreal.

You have to come and see us. Nat's just getting checked over, but I think we'll be home tonight.'

Amy pictured Natalie's joy at the thought of Ben's family descending on her the moment she arrived home from hospital.

'You might want to give it some time before you start handing out the invitations, brother,' Amy laughed. 'Why don't we say we'll come over after I pick Brodie up from school on Monday, but only if Natalie is totally fine with that, OK?'

'Sure, sounds like a plan. I'll send over some pics in the meantime though. Wait till you see her, Amy, she's absolutely beautiful.'

'I bet she is.'

Amy ended the call and watched her phone start immediately buzzing as Ben sent through pictures. Brodie began wriggling in the bed next to her, his eyelids flickering open.

'Have a look at this.' Amy tapped on the first picture of her brand new niece and showed Brodie the screen. 'This is your new cousin.' She swiped through the four other photos Ben had sent.

Brodie studied each of the pictures closely. 'What's his name?'

Amy laughed. 'No name yet, I don't think. And I'm afraid to tell you that he is a she. It's a baby girl cousin for you.'

'A girl?' Brodie screwed up his small features into something resembling distaste. 'But a girl won't want to play with me. None of the girls at school play with the boys. Except for Zara, she plays with Michael sometimes. But only because she wants to kiss him.' Brodie stuck out his tongue.

'I'm sure your cousin will play with you, eventually. Not for a while though because she's very little just now. In fact, you're quite a bit older than her so you'll probably need to look after her a bit, teach her stuff.' Amy kissed her son on the cheek. 'Come on, let's get you some breakfast. We're going to visit Nana today.'

Amy's mother Judith was reinventing herself again. It all stemmed from a conversation they'd had back in the early summer of 2017. Amy and Judith were in the Marks and Spencer café on Princes Street one Friday afternoon where Judith had a job in the men's suit department, a position which allowed her to flirt outrageously while being paid, and all without having to get involved with or, thankfully, marry another man.

They were drinking lattes and eating toasted sandwiches Judith's colleague Sandra had given them for free, while Amy tried to interest her mother in the latest book she was reading.

'It's called *Life After Life* – it's kind of about getting a second chance if you mess up the first time around.' Amy took a bite of her sandwich. Her mother hadn't touched her food but was distracted by something on her mobile phone. 'I couldn't imagine wanting to go back and change my life, not now Brodie's here,' she went on, taking another large bite. 'What about you? Mum?'

'Hmmm,' Judith was waving at a customer she'd served earlier.

'Mum? Did you hear me? I was saying I couldn't imagine going back and starting my life all over again, could you?'

Judith picked up her sandwich, inspecting either side of it before placing it back on the plate. 'Sorry darling, could I what?'

Amy sighed; it was easier to have a conversation with Brodie than her mother.

'I'm reading a book,' she began again, 'about getting the chance to start life all over again if you could. It's really good . . . anyway, I was just asking, if you could start life all over again, would you do anything differently?'

'Oh, yes.' Judith looked thoughtful for a moment. 'I'd love to start over. There's no chance I'd marry your father again, or Ken for that matter. Despite the perks of that marriage.'

Amy chose not to challenge her mother on the point that if she hadn't married her first husband, Tony, neither she nor Ben would exist.

'But if you could do it all again, would you do something else? Is there a career you would've chosen?'

Judith had looked straight ahead, her eyes unblinking. After a moment she said, 'You know Amy, I think I'd go to art college if I could do it all again. I always fancied myself as a bit of a painter. I was good at art, at school.'

'You could go back,' Amy said, slightly distracted by a work email that pinged through on her phone, despite Friday being her day off.

'Oh, they wouldn't have me. I didn't even leave school with so much as an attendance certificate let alone any qualifications.'

'That doesn't matter these days, Mum.' Amy put her phone face down on the table. Work could wait until Monday. 'There're courses for adult returners you can go on, for people that didn't get the right qualifications first time round. I saw something at the Meadows Festival a few weeks ago. I'm sure I've got a leaflet at home.'

Amy forgot almost instantly about the conversation, but Judith, who had managed to master googling, found the access course, applied, had an interview and then arrived a few weeks later one evening at Amy's flat, brandishing a bottle of Prosecco 'to celebrate going back to school'.

Amy, although dubious about the swiftness of her mother's change of direction, was slightly in awe that she had managed to find funding, organise with her bosses at Marks and Spencer to keep her job on a part-time basis and was glowing with a purpose that she hadn't witnessed in years.

Judith had been on the course since September the previous year and seemed to be quietly enjoying her new challenge, but when they discovered just before their grandmother's accident that their mother had sold her flat and bought an artist's studio in a converted factory off Easter Road, Amy secretly began to worry. Their mother's single-minded determination had always been a source of marvel and horror in equal measure for them, and Amy could see Judith was getting carried away, the access course was her new Tony or Ken, her latest obsession to lose herself in. At least this time, Amy was glad it wasn't dependent on a man. At least this time it might make her happy.

The studio was in a huge red-brick building that was once a lemonade factory. A plaque on the wall next to the door that was now the main entrance to the building gave acknowledgement to the workers who supplied the city with fizzy pop for over thirty years. Amy wondered what the factory workers would make of the new inhabitants; if they would find the abstract sculptures and huge canvases splattered with paint interesting or irrelevant.

With everything that had been going on, Amy had been avoiding facing up to the reality that her mother was now living in some kind of artists' commune, and in turn had evaded visiting Judith in her new accommodation so far. But as her mother seemed to be fully immersing herself in her new world, she had decided there was no other option than to turn up and see the real situation for herself.

They eventually arrived just after lunch that Saturday afternoon, having followed the directions Judith had given them which had landed them somewhere around the back of the Hibernian football stadium.

'Can we go to a football match one day, Mum?' Brodie asked as he stared up at the huge structure.

'One day,' Amy promised, mentally making a note to ask Ben to do the honours.

The studios were up a lane somewhere between the stadium and the main road but there were no other people around and Amy felt as though she had walked into some kind of disputed territory. The derelict building opposite the old factory was all jagged panes of glass and peeling iron bars. She imagined someone with a sniper rifle, following them through a lens from one of the top windows and she quickened her step. Although her overactive imagination was really to blame, the place was definitely a bit creepy too. She covered her fingertip with the sleeve of her jumper to avoid having direct contact with the entry system at the front door. There was a sticker next to *8*, which said simply, *Jude*. She'd been making everyone call her that since she started the access course last September. 'Judith makes me sound like such an old fuddy-duddy,' she'd said.

It wasn't just the intercom that was filthy; everything at the studios seemed to be covered in paint or other unidentifiable substances. Amy could feel mild pangs of the desire to take a bottle of bleach to her immediate surroundings growing with each second she stood there. There was no answer on the intercom, which she began to doubt actually worked, and so she tried her mother's mobile again. It rang out and went straight to voicemail, as it had on the previous four attempts. Brodie was beginning to get impatient, trying to wriggle his hand free from Amy's grasp.

They both jumped a little as a girl wearing dungarees and a headscarf silently appeared behind them, her keys jangling as she indicated to get past. She pulled an earphone out as she waggled her key in the tarnished lock.

'Are you looking for someone?' she asked. Amy noticed the Irish accent as she clasped her hand to her chest in an attempt to still her heart from thumping. The girl was petite and pretty with dark kohl-lined eyes and bright red lipstick, certainly nothing to be frightened of. Brodie stopped squirming and stared at her. She wasn't much taller than him.

'We're trying to get in to visit my mum. She lives at number eight.' Amy pointed at the buzzer.

The girl stopped opening the door and looked up at Amy, her expression solemn. 'You know you're not meant to live in here. It's about the insurance.'

She turned the key and swung the door open wide, stepping back to let them pass.

'Of course, no one pays attention to that rule.' She laughed gently and winked at Brodie, who stared straight back at her and tightened his grip on Amy's hand.

Amy smiled. 'Thanks for letting us in.'

'No problem,' the girl said. 'Your mum, in studio eight. She's Jude, right?'

Amy nodded. The girl laughed her gentle laugh again. 'Sure, your mum's brilliant, a real hoot, so she is. I think it's just amazing what she's doing. Never give up your dreams, eh? Tell her I'll see her tomorrow, will you? I've lost my phone again.' She shrugged as if losing her phone was a regular occurrence and walked away, down towards the end of the corridor. Amy looked at Brodie who was still staring after the girl, transfixed.

'Come on, cheeky,' she said, squeezing his hand and leading him up a set of stone steps, covered in more paint splattering. 'Let's find out what Nana's been up to.'

*

83

It took five knocks for Judith to finally answer the door into her private studio. The painter's smock she wore billowed as she ushered Amy and Brodie inside.

'Sorry, darling,' she indicated the earphones now slung around her neck. 'I was painting to Elkie. What a woman, such grit in her voice. Real emotion too. So inspiring.' She waved a paintbrush around as though conducting an orchestra.

Amy noticed an easel at the far end of the room, the painting covered by an old white sheet. She realised she was yet to actually see any of her mother's artwork.

'What are you painting?'

'That, my darling, is a secret, a surprise!'

Amy shook her head. 'You've heard Ben's news, I take it?' she asked.

Judith clasped her hands over her heart. 'I have indeed! My lovely boy has a lovely girl. Isn't it wonderful?'

Parents weren't meant to have favourites, but Amy had long since known that Judith would save Ben first if both she and her brother were drowning simultaneously.

Amy bent down and picked up an empty bottle of wine from the floor, raising an eyebrow.

'Now, now, Amy darling, that's from last night.' Judith swept over to the counter next to where an old Belfast sink was plumbed into the wall and picked up a large glass of clear liquid with a slice of lemon floating on the top. 'Today, I'm on gin!' She laughed and took a long drink.

'For goodness sake, Mum, it's not even two o'clock.' Amy pulled Brodie's jacket off, laying it on the only chair; a huge round wicker basket affair filled with brightly coloured cushions. He ran over to look out of the window at the other end of the room.

'Is this what you're sleeping on?' Amy asked, indicating the chair.

84

'Of course not, look.' Judith dashed across the room and began unlocking what looked like a cupboard in the wall. She pulled down a full-size double bed, which landed on the floor with a loud clunk. 'Isn't it marvellous? The man who owned the studio before me built it by hand. A hidden bed!' she exclaimed.

Brodie kicked off his trainers and jumped onto the mattress. 'And a trampoline to boot!' laughed Judith, ruffling Brodie's hair.

Amy's phone buzzed in her pocket. Taking it out she saw another message from Nick:

Any thoughts?

She'd forgotten to get back to his text from earlier in the week. She stabbed out a quick reply.

Busy this weekend but maybe next Friday?

His reply was immediate:

Perfect x.

Amy winced slightly at the hopefulness of the kiss and put her phone back in her pocket. She looked around at the room again. It was fairly large, she supposed, and the huge windows at the far end let in so much light that it wasn't an unpleasant space. It just wasn't a home.

'Where's the toilet, Mum? And the shower. Where are you washing?' Amy was beginning to feel increasingly anxious about the situation her mother had created for herself. 'Do you still have money left over from the flat sale?'

'Oh, stop fussing, it's fine.' Judith waved her hands around. Liquid sloshed in her glass, threatening to spill. 'There's a toilet at the end of the corridor and I go swimming every morning at seven. I shower there. So, you don't have to worry, I'm not going to become an unwashed embarrassment to you.'

Amy wasn't convinced.

'We met a girl on the way in who told us you're not meant to sleep here. She let us in. Does the buzzer not work?'

Judith ignored her daughter's question; she was busy showing Brodie how to make great wide brushstrokes of colour on a blank white canvas.

'Try not to get very messy,' Amy warned, before immediately feeling like a spoilsport as Judith tutted and whispered loudly.

'You get as messy as you like little man,' she said, patting him gently on the back.

Amy rolled her eyes. 'She said she'd see you tomorrow, by the way.'

'Who did?' Judith picked up her mobile phone and began typing slowly with one finger, holding it at arm's length and squinting at the screen.

'The girl from downstairs. Small, Irish. Dungarees.' Amy opened the fridge under the counter next to the sink and took out a bottle of white wine. She noticed the only food present was a box of leftover Chinese takeaway.

'Oh, you mean Sian?' Judith smiled, still distracted by her mobile. 'Sian's a sweetheart. She's already at the art college. Says she'll show me around in September.'

'So, you're still going through with it then?'

Judith's head snapped up from her phone.

'Of course I'm going through with it. I thought you knew I was serious about this.' The phone pinged, distracting her again.

'Anyway, Mum, I need to talk to you about Grandma. You know she's staying with us?' Amy searched in the only cupboard in the makeshift kitchen for a glass. All she could find was an old mug she recognised from when she was a child. It made her wonder momentarily where her mother's belongings were from the flat. No point in asking. She poured some wine into the mug and drank a mouthful.

'Hmm?' Judith's eyes stayed glued to the phone.

'Mum!' Amy snapped loudly. 'Will you please listen to me? I need your help with Grandma.'

Brodie turned from his painting; his eyes wide. He wasn't used to hearing Amy raising her voice. After Nick left, she'd made a promise to herself that they would live in a non-shouty household. It was a utopian ideal that on a rare occasion she failed live up to, but for the most part, their home was a peaceful one.

'Calm down, sweetheart.' Judith placed her phone on the small coffee table next to the chair full of cushions. 'You have my complete attention. Now, why do you need my help with Grandma?'

'We're going away, the weekend after next. Just down to Dad and Muriel's caravan.' At the mention of Tony and Muriel, Judith's brow furrowed. 'Grandma's still staying with us. She can't be on her own for too long, so I need you to look after her for a bit while we're away. I was thinking maybe you could stay with her, at my house?' Amy adopted her best pleading face.

They were interrupted by a knock at the door. Judith clapped her hands together, delighted at the interruption.

'Oh, he's early!' she gasped.

Amy gathered up Brodie's coat. 'Come on,' she said, taking the brush from his hand, placing it on a pile of paint-soaked newspapers. 'I think we're going.'

Judith opened the door to reveal a tall, dark-haired man whose arm she grabbed on to so she could pull him into the studio.

'Come in, come in,' she coaxed. 'This is my daughter Amy, and her little boy Brodie.'

'Hi,' he said simply, giving them both an awkward smile and a small wave with his free hand.

'This is Robbie,' Judith twittered on. 'He's agreed to do some life modelling for me.'

Amy looked directly at Robbie. 'Really?'

Robbie shrugged; his face reddened slightly.

'Robbie is on the access course with me. He's going to be at the art college in September too.'

Amy looked from Robbie to her mother.

'That's nice,' she said finally. 'Anyway, we better be getting off. Can you let me know about Grandma?'

'What about Grandma?'

Amy sighed. 'About looking after her, when we're away?'

'Oh yes, yes.' Judith flapped her free hand; the one she wasn't clinging to poor Robbie with. 'Phone me to remind me though, darling, or I'll forget.'

Judith turned and stared up at Robbie, mesmerised. Amy noticed a familiar syrupy gaze that she'd seen many times before, which caused an equally familiar sense of mild dread to start weaving its way into her gut. Her mother was well known for getting involved with unsuitable men. Not that Robbie looked unsuitable; just far too young for her mother and at that moment he had the look of a trapped animal.

Amy kissed Judith on the cheek.

'Nice to meet you, Robbie.' He gave her a small nod and a slightly lopsided smile.

She closed the door. Brodie raced ahead towards the stairs at the end of the corridor. She could hear her mother chattering away inside and the occasional lower sound of a male voice as she pulled her jacket on and slung her bag across her shoulders. *So, he does speak then*, she thought, before making her way back along the corridor and out into the thankfully paint-free world beyond.

7

Edinburgh, 1987

My dad once brought a toad home in a bucket. He liked to fish down at the water of Leith, near where we lived, but only when he had a day off. He drove buses or sat in his chair watching black-and-white films on the colour TV the rest of the time.

The day Dad brought the toad home, he called my brother Ben and me into the living room where he was crouching over his old scratched red fishing bucket, his hand placed firmly on the white plastic lid. 'Come and see this, kids,' he said. I wasn't too excited because I thought it would just be more of the same fish he usually brought home, and I was in the middle of my reading book for school, but I always did what I was asked to do. Especially by my dad.

Ben and I knelt next to him on the carpet as he peeled the lid off slowly. 'Wait for it,' he teased, until it was only half off and we could see through the gap: slimy brown skin and the bulging eyes of a big ugly brown toad. The toad quickly saw its chance to escape and leapt out of its prison, causing dad to fall backwards, laughing loudly as he landed on his bum, still clutching the lid, and Ben and I screamed and jumped up onto the couch.

Mum came through the living-room door just then and Dad shouted, 'Watch out, Judith!' It only took her a moment to see what all the fuss was about, and she screamed too and ran out the room, slamming the door behind her. Dad dived around after the toad until he managed to grab it in both of his hands, and he shouted for Ben to get the lid for the bucket.

After he went back down to the river, Ben and I slumped down on the sofa giggling and Mum came back into the room with a cloth, asking us to point to anything the toad had touched. That was a good day. We had bad days too, the four of us. The worst day came when I was eight and a half. It was 1987 and everything was about to change.

We are in the living room, me, Ben and Mum. All of us, except Dad because he's on a late shift on the buses. I'm sitting on the floor, my back against the warmth of the radiator because I'm always cold. Mum says I have thin blood and she makes me a hot-water bottle every night for my bed, even in the summer. There is a mug of milk on the carpet next to me that I haven't started drinking yet.

My mum Judith is on the couch, in her usual place, legs curled under her bum, a cigarette in one hand, the soft silky ribbon of smoke dancing through the air above her head. On the small table next to the couch is a can of lager with a picture of a lady on it. It's her 'Thursday-night treat' because it's almost the weekend. Ben is sitting on the floor beneath her, on a large red cushion that spills stuffing whenever it gets moved, because our pet rabbit chewed its way through everything in the house one day when we let it hop around. Dad got rid of the rabbit the day after it did that. He got rid of our cat too, because he thought it might be why Ben sneezed a lot. There was also the time the cat had peed on his bus-driver's jacket and he'd spent a whole shift at work in the cab of the bus listening to passengers complain about the smell from their seats behind. But he didn't say that was the reason.

We're watching *Top of the Pops* together. We do it every Thursday after tea; sometimes with Dad, sometimes without. The TV screen flashes brightly but the volume isn't too high because Mum says the walls are thin in these houses and she doesn't want to upset Mrs Nisbet next door.

We don't know that my dad is in the hallway right then, locking the front door from the inside, listening to the sound of the television mixed with laughter, leaking from under the crack of the living-room door.

By the time I was eight years old, we'd only had one family holiday that I could remember. We'd gone up north, to the Highlands, where the sky was grey, and the rain kept us captive for too many hours in the small caravan that belonged to one of the other drivers at Dad's work.

Dad took my brother fishing on the pier while Mum and me went to a café one day. They got chatting to some of the men that lived in the town but didn't catch any fish. Dad bought some already cooked from the chippie instead and joked with my mum about his 'catch'. One of the men told my dad he should join them in the pub that night, which he did. He came back to the caravan when we were all in bed, but I was awake, and I could hear him tell my mum to shut her mouth about it. Nobody said anything about his black eye at breakfast and we left that afternoon, two days before we were meant to.

Sitting next to the radiator means I'm closest to the living-room door. I hear a floorboard creak in the hall and say without thinking, 'Dad's home,' and Ben says, 'Oh no,' and the three of us laugh but it was just a joke. The door suddenly explodes open, banging loudly against the radiator and I knock my cup of milk over. The liquid seeps down into the brown carpet and I start to worry because I know it will smell if it doesn't get cleaned up right away, but my dad is standing in the doorway shouting by then.

'Having a good laugh at me?' His hair is sticking up in funny clumps, reminding me of the clown from playschool, and he looks over us all, but there is something different about his eyes; they are darker and I can feel a fluttering in my tummy because I know it is my dad but he seems like a stranger at the same time.

His work boots thud across the carpet, the floor shakes with each step, and then he's at the other end of the room, struggling with one of the catches on the window before it pops open suddenly and he leans half of his body out in the cold evening air.

'Stop it, Tony, the neighbours will hear,' my mum says, but she doesn't stand up, just stays curled into her corner of the sofa.

'Come on, Judith, let the neighbours hear what a bastard I am,' he shouts, and Mum says, 'Ben, take Amy through to the bedroom and keep the door shut.' But my dad is marching back towards the sofa and he's grabbing my mum and pulling her towards the open window and Ben starts shouting for him to stop it, and I close my eyes because all I can think about is the milk, festering, heating up next to the warmth of the radiator. It is going to smell bad.

It's a while before the shouting and smashing stops. Ben stands guard at my bedroom door, his foot pressed tightly against the bottom, his white knuckles showing through his skin as he grips the handle, holding it up, keeping us safe.

The curtains are still open and the windows are inky black with the night beyond. I can see myself reflected in the glass, a ghostly pale girl sitting on the edge of her bed. Ben keeps warning me to stay where I am, but I don't want to move; I'm not sure that I can.

Eventually, when it's been quiet long enough, Ben stretches his hand out for me to take. Opening the door just a crack, we edge out and hold our breaths as we make our way along the hall, past the familiar furniture in the dark, to the top of the stairs. We stand for a few moments, both of us trying to hear some noise among the silence that has fallen over the house. We creep slowly down the stairs, careful to avoid the middle step and its giveaway creak. At the bottom, Ben looks into the downstairs box room that Dad keeps all of his fishing stuff in. 'She's not here,' he whispers, and I think it would be unlikely for her to be in that room but again I don't say anything. We keep going, along the hall, the living-room door is half open and we can see our dad sitting on the sofa, his head in his hands, his body shaking. As Ben pushes the door open, Dad looks up and blinks, surprised to see us, as though he'd forgotten we even existed. His eyes are red, but I can see my dad in them again. I rush forward to hug him. 'Where's Mum?' I ask, suddenly finding my voice.

'She's gone,' is all he says.

I can't remember anyone speaking after that. I watch my dad and my brother moving around the room and I follow Ben dumbly to pack some things in an overnight bag: pyjamas, a toothbrush, underwear for the next day. Then we sit down, side by side on the sofa, waiting for something to happen although I'm not sure what. The television set still flickers silently in the corner, but no one watches it now.

It is way past my bedtime when the doorbell rings and I hope that it's Mum, but it isn't. Instead, Dad's sister Sharon comes into the room and walks past us into the kitchen, telling my dad to follow her. They shut the door and we hear their voices getting louder before Sharon comes back out and stands in front of Ben and me, tossing her car keys in one hand while she chews on an off-white piece of gum that pops into view when she speaks. 'Come on then,' she says, and we follow her outside and into her car. She drives us through the quiet streets to her flat and we climb up to the second floor of the building. I count up forty-eight stairs, and then we sit on high stools at a tall table that splits the living room from the kitchen, while she makes us toast. Sharon tells me to change into my pyjamas and says I can sleep in with her and that Ben will have to sleep on the sofa. My brother shrugs at this and says nothing. Sharon is brushing my hair in front of the bathroom mirror when I ask again, 'Where's my mum?'

She locks her eyes with mine in the mirror but doesn't say anything for a while. I think she isn't going to answer me at all until she says finally, 'I'm not sure, but don't worry, I'll find her.'

'Promise?' I ask.

'Promise,' she says, tugging the brush through a stubborn tangle at the back of my long hair. 'Besides,' she goes on, 'it's not like you can stay here more than one night.'

Sharon kept her word and found my mum. She phoned Grandma, who said she had a 'bloody good idea' where Mum would be.

She dropped Ben and me at Morag's house early the next morning. Morag is our grandma's best friend. She's known Grandma since they were both five years old, and my mum since the day she was born.

Morag said Mum was still sleeping and made us pancakes and hot chocolate and we snuggled up under blankets on the sofa and watched *Mary Poppins* on Morag's video player, which jumped a bit because it's her granddaughter Molly's favourite film.

It was well after lunchtime when Mum woke up and plonked herself down on the sofa with us. She pulled me into a hug, kissed the top of my head and held on to me for a long time. She didn't smell very nice, a bit like one of the ashtrays she keeps next to her spot on the sofa, but I was just happy she was there, so I didn't say a word.

I wet the bed that first night at Morag's. I'd never done that before. Mum fussed about the bed sheets. She didn't want to be embarrassed. Morag had taken us in, and she couldn't put them in the washing machine, they were dirty. I felt like there was something wrong with me, like I was dirty too. She put them in a bin in the end, then went to the charity shop on the way to school and bought some more. I heard Morag telling Mum off when she found the second-hand sheets.

'You should've told me the truth, Judith – it wouldn't have mattered,' Morag insisted.

'I'm so sorry,' I heard Mum reply. She was sitting at the kitchen table crying. She did that a lot in those first few weeks.

Morag's flat is huge. Our whole house could fit into the hallway. I love living with Morag, mainly because Grandma Jeannette comes and visits us here but also because there are always nice things to eat on the long kitchen table: big scones with home-made strawberry jam and splodges of cream, or sticky golden muffins that mushroom out the top of their cases, bursting with blueberries or chocolate chips.

Mum says she remembers Morag making all the same things when she was a little girl. That was when Morag's husband Tom was still alive.

Ben told me Tom died when he was out working on the farm one day; he'd asked Mum what had happened to him and she told him that there was something wrong with one of the machines and it had fired him halfway across a field, like he'd been shot from a cannon at the circus. He was dead before he landed on the ground. Mum told Ben that Morag couldn't stay on the farm without Tom after that, so she gave it to her eldest son and his wife, and moved back to the city she'd grown up in.

Morag talks about Tom and tells stories about him a lot. 'When someone is snatched from you in an instant, you don't get to say goodbye,' she said to me one day as I helped her with some baking.

'Do you wish he was still alive?' I asked.

Morag smiled, not taking her eyes off the mixture she was stirring.

'I spend a little bit of every day just wishing I could tell him I love him, just one more time,' she replied, before telling me to go and wash my hands.

I knew Morag was sad about Tom, but she always looked happy. She smiled and laughed lots and made everyone feel welcome. I hadn't realised I wasn't happy before. Even Mum began to cheer up after a few weeks. She couldn't eat at first, she said. She could drink though. While Ben and I sat at the table with Morag and any other visitors she had, Mum would stand at the kitchen window, a glass of wine in her hand, looking out into the distance with a heavy frown on her face. She would have had a cigarette too, but Morag wouldn't let her smoke inside. Not after that first night anyway, when Mum had turned up, sobbing and stammering until she'd been given a large brandy, shaking as she struck a match to light a Silk Cut.

Dinner at Morag's is always something to look forward to; a huge piece of meat, roasted for hours, the smell wafting through the kitchen making us all feel more and more hungry throughout the day. There are trays of creamy potatoes and shiny, buttery vegetables to go with it and Morag likes us to eat seconds and sometimes even thirds, because she's says we're all skin and bone.

Eventually Mum started eating again too. She'll sit with us if Grandma isn't there.

Grandma visits us lots now we live with Morag. She meets me some days at the school gates and walks me back home. Ben started at the high school after the summer holidays and is always off with his new friends. Morag tries to get my mum and Grandma to talk to each other, but Mum just walks away. 'I can't deal with this right now,' she'll say and then leave the room.

I hear Morag and Grandma speaking every time, after it happens. They sit at the kitchen table, sometimes whispering and sometimes saying things loudly enough for me to overhear. Grandma says she spoiled my mum and Morag listens then disagrees and tells Grandma that it isn't her fault, that it had been hard, and that Grandma had always done her best. One day they were talking about someone called George as I poured myself a juice from a jug at the far end of the table. I can quite often be in a room for a long time before people realise I'm there. It's how I hear things I shouldn't have heard.

'Who's George?' I asked, startling them both. Grandma patted the wooden bench next to her and I sat down. She put her arm around my shoulders and told me that George was my grandfather, my mum's dad, and that he died a long time ago.

'So, he was your husband?' I'd asked.

Grandma and Morag looked at each other and smiled and Morag said, 'You're a clever girl for an eight-year-old.'

And I said, 'I'll be nine soon.' Then Morag got up and took two of the iced buns from the kitchen counter and told me to take one to Ben and to put the TV on if I wanted to.

8

Edinburgh, 1989

My mum has a new boyfriend. He's called Ken and she says they knew each other at school. Mum says it's fate. That they didn't have a chance the first time because my dad tricked her and got in the way, but now they've found each other again. She says it's true love.

We're meeting him today for the first time. A car arrives to pick us up, the driver waits on the street outside Morag's and Mum jumps up and down at the window, shouting at Ben and me to get our shoes on.

Mum sits in the front of the car, next to the driver and Ben and I strap our seatbelts on in the back, each next to our own electric window, which Ben keeps playing with, sliding it down and then up again. I'm too frightened to touch it in case I break it. I'm wearing my new pink denim shorts, the ones Mum bought me from the catalogue, and I'm already thinking I shouldn't have, because my bare legs are sticking to the grey leather seat. Mum talks to the driver the whole way about Ken. He nods when she asks if he knows him well, but then goes on and on, telling him things that I'm sure he already knows. I hear her tell him that Ken is a pilot. I think that is her favourite thing about him. She told me he's not just a pilot, that he owns lots of businesses, but she doesn't know too much about that, so she brushes over this when she's talking to her friends about him. They all seem pretty impressed with the fact that he's a pilot anyway.

Mum turns in her seat to look at us.

'Now remember, you two,' she warns, 'best behaviour.'

Ben and I nod but I think to myself that she didn't really need to tell us that. Neither of us are ever badly behaved. I wonder for a moment how she would react if I told her to be on *her* best behaviour. *Perhaps you shouldn't drink so much wine*, I'd say. *Perhaps you shouldn't sit on that man's knee when his wife is sat right next to him, looking at you like she wants to slap you.* She'd done that at Morag's New Year's Eve party last year. It wouldn't make any difference what I said to Mum though. She doesn't really listen to anyone; not Grandma or Morag, and least of all me.

When we arrive at Ken's house, my brother whistles softly.

I don't think either of us have ever seen anything like the house we are now parked in front of, not in real life anyway.

As the car stops, one of the huge front doors swings open and a grinning man in a pink shirt runs down the stairs towards the car. He opens Mum's door first.

'Darling,' he says loudly, offering her his hand. He pulls Mum into a tight squeeze of a hug that makes her giggle and then peers into the back of the car at us, pretending to be surprised to see us there. Ben and I glance at one another. I'm grateful that he's sitting on the side of the car nearest to Ken. He pushes the door open and gets out first.

'Young man,' Ken sticks out his hand for Ben to shake. 'Do you play rugby?' Ken has a loud voice; he booms rather than speaks.

Ben shakes his head and says, 'No, sir.'

'Never mind,' Ken booms again, slapping Ben on the back. 'Magnus is out back tossing a ball around. He'll be happy to teach you.' Ken bends down to investigate the back seat of the car once more. I am sitting very still in the hope I may have been forgotten about.

'And who is this beautiful young lady? Come on, come out here.' Ken slaps his thigh as someone might call on a dog.

I try to slide along the seat, but my legs stick to the leather and my foot catches on the rim of the car door. I fall out and land on the gravel at Ken's feet. Mum fusses.

'Silly girl,' she says, grabbing my arm to pull me up.

'No harm done,' says Ken, patting my head, before we all head towards the house.

It's obvious that Mum has been here before because she knows exactly the way to take us. I follow her through the huge entrance hall with the sweeping staircases, two of them, one on either side; they make me think of a Disney cartoon, I can see a princess wearing a ballgown gliding down them. We walk on towards the back of the house, past a games room, a dining room and a room that looks like a real cinema, before we're led through into a gleaming white kitchen, the back wall of which is made entirely of glass doors, half pulled open like a concertina split in two. Various groups of people stand out on the striped green lawn, a few heads turn to look at us. One woman spots my mum and begins waving frantically as she teeters over the grass wearing incredibly high heels.

'Judy!' she shouts, more than once, as if anyone couldn't have heard her the first time. The woman kisses my mum on each cheek and gives her a strange half-squeeze half-hug, their bodies not touching. 'Are these your children?' She stands with one hand on her hip and hooks her other arm with Mum's.

Mum nods, pointing at us in turn. 'Ben. Amy.'

'Lovely,' she replies, giving us a glimpse of her teeth before leading Mum off to a table full of bottles and glasses of varying colours and sizes.

Ken bellows for his son Magnus, who jogs over and takes Ben away to show him the tennis court and his way around a rugby ball, and then he waves for his daughter Sasha to come and take charge of me. She is taller and thinner than me, with a long mane of highlighted wavy blonde hair that sways as she walks towards us. I know she is thirteen because my mum told me, but she seems more like one of the grown-ups and I start to blush and feel stupid.

'Sasha, this is Judith's daughter Amy. Look after her, there's a good girl.' Ken kisses the top of Sasha's hair and leaves us to it.

Sasha raises her sunglasses to take a good look at me, her eyes travelling down to my new pink shorts and then onwards towards my trainers which suddenly looked scuffed and old.

'My goodness,' she says finally. 'Has no one ever shown you how to shave your legs?'

I shake my head and take a peek at them, contemplating the blonde fuzz that catches the sunlight, creating a dusty covering over my skin. I'd never given it any thought until that moment.

'Come on,' Sasha beckons, and I follow her back towards the house. She takes me to her enormous bedroom on the first floor, which has a door into a bathroom all of its own and another room attached, which is bigger than any bedroom I've ever slept in but for Sasha is just somewhere to keep her clothes and get dressed.

'This isn't even all of my clothes, my good stuff's at Mummy's,' she tells me. 'That's where I stay most of the time.'

Sasha then says I've to sit on the side of the bath while she uses the shower head to wet just my shins, then lathers on some gel, which erupts into foam as it hits my skin. She doesn't seem bothered about touching me, even though we've only just met, and I think that it would be wonderful to be like Sasha; to be as confident as she is.

When my legs are fully foamed, she takes a razor out of a shiny plastic packet.

'It's a new one, don't worry,' she tells me and I wonder what I would have to be worried about but then she slides it up my leg from my ankle to my knee, rinses it under the bath tap, then repeats a few times, after which a trickle of blood slowly seeps from a tiny scratch that I didn't even feel.

'Shit,' she says, but she keeps on going, more carefully I notice, then after a few more strokes she says, 'There, now you do it,' and hands me the razor. I copy her technique until my legs are completely smooth and my skin is glossy from all the soap and water.

'Much better.' She hands me a fluffy white towel and I dry my legs, trying to avoid the scratch.

'You don't say much, do you?' Sasha says.

'I suppose not,' I reply quietly. The truth is I don't really know what to say to someone like Sasha; I am completely terrified of her.

We go back to the garden and sit on two loungers positioned in the sunshine at the edge of the lawn.

'Why don't you get some food from the barbeque,' she says. 'I'm not eating because I'm going on holiday in a few weeks and I don't want to look fat in my bikini.'

Given there didn't seem to be an ounce of fat on her (I'd noticed how her wrist bones stuck out as she held the razor) I didn't think there was any way she would ever be fat.

'I'm not really hungry,' I say, even though I am starving. To make it worse, my brother waves a burger at me from across the garden; he's chatting and laughing with Magnus, another new friend.

Sasha flicks through a magazine for a while and I sit with my legs hugged up to my chest, just watching people. I wish for a moment I'd brought a book but then think I wouldn't want Sasha to see the books I read; I can't imagine her being too impressed with the girls in *The Babysitters Club* books I got for my last birthday.

Suddenly someone is standing at the side of my lounger, blocking out the sun. I look up to see Ken's son Magnus, Ben standing just behind him, grinning.

'Do you two want to come for a swim?' Magnus says without introducing himself. I notice he talks with the same loud voice as his father.

I shake my head. 'I haven't got a swimming costume.'

'I can lend you one,' Sasha offers and I cringe at the thought of not being able to squeeze into any swimming suit she owned.

'Aw, come on, Amy,' Ben pleads. 'The pool's inside the house, it looks amazing.'

'No thanks, I'll just stay here,' I say.

Sasha lifts her sunglasses and considers Ben. 'I'll come,' she offers, standing up and linking arms with him. Ben laughs. 'OK then, let's go.'

'Sure we can't tempt you?' Magnus hasn't moved and his presence is causing me to curl into myself.

I shake my head. 'No, thank you.'

He smiles and I think he looks kind, despite his loud voice. 'OK, little one,' he says. 'We're in through those glass doors over on the far side of the house if you change your mind.' He breaks off into a jog to catch up with Ben and Sasha.

I release my held breath as I spot my mum swaying across the grass towards me.

'Everything all right, honey?' she asks. Her large glass of white wine sloshes around as she sits herself down on the lounger next to me. 'I saw you chatting with Sasha, she's a lovely girl, isn't she?'

I nod.

'What do you think of Ken?'

I pause, trying to work out what the right answer would be. 'He's OK,' I try, which I know is a mistake the moment it comes out my mouth.

'OK?' she shrieks, throwing her head back in one of her over-the-top laughs that makes me feel a bit funny inside. 'He's more than OK, honey, look at this place, look at him . . .'

Mum gestures over to where Ken must have been standing a few minutes ago. She frowns for a moment.

'He must've gone in to get more wine,' she says, before pulling a cigarette out of a packet and lighting it, taking a long, slow drag. I hate it when she smokes.

'I'm going to the loo,' I say, but she's already distracted by the magazine Sasha had been reading.

All the grown-ups at the party seem quite merry; the volume of the music has gone up and people are talking and laughing loudly. The barbeque has been put out, but I grab a bit of chicken as I pass the food table and stuff it in my mouth as quickly as I can in case Sasha can see me. No one takes any notice of me as I wander into the house. I do need the toilet and think there are probably a few to choose from on this floor alone. I walk back through the kitchen and past the cinema room and the games room. I try a couple of doors. One door leads into a library. Book spines line the room from floor to ceiling. I can't imagine being lucky enough to live somewhere with its own library.

I gently shut the door to my new favourite room in Ken's house and then remember that I'd spotted a toilet on the way in, near the front door. When I push down the handle and nudge the door slowly open, the first thing I see is the toilet and I think, *Thank goodness*, because I'm really needing by now. The second thing I notice is the two bodies wriggling against each other at the sink, their faces pressed together and arms grabbing at each other's body parts like octopuses. It's the pink shirt that really catches my attention. I just stand there, unable to move, my need to use the toilet growing. It seems like forever before they see me. When they do, they gasp and Ken wipes lipstick off his mouth onto a towel and the woman, the one who had rushed over to see my mum when we arrived, makes funny twittering noises like a little bird.

Ken pushes her past me, telling her to calm down and go home, then instructs me to sit down on the toilet lid. I do as he says. He shuts the door and turns the lock (so he does know how), then crouches down in front of me.

'I don't think you understand what you just saw . . .' he begins.

And I think, *Yes, I did*. But I don't say anything.

'Cheryl is just a friend,' he continues, 'and sometimes we need to comfort our friends.'

'OK,' I manage to say. I really need to pee.

'The thing is,' he goes on, 'your mother doesn't know Cheryl very well yet and she might not understand why I was having to give her a hug.'

Ken stands up and reaches into his back trouser pocket, producing a bulging black leather wallet. He flips it open and takes out three crisp twenty-pound notes.

'How about you take this, and we agree not to tell Mummy about Cheryl just yet?' He holds out the money for me to take. I sit frozen, my hands gripping either side of the toilet-seat lid.

'I really do love your mother, you know.' Ken lets his hand drop down and he sighs loudly. 'Oh, who am I trying to kid. You're a clever girl. You know I wasn't just hugging Cheryl. Listen,' he bends down again so our eyes are level. 'Cheryl and I have been a bit more than friends, I'll admit that. But it's your mother I want to be with now. I was just saying goodbye to Cheryl. Nothing like that will ever happen again. Do you understand?'

I nod. Ken hands me the notes and this time I take them because I need him to get out of the room or I am going to wet myself.

He seems satisfied. 'Good girl,' he says, before patting me on the head for the second time that day. He leaves the room.

I jump up and snap the lock shut.

A bit later, after I've peed and sat back down on the toilet-seat lid, not sure what to do, there is a knock on the door. I think it might be Ken, coming back to make sure I'll keep his secret. I stuff the notes into my short pockets, not noticing that one falls to the ground.

It's not Ken.

'What are you doing in here?' Ben glances into the room as if checking I'm alone.

'Nothing, I just needed the toilet.'

'The swimming pool was great you know, you should've come with us.'

I nod. At that moment I really wish I had.

'Mum says we're going to stay the night here. Ken's just set up the cinema for us to watch a film. Sasha and Magnus are watching it too. Come on.' Ben looks down at the bathroom floor, noticing the twenty-pound note. 'Whoa, look at that,' he says, squeezing by me to pick it up. 'Do you think we should see who it belongs to?' He turns the note over in his hands.

I shake my head. 'Just keep it,' I say. 'They won't even know who dropped it.'

'Good point.' Ben still looks unsure.

'Honestly, I don't think anyone would even mind if you had it. They've all got loads of money here.'

I take it from his hands and shove it into the pocket of his trousers.

Ben smiles. 'I'll split it with you.'

'No need,' I say, following him through the hallway. The other two notes burn hotly in the pocket of my pink shorts.

9

Edinburgh, 1991

A wedding. Today is the day we become a real family, or so Mum says. They've been waiting for the divorces to come through and we've been living at Ken's for almost two years now, putting up with their unfunny jokes about living in sin. I am completely sick of anything wedding-related and looking forward to tomorrow when we can hopefully all get back to normal; although I'm not sure I really know what normal is anymore. Being my mum's bridesmaid is my worst nightmare; there are the spots that decided to erupt on my chin last week and the fact that my mum keeps commenting on my puppy fat and tutting whenever she sees me eating anything with sugar in it. To make matters even more horrendous, she has chosen the most disgusting yellow bridesmaid dresses I've ever seen. Not many people suit yellow, especially not someone as pale as I am. There was no changing her mind though. Even when I tried it on and she made a face, openly disappointed with how I looked wearing the dress, there was no convincing her. It had been in a magazine, you see, one of the glossy kinds that show pictures of semi-famous celebrities pretending to relax on a white sofa. The exact same dress had been worn by the bridesmaids of an actress from one of the soap operas and, as Ken says, nothing is too good for my mother.

I wondered at one point if she might replace me rather than the dress and found some momentary joy in the prospect, particularly because I didn't think it would be beyond my mother to cut her own daughter from her perfect wedding. She wouldn't want the photos ruined.

Unfortunately, I am not going to be lucky enough to get a reprieve from wearing the hideous dress and I will appear in the photos, hopefully hidden behind Ken's niece Sophia, who overshadows me in every sense, with her deep suntan and glossy brown hair. The dress looks like a different garment on her.

The wedding is taking place on an estate on the outskirts of Edinburgh. The ceremony is going to happen in the old grand house, after which everyone gets kicked out into a less grand, large white tent pitched on the lawn.

The yellow dress has been paired with baby blue to create the colour theme for the day. Yellow and blue metallic helium balloons are tied to any available object and there are thousands of metres of pale yellow and blue satin ribbon laced through chairs and spiralled around every visible pillar or post.

The ceremony room in the old house is completely draped in garlands of flowers, which hang from the walls and the back of the chairs. It looks like a botanical bomb has gone off and the staff I saw setting up the room were all snuffling and rubbing their eyes by the time they'd finished.

The women in the wedding party have been given a room upstairs in the big house for getting ready. I've been squished into the offensive yellow garment and am having my hair put up by the hairdresser who keeps swearing under her breath and commenting that my hair is too thin, when my mum appears from the room next door in her wedding dress. Her hair and make-up have already been done and it occurs to me that she hasn't shown me the dress before now. Why hadn't I even thought about seeing it? I suppose I'd imagined she would wear some ridiculous over-the-top puffball and had probably wanted to block the embarrassment from my mind. I was wrong about that. She's chosen a long champagne-coloured silk dress that falls slightly off one shoulder. The dress skims over her hourglass figure and I think in that moment that she looks like a film star. My mum has become more and more glamorous since we moved in with Ken, and she is going to be the star of the show today.

As I watch her standing there, smiling her dazzling white smile (thanks to Ken's award-winning dentist), something niggles at me, something I've tried to forget since the moment I stepped into the bathroom in Ken's house on the day of the barbeque. Of course, neither Ken nor I have ever forgotten it. We are polite but mostly avoid eye contact. He still gives me money. I find twenty-pound notes in my jacket pocket that I know weren't there the day before, or when I pull my gym kit out of my school bag, a couple of ten-pound notes will waft out and drift gently, like feathers, to the changing-room floor. I know it's so I won't say anything about that day, but what Ken doesn't know is, with or without the money, I probably wouldn't say anything anyway. I do think about telling Mum about what I saw that afternoon, or Ben at least, but I never quite find the right moment and then I think I've probably left it too long now, and anyway, I don't want to ruin things. When Mum is with Ken, she just seems so high and so happy, I don't want to be the one responsible for bringing her crashing down. So, I stay quiet, and the secret stays locked away.

*

Everyone *oohs* and *ahhs* as Mum walks down the aisle and Ken wipes at his eyes, but I can't see any tears. They hold hands facing each other and the registrar begins to speak and an overwhelming urge to laugh bubbles up inside me and I have to hold my nose but I'm shaking with the effort not to make a sound. Just before the actual bit where they say 'I do', someone gets up to sing a song as part of the whole performance and I manage to control myself and my mind drifts a little and I am looking around the room at who is there and the decorations, and then without thinking I glance towards Mum and accidentally catch Ken's eye, just briefly, but enough to make the niggle in my tummy grow; something unfurls. For the rest of the ceremony I look down at the deep-red carpet with its golden swirls and concentrate on how badly it clashes with the pale yellows and blues of the decorations and I wonder if Mum had suggested re-carpeting the whole room at some point to the wedding organiser.

When they've signed the register and it is over – or perhaps just begun – I join the stream of guests spilling out onto the lawn, glad to be out of the stuffy, flower-filled room. I ignore the confetti-throwing crowd and wait as patiently as I can, kicking at the grey gravel with my horrible yellow shoes, until I'm called for the photos.

When the photographer has stopped shouting at me to 'get behind the pretty one' for the final time, I edge away from the wedding party and the people drinking glasses of champagne, until I find myself leaning back against one of the large oak trees on the edge of the estate, closing my eyes until I hear a familiar voice say, 'Penny for them?'

Grandma Jeannette always says she can read me like a book. I hate hiding anything from her and so when she takes hold of my face under the tree that day and stares straight into my eyes, I feel the words piling up on my tongue and I want so badly to open my mouth and let them tumble out. But I swallow over the great lump of guilt in my throat and instead let out a loud sob and she pulls me into a hug and shushes me, while I cry against the lovely pale-silver jacket I helped her pick out in Debenhams the weekend before.

I tell her it's the dress, that I hate it and feel so uncomfortable and she looks me up and down and raises an eyebrow and says, 'Well it's not the best I've ever seen you look.'

She laughs then and I look down at myself and notice two dark splodges on the sickly yellow satin that I must've made without noticing and then I start laughing too, because the whole thing – the dress, the wedding, my new life – it all just seems so ridiculous.

Grandma tells me to go and get changed into the clothes I'd worn that morning.

'Your mum probably won't even notice; she's far too caught up in herself today – even more so than she normally is.'

I run upstairs to where we'd all got ready that morning, kicking off the hideous matching yellow shoes as I go and am surprised to find Mum standing in the room, alone, in front of the full-length mirror, staring at her reflection. She turns at the sound of the door closing behind me and smiles, but her eyes are glistening with tears. We stand across the room looking at each other and just as I say, 'Grandma says I can take the dress off,' she says, 'What do you think of the wedding?'

I say, 'It's good,' and then, 'So can I take it off?' But Mum has gone back to looking at herself in the mirror again and doesn't answer so I just struggle out of the horrible dress and gratefully pull on my favourite jeans and a T-shirt. I sit on the bed, waiting for Mum to move or to say something but she doesn't so I ask eventually, 'Are you OK?'

She turns around and sighs dramatically, taking on the lead role in her own movie and says, 'I'm probably being silly. It's just that I can't help feeling like this is all a bit of a dream. Do you think he really loves me?' She then adds, 'Ken.' Just in case I might be in any doubt that she was talking about the man she'd just married.

The black crow in my stomach begins trying to flap, but it's trapped by the lies that have wound their way around its wings and through my gut, creeping up my throat and threatening to strangle me. I can't speak. I don't know whether I should nod or shake my head. I suppose I think Ken does love my mum really; he'd let us move into his house after all. He must have wanted her around. But I am paralysed.

I'm saved by a small knock at the door. Grandma appears and looks at me and then at my mum and asks, 'What's going on?' and Mum frowns and pouts and says, 'Nothing,' and puts her hands on her hips. 'What are you doing up here anyway?'

Grandma points at me and says, 'I was just looking for Amy. She was upset. Not that you'll have noticed.'

This seems to be the worst thing she could've said because Mum hoists up her dress and stomps out of the room making a low growling sound.

Grandma sits down next to me on the bed.

'A problem shared, is a problem halved, you know.'

The black crow keeps trying to flap, and I wonder what it would feel like to set it free. I look at my grandma and know, if there was anyone in the whole world I can trust, it's her. I take a deep breath and tell her. 'Grandma,' I say, 'I've got a secret.'

*

Grandma was right. I feel instantly better. Then I feel worse because I know she wants to tell my mum and I can't stand the thought of everyone being upset, not today. I beg her not to say anything, but she isn't listening to me as I follow her out of the room, down the long staircase and out onto the gravel where the wedding guests are all still hovering around in small clusters. She walks straight up to Ken and stands with her hands on her hips, waiting for him to finish telling one of his stories to a group of wedding guests.

When he delivers the punchline and the audience all titter politely, Grandma taps him on the shoulder.

'Excuse me,' she says, her voice low. 'I need a word.'

Ken tries to put his arm around Grandma's shoulders, but she takes a sidestep.

'Jeannette,' he bellows. 'Or can I call you *Mum* now?' The usual charming smile begins to form on his lips until he glances over and catches sight of me. The colour drains slightly from his face and he coughs and straightens his tie and puts his half-empty champagne glass down on one of the tall tables dotted around the lawn. 'Of course,' he excuses himself from his guests who are glancing between my grandmother and Ken, their minds already creating theories to gossip about later.

'Let's go somewhere private.'

Ken looks back at me twice. I don't follow them into the main house, don't need to hear the conversation they're about to have. I wonder though, if there is now a crow flapping its wings inside Ken's stomach.

10

Edinburgh, 1993

When Sasha had shown me her room in Ken's enormous house the day of the barbeque, I'd never imagined that one day it would be mine. But four years later, here I am: sitting on her old bed, propped up by a pile of plump feathery pillows, listening to my Take That tape for the four-hundredth time and staring at the posters I've carefully extracted from various magazines to hide the elaborate Laura Ashley wallpaper that covers most of the walls in the house. Sasha said she 'didn't give a shit' that I'd been given her room when we moved in with Ken. She regularly refers to her dad as 'that arsehole' and says she didn't want to stay at his house anymore anyway. She is almost seventeen, has been expelled from Mary Erskine's, sports a pierced nose and made Ken lose his temper in a way I hadn't witnessed before by getting a large tattoo of angel wings across her back. She flaunts the illegal artwork openly by wearing vests with spaghetti straps, even when it's freezing cold outside. Despite her promises to stay away, she still visits the house and occasionally stays over, moving back into her old room alongside me as though she never left. She sweeps in and flops down on the bed, telling me about the latest in a string of men that she's involved with, all of whom seem to mistreat her in some way or another. I'm still a bit terrified of Sasha, but I've seen enough of the cracks over the years to know that under all her boldness, Sasha has a softer side, and when she lets that side of herself show, she's one of my favourite people.

I go to Sasha's school now, the one she got kicked out of. I wear her old uniforms, the red and blue kilt and the stiff navy-blue blazer, and I use her hockey kit at the weekend. I suppose it looks from the outside that I've stepped straight into Sasha's life. I suppose I have.

She's taught me some other things over the years, besides how to shave my legs. She showed me how to do my make-up (lots of dark eyeliner), how to smoke a cigarette (never inhale fully) and how to give a blowjob (this she demonstrated with a Calypso ice lolly, to my complete embarrassment and to her complete amusement). I'm yet to put the latter training session to use. She sighs and rolls her eyeballs quite a lot around me and will make a point of telling me that she has much better people to be hanging out with and she is only spending time with me because she feels sorry for me. But she stays lounging on the bed long after she's said she'll leave. We are the most unlikely of friends, but somehow, that is what we are.

Apart from wearing her hand-me-down uniforms, I'm nothing like Sasha at school. I don't hang out with the popular crowd like she had. I'm not one of the geeks or nerds either. I'm just somewhere in the middle, mostly unnoticed, with a couple of other girls similar in temperament and ambition (our main ambition being not to attract the attention of the popular crowd). I do reasonably well at most subjects, and I like upper school: moving around classrooms, soaking up new ideas, discovering I can remember most of what I learn and recall it easily in tests. I'm not so keen on studying at home though, much preferring to lose myself in books that would be of no use when it came to exams. I spend most of my time working through the fiction novels in Ken's library, books that have never been touched before I came in and started folding over pages and reading them by the swimming pool where the dampness would wrinkle the pages. Ken is keen to keep me happy, so he orders any books I want, and he even bought more shelving to fill. I love fiction, any kind, anything that takes me away into another world. If I can escape into someone else's story for a while, I'm happy. Ken ordered me the entirety of Judy Blume's back catalogue and I've been getting quite a bit of sex education from them, so when Sasha finished showing me how to perform the thing with the Calypso, I asked her, 'What about actual sex. How do you do that?'

She looked at me, a little shocked I think, and then with a flick of her hair she said, 'Oh, penetrative sex is different. You won't have to do much; the guy will do most of it and please himself anyway. Now close your eyes,' she instructed. She was doing my make-up, hovering a black kohl pencil dangerously close to my eyeball. I watched her consider her answer before I did as I was told and heard her say, 'Unless he wants you to be on top. If that happens, just bounce up and down a bit.'

Sasha has an answer for everything.

Magnus comes back to visit Ken sometimes too. He's at university in Bath. His visits usually coincide with some social event for one of his old Edinburgh school friends and so he tends to come back to the house in the middle of the night. I hear him stumbling around in his old bedroom, the one next to mine. Sometimes he comes in and wakes me up to chat and offer me cold chips from crinkled white paper. He throws them up in the air and catches them in his mouth, whooping each time he gets one in and leaving the ones he doesn't on my bedroom floor.

*

A month or so ago, Magnus woke me up and begged me to come downstairs and into the garden. I followed him, rubbing my eyes and telling him I didn't really want to, but he wouldn't listen. He lay down on the grass and told me to lie next to him. When I eventually agreed, he spread his arms wide, gesturing up at the clear night sky filled with a million stars.

'Isn't it amazing, little one?' he said.

I had to agree with him; it was incredible. I didn't think I even knew there were so many stars in the sky; no one had ever asked me to lie down and look at them before.

'Do you know what I think?' he went on. 'I think there's another universe beyond all of that. Can you imagine?' He turned his head and I turned mine to look at him and he grinned widely. His eyes were glassy, and his floppy blonde hair was stuck to his forehead, but I felt a little flutter of something and quickly turned away to look again at the stars.

'What kind of universe?' I asked, my voice tiny in the vast darkness of the garden.

Magnus looked back up at the sky and rested his head on his clasped hands.

'Maybe it's just another universe like this one. Maybe there's a boy and a girl just like you and me, lying on the grass, looking up at the sky and wondering what the other universe is like too.' He laughed quietly and removed his hands from behind his head, laying them back down by his sides. His fingers touched mine. I leapt up.

'I better get to bed,' I said before racing up the garden towards the house. I think he slept on the grass that night.

The thing about my new life is, it gets harder to believe I had an old one. We have a swimming pool in the house. We don't have to go and queue at the local baths anymore, waiting to slip fifty pence under the iron grate to the lady that operates the turnstile, making sure not too many children are let in without at least one adult to watch over them. We don't have to change in the cubicles with chewing gum stuck to the underside of the bench, or take a shower, looking down at other people's hair clogging the drains. I swim every day now, just because I can.

We've all become so busy; I sometimes go for days without having to bump into any of the other members of my 'family' because they're off doing some activity or another. We pass each other on the stairs, in too much of a rush to get to school, or work (only Ken), or a charity event (Mum), or hockey practice. Except for Marisol of course. She's the housekeeper; an almost permanent fixture in the vast white kitchen. If we'd been brought up in Ken's house from birth, I would've probably developed some kind of maternal attachment to her. She's from the Philippines and has a family of her own at home that she sends money to. Ken pays for her to go back three times a year, two weeks at a time, which is when the agency staff come in and something inevitably goes missing from the house. Last time it was a pair of diamond earrings Ken bought for my mum's birthday, although I suspect that had nothing to do with the agency staff and more to do with Mum's carelessness.

Marisol has pictures of her two children stuck all over the walls of her room above the garages. I sometimes see her watching my mother, frowning. She probably thinks our mum takes it for granted that she lives with her children. She's right about that. I hardly ever see her. She's become involved with so many women's groups and is a member of every club possible. I wonder, sometimes, if some of the events are made up and if she's having an affair and this makes me feel hopeful because it would serve Ken right. Not that he would be bothered, I don't think. He's currently seeing at least one other woman. I know this because I look at his credit card statements – the paper ones that clog up the mail basket at the bottom of the driveway. I didn't mean to start snooping, but they make for quite interesting reading. Looking at them wasn't really my fault. He'd shoved one in the back of a kitchen drawer, probably in a panic to hide it, and I could hear the paper scraping every time the drawer slid in and out. So I stuck my hand right to the back and managed to grab it. There were hotels and meals out, mounting up to hundreds and even thousands of pounds. I saw the name of one particular restaurant in Edinburgh and casually asked Mum if she'd ever been there. She hadn't.

I do still think about telling my mum what I know. Pretty much every night before I go to sleep, I convince myself that when I wake up the next day, I'll be able to tell her. The thing is, I still don't want things to change; for me and for Ben mainly, but also for Mum. She's got a whole new life. She looks younger now than she did ten years ago. Ken paid for her to have her boobs done too. She had the operation when I was away on a skiing trip with school and when I returned, it was the first thing she rushed to show me. I hadn't seen my mum's boobs since I could remember, but suddenly she was parading topless in front of me in her bedroom, the shiny skin stretched over her new assets, like overfilled water balloons. She never did ask how my skiing trip went.

I only really think about my old life, about my dad, when something reminds me of him; a film he'd taken me to watch at the cinema or if I see someone fishing. Things like that. I don't miss him, at least I didn't think I did.

Marisol is in the kitchen when I get home from school. She's cracking eggs into a food mixer and I assume she's making a cake, which Mum will probably be taking to an event, where she'll pass it off as her own.

'Hello,' I say, opening the fridge, searching for something to eat.

Marisol comes over and slaps my hands away from a plate I'm about to remove.

'Not that one. Here.' She takes out a box containing some of the savoury pastries she makes each week and hands it to me. 'Your father phone,' she says.

Without thinking, I reply, 'Ken's not my father,' to which Marisol tuts and shakes her head slowly.

'Not Mr Richards. *Your* father.' She thrusts a Post-it note into my chest. 'He wants you call him,' she says, before pushing me gently towards the hallway. 'Go. Phone him.'

I don't call him straight away, of course. I go up to my room and lie on the bed, staring at the ceiling, acutely aware of the Post-it note crunched up in my left hand. I wait for Ben to come home and pick at the pastries.

It's Thursday, rugby training after school, and Ben is still in his kit, covered in mud, his hair soaking wet and plastered to his head when I leap from my bed and grab him in the corridor.

'What should we do?' I ask, following him to his room.

'That depends,' he says, 'which one of us did he ask for?'

I hadn't thought to get any more details from Marisol. She was in her room for the night now anyway, not to be disturbed.

'I'm sure it would be both of us,' I say, not sure at all.

Ben unpacks books from his schoolbag onto the desk. He's studying for exams between rugby training because he wants to be a doctor. 'Let me have a shower first, Amy,' he says, but he's frowning, and I think he will be going through all the same thoughts I've been having.

'Come to my room after,' I tell him before going back to lie on my bed and stare again at the ceiling.

After an unusually long shower for Ben, we sit on my bed, Sasha's bright-pink landline phone and the uncrumpled Post-it note on the quilt between us. Neither of us really wants to make the call.

'He'll be expecting you,' I say, attempting to put the onus on my brother.

'Why?' Ben looks as unwilling to pick up the receiver as I am.

'Because you're the oldest,' I reason.

'Only by a year!'

'Fine.' I know full well that Ben won't do it so I snatch up the handset and quickly punch the number in before I can change my mind. I hold the receiver out in front of us so we can hear the distant ringing. I am about to hang up when, after five rings, we hear a faint, 'Hello,' from the other end. Ben and I look at each other, eyes wide. The voice says hello again, this time a little louder. I close my eyes and bring the receiver up to my ear.

'Hi Dad,' I say. 'It's me. Amy.'

We spoke for an hour that night. Some crying went on, mostly from me. Speaking to my dad made me feel guilty because I really hadn't given him much thought in such a long time and because suddenly he was a real person, a man I remembered, but I felt like I was betraying Mum by speaking to him too. Ben was short with him, giving him monosyllabic answers before handing the phone back to me. My dad was sorry; that was the message he wanted to get across. That, and he missed us. He told us about his friend Muriel who lived next door and how he went to church with her on a Sunday. He said that Muriel had helped him and that she was the person that had said he should try and get in touch with us.

'I didn't think you'd want to hear from me, after all this time,' he said. 'But Muriel said that it wasn't for me to decide what you wanted, and I should at least give it a try.'

He went on. 'No pressure at all, but Muriel would like to invite us all round to hers for dinner next Sunday. Five o'clock. You don't need to decide now but if you could let me know what you think, during the week, that would be grand. You know where we are now.'

An image of our old house flashed into my head. I had always known where he was. I didn't think I was that little girl anymore; the one sitting on her bed, listening to the firecracker sounds of her parents shouting at each other. I wasn't sure if I wanted to go back, didn't want to find out that perhaps I was still that little girl. We hung up the phone and sat in silence for a while.

'I suppose we have to make a decision,' I said at last.

Ben nodded. 'I'm hungry.'

'Me too,' I said, and we went downstairs to upset Marisol's overly organised fridge.

II

Edinburgh, 2018

Ben answered the front door, his hair sticking up in all directions and a slightly manic look in his eye. Amy wondered if he had, at any moment, stopped grinning since the arrival of his daughter, or indeed managed to get any sleep at all.

'Come in, come in,' he ushered, taking hold of Jeannette's arm and helping her up the step. 'How's that bump healing, Grandma?'

'It's mending just fine, thank you, sweetheart. You'd have thought it would've knocked some sense into me. Doesn't seem to have done the trick though.'

Ben laughed. 'Amy wants me to give you the once-over while you're here if that's OK.'

'Oh, she does, does she?' Jeannette turned to give Amy a withering look.

'Come and meet your latest great-grandchild first, though.' Ben held on to Jeannette's arm and led her through the hallway.

Amy and Brodie followed them into the large open-plan living space at the back of the house. Natalie was sitting in a nursing chair, her baby held closely to her chest, wrapped in a pale-yellow blanket.

Brodie approached cautiously; his eyes fixed on the bundle.

'It's OK, Brodie, come closer and meet your cousin.' Natalie loosened the blanket. The baby squirmed; a tiny hand wriggled free and stretched upwards.

'Can I touch her?' Brodie asked.

'Of course you can, go ahead.' Natalie smiled encouragement.

Brodie reached across slowly. Amy noticed instantly how big her son's hand looked in comparison to the tiny delicate fingers of the newborn and felt something close to sadness wash over her briefly; another reminder that her boy was no longer the baby.

Brodie turned and grinned at his mother. She gave him a thumbs up from where she was filling the kettle at the kitchen sink.

'What's her name?' Brodie asked his aunt. Amy noticed Ben glance up and share another moment with Natalie. They both smiled.

'Do you think you can guess?'

Brodie looked thoughtful for a moment.

'Is it Kirsty?'

Natalie shook her head.

'Cara?'

Amy smiled; he was guessing the names of the girls in his primary-school class. He tried a few more.

'It's probably not a name that you've heard before.' Amy was intrigued; her brother had been vague on whether they'd settled on anything yet.

'Shall I just tell you?'

Brodie nodded eagerly.

'She's called Etta.'

Brodie tried it out. 'Etta.' Amy looked at her brother who had taken a seat next to their grandmother, his arm resting behind her on the back of the sofa.

'Etta,' Jeannette repeated the name.

'Just a small nod to you, Grandma. We'd have called her Jeannette but there's only one of you,' he teased.

'That's lovely, sweetheart,' she patted her grandson's leg. 'Now if Mummy doesn't mind, I'd like to meet little Etta properly, please.'

Natalie stood slowly, all the time rocking the baby and crossed the room, placing her gently into Jeannette's arms.

'Where's your phone, Ben, get a photo will you.' Natalie stretched, reaching her arms towards the ceiling and bending slightly backwards.

'My goodness, you look amazing.' Amy glanced down at where there had been a neat little bump only the week before. Natalie instinctively placed her hands on her belly. 'It's a bizarre feeling, isn't it? After months of feeling full and heavy, suddenly being empty.'

'I think I felt quite relieved, although I know what you mean. Pregnancy seems to last forever and then before you know it, the baby's here.' Amy looked over at Brodie who had already lost interest in his new cousin and was now trying to guess the passcode for Ben's iPad.

'And then all of a sudden, they're six years old.' Amy squeezed her sister-in-law's arm. 'Treasure every moment, even the tough ones. That's the only nugget of advice I have for you.'

Natalie laughed. 'I was kind of hoping you'd have more than that for me. I'm expecting you to know it all, especially seeing as you've done it all by yourself.'

'I'm sure I can help out a bit, but I certainly don't have all the answers. Most days I just make it up. I think the secret is that most people do.'

'Well you've done a fantastic job of making it up then. Brodie's such a lovely wee boy.'

Amy looked again at her son, a bubble of pride rising in her chest. She wiped at a tear that had escaped unexpectedly and sniffed loudly. 'Right,' she said. 'It's my turn to meet Etta properly now. Pass my niece over please, Grandma.'

An hour later, the doorbell rang.

'Listen, we'll get going, we shouldn't have stayed so long. It was only meant to be a quick visit. You both could do with a snooze, I'll bet.'

Natalie didn't look as though she wanted to argue.

'That'll be Mum,' Ben said, making his way to the hall.

Amy could hear her mother before she came billowing into the room. She was wearing another arty outfit; a bright and baggy flowery dress, accessorised with oversized necklace and bangles in primary colours. Her hair was piled messily on top of her head and she was wearing deep-red lipstick, similar to the colour the girl in the dungarees had been wearing at the studios.

'Sorry I'm late, everyone,' she announced to the room, 'but I did bring food.' She brandished a large paper bag. 'Fish and chips!' she announced. Brodie cheered.

'I think we were just about to get going, Mum,' Amy said. 'Natalie's a bit tired.'

'Nonsense.' Judith put the bag down on the island counter and began unpacking the boxes. The smell of freshly cooked fish and chips wafted through the room.

'I am quite hungry actually,' Natalie said, wandering over. Ben was already attacking an open box. 'I'm starving,' he said through a mouthful of fish. 'I think we've forgotten to eat.'

'Hello, Judith,' Jeannette called over from the sofa.

'Hello, Mother,' Judith replied, not looking up.

Judith produced a bottle of Prosecco from her oversized handbag. 'Let's get this open, shall we? Glasses, darling?' Ben put the box down and wiped his fingers on a towel.

When they had all eaten some fish and chips and drank a toast to the newest family member, Judith tapped the side of her glass.

'I've got an announcement to make.' Amy felt her stomach flip. Jeannette muttered something incomprehensible.

Judith flashed her mother a quick look of contempt before returning her wide smile to the rest of the group.

'I'm having a gallery showing.'

Amy glanced at Ben. 'You're having a gallery showing? But you haven't even started art college yet.'

'Well, dearest daughter, it just so happens that my talent has been discovered far earlier than even I had imagined.'

'Have you got a new boyfriend?' Amy could sense, as she always did with her mother, that there was more to this story than she was letting on.

'No, I have not got a new boyfriend.' Judith pretended to be offended momentarily. 'I do, however, have a friend who knows someone who owns a new art space in town, and they were looking for unknown and emerging local artists to create their opening show.'

'A *friend*.' Amy shook her head. 'I knew it.'

'Now, now, he really is just a friend.' Judith paused. 'In fact, you met him, at the studio the other day. Handsome young Robbie, you remember?'

'The guy who was going to pose nude for you?' Amy thought back to the brief meeting. Had he been handsome?

'You have men posing nude for you?' Ben asked through a mouthful of chips he'd scavenged from the leftovers.

'Not completely nude, darling. He was wearing a sheet over certain bits. Anyway, that's not the point. The point is that my paintings are going to be on display, and you're all invited to the opening night.' Judith clapped her hands together with excitement.

'Good for you, Mum.' Ben smiled at Judith.

'Yes, well done.' Natalie joined in. Amy said nothing.

'Now.' Judith clapped her hands together again. 'Pass me this gorgeous new grandchild of mine. Does she have a name yet?'

Amy shared a look with Jeannette.

'Well she's not called Judith, if that's what you're wondering.'

Judith ignored her mother and began cooing and exclaiming at how delightful the baby was. She wrinkled her nose a little as Natalie told her the name. 'Bit odd, isn't it?' she remarked, before returning her attention to the baby, humming a soft tune and rocking her gently from side to side.

'When is this gallery thing?' Jeannette asked, ignoring her daughter's crass remark.

'Not until September. The twenty-first, I think. I'm not sure it'll really be your cup of tea, to be honest. You might not want to bother.'

Amy suddenly realised, 'But that's your birthday, Grandma. Mum, that's Grandma's ninetieth. Friday, twenty-first of September.'

Judith shrugged. 'Well, I can't change the opening night. It's not up to me.'

'But Mum, we've decided to have a party.'

'*You've* decided to have a party,' Jeannette added.

'Amy. There is nothing I can do about the date of my show. Surely you can throw your little party on another day?'

Amy simmered. She knew there was never any point in trying to make her mother see things from anyone else's point of view.

'What time will your opening be at? Maybe we can do both things.' Ben had finished shovelling the leftover chips into his mouth and slumped back down on the sofa.

'I don't have any of those details yet, darling.'

'We'll work something out,' Ben assured his sister. 'We certainly can't let your ninetieth birthday go by without a massive fuss.' He smiled at Jeannette, who rolled her eyes.

Amy's phone buzzed on the coffee table. She noticed Nick's name flash up on the screen. Ben noticed too. He looked at Amy and pointed at her phone, a dark cloud crossing his face.

'What on earth is he doing phoning you?'

Amy swiped the screen to reject the call. 'I was going to tell you he'd been in touch,' she said, already feeling the defensive prickle creeping up the back of her neck.

'Please tell me you're not getting involved with him again?'

'Involved with who?' Judith had placed the baby back in the Moses basket next to the patio doors and was pouring the last bit of Prosecco into her own glass.

Amy sighed. 'Nick's been in touch.'

'Nick who?' Judith looked confused.

'For goodness sake, Mum, surely you remember Nick.' Amy indicated Brodie who didn't look up from the iPad.

'Oh, that Nick. Christ.' She pulled a face. 'What does he want?'

'He turned up outside my work the other day. He's got a new girlfriend and they're having a baby. I think it was the girlfriend who convinced him to do it actually.'

'But what does he want?' Ben's state of elation was faltering under the reminder of his sister's ex-boyfriend.

'He says he wants to see Brodie.'

At the mention of his name Brodie's head snapped up. 'Who wants to see me?'

'Just an old friend, kiddo. Someone who knew you when you were a baby.'

'Again, please tell me you're not seriously thinking of inviting him into your life again?' Ben was shaking his head in disbelief.

'I'm not doing anything yet.' Amy raised her hands. 'He says he's changed. I had to give him a chance to apologise.'

'And did he? Apologise?'

Amy thought back to the meeting in the café. She couldn't quite remember the exact details of the conversation. In fact, the memory of the meeting was a bit of a blur.

'Look, he's got a whole new life. Perhaps he just wants to make amends. It's not like he's going to try and get back with me or anything.'

Ben looked unsure. 'Just be careful, Amy.'

'I will be.' Amy stood, lifting her phone and sliding it into her back pocket. 'We should really get going now anyway. You guys definitely need to get some sleep.' She leant down and gave her brother a quick hug. 'Come on, Brodie. You too, Grandma. Mum, do you want a lift?' Judith was stabbing away at her mobile phone.

'No, thank you. Robbie's just arrived to pick me up. We're going for a drink.'

Amy looked at her brother. *Told you*, she mouthed, shaking her head.

'It made me think about when Brodie was born.' Amy placed the mug of tea on the side table next to her grandmother's armchair. 'It seems like so much has happened since then but then it feels like it was only yesterday at the same time, if that makes sense.'

'It does, dear.' Jeannette lifted the mug with two hands, trying to steady the shaking. 'It sometimes feels like not that long ago your mother came crashing into the world.'

'Was he there?'

'Who?'

'The affair man? Did he come to the birth?'

'Don't call him that.' Jeannette tutted. 'And no, he wasn't at the birth. That's a new thing anyway. Most men didn't see their offspring being born back in those days.'

Jeannette closed her eyes for a moment. He was there again, just behind her eyelids. She could see him striding into the room. Amy looked at herself in the mirror over the fireplace and ran her fingers through her hair, pulling it up into a ponytail. 'You need to tell me more about what happened. Why was he never going to leave his wife, there must've been a reason he couldn't?' She slumped down on the sofa.

'They were married, dear. It wasn't as easy in those days just to walk out – you young folk think getting married is a good excuse for a party. Back in my day people meant their wedding vows. Marriage was for life. He,' Jeannette paused to take in a deep breath, 'George, was a good man, despite everything. He didn't want to bring shame on Annie's family.'

'But what about the shame he brought on you? I don't think that was very honourable of him.'

'Ah, but I'm to blame for that too. I didn't have to agree to meet him all those times. I could've said no.'

'It sounded like he made you promises though, Grandma. I don't think you would've done it if he'd admitted right at the beginning that he'd never leave his wife.'

'Well . . .' Jeannette thought for a moment. 'I'm not sure that's strictly true. We all do silly things when we're in love, or at least when we think we're in love. You should know all about that, dear.'

Amy raised an eyebrow. 'Ouch!' She laughed.

'I'm sure your feelings at the time for Nick made you overlook the obvious flaws for quite a while, that's all I'm pointing out.'

Amy shook her head. 'I certainly didn't do everything the way I would now. God, if I could go back in time and give myself a shake.'

'No point in thinking about changing what's done. You are where you are now because of all the choices you've made – and I think you're doing all right these days. Just think, if you hadn't made the decisions you had, Brodie might not be here.'

Amy thought back to the conversation she'd had with her mum the year before; the catalyst for Judith making the change to her life. She still felt the same, like she wouldn't do anything differently. The future was another matter though.

'Another cup of tea?' Amy stood, holding out her hand for her grandmother's cup.

Jeannette shook her head. 'No thank you, dear. I'm just going to pop the TV on for a bit though, if you don't mind.'

'Of course not. I'll just go and check on Brodie.'

Amy wandered through to her bedroom where Brodie was tucked under the covers, propped up on pillows, his latest favourite book about dinosaur's pooping planets spread out in front of him. She climbed up beside her son and tucked an arm round his back. 'Shall we read it together for a bit?' she offered. Brodie nodded sleepily. Amy began reciting the rhyming words, trying to lose herself in the ridiculous world of Brodie's book. There was a figure in the back of her mind that just wouldn't go away though, no matter how hard she tried. She was going to have to decide what to do about Nick, once and for all.

An hour later, Amy went to help Jeannette through to bed. Thoughts of the past, of Brodie's father, of Nick, had been whirling around her head since Brodie had nodded off. It was impossible, it would never go away, she knew that now, not until she faced up to things. She sat on the arm of her grandmother's chair. They looked at one another, both aware the conversation from earlier was unfinished. Amy cleared her throat.

'Grandma,' she said, 'I've got a secret.'

12

Edinburgh, 2010

Sasha is already sitting in the bar when I arrive. We go for a drink every Thursday and have a usual place to meet, but this week Sasha has chosen a new bar that's opened on George Street. It's decorated in Liberace-style decadence and serves small measures of wine in glasses the size of balloons. The bar is perfect for Sasha, who spends half her life being plucked and polished at the beauticians, but less so for me. I would be quite happy in the Rose and Crown around the corner, with its dated wallpaper and sticky tabletops. I know how to fake it when I have to though; after all, I spent most of my teenage years pretending to be something I wasn't, in a world I didn't belong in. My stepsister stands to greet me, planting air kisses somewhere east and west of each of my cheeks.

I take off my jacket and sit down opposite Sasha. She pours some wine for me into an empty balloon-sized glass from a bottle in an ice bucket.

'Don't look now,' she says, 'but there a guy from television over there. I told you this place would be interesting.'

'Who?' I start to turn in my seat, but Sasha grabs my wrist.

'Don't *look*!' she hisses. I take a drink of wine instead and notice something floating on top of the liquid.

'He's one of those folks that does those thingy bits on the news.'

'Thingy bits?' I try to fish the unidentifiable piece of something out of my wine with my index finger.

'You know, like when the camera cuts away and some reporter's standing outside Parliament or something. That's what he does.'

'Well seeing as you won't let me look at him, I guess I'll never know if I know him. How's the business doing?'

We spend the next hour working our way through the bottle of wine before ordering a second one. Halfway through that, Sasha leaves me to go to the toilets and I take out my mobile phone and read a text from my brother asking me if I've got time to take his car to the garage. He started a new job at the Royal Infirmary a couple of months ago and seems to be at work all the time. I text back.

No problem, phone me tomorrow x

A minute later, a reply pings in.

Cool, thanks sis! What U up 2? X

I hate that even my intelligent brother uses text speak. I type out the reply.

Out with Sasha for a drink x

I watch my phone until the screen lights up again.

No such thing as 1 drink with Sash! Make sure UR OK 2 drive my car 2morrow x

I put my phone down on the table and twist around to see if I can spot Sasha coming back from the toilets. I'm about to turn back when I spot her talking to a man at the bar. She's flicking her hair and standing with her hand on

137

her hip, pelvis thrust slightly forward. Classic Sasha mating ritual. The man points over to me and smiles. He's incredibly handsome, a bit on the short side, but really nicely dressed. Perfect for Sasha. She turns and walks back towards our table.

'Have you—' I start, but she interrupts me.

'I was speaking to that guy, the one from the television,' she points over in his direction.

'Stop it, he'll see you.'

'That's the plan,' Sasha laughs, beckoning to him.

I sit back, folding my arms, and fix Sasha with my most contemptuous stare.

But Sasha just responds with one of her brightest smiles.

'Hello again,' she says simply, batting her eyelashes. The man looks amused by her.

'You wanted me to meet someone?' he asks.

I try to hide my face behind my hand.

'Yes! This is my sister, Amy.'

I form a graphic image in my mind of my hands around Sasha's throat.

'Nice to meet you, Amy, I'm Nick. Can I get you girls a drink?' I begin to protest but Sasha stops me.

'I'm afraid I can't stay but I'm sure Amy would be more than happy to join you for one.' She begins gathering her coat and bag.

'White wine, is it?' He indicates my empty glass.

'That'd be lovely, thank you.'

Nick goes back to the bar. I turn and see one of the men he was talking to before slapping him on the back.

'Why on earth did you do that?' I hiss.

'Because you've been single far too long, and you need to loosen up a bit. And he's a total dish.'

Sasha gives Nick a small wave. 'Also, I did see him checking you out earlier, when you went to the ladies'.'

'He was not!'

'Was too. Now have fun. I'll call you later.' Sasha does another round of air kisses before deserting me.

Nick returns from the bar, placing another of the bulbous glasses in front of me.

'Your sister's quite unsubtle,' he says, sliding into Sasha's empty seat.

'She's my stepsister actually. No blood relation. Our parents aren't even married anymore so I can probably legitimately disown her now.'

Nick laughs, revealing a set of perfectly straight white teeth.

'So, what do you do, Amy?'

'Oh, you know. What everyone does; something in marketing. Very boring. Although Sasha says you work in television. You're some kind of reporter?'

'What, you mean you don't know who I am?' Nick feigns outrage.

'Sorry, no. I tend to avoid the news. Too depressing.'

'You're right about that. I mostly cover Scottish politics, so it gets pretty dreary sometimes. I do get to do the occasional good news story though. The other week I was sent to cover a story about a woman who wants to marry her horse.'

'No way. You're making that up.'

'Sadly, I'm not.' Nick takes a drink of his beer. 'Have you eaten?'

I shake my head.

'There's a tapas restaurant a couple of streets away that I've been meaning to try. Don't suppose you fancy grabbing a bite with me?'

After he leaves my flat the next morning, I ring Sasha straight away.

'Good for you, when are you seeing him again?' she says.

'I don't think I am. He doesn't even have my number.'

She tuts loudly on the other end of the line.

'Oh for goodness sake, honey, don't be so stupid. Nobody needs to have your number to get in touch with you these days.'

'Anyway, I'm sure it was just a one-night thing,' I tell her. 'He's far too good-looking for me.'

This statement evokes another loud tut and an instruction to get some wine chilling in the fridge because she's inviting herself to my house later for a Friday night takeaway and a full debrief on what went on.

We spend the evening eating Chinese food and drinking too many bottles of white wine. Just after midnight I open my laptop and check my Facebook messages and find one from Nick; Sasha was right, he didn't even need my number.

'He wants to come over tomorrow,' I tell her, and she grabs the laptop, typing in a response before I can stop her. Admittedly I don't try very hard.

I am shitting a brick by the next day. Sasha insists on doing my make-up and leaves me ten minutes before he's due to arrive, looking as though I've been involved in a car crash. I'm rubbing at her age-old idea of smoky eyes when the buzzer rings.

'You look lovely,' he comments as he comes in through the front door and kisses my cheek.

'Through here.' I point towards the living room.

'I know,' Nick smiles and I predictably begin to blush, forgetting he was here only a few nights ago.

We drink the champagne he brought, and my stomach does somersaults when he kisses me and then he says he has to go because he's working in Glasgow tomorrow.

'Can I see you again soon though?' he asks as he's leaving.

I agree because I can't quite believe he actually wants to, but I think to myself that this can't last; he is literally too good to be true.

Famous last words.

13

Edinburgh, 2011

I have really messed things up. When I met Nick, I couldn't believe he was interested in me, not genuinely. But then he whipped me up into his whirlwind social life and it wasn't long before he was calling me his girlfriend.

'I don't remember you ever asking me to make it official,' I joked one night. We were wrapped in the duvet in my bed, my head resting on his chest.

He laughed. 'Should I phone your dad and ask for his permission?'

I sat up and whacked him softly with my pillow. He pulled me down and climbed on top of me, pressing his lips against mine. I felt myself melting into him. He can do that to me with just a look.

Sasha had been right about how boring I'd become. Nick knows so many people and they love having him around, so there's always some excitement to be had, another party to go to. And if I'm being completely honest, then I have to admit that being with Nick has done my ego the world of good; other girls comment on how jealous they are; he is so handsome, so much fun to be around. I am so lucky. Of course it would be me that messed things up.

*

I'm sitting on the toilet praying that the first test was faulty. How many women have experienced the same delusional hope I wonder? It really is Sod's law; so many people desperately wishing to see those two lines appear, month after month, feeling that sinking disappointment when they realise their dreams aren't coming true yet again. While other women, like me, try to convince themselves that it could be inaccurate, even when something inside them is screaming the truth.

I am lamenting, scared to leave the toilet and face up to the reality on the other side of the door. Beyond it exists a world in which I am *pregnant*. How could I have been so stupid? Worse still, there is no one I can call; no friend that I want to sit with while the urine soaks up the stick. Sasha would love the drama but there is a very good reason why I don't want her here; a reason that I've been trying to bury deeply since the night of her birthday party.

I try the second test from the two-pack I bought in Boots. Same result. I go straight to bed and lie under the covers with my hands on my stomach, imagining all the activity going on in there. I try to work out when my last period was. How far gone would I be? I have no idea: two months, three months maybe. I reach my hand out of the covers and feel on the bedside table for my mobile phone. I haven't seen or heard from Nick in a couple of days. He hasn't responded to my texts. He said he was tired of me not believing he wanted to be with me. He said I needed to think about whether it was actually me that didn't want to be with him. When I think about Sasha's birthday party night, I wonder if he's right.

I type out a text.

Hey, really need to see you. Kind of urgent situation. Please reply? Xxx

The light outside my flat begins to darken as I wait for a response, not moving from beneath the covers. At some point I fall asleep because when I wake up, it's pitch black and I quickly check my phone. My heart lurches at the sight of the message from him.

Busy now, tomorrow? X

Only one kiss. He must still be upset with me. I quickly type back.

Perfect, let me know where and when would suit you xxx

I stick to three kisses to show him that I want to be with him.

We meet in a pub on the Shore, in Leith. It's the kind of place where salt-of-the-earth locals mix with the trendy folk from the new digital agencies springing up in the shared offices around the area. I'm already there when he arrives, a pint of beer and a glass of white wine in front of me. He leans down, kisses me on the cheek. He sits.

'So what's up?' he says, raising the pint glass to his mouth and taking a sip.

I blurt it out.

'You're what?' I know he's heard but I repeat it again anyway.

'I'm pregnant.' The words feel ridiculous coming out of my mouth, like they're not mine to own.

Nick stares at me, his features twisting, and I see an anger sparking in him, like a match being struck. His muscles tense.

'Is this some kind of joke?' he asks, and I shake my head slowly from side to side. 'How?' he says it through clenched teeth.

I don't want to anger him further by giving the obvious response to his question.

'I'm not sure really, maybe it was that time,' I lower my voice so the people at the next table can't hear, 'when the condom, you know, slipped off.' My voice is a whisper.

Nick looks incredulous, so I continue.

'We've not exactly been careful. Think about all those nights out. We've probably had sex and not remembered it in the morning.'

Nick makes an ugly snorting noise. I can tell I've made him think about it though; can see he is battling within himself. He takes a long drink from his pint glass and puts it down with a heavy thud.

'Is it mine?' he asks in a low growl.

It's the question I didn't want him to ask, not only because of what had happened the night of Sasha's birthday party, but because it would mean either he didn't trust me, or worse, he was sleeping around himself.

'Of course it is.' I take a drink to try and cover the blush I can feel rising up my neck and into my cheeks. I'm an expert at keeping a secret, but this is different. Nick is staring at his pint glass. I wait; the silence stretches. I take a second gulp immediately after the first and have almost finished the glass when I remember I shouldn't be drinking.

Nick drains his pint and without looking at me says, 'You'll need to have an abortion.'

'I'm not sure—' I begin, but Nick stops me by crashing his fist down on the table. Both of our glasses jump, along with the people at the next table.

Nick stands to leave. 'Have an abortion,' he says again, looking directly at me this time. I feel a shiver running the length of my spine as I watch him turn and walk away. The pub door bangs loudly as he shoves his way outside.

14

Edinburgh, 2012

Nick does a disappearing act the minute my contractions start. Scotland are playing rugby at Murrayfield and high-spirited fans dressed in blue and white, some with Scotland flags draped around their shoulders, are making their way towards the stadium, most likely with a stop at a pub en route. I stand at the living-room window, looking down at the junction below, concentrating on the traffic lights changing from red to amber to green and then back again. The contractions are still quite far apart, more like strong period pains, and I am trying to follow the advice of the lady at the NCT classes and go on as normal during the first part of labour.

'The more you move around the quicker labour will progress,' she'd assured us. I'd joined the classes not fully understanding what the National Childbirth Trust were all about. Nicola from the office had told me she'd been and still kept in touch with all the other mums she'd met. It sounded like fun. I walked in to my first group, without Nick, and mistakenly put up my hand when the lady asked cheerfully, 'Is anyone planning on having an epidural?' That was when I discovered that the *N* should have stood for *Natural*. We all sat around, watching a volunteer and some coloured balls of strings demonstrate how awful and uncomfortable an epidural is. When she asked afterwards if I'd changed my mind, I hung my head and nodded in the manner of a chastised schoolgirl.

Nick had *really* disappeared before the contractions started. We were watching a movie on the sofa last night, having finished a takeaway from the local Thai restaurant. I'd eaten a chilli by mistake and made a comment about how spiciness is said to sometimes induce labour. When I said I was feeling a bit funny later, and that the baby was moving, he grabbed his coat and said he was going to get me some indigestion tablets. He didn't come home.

Rather than panic, which I'd done the first few times he'd disappeared for the night, I am quite relieved. Nick has been living in my flat for the last few months, ever since he decided he wanted us to try again, he wanted us to be a family. Of course, I'd already made the decision to keep the baby before that, with or without Nick's support, because I'd spoken to my grandma and she'd told me that she would be there for me and to remember that she'd managed to do it all alone way back when people's views weren't quite so accepting. I'd visited an abortion clinic on Nick's request but when the doctor had asked me why I'd wanted a termination, I paused and then told her I didn't. She sent me on my way that day with an antenatal appointment instead. But when Nick had reappeared, I welcomed him back. He was sorry, he'd freaked out. He said it was probably something to do with his parents not being alive, he was frightened of life, and death. We'd had something special and I wanted that back. I also didn't really want to do it alone if I didn't have to. Not that it's all gone swimmingly so far. I've started seeing another, unfamiliar side to Nick. I've found out that he bounces between extremes; one minute being distant and spending a lot of time out of the flat, the next buying me expensive gifts and rushing around to make sure I have everything I want. He tells me constantly that he loves me and I believe him, perhaps because I love him too. He explained to me once, after the second time he'd stayed out all night, that he's frightened of the love we have for each other; he's never experienced anything like it and, in a way, it kind of made sense. I certainly haven't felt anything like it before either.

I give up on the advice of the NCT lady and go back to bed, spreading myself out to try and get comfortable, sleep coming in fitful waves as my stomach gurgles and the baby continues to wriggle, pushing its limbs against the tight confines of my fully stretched uterus. I eventually give up on any more rest at around 2 p.m. and pour a bath to ease the ache in my back.

The first proper contraction comes as I sit at the dressing table in my room trying to dry my hair. I can hear the roars from the rugby stadium by then; my cries drown them out.

I haven't called anyone yet, haven't wanted to bother anyone this early on in labour but as I feel the surge of the contraction sear through me, taking me by surprise with its force, I begin to panic. I realise I am alone, and the pain is searing hot and disorientating. Then, just as soon as it starts, it stops, and I think, *That wasn't so bad*.

Until the next contraction comes, about ten minutes later, that is. I scroll through the contacts in my phone and hover over Ben's number, then Sasha's. For some reason, I phone my mum.

'How many minutes apart are they?' she asks.

When I tell her around ten, she laughs and says I've to relax, that she'll come over in a bit. 'Tell Nick to rub your back until I get there.'

'He's not here,' I start crying. 'He left last night to get some indigestion tablets and didn't come home. I've no idea where he is.'

I hear her mutter something about men and childbirth before she promises to be there as soon as she can.

Mum arrives half an hour later carrying two lattes and a bag of sweet pastries.

'I don't think I can eat or drink anything,' I say, retching at the smell of the coffee. Another contraction starts along with an added wave of panic. I am finding it difficult to get any air into my lungs.

'You're not breathing properly,' my mum is saying. She kneels beside me and places a hand on my lower back. 'Take a deep breath in, through your nose,' she instructs. I do as I'm told. I am five years old again and want to be cuddled into her on the sofa, watching TV.

'Good. Now slowly sigh the whole breath out through your mouth – that's it, push it right out and relax those muscles.'

I am amazed that it works. 'I have given birth twice, you know,' Mum tuts.

We wait for a bit, Mum drinks both lattes and takes a bite of one of the pastries, then decides it's time to call the hospital. The contractions are three minutes apart. I hide my true condition well at first from the taxi driver until halfway to the hospital when I let out what can only be described as a demonic sound.

'You're not about to drop, are you, hen?' he says through the glass plate dividing us, as we stop at some traffic lights. 'It's just, this is my new taxi.'

My mum tells him to shut up and drive but by the time I reach the hospital I fully believe that the baby is already halfway out.

149

I'm ushered through to lie on an examination table.

'Only five centimetres,' the nurse states, snapping off the rubber gloves she'd been wearing and tossing them into a bin. 'Usually I'd send you home for a bit but we're quiet in the midwife-led unit so if you'd like to go over there for a bit . . .'

'I want an epidural,' I am completely sick and tired of the pain. How do women do this every day? It is the most unnatural hell to be going through.

'Too early for that too I'm afraid,' she smiles, and I ignore the wild urge to call her a bitch as another contraction tears through me. She waits for me to finish writhing around in pain and then says, 'Let's get you down to the new wing, they've got birthing pools. How about a nice warm bath?'

I had no intention of having a water birth, but that's what is happening. By the time I screamed for an epidural again, too early had turned into too late. I have, however, discovered the delights of gas and air and am floating around naked, wittering on about halloumi cheese when my grandma arrives. She's eighty-three but still fit as a fiddle, as she's fond of pointing out, and she marches into the room, tells my mother to go and have a break and then talks in her soothing voice to me, reassuring me that everything will be OK as she ties my straggly wet hair up into a ponytail.

She doesn't mention Nick and I'm glad because if he was here, I might be telling him things that I shouldn't, things that would make him run away forever, and I don't want that.

Mum comes back into the room and in one of my more lucid moments I realise she's adopted her sullen-teenager face. It happens every time they're in the same room. In my exhaustion and slightly elated state from the gas and air I begin shouting at them both to get along, to love each other. The contractions are only a minute apart now and the midwife is telling me we're ready to go on to the next stage.

'What next stage?' I am continually shouting now, although my throat is sore and my voice croaky.

'You're going to start pushing, baby is on the way.'

I can feel an urge to push bearing down on me, but I'm not ready.

'You two,' I jab the gas and air nozzle at my grandma and mum. 'You need to stop it.' They look at each other then back at me. 'I need you both! This baby needs you both. I'm not having this baby until you agree to make up. Put the past behind us. Let's put the past behind us all. It's shit, the past.' I know I am rambling, but the gas and air is making me feel so emotional and, I think, a little bit drunk.

Of course, I can't stop the urge to push and before I know what is happening, the two of them are behind me, one over each shoulder as the midwife plunges her hands under the water and starts reciting instructions.

'Your baby's head is almost out now,' I can hear her saying. 'Would you like to touch it?'

I open my eyes at that moment and must give her a look of utter disgust because she says cheerily, 'No, OK, let's just keep going then.'

I've never known pain like it. I feel like my bottom is going to explode. Then, suddenly, the baby, my baby, slides out and the pressure stops and a blanket of silence falls over the room.

'I'm going to hold him under for a minute and then bring baby up onto your chest. Try and sit up out of the water a bit.'

My whole body shakes but Mum and Grandma help me up and then the bluest, most scrunched-up bundle of head and body and limbs is scooped out of the water and into my arms and I hold him tight to me and say over and over, 'My baby, my baby.'

There is a lot of stuff that happens afterwards, involving a placenta that is too eager to slide out while I step from the birthing pool and some stitching that's required because apparently I didn't listen to the midwife telling me to 'pant baby out'. Nobody tells you too much about those bits before you give birth the first time. There is also the shock of the breastfeeding, which I had given absolutely no thought to prior to the birth, but which feels as though tiny shards of broken glass are trying to pass out through my nipples. I am finding the whole experience a little underwhelming in the pleasure stakes, but then it happens.

The midwife lets me go for a shower and I come back to find my tiny baby boy being wrapped tightly – *swaddled*, Grandma calls it – in a white hospital blanket. I am wearing fresh pyjamas and feel clean and warm and, as I sit up on the bed, she passes my little bundle to me.

'We've been through it today, haven't we, Brodie?' I whisper. His lips are moving around, presumably looking for something to suckle on and he opens his eyes just a little to reveal black pools behind slightly purple eyelids. The birth had been so surreal, so alien, that it had been difficult to register any feeling or emotion at the time. My body had been in shock when he was handed to me in the water. But I feel it now, feel every part of me filling with love for this tiny fragile human being I've been growing inside me for the last nine months. Mum and Grandma slide through the curtain just then and I look at them and they look at each other and for the first time ever in my whole life, I see them smile at one another. 'Come and meet Brodie,' I say, and Grandma nudges my mum forward.

'Go on, Granny,' she says.

'Oh no, not *Granny*. I'm not quite lavender and cardigans enough for that.' My mum thinks for a moment. 'I'll be *Nana*.'

Grandma and I share a look and laugh. I pass my son to his nana, and my grandma comes and sits next to me on the bed and holds my hand in both of hers and says, 'I'm so proud of you, kiddo,' and I cry big fat happy tears, because I know right then, that Brodie is going to be a very loved little boy. All we need now is Nick.

15

Edinburgh, 2018

Her grandmother's past had been tumbling around Amy's mind for weeks. She had of course always known that they shared the experience of lone parenting; the thought had given Amy strength at times, when she'd struggled with the solitude and the pressure of responsibility. But to discover that there was more; another family, a half-brother - her grandmother, it seemed, could keep secrets for a long time too.

She had spent an afternoon at work that week surreptitiously googling the family that her grandma had once been on the periphery of, and that her own mother, and in turn she supposed, herself and Ben, even Brodie, were related to by blood. That was the thing about families; they spread, just like in the branches of Brodie's clumsily drawn family tree, and although you could ignore some of those branches if you wanted to, you could never break them.

Details of Annie's father's law firm were easy to find, and she discovered that it had transitioned throughout the years; merging with others until sometime during the seventies, the Forrest name no longer existed on any of the brass plaques of the city's law-firm doors. It always amazed her how much you could find out about strangers on the internet so quickly and the more she looked, the more she became determined to find some trace of the family who were connected to her own.

David Forrest had become a lawyer, as his parents had planned for him, and she found a trail of him right up into the 1980s where he worked for a law firm in London. Feeling brave about meddling in someone else's life, rather than facing up to her own current issues, she sent an email off to the place he'd last been known to work. Christine had emerged from her office, on the warpath for some perceived misdemeanour or another and so Amy shut down her computer quickly, the thought of the email she'd sent almost immediately fading from her memory.

As well as her grandmother's past, her own life decisions were also reverberating, forcing Amy to revisit forgotten memories; which made her far from comfortable. Like Jeannette, she'd faced a crossroads in her life; a point at which she could have made a very different decision than the one she had, and which would have created a completely different reality for her today.

She glanced at Brodie in the rear-view mirror. They were driving to the Botanical Gardens to look at a venue for her grandmother's ninetieth birthday party. Her little boy was staring out of the window, watching the world go by. She wondered what he was thinking about; wondered how often he thought about the absence of a father in his life. Her own father had been absent for a number of years and she couldn't be sure if she'd missed him, even now. She supposed there had been some sadness in the beginning, and perhaps when she saw her friends with their fathers, she had felt a pang of something close to jealousy. But he had been there for the first eight years, a permanent fixture. Brodie had never known any father figure; from ever since he could remember, it had just been the two of them. Not having a dad was Brodie's normal. She supposed that didn't mean it wasn't something he missed.

Amy pushed the thought from her mind. When they arrived at the Botanical Gardens, a woman wearing a tight pencil skirt and block-heeled court shoes came clopping out of the building they were about to view to greet them.

'I'm Janice,' she smiled and offered her hand for Amy to shake. 'We spoke on the phone.'

Amy followed Janice into the venue, admiring the ornate doorway that opened into a rectangular room with shiny parquet flooring bathed in light from the floor-to-ceiling windows that lined the front wall. It was the perfect size: not too big.

'It's a wonderful venue in the daytime or the evening really,' Janice, the assistant manager, was saying. Brodie was racing round the perimeter of the room, shouting out a number each time he completed another lap.

'Brodie, stop that, please,' Amy called. She was finding it difficult to concentrate due to the thumping headache that was currently pulsating inside her skull. She felt around in her bag for some ibuprofen.

'Just one more, Mum,' Brodie shouted back as he continued to thunder around the room.

'I bet he listens to his dad,' Janice commented, 'my two boys run rings around me, but the minute their dad barks an order – that's it!' She laughed and continued, 'I'm probably too soft with them, let them get away with murder so they don't take a blind bit of notice when I ask them to do something.' She was laying out promotional brochures on the make-shift bar in the corner of the room.

'Brodie!' Amy shouted more loudly this time, taking her phone out of her bag and handing it to her son. 'Do me a favour and just have a wee seat over there while I talk to the lady, OK?'

'Sorry about that.' Amy smiled sweetly. 'I think we'd like to hire it in the evening if that's possible. It's Friday, twenty-first of September we're thinking of.'

Janice pursed her lips and stabbed at her mobile phone. 'Let's just see . . . Oh dear, sorry, that date is already taken, I'm afraid. Wedding.' She continued to stab. 'I could do you the Saturday though. The twenty-second? I've had a cancellation so I could slot you in quickly if you were able to get the deposit over ASAP.'

Amy sighed; her mother would have her own way, as usual; everyone would be able to attend her gallery opening. She looked around the room. It was perfect. Her grandmother had taken Amy to the gardens regularly when she was a child, so she knew she would love the venue. It was important that everything was just right for her.

'That's fine. We'll take the Saturday then.' Amy tried not to be too disappointed; Jeannette wouldn't mind the party not being on her actual birthday, and besides, more people might be able to make the Saturday, especially now it wasn't going to clash with Judith's event.

Janice nodded and took down some details. Amy promised to send over the deposit that afternoon and then wandered over to the hothouses she'd raced around as a child.

As they strolled through the huge glass houses, condensation streaking the glass, they exclaimed at all the weird and wonderful tropical plants (*could that one eat you, Mum?*) and Amy made a mental note to talk more with Jeannette about her past that evening. She was beginning to hatch a plan and wanted to give her grandmother the best birthday ever. After all she'd been through in her life, she deserved it.

16

Amy's dad, Tony, had found God. He didn't find God by himself. Tony's neighbour, Muriel, saw him walking each day to the pub or the shops and then home again and decided he was lonely and miserable. So, she knocked on his front door every Sunday morning, offering him a lift to church, which he resolutely refused each time. One day, however, when he had a particularly bad hangover from watching the football in the pub the day before, Tony thought it might just be easier to go and sit quietly in church, rather than to listen to Muriel standing at his front door giving him the reasons why he should just go and sit quietly in church.

Muriel moved into the house next door to Tony a few months after Judith left. Amy didn't see her dad at all by then. They'd tried to keep in touch with him at first, Morag walking them back to their old house, promising to pick them up in a couple of hours. But Tony didn't want to talk and would just sit in his chair, cracking open cans of beer, watching old black-and-white films. One Saturday, he didn't answer the door and so Morag took them for ice cream instead. When the same thing happened the following week, they just didn't bother trying again. Soon after that, Judith changed her own and her children's surname to her maiden name, Aitken. It was her way of letting him know that he'd lost his children, not that he seemed to care at all at the time.

Muriel and Tony started as friends. She drove him to church every Sunday for almost a year before he agreed to let her cook him Sunday lunch. They'd shared snippets of conversation in Muriel's old Citroen 2CV on the way to church, but it wasn't until he sat opposite her at the table for two in her tiny kitchen, and she served up another dollop of mashed potato, that she told him about the son she'd lost. Her little boy had been diagnosed with leukaemia when he was two and died within six months. 'Two weeks off his third birthday,' she told him. 'It was why I started going to church.'

Muriel's husband ran off with a barmaid from their local pub a few months later and she'd been on her own ever since.

By some miracle, perhaps it was an act of God, Muriel managed to get Tony to open up a bit about his past, something he'd never been able to do before. He wasn't the type of dad that said things like, 'when I was a boy'. Amy hadn't seen any evidence of him ever having had a childhood; no photographs, no memorable tales of mischief. She had always just pictured him entering the world as a fully formed man.

After Muriel got him talking that day, he began talking more and then he cried, and Muriel wondered momentarily if she'd done the right thing because he didn't seem to be able to stop crying. But she took him to the doctor and he was OK after that.

When Amy and Ben had phoned their dad from Ken's house and arranged to go and meet him and Muriel for dinner, they hadn't known what to expect. What they discovered was a man they barely recognised, but in the nicest possible way, and neither of them wanted to question the transformation.

It wasn't until Amy was pregnant that she discovered more. They were making tea together in the small kitchen at Muriel's, where her father had lived for a few years. He'd given up the house Amy had grown up in and now a new family occupied the space next door she'd once called home. She hoped they were happy there.

Tony passed Amy the teabags and went to fill the kettle. She dropped one into each of the three mugs and noticed her dad staring at the bump.

'Is it strange for you to see me pregnant?' she asked.

'It is a bit, yes.' He flicked the switch on to boil the water and leant back against the worktop. 'And you say it's a boy?'

Amy nodded. 'Indisputable apparently.' She thought of the image on the screen at the scan; a cartoon-like penis shape with two little balls. The sonographer said she had no doubt. Touching her bump, neat and round, she gathered some courage. 'It's bizarre to think that everyone starts off like this – even you.'

Tony nodded curtly, his jaw tensing.

'What was she like, your mum?' Amy went on.

Tony picked the kettle up and silently leant over to fill each mug slowly.

'Sorry, it's fine if you don't want to talk about it.'

'It's not that, love. It's just that I haven't ever spoken to anyone about it, except Muriel.' He placed the kettle back on its base and reached across to open the fridge for the milk.

'Honestly, you don't need to tell me. Just forget I asked. It's fine.' Amy touched her dad's arm. He placed his hand on top of hers and patted it twice.

'It's OK, it's just . . .' Tony sighed. 'Muriel told me about her son. He died you know, when he was just a baby, only two. Did she tell you about that?'

Amy nodded.

'And I suppose, looking back, I thought she'd been through something so terrible that actually what I'd been through didn't seem as bad.'

Amy fished the teabags out of the mugs one by one.

'When I was about six, you see, I got home from school one day and found my mother sitting on the kitchen floor. I thought she was just resting at first and so I went towards her to wake her up and I slipped on something wet on the floor.' Tony stopped talking to put a splash of milk into each of the mugs. 'I fell down into her lap and I came right up close to where all the wetness was seeping out of her.' He touched his own wrist.

Amy put a hand to her mouth. 'Oh my God,' she said before remembering where she was and muttering an apology for the blasphemy.

Tony tutted. 'Don't be silly, love, it's Muriel you've to watch your language round, not me.'

'So what happened then? Was she dead?'

Her dad shook his head slowly. 'The neighbour came in behind me and sent her son for the ambulance. She got to hospital in time, but she was never quite right again. They put her in a hospital for people who were . . .' Tony tapped the side of his head. 'And I never saw her again after that.'

'What about your father?'

'I stayed with him for a bit until the neighbour that found me that time phoned the police. My old man had a bit of a heavy hand and so they took me to a children's home and then the rest, as they say, is history.' Tony picked up two of the mugs. 'Come on, we'll get these out to Muriel before they get cold.'

Amy lifted her own tea and followed. 'I'm sorry I never knew that about you, Dad. Really sorry you went through that – it must've been horrible.'

'All in the past now, love.' Tony smiled down at her bump. 'I tell you what though. That little boy in there will never have to go through anything like I did. What a lucky boy he's going to be to have you as a mum.' Amy swallowed. She'd been struggling to keep her emotions in check as the pregnancy progressed.

'Thanks, Dad,' she managed, before the tears burst forward, despite her best efforts.

Muriel told Amy once that Tony had never been loved as a child and that's what made it difficult for him to be able to love other people.

'Tell someone they're worthless for long enough and they'll begin to believe it,' she'd said.

So, Muriel started telling Tony he was a good man and he began to believe it, a little bit at a time, until one day, the old Tony, the man so full of bitterness and anger, had sloped off and left a quiet, kind, slightly abashed man in his place.

When Amy was little, she thought her dad was great fun. She supposed she must have known there was anger in him, but he didn't ever direct it at her. She had hoped, when Muriel helped him get rid of the anger, that the fun side of him would still be there but, disappointingly, it seemed to have faded too. Tony wore a thinly masked pained expression when he thought no one was looking and when he smiled, it didn't quite reach his eyes. But at least he wasn't alone anymore. He had Muriel. And God.

Amy had grown increasingly fond of Muriel over the years, not least for saving her dad. She didn't doubt that if it wasn't for Muriel's staunch Catholic method of persever-ance, he would still be sitting in his armchair, rolling ciga-rettes and drinking six cans of lager every evening. She was a big woman, not overweight but tall with broad shoulders and a generous bust. Grandma Jeannette said Muriel had a 'good arm for washing steps', which Amy thought was a bit unfair as it made her sound burly, when she was really just strong, on the outside and on the inside too.

Muriel and Tony had invited them to spend the weekend in their caravan in Pease Bay, near Dunbar, just down the A1 from Edinburgh. It was a proper caravan park, with a clubhouse and a reception full of posters letting the residents know about the rules they had to abide by in order to be respectable members of the caravan-site community. Brodie loved Muriel's caravan, especially the tiny twin room he shared with his mum, with the fish-finger beds – nicknamed as such due to their similar shape (and size) to his favourite frozen food. The caravan was set on a hillside and had sweeping views across the bay from the window that filled one whole end of the metal box.

'Not one of the ones shoved in like sardines on the flat bit in front of the beach,' Muriel was keen to point out as she stood at her window, elevated above the rest of the site. Amy did occasionally have an urge to point out that pride was a sin, but knew the caravan was Muriel's only real vice.

Amy and Brodie arrived on schedule at 2 p.m. (lateness *was* a sin) to find Muriel standing at the barrier, ready to swipe their car through with her residents' pass. Upon spotting Muriel's familiar figure, it struck Amy, as it always did, how opposite she was to her own mother. If they had been at school together, Judith would've been the one smoking round the back of the bike sheds while Muriel led an outdoor expedition training course for other students in the main hall. Muriel wore walking shoes and a Berghaus jacket, her hair cut sensibly short for a woman of her age. Amy's mother still sported the same wavy shoulder-length haircut she'd had in the eighties, although these days she was morphing into an art student and was in the habit of piling it messily on her head in the same 'just got out of bed' style all the nineteen-year-olds were wearing.

Muriel waved at them as the barrier lifted and Amy stopped the car to let her hop into the passenger seat.

'Welcome, welcome,' she said, clapping her hands together as she got in. She stretched around to give Brodie a smile in the back. 'Hello there, how are you?'

Brodie gave her two thumbs up; he was chewing on some Haribo he'd found down the side of his seat. Muriel turned and fastened her seatbelt, never one to break the rules even in a five-mile-per-hour zone.

'Your dad was having a nap, but he should be up by now. I told him, "Tony, get the kettle on the minute you get up – Amy will need a nice cup of tea after the drive."' Muriel was fond of recounting the conversations she had, verbatim.

Tony had retired a couple of years ago. No longer Tony the bus driver, he was now Tony the pensioner with a bus pass and a newly acquired golfing habit, the normality of which Amy found strangely comforting.

Sasha had once asked Amy a long time ago, as she painted her nails a lurid colour of green, if she loved her dad. It had been obvious Sasha was thinking about Ken and wondering if she was meant to love him just because he was her biological father. Amy hadn't been able to answer the question straight away and it had got her thinking.

'I suppose I do,' she'd settled on in the end. Her father had been a bit of a mystery to her at that point, but she was sure of the answer now. She had watched him change into the man he was with admiration. He'd given her hope that people could change. It was perhaps the reason she'd believed Nick could change, all those times when he promised he would. It was perhaps why she was beginning to believe he'd really managed it this time.

Tony was standing at the bottom of the hill when they pulled the car into a space, ready to help them carry their bags.

'Kettle's on,' he nodded in the direction of Muriel, 'as per my orders.' He gave Amy a quick hug and went to the back of the car to open Brodie's door. 'Hiya, wee man,' he said, helping his grandson climb out.

'I've got a new wetsuit, Granddad,' Brodie grinned proudly.

'A wetsuit?' Tony feigned confusion. 'Where on earth are you going to use a wetsuit around here?'

'In the sea, silly. I'm going boogie-boarding. Mum says I can.'

'Well if your mum says you can, I'm sure you can.' Tony gave his daughter a small wink and lifted the rucksack out from the back seat. Taking Brodie's hand, they started walking up the hill towards the caravan together.

Amy followed, listening to Brodie telling her dad all about sports day at school and how he was fourth in the running race but should've been third because Fergus Henderson cheated and started before the whistle was blown.

When they had dumped their bags in their room, Muriel gave them the usual introductory speech: clean towels were on the end of the beds; they had sole use of the shower room because the master bedroom had an en suite (another point of pride for Muriel).

They made hot drinks and ate biscuits and then Muriel sent the three of them off for a walk to get some fresh air. 'I'll meet you at the clubhouse in an hour,' she said. 'I've booked a table.'

Amy and her dad walked with Brodie down to the beach and began ambling along where the waves were breaking, bubbles of foam fizzling on the sand as each wave ebbed.

'He's stretched up a bit,' Tony commented as they watched Brodie race ahead along the shoreline, getting close to the water then dodging the waves at the last possible second.

'He's growing so much. I'll need to buy some new school trousers soon, his old ones are flying half-mast.'

Tony chuckled. 'I'll give you money for them.'

'You don't need to—'

'I want to. Just let me know how much they are and I'll put the money in your bank account.'

Amy was always grateful for the help her dad gave her. It wasn't as though he and Muriel had lots of spare cash, but he would insist on contributing, even just a little.

Brodie ran back towards them and deposited some mussel shells into Tony's hands, with the stern instruction to keep them safe, before haring off again.

'How's work?' Tony asked.

'Oh, you know. Never enough time. Boss from hell. The usual.' Amy was used to her dad's line of questioning these days. His next question would be about her love life. She pre-empted him. 'Nick got in touch.'

Tony stopped walking. 'What?'

'He turned up outside my work one morning. I nearly threw up on his shoes.'

'Shame you missed. What did he want?'

'To see Brodie, mainly. He's got a new girlfriend. She's pregnant.'

Tony let out a low whistle. 'And are you going to let him see Brodie? Has he already seen him?'

They started along the beach again.

'No. I met up with him on my own. The girlfriend was there too though. He was a bit, I don't know, different, I suppose.' She thought for a second. 'Calmer, maybe.'

'Be careful, Amy.' Tony frowned. 'Try to remember what he did to you, and to Brodie.'

Amy prickled slightly, although she was unsure why. 'He might have changed. Maybe he's realised. Maybe he got help.'

'Maybe not though.'

'You changed.' Amy poked back at him, instantly feeling guilty.

Tony stopped walking again and looked down at the sand. He kicked at a small stone with the tip of his canvas trainer.

'I did,' he agreed, 'but I know how hard it was, and I know that it takes a long time.'

They started walking. Amy linked her arm through his.

'Sorry Dad,' she said.

'No, I'm sorry, Amy. I'm not trying to tell you what to do and I'm not saying he won't have changed. I know you'll do whatever's best for Brodie . . .' He paused, 'Just try to also do what's best for you.'

'I will.' They were almost at the other end of the bay.

'Because if he gets up to any more of his nonsense, he'll have me to answer to,' he added, making a limp fist with his free hand.

'I'm sure if he knows that, he'll be on his best behaviour.' They both laughed.

'Seriously though, Dad, please don't worry. He can't hurt us again, it's not like it was before. I'm in a completely different place. And I think he might be too.'

'Well if you're sure, then I'm sure, I suppose. Just remember I'm here if you need me.'

'I know, Dad, thank you.' Amy planted a kiss on his cheek. 'Come on, we better not be late for Muriel.'

*

They arrived back at the flat late on Sunday afternoon, the car and all of their belongings full of sand. Judith had replied to her daughter's nagging texts the day before in her usual manner.

Are you remembering to go to my house first thing tomorrow? x

Amy had waited impatiently for a response. Eventually the reply came back:

Yes. I'm not an idiot, darling. Give your father my love x

That had been her mother's attempt at sarcasm.

'We're home,' Amy called out as they pushed through the front door, dropping their bags in the hall. Brodie raced into the living room, desperate for the television fix he'd been deprived of all weekend.

Amy followed, surprised to find that her grandmother wasn't in her usual chair. Frowning, she went through to the kitchen, which was also empty. The flat was eerily quiet. Perhaps they'd gone out for a walk, she thought. The wheelchair they'd hired the week before wasn't in the hallway. Amy couldn't quite imagine her mother suggesting she push Jeannette to the park, but you never knew. For a moment she was hopeful. Perhaps they'd even made up.

The door to Brodie's room was slightly ajar. When she put her head around to peer in, Amy found Jeannette lying in Brodie's bed.

'Grandma!' She rushed into the room. 'Are you OK, are you not feeling well?'

Jeannette opened her eyes. 'Oh, hello, Amy dear, did you have a nice time?'

'Did Mum not come to help you today? That woman!'

'Stop that now. Your mother did come to see me. She was wafting about as though I should be so grateful that she'd given me a minute of her time. So I told her to leave.'

'Have you been in bed all night and all day? Why didn't you phone me?'

'You were having a lovely time with Brodie. I wouldn't want to ruin that. I'm a bit hungry now though, dear, maybe you could help me up to get something to eat. I managed to get through to the bathroom earlier, but it took it out of me.'

Amy thought she might like to genuinely kill her mother at that exact moment.

'Come on, let's get you sorted.' She helped Jeannette out of bed and through to the bathroom. She would have to deal with Judith later.

On Thursday Sasha picked Brodie up from after-school club and took him home so Amy could meet Nick after work. He wanted to talk more. His text messages had been persistent but gentle, and hopeful rather than pushy. It was a while since their café meeting, and she was well aware she had been avoiding the inevitable; the very least she had to do was tell him the truth.

They arranged to meet in an unfamiliar bar: somewhere the walls wouldn't be whispering stories of their history in the background. Amy had no desire to cover old ground where they didn't have to. Her preferred option when it came to Nick was to leave the past firmly where it belonged.

He was already there when she arrived, a glass of red wine and a glass of white on the table in front of him. He stood awkwardly, rubbing the palms of his hands on the sides of his trousers.

'Hi,' he said.

'Hi,' she replied, leaning in to brush his cheek with a non-existent kiss.

Amy took off her jacket and hung it on the back of the chair, noticing how damp her own hands were.

'Is this for me?' She indicated the drink as she sat down. 'Or is Vanessa here too?' Amy looked around the bar.

'No, she's not here tonight. And apologies, it was presumptuous of me. You might not even want wine, sorry. Can I get you something else?'

'Wine's fine.' Amy took a sip. 'So?' she said.

'So,' he replied.

They both started to say something at the same time then stopped.

'Sorry,' Nick said. 'You go.'

'I was just going to ask how Vanessa is, with the pregnancy and everything.'

'Yeah, she's good, thanks. We've been looking at flats, trying to work out where we're going to put down roots. I've been offered some work in London and Vanessa's family are down there. But, of course, I'm now thinking about Edinburgh, because of Brodie mainly.'

'About that . . .'

'Hi guys!' One of the overly buoyant bar staff appeared at the side of the table, beaming. 'Are you guys eating tonight?'

Nick looked questioningly at Amy. 'We could. If you want to?'

Amy nodded. The barman offered them each an oversized menu.

'I'll give you guys a minute, more drinks in the meantime, guys?'

They ordered another two glasses of wine and Amy and Nick smiled at one another. In the past they would've laughed at the enthusiasm of the young barman and his overuse of the word *guys* – they would've called him the 'Guy guy' or something and shared the private joke beyond that evening. But she knew they would never be back at that place.

'Sorry, we were interrupted. What were you going to say?'

'It's nothing.' Her nerve had gone. They should talk more first, she thought. 'Tell me about the work you've been offered in London.'

The food didn't arrive until Amy had managed to consume three large glasses of wine. The alcohol was making it all surprisingly easy and the conversation was flowing between them. She phoned Sasha from the toilet.

'Honestly I'm fine,' she reassured her stepsister. 'I'll be home in less than an hour to put Brodie to bed.'

'Amy, it's after nine o'clock. He's tucked up already. Your grandmother and I are just having a small libation and a chat, mainly about you, of course.'

Amy agreed not to do anything silly and hung up. Looking in the mirror she noticed her eye make-up had smudged. She went to grab a tissue and stumbled slightly. Holding onto the sink to steady herself, she stared straight ahead at her own reflection. What was she doing? She needed to sober up. She splashed some water on her face, wiped at the black smudges and gave her cheeks a quick slap. Despite her earlier resolve to tell Nick the truth, she knew that she wasn't going to be able to do it tonight.

Her grandma had insisted that it was time to tell Nick.

'If you don't make the decision to get it over with soon, the weight will only get heavier.' Jeannette had wagged her finger at Amy. 'Trust me, dear, I know what I'm talking about.'

Amy had agreed; it was the right thing to do. Just perhaps not this evening.

17

Edinburgh, 2011

Sasha wanted me to help organise her thirty-fifth birthday party.

'Halfway to forty,' she said, attempting to justify her decision to throw an extravagant event on a non-significant birthday.

'Any excuse,' I'd retorted.

Although we grew up for a while in the same surroundings, I've always known that Sasha has no idea how people live in the real world. She'd never known anything other than ponies for Christmas, or cars for birthdays. The people I'd grown up with until my mum left my dad had never quite escaped my thoughts, and the extravagance of our new life with Ken had often lain heavily on my conscience, guilt always present, even among the enjoyment. I had sometimes wished we could go back to our old house, back to our old life, especially on the occasions when Mum would disappear with Ken for days on end and Ben and I would be left with only the housekeeper for company. When my parents were still married, Mum was always at home in the evenings. I would crawl up next to her on the brown corduroy sofa and lay my head on her chest, listening to the soft thump-thump of her heart. I missed those times so much when we moved in with Ken.

I didn't know Sasha's mother very well and only met her a few times, but on all those occasions I had been completely terrified by her. Agatha was an angular woman, tall and slim and undeniably from aristocracy. She wore knee-length cream pencil skirts with pastel-coloured silk blouses and her glossy brown hair was permanently whipped up in a chignon so rigid I suspected it wouldn't be troubled by a force-ten gale. Agatha doted on Magnus and always appeared slightly irritated by Sasha. From what I could gather, Agatha's family had been disappointed at her choice to marry Ken; he would undoubtedly dilute the lineage of any offspring. It was a concern they needn't have had; Sasha and Magnus both navigated life with the certainty that they were at the very top of the food chain.

Sasha arrived at my flat one Saturday afternoon with a bottle of champagne and a joint she declared would blow my mind.

'You know I don't smoke,' I told her. To which she replied that I was boring.

It turned out all she wanted me to do was send her friends a group text to invite them to the party so it didn't look like she was organising it herself.

'Why can't you be organising your own party?' I asked, completely bewildered.

'For goodness sake, Amy, no one organises their own birthday party. We could pretend it was a surprise party,' she looked thoughtful, 'but then I'd have to wait until everyone had arrived and would miss half the night. No, it's fine, just make sure you get people to agree to come. Tell them it's free booze all night, that'll do it.' It always amused Amy that some of the richest people were the most delighted at the idea of a freebie.

'Do you want me to invite your mum and dad then?' I couldn't quite picture Agatha stepping inside a nightclub.

'Fuck no! No old people. Just the ones on that list. Oh, and you can add lover boy, and Ben.'

'I'll ask Ben.'

'What about Nick? Don't tell me you've fucked that one up, please.'

'I do not fuck things up, thank you very much. I'm just not sure if he's working.' It was a lie. I wasn't sure if he was speaking to me. He hadn't replied to any of my texts in the last forty-eight hours.

'Well it would be good if you could convince him to come along. He's gorgeous, and on TV. He can be one of my celebrity guests.'

For the next two weeks I became Sasha's party secretary. She phoned regularly, wanting updates on who'd replied.

'What do you mean Charlie can't come?' She sounded furious. 'I went to his fucking crappy thirtieth in the Balmoral and spoke to his decrepit old aunt for most of the night. Her teeth kept falling out and she stank of blue cheese. He owes me.'

'Apparently the stinky old aunt has died,' I said. 'That's why he can't make it. The funeral is on Saturday in Buckinghamshire. He won't be back until late on Sunday.'

Sasha was quiet for a moment.

'Still,' she finally went on, 'he could've got a train back up or something and been at the party by midnight. That's when all the fun starts anyway. I think I'm going to phone him and tell him that.'

'I thought you weren't meant to be organising your own party?'

'Ah, yeah, of course, can you text him with the suggestion then?'

I agreed I would, having absolutely no intention of fulfilling the request.

I always knew, deep down, that my life at Ken's was temporary. Apart from knowing about his infidelity, which was bound to cause problems eventually, I could just feel that I didn't fit; I was only borrowing. It really wasn't until I got my first pay cheque from my first real job, and had divided it out; rent, bills, food, that I realised how ridiculous our life with Ken had been.

It was 2001 and I was in third year at university when it all came crashing down a second time for Mum.

I'd followed Ben to Glasgow. He was nice about it because he's nice about everything but the minute I arrived for freshers' week, it was clear that I would need to make my own way, find, my own friends. He was studying medicine and playing for the university rugby team. A rugby-playing doctor was pretty high in the social popularity stakes, so I didn't really get a look-in.

Sasha had dropped out of numerous universities by then and took to visiting me almost every weekend so she could leech on my experience. She made far more of a go of the whole thing than I did. Usually she ended up going home with some poor unsuspecting undergraduate, but if she wasn't in the mood, she would come back to my halls and squish into the single bed with me. At some point in the night, I would end up on a camping mat on the floor.

I wasn't meant to still be in halls in my third year but I couldn't stand the thought of sharing a draughty flat with five other people who wouldn't do their own washing up, so I made an application to stay in the postgraduate accommodation where my room would be small but I would have my own private bathroom. The accommodation was also catered for which meant it was almost like living at home, except that the food wasn't quite up to Marisol's standards. Most of the other residents were wealthy international students but Ken was paying, and he knew someone at the university who managed to pull some strings. As usual, he could get anything he wanted.

I'd made a last-minute decision to go home that weekend, probably because I had no clean underwear. My mum wasn't replying to my text messages, but I knew Marisol would be around and I could spend the weekend being fed and lazing around by the pool. I'd become so complacent by then, not thinking it would last, but not expecting it to end any time soon.

The main rush hour had passed when I got to Queen Street station, most of the commuters already sitting behind their desks. I managed to get a seat at a table and laid out the coffee and the bacon roll from the kiosk in the station. At each stop, as we got nearer to Edinburgh, the carriages filled up.

A man and woman boarded the train at Linlithgow and, annoyingly, sat on the two seats opposite me. They opened out a newspaper in front of themselves and started doing the crossword together, brushing hands occasionally, glancing at each other in a way that suggested they were more than just friends.

I'd been single at that point since I broke up with Matthew two weeks after I started university. He was a year older than me and already at university in Edinburgh, while I completed my final year at school. Looking back, he obviously chose to stay in Edinburgh for me, because when I told him I was going to Glasgow he looked pained and said, 'I suppose we can make that work, it's not too far a distance.' I had hoped I wouldn't have to say the words to Matthew but when he turned up uninvited on my second weekend in Glasgow, I decided it was the right time to finish things. In typical Matthew style, he didn't get angry or upset with me. He said if it was what I wanted then, of course, he would let me go. But he would wait. He was always so reasonable. It was quite annoying at the time but I sometimes picture him now, sitting on his bed in his parents' house, waiting for me and I feel ashamed of the way I treated poor Matthew; he was just too nice.

Matthew was the only person I'd slept with by then. It was his first time too, the night we awkwardly moved from kissing to touching each other in a more grown-up way. We'd talked about it first. Matthew didn't want me to feel pressured, but we talked about it so much that one night when he was in my bedroom watching a movie, I said to him, 'Oh for goodness sake, will you just do it already.' And he did. Afterwards, I lay on my back, staring at the ceiling, thinking; is that it? Matthew had been as gentle as he could be, but it had still hurt a bit and I certainly didn't experience any pleasure even close to what Matthew had when, after a few jerking movements, he'd appeared slightly alarmed and declared, 'Jesus Christ, I'm coming.' It got a bit better as time went on, thankfully, it was just never really good enough.

I got off the train at Haymarket the day my mum's world imploded for a second time, leaving the man and the woman to enjoy the few minutes to Waverley by themselves. The crossword was only half finished.

I jumped in a taxi and told the driver where I was going. He whistled and said, 'Some right nice houses there, darlin',' before going on to list all the famous people he'd had in his cab as we drove through the city.

When the taxi pulled up at the gates to the house, I knew something was wrong. Ken's Porsche was abandoned in front of the house, the driver's door flung out to the side. The front doors were both wide open. I walked into the hallway to find Marisol at the bottom of one of the staircases, pacing and looking up, ringing her hands together under an imaginary tap.

'What's going on?' I asked. She jumped.

'Oh, Amy,' she said. 'Please go up, go up,' she put her hand on my back, guiding me to the bottom step. 'Your mother.'

My first thought was that she might be dead. I dropped my bag and took the stairs two at a time. Ken came thudding towards me along the corridor.

'She's a fucking madwoman,' he declared loudly as he stormed past.

I ran along the corridor to their room and found my mum sitting on the carpet in the middle of a pile of clothes. She looked like a little bird sitting in a nest. On closer inspection I could see that the clothes making up the nest were all torn and sliced. All of Ken's expensively tailored suits and shirts, slashed into shreds, and she was sobbing and clutching a large pair of scissors.

'Mum?' I said. She looked up. Her cheeks were streaked with mascara, her eyes burning red.

'What's going on?' I asked, settling down beside her and taking the scissors gently from her hands. She continued to cry, great big wracking sobs that shook her entire body. I put my arms around her and tried to hold her still. 'What's going on?' I asked again after a few minutes had passed.

'He's . . .' she started but then stopped again and I could see she was processing something, thinking beyond this room, beyond me. Then she let out a howling noise that was so guttural and animalistic that it made every hair on my body stand on end and I put my hands over my ears instinctively. She crumpled into herself when there was no more noise left, a heap in the heap, and managed to spit out some words. I didn't hear what she said the first time, perhaps I didn't want to hear it, but I asked her to say it again and she lifted her head to look right at me and said, 'He's leaving me.'

I'm ashamed to say it, but my immediate thought was completely about myself.

'He can't,' I said, and my mum choked out a bitter laugh.

'He's been having an affair. With an air hostess. A fucking air hostess!' She raised her voice. 'What a fucking cliché. And now he wants to *marry* her.'

My mind raced with the implications of mum no longer being married to Ken. I kept thinking about the money; he would stop giving me money. My mum started sobbing again and I shook myself for being so selfish.

'What are you going to do now?'

She shrugged, blowing her nose on one of Ken's shirts that hadn't been attacked as much as the others.

'I don't know, Amy. What am I going to do?' She wiped at her eyes. 'He's selling the house.'

My mum breathed out heavily, as though deflating.

'You don't need to think about that right now, Mum,' I said. 'Maybe you should get a bit of rest. You look exhausted.'

It took another half-hour for me to coax her up from the floor into the bed. I tucked her in like she used to do to me when I was very little. Downstairs, Marisol was kneading dough on the marble worktop, her eyebrows knitted together.

'She's sleeping,' I told her.

Marisol shook her head. 'He never happy that man, always want more and more.'

*

Mum had a bit of a crash course into reality after Ken sold the house, pushing their divorce through quickly so he could get married to the air hostess. He bought her a flat and gave Ben and I money to put down as deposits on our own flats, after which there was nothing more. I felt strangely numb about the whole thing. It was as though the house and the money and our whole lives with Ken had been an interlude. I got a job when university finished and eventually bought a tiny one-bedroom flat using the money Ken had given me. The only reminder of the life I'd borrowed (other than being a homeowner which would've been impossible without Ken's money) was Sasha, who had stopped speaking to her father altogether because he was a 'fucking useless shagging piece of shit'.

Sasha's thirty-fifth birthday extravaganza (her words) is taking place tonight in a club in George Street. She's spent the whole day at my house getting ready, which involved opening a bottle of Prosecco at 11 a.m. and doing then redoing her make-up and hair several times.

'You'll need something to eat, Sash, or you won't even make it to the club,' I say.

'Eating's cheating,' is her reply before she pushes up the stiff window in my living room and leans out to light up a menthol cigarette.

Later, when I manage to sit her down at the table in the kitchen and convince her to eat a few crackerbreads with low-fat cheese spread, she asks again if Nick is coming to the party.

'He's got a work event, or something,' I lie. It's becoming a habit of mine when it comes to Nick, lying. I don't want anything to ruin what we have because most of the time it is so good, but we'd been out the previous weekend and bumped into Ben in a pub and something had shifted between us and I was worried I was going to lose him. I thought we'd had a good time but then, in my bed, later that night, Nick started to tell me how nauseating he found my brother.

'He's just so *nice* all the time,' he'd said.

'What's wrong with being nice?' I'd tried to cuddle into Nick's side, but he'd turned away from me.

'No one is ever really that nice. I just think it's a bit of an act. "Look at me, the helpful doctor,"' Nick had sneered. I was surprised at how annoyed he seemed.

I'd tried to defend Ben. 'He's just a good guy, I really don't think he's like that.'

'You're too weak when it comes to him, Amy.' Nick had slid out from under the covers and pulled his trousers on. 'You let him belittle you in front of everyone.'

I was confused then. 'He didn't . . . Where are you going?' Nick was fully dressed and walking towards my bedroom door.

'I need some space, sorry.'

After he'd left, my stomach had churned and I'd sent him a text. We'd obviously had a misunderstanding; I just wasn't sure why. He hadn't replied since.

Sasha and I head off towards George Street just after seven. I told everyone the party was to start at eight but as Sasha pointed out, that meant people wouldn't start to show until around ten. She's already a bit drunk and I have to hold her firmly by the arm to get her down the steps into the club. There are a few people in the front part of the bar having early-evening drinks. The barman looks at Sasha with a raised eyebrow before leading us through to the VIP room at the back, which cost an eye-watering amount to book out on a Saturday night and I'm reminded again of the contrast between our lives these days.

'We might let a few of the members through after midnight, depending on how many people you end up getting if that's OK?' Sasha is too busy concentrating on opening a bottle of Prosecco she's removed from one of the huge silver buckets of ice.

'I'm sure that'll be fine.' I smile at the man and wonder how long it will be until I'm able to get home, remove the expensive dress I've borrowed from Sasha, which is nipping me under the arms, and crawl into my lovely comfy bed.

We sit until after nine, Sasha disappearing to the toilet frequently, each time coming back more alert before diving into the Prosecco again.

'You need to slow down,' I tell her, but she brushes me off and calls me a boring nag.

At around quarter to ten the guests begin to arrive in dribs and drabs and I automatically take on the role of waitress, wandering around filling up people's drinks. By eleven, there are about fifteen people altogether, including Sasha and myself. She staggers over to me as I'm opening another Prosecco and hisses loudly in my ear, 'Where is everyone? You need to texscht them all.' Her eyes are going in and out of focus, so I suggest she should have a drink of water, but she makes a face and flaps her arms at me and goes off towards the loos again.

Ben arrives with his new girlfriend Natalie, who looks as uncomfortable in the surroundings as I feel. The music has been turned up and the whole place is pulsating with the beat.

Ben shouts in my ear, 'Nick not here?'

I shake my head. 'He's working I think.' I shout back.

Ben nods and takes a swig from his beer bottle. The three of us stand watching the party for a while. He leans in towards me again. 'I'm not sure about him.'

'Who?' I assume Ben is talking about the two men in the middle of the room, one of whom is trying to get the other into some kind of friendly headlock.

Ben rolls his eyes at me. 'Nick. I just think there's something . . . off, about him.'

'What do you mean?' The music seems to be getting even louder and I'm having to shout over it. Ben starts trying to explain what he means but I can't hear him, so he stops, shaking his head and then mouths, *Talk to you later.*

At midnight the barman comes over and asks if he could let some of the regular members in, to which I reply yes, because I don't think Sasha will notice, or care, who is here, as long as it's busy.

I pour a few more drinks and watch the room fill up, conscious that Sasha is still in the toilet. Not sure if I've made the right decision about opening her party up to strangers who are all now guzzling the free booze, I go to find her. There are two girls looking in the mirror, one of them pouting like a mesmerised fish while she applies thick layers of glossy red to her lips. The other is leaning in towards her reflection, sweeping black mascara in slow deliberate movements onto her eyelashes. They are having a conversation that seems to be dominated by the word *yah*.

'Sasha,' I call out as I push each of the cubicle doors in turn. The one at the end is locked. I knock hard. 'Sasha, it's me. The guy from the bar came and asked if we could let some of the members in and I said yes, I wasn't sure.' No reply. A flapping begins in my gut. 'Sasha,' I shout it this time and the yah-girls turn to look at me.

'She's been in there, like, forever,' the lipstick girl says.

'Yah,' agrees the other one.

I get down on my hands and knees, which isn't easy in the tightly fitting dress, and look under the cubicle. I can see Sasha's black Louboutins and her red lacy G-string around her ankles. One of her hands hangs down the side of the toilet as though she's slumped over.

I struggle to stand up, panic rising in my chest. 'We need to open this door,' I say to the girls, who continue to look at me as though I'm speaking a language they don't understand. 'The door,' I gesture to the little red rectangular patch on the opposite side of the lock. 'We need to get it open, do you have a credit card?' More looks of confusion follow. 'I need something to undo the lock with, I'm assuming you're not carrying screwdrivers but if you are . . .' I stop, knowing this will only complicate matters further. 'I just need a card or something I can slot in there,' I point to the lock again, 'so I can turn it and open the door. I think Sasha's unconscious,' I add, hoping this will increase the sense of urgency.

Mascara girl reaches into her handbag and passes over a platinum American Express card with the warning for me to be careful, she needs it back. I slot it into the lock and turn. The bolt slides easily backwards and the door swings open. Sasha's head is lolling on her chest, a trail of gooey-looking sick connecting the corner of her mouth with the bulge of her breast that's pushed up and out of her silver sleeveless dress. I grab some tissue and wipe at the sick, hoping the other girls haven't seen it, trying to preserve Sasha's dignity even in this situation. 'Call an ambulance,' I shout at them. I turn back to Sasha, unsure whether to remove the G-string or try and put it back on. I keep saying her name, trying to wake her, shaking her shoulders gently. She groans, which I guess is a sign that she isn't dead and take this as a positive. In the end, I decide to take the pants off, sure that the paramedics will cover her to take her out of the toilet. It's easier to concentrate on these little things than to think about the reality of the situation.

Sasha starts retching again just as the paramedics turn up and usher me out of the cubicle, taking control in that no-nonsense manner they have about them.

They put Sasha onto a stretcher and carry her out through the emergency-exit door rather than parading her through the club. I dash back to the party to grab our coats and bags. Ben and Natalie have gone and no one else seems to be noticing the birthday girl's absence.

Accident and Emergency on a Saturday night is a feral experience. Luckily, because Sasha is unconscious, we don't have to wait around, and she's taken straight through on a trolley into a cubicle where they ask me repeatedly what she's taken. I'm not sure but I guess that it might have been cocaine. There is nothing in her bag except some extra-strength codeine, so I can't even give them any clues from that. Someone grumbles at me that it's important they know, and I promise them I don't know for sure. Perhaps they think I'm lying.

I take Sasha's phone out of her bag and try to call Ken. The dialling tone informs me he's abroad. Sasha's mum's number goes straight to voicemail. I remember Magnus was supposed to be coming to the party but hadn't turned up, so I try him. I can hear loud music and chatter in the background when he answers.

'Sash! Where the fuck are you? I'm at your party but the birthday girl is missing,' he shouts over the noise.

'Magnus, it's Amy, can you hear me?' I try to keep my voice down as I look at the sign on the wall with a huge red line across a picture of a mobile phone. There's some shuffling at the other end of the line and I think he's hung up but then he says clearly, 'Amy, how the fuck are you? Where's my sister and why aren't you at this terrible party?'

Magnus arrives at the hospital half an hour later. Sasha is still unconscious and being moved out of the cubicle to a ward where the doctor says she'll likely be asleep for the next twelve hours.

'Dappy tart,' Magnus says, shaking his head at his sister and leaning down to kiss me swiftly twice, once on each cheek. 'I've got a driver outside; can I take you home? I assume this one is going to live?'

'They think she'll be fine, just needs to sleep it off. A lift home would be great, thanks,' I say.

My invite for Magnus to come up to the flat is an empty one and one I certainly thought he would politely decline, so I'm surprised and a little put out when he accepts. He sends his driver away for the night and follows me up the stairs to my flat saying he'll call a taxi after a nightcap. I go into my room to remove the dress and put on a T-shirt and leggings, while he pours us a couple of glasses of wine from a half-empty bottle in the fridge. It's been a long night but once I'm out of the dress and have taken a sip of the wine, I feel more awake than I have all evening. Magnus sits down in the corner of the sofa, his arms and legs spread, and undoes the top buttons of his navy shirt.

I have always been mildly aware that Magnus is attractive, but growing up, he'd been that bit older than me, not to mention the fact that he was from a class of men that I usually found unbearably archaic, with their private clubs and unshakeable sense of privilege. There was also the point that our parents had been married, which put an unseemly suggestion of siblings between us and which stopped me from having too many thoughts beyond the acknowledgement that he was a good-looking man.

I sit at the other end of the sofa and drink more wine and try to keep reminding myself that I do not fancy this man, who has made himself so comfortable on my sofa and who has clearly just come back from a presumably exotic holiday because his skin is tanned, golden and glowing. No, I'm not finding him attractive at all. I think of Nick, of how I feel about him, and pick up my mobile phone to see if he's replied to any of my texts yet. Nothing.

'She's probably upset about Dad,' Magnus offers.

'What about your dad?'

'The new girlfriend, the one he finished with Nicole for.'

'I didn't know he'd ended things with Nicole.' Mum will be delighted.

'Tanya or something. That's the new one. She was at school with Sasha. I don't think she took it too well when she found out. Called him a pervert.'

'And what do you think, of your dad going out with someone younger than you?'

'Good on him, that's what I think.' Magnus laughs. 'Sly old fox. What about you, Amy, what are you up to these days? Got a boyfriend?'

I feel the blush beginning to rise. 'I mean, I've been seeing someone, but I'm not sure,' I'm desperate to change the subject, to divert attention away from me, although I'm not sure why. 'What about you?' I ask.

'Ah yes, one girlfriend. Fiancé actually. Haven't told anyone yet because I'm not sure I really want to go through with it, not any time in the next year anyway. Her family know though, so there's probably not much chance I'll get out of it.'

'Why don't you want to marry – what's her name?'

'Felicity. There's nothing wrong with her, it's not that I don't want to marry Flick, more that I don't want to marry anyone at the moment.'

'Then why propose?' I honestly don't think I will ever understand some men.

'She was expecting it. I knew if I didn't, she would probably finish with me. I didn't even have a ring. Managed to convince her that the reason I proposed without one was because I wanted us to design one, together.'

'So, you'd rather be engaged to someone when you don't want to get married than get dumped?'

Magnus thinks for a moment, then flashes a smile. 'I suppose so, yes,' he laughs again, this time I join in.

'I think that makes you an egomaniac or something, Magnus.'

He nods and finishes the wine in his glass. 'Got any more?'

The thing about alcohol is that it can make you forget that your life doesn't just consist of the moment you're in when you're getting more and more sozzled. Magnus and I open another bottle of wine, red this time, and drink the whole thing, talking about Ken, about Sasha, about getting married or how to get out of getting married. We laugh about the times when we were younger and Magnus would wake me up after he'd been on a night out to talk. 'Those were the times I hadn't managed to pull, rare of course,' he says, and I reach across and punch him gently on the arm and tell him he's full of himself.

After we finish a third bottle, Magnus goes off to use the toilet and when he comes back, rather than sitting down in his corner of the sofa, he comes and sits right next to me, places a hand on the side of my face and kisses me full on the lips. Everything happens so quickly after that. I kiss him in return with the desire I'd held back for years as a teenager and before long we're undressing each other and then he's inside me and I open my eyes and come face-to-face with his smooth, muscular chest and think, *This is weird*. It feels unlike anything I've ever experienced and I have a sense of being detached from the whole thing, as though we could be two people at separate ends of the earth despite how physically close we are at that moment. I think briefly of Nick and how different it feels to be with him and I close my eyes again. Soon Magnus is making those noises that signal the end, then buttoning up his shirt as I pull my leggings back on and then he's saying, 'Sorry, Amy, don't know what happened there. I best be getting off, you OK?'

We hug each other awkwardly at the front door and then I crawl into bed, confused. We'd both drank too much, that was for certain, but there had been something lingering between us all these years and we'd obviously just mistaken what that was. I cringe at the thought of us ruining what had been an old friendship, based on late-night chats and looking at the stars, and pull the duvet over my head. I just want to forget about it, so I push it to the back of my mind and hope that I'll never have to think about it again.

18

Edinburgh, 2012

It started early one morning. She thought she'd been ill before but knew at that moment that any previous ailment she'd suffered had been minor. Nick took Brodie off to nursery; he was going to Glasgow for work; he couldn't get out of it, but he promised to come back as soon as he could once filming was finished. It didn't feel right. She hadn't let Nick do anything alone with Brodie since two weekends previously when he'd had another one of his outbursts, but she didn't have a choice. His moods had been changing more frequently since they'd found out she was pregnant again, but he'd promised to go back to the doctor. He'd promised it wouldn't happen again.

'You'll be fine. It's probably just a bit of morning sickness or something,' he said as he strapped Brodie into his buggy. Amy watched them from her horizontal position on the sofa. Looking at them together, it was so obvious to her then that Nick wasn't Brodie's father, but she was too unwell to feel the usual surge of guilt she experienced when she thought about the truth.

'Love you,' Nick said as he left. Amy didn't reply.

By 11 a.m., she could barely lift a limb but knew she had to; the warm wet fluid was beginning to slip out from between her legs. She was so hot her dressing gown was soaked with sweat, but she couldn't find the energy to undo the belt and take it off. Her body was telling her mind that she desperately wanted what was inside her to come out, because it instinctively knew it was the thing that was making her feel so terrible. Amy made it to the toilet just before the first deep ruby-red piece of jelly slid out. More followed, her muscles tightened, teeth clenched, and tears fell because she felt like she might actually be dying, and she was frightened she was going to die on the toilet, alone, like Elvis.

It took a while for her body to stop squeezing, for the desire to grind her teeth hard down against each other to wear off. When it finally did, she felt instantly better, like some great poison had been purged from within, and she let out an enormous sigh of relief, a moment that was almost immediately surpassed by a flash of searing white terror and the realisation that it wasn't a poison that was now sitting in the bowl of the toilet, it was her baby, Nick's baby. She slipped forward, twisting round to look. It was red, of course, bright-red toilet water, but she could also see the dark fleshy masses at the bottom and something inside her turned animal and she had to save her baby. Her hands plunged into the toilet, trying to grasp the pieces of jelly that kept slipping through her fingers, impossible to capture, and the desperation coursing through every part of her body quickened, leaving her breathless. She couldn't seem to get any air into her lungs but kept on scooping, and the baby kept slipping. She needed to save it – not from death, she knew it wasn't alive. It wasn't about that. She was trying to save her baby from disappearing, for its final resting place to be far away, somewhere unknown. Her mum used to flush the dead goldfish down the toilet. 'Off to the graveyard in the sea,' she would say.

It was Ben who found Amy later that afternoon, passed out on the floor, arms still clutching the toilet like a favourite teddy. He'd worried when they'd spoken the night before and she'd told him she was pregnant but there was a little bleeding and they'd argued because he said she was stupid for having another baby with Nick. She hadn't disagreed, she just didn't want to hear it said out loud. When he hadn't been able to get in touch, he'd driven to Amy's flat and let himself in with the key that she always insisted he had; the key that Nick had told Amy to get back from Ben (*why should your brother be able to swan in to our home whenever he wants?*). He tried to bring her round, but she was weak and listless and needed to go to hospital, so he phoned an ambulance.

When Amy came-to in hospital later that evening, dizzy and disorientated, her first thought was for Brodie. One of the nurses assured her he was safe, that he was with Ben. Her second thought, and one that made her insides twist with fear was, *Please God, let no one have flushed the toilet.*

Sometimes, the worst things happening end up being the catalyst for the best changes. Ben picked Amy up from hospital the next day, Brodie was in the back of the car, ten months old and joyfully oblivious. She sat next to him so she could hold on to his pudgy little hand and chat to him, tell him how much she loved him and watch him slavering in response. Nick wasn't home when they arrived and so Ben stayed and helped get Brodie into bed. He made her eat and drink something, even though all she really wanted to do was curl into a ball on the sofa and cry. He only left when she promised to call him if anything was wrong.

'Put the chain on and double-lock the door,' were his lasts words. She should've listened.

She'd been dreaming about walking through an overgrown garden, pushing thick, tangled weeds out of the way to move forward as it became more and more dense until she could feel something sticky on her hands and, looking down, she saw blood everywhere, all over her fingers and the weeds, which were tangling around her legs. The more she struggled, the more tangled she became. Amy woke suddenly, gasping for air, beads of sweat trickling down her back as she sat up and tried to catch her breath. She let out a small yelp when she saw Nick sitting in the chair in the corner of the room. His face was half bathed in the orange light from the streetlamp, seeping in through the thin white curtains. He was staring straight ahead, his gaze fixed until she said his name for a third time, and he looked at her as if something had switched on, as though he'd just noticed she was there.

'What are you doing?' Amy asked, pulling her legs round to sit on the edge of the bed. 'Where've you been?'

Nick rubbed at his eyes and groaned softly.

'Has the baby gone?' he asked.

Amy nodded.

'Come and get a drink.' She stood and offered him her hand, which he took, and they walked together into the kitchen. Nick sat down on one of the high stools at the breakfast bar as she flicked on the low lights under the cupboards and took the kettle to the sink.

'Where were you?' she asked again, gently. 'I could've done with you being around.'

Nick sighed. 'Ben left a message on my phone, said what had happened.' He paused, rubbing his temples. 'I couldn't deal with it, Amy. I had to get away. And I knew your *brother* would just take over everything.'

Amy felt something break inside her, just a small snap, but she was so tired, and just didn't have the patience, not after what she'd been through. Looking back, she didn't know why she said it, because really, she knew it would provoke a reaction. But at the time, it just came out; an innocuous enough thing to say.

'You know, Nick, this really isn't all about you. For once.'

His jaw tightened. She knew in an instant that she'd flicked the switch, strangely not regretting it this time. She was exhausted and weak but images of the last year were hurling around her mind and suddenly, as though a huge thousand-watt lightbulb had illuminated between them, she could see everything so clearly.

Nick was shouting, but it wasn't these words she could hear, it was all the things he'd said before now that slithered forward, vying for attention: *Your brother controls you, your mum's so flaky, I don't trust them, you're so much better than them, you don't need them, it should just be the three of us, we're a family now* . . . and the violence that he'd laughed off; he hadn't meant to hit her, of course he would never harm Brodie, he hadn't thrown the bottle of milk at her, she'd just been in the way. And the begging afterwards, for forgiveness, for love; it would never happen again, he would get help. Had she seriously thought another baby would fix things, make everything, including Nick, all right again?

The urge to laugh gurgled up inside her but he was in her face, screaming that she didn't love him, when she found herself pulled sharply back to the present and the thing that had fractured inside her only minutes before, snapped fully. She shouted back, baring her teeth, 'Love you? How could I love you after everything you've done? I hate you.'

He stopped at that. Froze completely. She had never fought back before, had always tried to calm him down instead. Amy held her breath and watched Nick turn, his movements robotic. He picked up a tumbler from the draining board, hurling it past her left ear at the wall. The glass exploded into a thousand tinkling pieces that rained down on the floor behind her. They stood, staring at each other, Amy's heart beating as though it would break out from her chest at any moment. Fight or flight. She ran from the room as he grabbed another glass and threw it, not towards her but at the same spot on the wall as before, and she knew then that she had to get out, that he was only beginning. Brodie was sleeping soundly in his cot, the nightlight casting a soft glow across his rounded cheeks. Amy lifted him gently, wrapping his blanket around him. She picked the car keys up from the table next to the front door and slid out into the stairwell wearing only her pyjamas. The grey stone stairs were cold against her bare feet as she moved quickly, hearing the sound of glass smashing growing distant as she tried to shush the wakening baby. Her hands shook violently as she strapped Brodie into his car seat. *I shouldn't be driving,* she thought. But she had to get away, had to get them both somewhere safe.

Ben opened the door before Amy even made it up the path to his house.

'I knew I should have stayed with you,' he said, scolding himself as he ushered them inside.

Nick left after that and didn't come back. He'd cleaned up the flat by the time they arrived home the next day. Ben came with her, again. He wanted her to call the police, said it was his duty as a doctor to report it, but Amy begged him not to. She just wanted to forget everything that had happened.

It didn't take long for Amy to realise that she could do it alone; that alone was better than what she had with Nick. And besides, she had Ben and Grandma, her dad and Muriel, even her mum, to count on when she needed an ear to bend or a shoulder to cry on. She knew she was lucky really. And so, life as they hadn't quite known it, went on.

19

Edinburgh 2018

In the end, her confession was inevitable. Amy had considered and reconsidered all of the possible consequences over and over and was unable to give the thought any more space in her head or it would threaten to overwhelm her entirely. She needed to stay sane for Brodie and it was the idea that she wouldn't be the parent she needed to be, if she was consumed by the lie, that spurred her on and gave her the modicum of courage she needed to face up to the truth.

When she'd emerged from the bathroom on the night they'd had dinner, slightly wobbly but sobering up by the second, Nick had called her a taxi to take her home, the look of concern on his face as he shut the cab door was genuine. His text messages since continued to be considerate, and as he grew in her mind as a changed man, her guilt and shame grew in proportion. He didn't deserve to be lied to, maybe he never had, despite the things he'd done. The past, the memories, were mixed in her mind, a confusing collection of good and bad, but none of that mattered any longer. As her grandmother had insisted, it was time to 'rip off the plaster' quickly and pray that it would only hurt momentarily.

She agreed to meet him one morning before work, a quick coffee, hopefully for the last time. As changed as he may be, she expected that Nick would hear the truth and slide from their lives, for good this time. He would have no reason to stick around now.

His face dropped as she walked through the coffee shop door that morning. He'd perhaps been hoping she would bring Brodie. Quickly rallying however, Nick smiled widely as he stood to greet her.

'I just thought there was a slim chance you might bring him today. I bought him this.' Nick handed over a brand-new iPad.

'I can't take this.' Amy placed it on the table between them and sat down. 'I'm so sorry, Nick. There's something I need to tell you. Something I should've told you a long time ago.' She took a breath and the words began to flow, freeing her from the lie. 'It's about Brodie. About his father.'

Nick frowned and started to say something. Amy raised her hand to stop him.

'Please, Nick, let me . . .' Amy sighed. 'The thing is, you're not Brodie's biological father. I wasn't sure at the time, but you were so keen to be around, and I just thought we would work it all out.'

He looked at her for a long time, his face expressionless.

'But I'm on his birth certificate. I'm his father,' he said eventually, pointing at his own chest.

'I'm so sorry, Nick. You're not. I slept with someone else around the same time.'

'You cheated on me?'

'I'm not sure it was cheating. Remember how things were a bit on-off sometimes. I didn't always know where I stood with you and then it just happened with the other guy. It was a total one-off.'

Nick looked as though he'd been punched in the stomach.

'Who was it?'

She had expected the question. 'No one you know.' It wasn't a complete lie; Nick had never actually met Magnus. 'I should've told you when you got back in touch. It just never seemed like the right time.'

'You should've told me when Brodie was born.'

'I know, I know.' Amy closed her eyes. 'It all just seemed so complicated. And the way things were between us, the way it all ended; I didn't feel like I owed you anything. I thought you would never come back, if I'm being honest.'

'And there's absolutely no possibility that I'm his dad?'

Amy shook her head. 'I'm so sorry.' She fleetingly remembered the moment, a month or so after Brodie was born, when she'd torn up the letter containing the paternity results into the tiniest pieces possible so that Nick wouldn't find the evidence in the kitchen bin.

Amy reached across the table. He looked so devastated right at that moment, yet there was none of the anger or vitriol she'd experienced from him in the past, nothing sinister flexing under the surface. He really did seem to have changed.

'I suppose it's just as well I've got Vanessa and the baby to look forward to.' He gave a half-smile. 'Listen, I've got to go. I'm reporting from Parliament in a couple of hours. I should probably sort my head out before I do that.'

'Shit, Nick, I'm so sorry. I didn't know . . .'

'It's fine. Well, not fine exactly, but it's OK. I'll be OK I mean. I don't think there would have ever been a good time for you to tell me any of this.' He got up to leave.

'Here, take this.' Amy offered him the iPad. Nick shook his head.

'Keep it.' She began to protest but he stopped her. 'Honestly it's fine, just give it to Brodie anyway. They need them for school these days apparently.'

Amy stood up; they were inches apart. Without thinking, she put her arms around him and hugged him tightly. 'I'm so sorry,' she whispered into his ear. Nick hugged her back briefly before pulling away.

'Got to go.'

He walked out of the coffee shop without looking back. Amy couldn't quite believe the conversation was over, or that Nick had responded in the way he had. It had all happened so quickly that she hadn't even ordered a coffee, Nick's was still sitting on the table, untouched. The relief washed over her and she felt a lightness where she hadn't been aware of a heaviness before. Her thoughts turned to another person on the list that needed to know. She had absolutely no idea how Sasha would react, but she couldn't help feeling positive about it now. Surely Sasha would be happy; she loved Brodie like an auntie anyway, it would now just be official.

20

Brodie hadn't spotted the iPad thankfully. Amy was trying to work out what to do with it and had shoved it on top of the wardrobe in her bedroom. Although Nick had told her to keep it, it just didn't feel right somehow. It was August and almost the end of the summer holidays. She'd taken some time off work to spend with Brodie and now two long weeks free from the office stretched ahead of her and she'd begun to unwind, trying not to ruin it yet with thoughts of the conversations she needed to have with her family and friends, now she was facing up to the truth about Brodie's father.

That afternoon, she dragged Brodie off the sofa where he'd been engrossed in a tenth episode of *SpongeBob SquarePants*, and insisted they get outside to do something.

The sun was shining and the park around the corner from their house was busy with other families trying to fill the endless school summer holidays. Brodie found a couple of other boys to race around with and Amy sat on a bench, watching them play, enjoying the feeling of doing nothing for once. At one point, she thought she saw Nick, standing on the far side of the park, his figure slightly obscured by the sunlight. She rubbed her eyes and squinted, looking at the spot again only to find it empty. She shook her head and gave a small laugh; her conscience was obviously playing tricks on her. She wondered how long it would take for the guilt to ebb. Later, they wandered over to the shops and bought ice creams, which melted more quickly than they could eat them as they walked towards home. They were just around the corner from their house when Amy stopped to dig a tissue out of her handbag and noticed the messages on her phone. They were from an unsaved number – Vanessa. It appeared she wanted to talk to Amy and wondered if they could meet. Amy assumed Nick had told her about Brodie not being his son and suspected Vanessa wanted to give her a piece of her mind. She deleted the messages and blocked the number quickly; that wasn't a conversation she needed to add to her list.

The following day, Amy, Jeannette and Brodie were enjoying a sunny spell in the back garden when the front doorbell rang. Assuming it was a delivery for one of her online-shopping-addicted neighbours who were never in, Amy opened the door without first checking through the peephole. It was Vanessa. She tried to shut the door again quickly, but Vanessa put her hand up to stop her.

'Please, Amy? I'm not here for trouble. I just want to talk.'

Amy frowned. 'How did you know where we live?'

Vanessa looked at her feet. 'I found your address. Nick had it written down on a piece of paper.'

'But how . . . ?' She tried to think if she'd given it to him at any point, but the idea was ridiculous, she wouldn't have. The fact that he hadn't known where they lived had always given her a sense of security; it was why she'd moved just after he'd left the first time.

'Maybe he got it from one of his contacts? I'm sorry, I don't know . . . and I'm sorry I've turned up here too, but I just really need to talk to you, please?'

A memory pushed at the edge of Amy's mind. *The taxi, he called the taxi the night we had dinner.* She must've told him the address then. She scolded herself for being so careless.

'Wait here.' Amy closed the door, leaving Vanessa standing on the doorstep and went back out to the garden.

Jeannette raised an eyebrow. 'What does she want with you?'

Amy shrugged. 'I'm not sure, but I don't think she'll give up until I agree to talk to her. Do you mind watching Brodie for half an hour?'

Amy and Vanessa walked in silence around the corner to the nearest pub. Vanessa insisted on buying the drinks and they sat at a table in the corner, furthest away from any of the other late-afternoon drinkers.

'I'm sorry for taking you by surprise. I just really needed to talk to you, and you didn't answer my text messages.' Vanessa took a sip of wine.

'Should you be . . ?' Amy pointed at Vanessa's stomach.

'Probably not. But that's why I wanted to talk to you. I've just got a bad feeling about this.'

'About what?'

'About the pregnancy. About Nick. About everything.' Vanessa took another drink, longer this time. 'The thing is, I asked Nick if he minded if I talked to you. I said it was about getting to know the mother of his son, but he reacted really strangely and said that I shouldn't talk to you directly, that you wouldn't like that. That was just before he turned up outside your work. I didn't really think anything of it, but after I met you that day in the café, he pretty much shut me down. Said that was the last time I would ever see you and that I should stop obsessing over his exes. I know he was trying to make me feel like I was the one with the problem, but I can just tell there's something he's hiding.'

Vanessa paused and looked down, studying her dark red nail polish.

'He's told me about everything that happened between you, but I just wanted to talk to you without Nick being here. To ask your side of the story.'

'What exactly did Nick tell you happened between us?'

'I'm not sure . . .'

'Go on, please.'

'OK, I'm sorry if this is hard for you to talk about though.' She took a deep breath and closed her eyes. 'He basically said that you had suffered from some mental health issues while you were together, that you were really jealous and possessive because of it, and that you made up lies about him being violent when he tried to leave you.'

Amy almost choked on her drink. 'He said what?'

'He said he tried hard to get you help but that the relationship between you was eventually so toxic that he felt the only thing he could do to make things better was to leave.'

Amy couldn't believe what she was hearing.

'I'm so sorry to bring all of this back up again for you. It's just, when I met you, I found it hard to believe some of the things he said you'd done. You seem so,' Vanessa searched for the right word, 'normal, I suppose.'

Amy felt as though she may be experiencing some level of shock; she was lost for words.

'Are you OK?' Vanessa had finished her glass of wine and was indicating to the barman for another.

'I hate to tell you this, but none of what Nick's told you is true. It was Nick that was possessive and jealous. He was also the violent one. Can I ask, how long have you actually known him?'

'We've been together for six months. He's been talking about us getting a place together, before the baby's born.' Vanessa shook her head, a pained expression settled in her eyes. 'I don't understand. You're telling me it was all the other way around? Why would he lie about that?' She groaned and put her head in her hands. 'I don't know what to believe.'

'Vanessa, I promise you that I'm not lying. Think about it. I know you haven't known him long but has there been any red flags that he isn't telling you the truth? You must have some inkling, otherwise you wouldn't be sitting here with me.'

Vanessa sighed. 'I didn't plan to get pregnant, but when I told Nick, he broke down in tears and told me he had a son he didn't have contact with. When I asked why he didn't see his son, he told me all that stuff about you. I'm finding it hard to believe that all that emotion was fake. He was really upset.'

'He does the emotional bit really well. It was why it was so difficult for me to see how dangerous he was.'

'You think he's dangerous?'

'He certainly was back then. I'd like to believe he's changed, Vanessa, but now I know what he told you about me, I'm not so sure.'

The barman placed another glass of wine in front of Vanessa and she handed him a ten-pound note.

'Keep the change,' she said, waving him away. The man stood awkwardly.

'You know,' he faltered, looking at the note in his hands, 'it's not really table service in here, if you want any other drinks . . .'

Vanessa flashed him such a look of contempt, he started to back away from their table. 'We won't be needing any more, thank you,' she sniped before turning her attention back to Amy. 'Where were we?'

'Has he ever lost his temper with you?' Amy asked

'Not really.' Vanessa thought for a moment. 'I suppose there was the time he threw a glass at the wall outside a pub we'd been in. But that wasn't directed at me. He'd had an argument with the barman about his pint being off. He was very drunk. I just thought it was a one-off.'

'That's what I thought. But then it happened again, and again. The thing is, he was always so sorry and always said he would get help to change. It wasn't until I was pregnant the second time that I realised what he was really like, to be honest.'

'Wait. What second time? Do you and Nick have another baby?'

Amy shook her head. The memory still caused black clouds to come rolling into her mind.

'I had a miscarriage. That's when he finally left.'

'Oh. I'm sorry, that must've been horrid.' She took another drink and then laughed bitterly. 'You know, if I'm being honest with myself, I think I've always had a sneaking suspicion that he might be a complete bastard underneath all those charming smiles. When my sister met him, she said she thought there was something a bit creepy about him, but I thought she was just a bit jealous. Can I ask you, Amy, did he ever hit you?'

Amy nodded. 'Only once though.'

'Once is enough.'

'He preferred smashing things up, I think.'

'Why didn't you ever report him to the police?'

Amy swallowed a mouthful of warm white wine. It was another source of guilt that she'd never reported any of the incidents. He'd always managed to convince her she was over reacting, that the police would think she was wasting time. Then, when he left, she just wanted to forget all about him. He was gone and he couldn't be a threat to them anymore. She supposed it had been selfish.

'Looking back, I should have. As time went on and I didn't hear anything from him, I just kind of tried to pretend he didn't exist. To be honest, despite him lying to you about the situation with me, he does seem like he's a lot less angry than he was.' Amy thought back to his reaction to her revelation about Brodie.

'Well, whatever's happened, he still lied to me about you. I can't trust him, can I?' Vanessa was beginning to slur slightly.

'You are having his baby though.'

Vanessa looked down at her stomach. There was little indication that she was pregnant, even now, perhaps just a slight rounding.

'I didn't ever think I would have children. I'm not very maternal.' As if to demonstrate Vanessa swept her manicured fingernails through her long glossy hair and took another gulp of wine. 'It was a mistake. I've already got an appointment at a clinic. I wasn't sure if I was going to go through with it, but I'm pretty sure now.'

'What? You're having an abortion?'

'Looks like it.' Vanessa drained her glass.

'You can't make a decision like that based on my experience with Nick. Please, take some time to think about it. It's such a big thing.'

Vanessa laughed. 'Not really. As I said, I've never much wanted children. I certainly don't want to have them with a liar. It was bad enough for me growing up with my dad constantly lying to my mum and cheating on her. I don't need that for me or for any child.'

An image of Ken flashed through Amy's mind.

'You're right there. No child needs to grow up with all that going on.'

Vanessa gathered her coat. Her eyes were glistening. She stumbled slightly as she stood from the chair, steadying herself by holding onto the back. 'Listen,' she hiccupped, 'thanks, Amy. I appreciate you coming here with me and for telling me the truth. I do believe you. I can feel it in here.' She patted her stomach. 'Do yourself a favour though, honey. Stay away from him. Don't let him back into your life, or your son's. Just because he fathered the boy, doesn't mean he can be a dad.'

Amy winced at the reference. Nick hadn't told her about Brodie. That was strange. She had an overwhelming urge to confess everything, but Vanessa was walking away from the table, unsteady on her eye-wateringly high heels. She turned back at the door to the pub and gave a small wave and the saddest smile Amy had seen in a long time. Amy drained her glass and thought about ordering another but knew she should get home. She had the distinct feeling that she had just participated in the opening of a huge can of worms that would only serve to slither Nick back into her life.

When she returned to the flat, Brodie had helped Jeannette into the kitchen, and they were both sitting at the table peeling carrots.

'We're making lentil soup, Mum,' Brodie informed her.

'Sounds good, kiddo.' Amy began clearing away the peelings into the food bin.

'How was your friend? Did she have anything interesting to say?' Jeannette asked.

'Oh, she had lots of interesting things to say.' Amy shook her head. She had been so convinced Nick had changed, but it looked as though he was still pretending to be something he wasn't. She thought about her own secrets and remembered the email.

'Actually, Grandma, there's something I've been meaning to tell you.'

'Yes, dear?'

'You know you told me about the Forrest family, about Mum's father? I did some digging and found out where David Forrest worked, it was a firm in London . . .' Amy stopped. Her grandmother was glowering.

'You've what?'

'Eh, I just . . .' Amy hesitated, 'I thought if we found him we could get in touch . . .'

Jeannette pursed her lips and tutted. 'Well you shouldn't have done that. It's not your business to go snooping on my behalf. Do you not think, if I'd wanted to, I'd have looked for him myself years ago? The poor boy played no part in the whole thing. He shouldn't be troubled by any of it.'

'Oh but, Grandma, he's Mum's half-brother. I just thought . . .'

'No, you didn't think at all, missy. You didn't think about talking to me about any of it first, did you?' Jeannette looked over her reading glasses at Amy and pointed the potato peeler. 'You have enough of your own business to sort out, so stop meddling in other people's and get on with that.'

Brodie looked up at his mother and pulled an *oops* face. 'Gee-gee just gave you a row,' he said.

'That's right, my wee scone, I did.' The two of them continued with their task. Amy busied herself tidying the kitchen and thought briefly about the email she'd sent inquiring if anyone at the London firm remembered a David Forrest. Probably best not to mention it now.

21

Edinburgh, 1962

It was April and Edinburgh was flourishing, waking from its dark-grey winter of sleep, the city brightening as the light stretched a little longer with each passing day. Spring was Jeannette's favourite time of year, bringing a sense that new beginnings were possible, that hopes and dreams would perhaps have a chance of blossoming into reality. Judith had recently turned four and would be going to school in August that year, a terrifying prospect for Jeannette, not only because the days and months and years seemed to be slipping by so rapidly, but because the school day just wasn't long enough. The nursery opened at eight and closed at six, giving Jeannette plenty of time either side of her working day to drop off and collect her little girl. School would finish in the middle of the afternoon, two long hours stretching between the bell ringing and Jeannette being able to hurriedly grab her coat and bag and race down the office steps. School and home were at the opposite end of Princes Street to the office. Jeannette could walk it at a fast pace in twenty-five minutes, sometimes quicker than using the bus, which stopped and started with irritating frequency. It would be half past five before she would be home. The woman who lived on the ground floor of their tenement had already offered to watch Judith for a few hours a day after school. There would be a cost for this, another nibble out of the already stretched weekly wages. George would give her the money, she knew that, but something always stopped her from asking, pride perhaps, and he'd already given them enough when he gave them their home.

Jeannette woke that Saturday morning in April with a restlessness that drew her from her bed earlier than usual. The weekend was much coveted in their home for the pleasure of waking and realising that today there was no work, no nursery, no pressing need to get up and go anywhere. The duvet could be pulled around tighter, snuggled further into, and even if sleep wasn't possible then dozing and daydreaming were a close second. That morning however, she was dressed by seven thirty, the kettle boiling on one ring of the stove, a small pan of porridge keeping warm on the other. Judith was still asleep when Jeannette perched on the edge of her daughter's bed and stroked wisps of dark hair from her slightly clammy pink cheeks, tucking them gently behind her ear. Her daughter stirred, frowning and pursing her lips, reluctant to leave the comfort of slumber, opening her eyes slightly, then quickly scrunching them shut again.

'Time to wake up, poppet,' Jeannette whispered, drawing back the covers and hooking her hands under Judith's arms to pull her onto her lap for a cuddle. Judith squirmed a little then nestled into her mother and Jeannette rocked gently from side to side, singing softly and breathing in the comforting sweet familiar scent of her child.

'We're going on an adventure today,' she told Judith as she tied the belt of her dressing gown and led her through to the sitting room. 'First, we'll go on a bus, then on another bus, then a boat and then we'll do the same all the way back again. Does that sound like fun?'

Judith nodded sleepily as she climbed up onto a chair and sat at the table, spooning porridge into her mouth with one eye still closed, squinting at her mother as she ate. Judith's morning muteness was a source of amusement for Jeannette, the origin of the characteristic proving a mystery. It would normally take around half, sometimes a whole hour for her daughter to utter her first words of the day. Once she began though, there was generally no stopping her.

As if reading her mother's mind, Judith finished her porridge and asked, 'Why does Daddy not live here?' and then, 'Eilidh's daddy lives with her, and her mummy.' Jeannette was sure little Eilidh made a point of reminding Judith daily that she didn't have a daddy. Not that she was accusing a four-year-old of being deliberate.

Jeannette thought of George. It was difficult not to every time she looked at her daughter. What would he be doing right now? He was probably eating breakfast and reading the newspaper. She could picture him sitting at a grand mahogany dining table. Annie walked into the scene in her head, spoiling her thoughts. She pushed them out of her mind. An uneasiness had settled within her over the last few days. George hadn't been in touch for over a week now. Usually he would send a little something if he couldn't visit; a note to let them know he was thinking of them, sometimes even just a postcard with his initials signed on the back, but nothing had arrived.

'Your daddy has to work so hard that he can't live with us all of the time.' Jeannette gave her usual answer, one she hoped would suffice for some time to come. Other men worked away from their families, it wasn't too far-fetched a notion. So long as no one found out that Judith's daddy lived with his wife and teenage son on the other side of town, the story should be watertight enough for the time being.

She was still in love with George, of course. Even now, after all that had happened and all the time that had passed. Despite the love, there were times when Jeannette swung from being completely accepting of their situation to feeling utterly bereft whenever it was obvious that she and Judith were not his priority. She had to constantly remind herself of all the reasons he recounted to her when she doubted his love, sensible reasons why he couldn't just up and leave his wife of twenty years.

There had been times when she thought that even he was tired of their situation and regardless of the reasons why he couldn't leave, she had felt that he may one day just do it: simply arrive at the flat and stay the night, then the next night and never leave. When he'd visited a month or so ago, soaked from the rain, and Jeannette had undressed him, hanging his clothes by the fire, he had looked at her with such longing, she thought that perhaps he was on the verge of taking some action, that something was about to change. They made love that night and he wrapped his arms around her afterwards and Jeannette felt closer to him than she ever had to anyone. He told her he adored her, that he couldn't live without her, and she truly believed it because there was something between them; an invisible thread that connected them, woven through their hearts and their minds. The closeness she felt in those moments failed to stop the familiar sense of disappointment creeping back as he dressed early the next morning and began making small talk, telling her about some renovations they were having made to the house, about a case he was dealing with at work. The bubble of their togetherness drifted away as his mind went back to his real life, to the life he belonged to. It happened every time, and yet she felt powerless to refuse herself the moments of closeness that preceded.

Jeannette gave herself a small shake. She wasn't going to let thoughts like that ruin today. The sun was shining. Count your blessings, that's what her own mother used to say.

It took two bus journeys to get to South Queensferry, a town that sits on the Firth of Forth, under the shadow of the giant red metal rail bridge. The pier was busy, a line of cars waiting patiently to drive aboard. Jeannette and Judith joined the steady queue of foot passengers traipsing up the gangway, presenting their tickets to the smartly dressed officer at the top, who welcomed them on board with a smile and a nod of his head.

They stood on deck for the beginning of the short journey, Jeannette holding on to the cold white rail with one hand and her daughter with the other as the ferry chugged away from the land and Judith squealed with delight at the water lapping against the side of the boat. The wind whipped its chilly fingers through their hair and played with their skirts. Jeannette bent down to fasten the large black buttons on Judith's red coat, another present from George, another reminder.

'Are you having fun?' she asked, and Judith nodded.

'Can I have a treat, Mummy?'

Jeannette laughed. 'Of course you can. We're going to have a very lovely treat soon, just over there.' She pointed to the land the boat was heading towards. This was a trip she had made with George, before their secret had been discovered. She intended to take Judith to the little café on the main street where she and George had sat together on a few occasions. They had shared a pot of tea and picked at the toasted teacakes the jolly woman who ran the café had insisted they try. Getting on the ferry with George seemed like a lifetime ago. Jeannette remembered the sense of freedom as the boat unhooked from the dock and began ploughing through the choppy waters. She had felt as though they were leaving the real world behind; that the further away from South Queensferry and Edinburgh they sailed, the more he became hers and she could pretend to herself that they were like any other normal couple. He had even dared to hold her hand on the first crossing, his fingers curling around hers as they sat next to each other on the rigid chairs bolted to the floor, looking out at the rail bridge towering above. The woman in the café had assumed they were a married couple, had smiled at them and talked a bit about the weather and then left them to have some privacy once she'd served them. They'd returned a few times, each occasion giving Jeannette the much-needed feeling that she was, for once, his priority. Even if it was only for a few hours.

The little bell above the door tinkled as Jeannette led Judith out of the cold and into the warmth of the café. They were greeted by the same warm smile Jeannette remembered and ushered to sit down at the table she had shared each time with George.

'Haven't seen you in a while,' the jolly woman said, and Jeannette smiled politely, suspecting that she was being mistaken for someone else until she continued, 'And where's that lovely husband of yours? Such a tall man, his legs didn't quite fit under the table if I remember correctly.' She laughed at her own memory and waited expectantly for Jeannette to respond. When no response was forthcoming, she turned to Judith and innocently asked, 'Where's your daddy today, sweetheart?' To which Judith said simply, 'I don't know.'

Jeannette panicked.

'I'm afraid he passed away,' she said, before immediately scolding herself for telling such a wicked lie and perhaps tempting fate.

The woman (the stitching on her tabard read *Beverley*) placed her hands over her heart and said, 'Oh my, how terrible, I am so sorry.' Then reached down and touched Jeannette's shoulder. 'Was it recent, love?'

A prickle of shame crept up Jeannette's neck. 'A while now,' she managed to say before busying herself with removing her gloves.

Beverley offered a reassuring smile. 'Ah well,' she said, 'at least you have his beautiful wee girl to remind you of him.' She touched Judith's cheek, who looked over at her mother, frowning. 'Now, what can I get you? I've got some lovely home-made cakes up there at the counter for you to choose from.'

Beverley wouldn't let Jeannette pay for the afternoon tea and even came around from behind the counter when they were leaving to give her a hug. 'My treat,' she said. 'I'm so sorry again for your loss.' It made Jeannette wince and regret the lie even further; she would never be able to return to the café again and if George was ever to happen upon the place, Beverley may collapse in fright.

As they walked down the main street towards the ferry that would take them back to South Queensferry, Judith asked, 'What's "passed away" Mummy?' And Jeannette distracted her daughter by pointing out a train that was rattling across the big red bridge overhead. The lie had come out of her mouth before she could stop it, but she wasn't sure whether it was the lie or the truth that was making her feel more ashamed now. She'd grown used to being alone with her daughter, yet she still wore her mother's wedding ring. She was never without it, as if it protected her and Judith from anyone realising the truth; that she had never been married and it would be her child that would forever carry the consequences of her actions. At times, the guilt threatened to completely overwhelm her, filling up every part of her body until she felt almost consumed by it.

Despite herself, Jeannette tried to keep outwardly cheerful, as she always did, for Judith's sake. This was meant to be a good day.

They travelled once more on the bus back into town. It slowed, brakes screeching noisily above the rumbling engine as they pulled into a stop halfway along Princes Street. It was only just after three and there was still time to have a wander along towards the East End, then home, perhaps stop on the way and buy something nice for dinner. The late-afternoon shoppers were beginning to disperse, some laden with bags, others having had a less successful day at the shops. Jeannette barely noticed anyone going by as she walked, holding her daughter's hand and listening to Judith's excited chatter about the boat trip. It wasn't until she tugged on her mother's hand for a second time and said quite loudly, 'Mummy, look, there's Daddy,' that Jeannette snapped her gaze up from the pavement and followed the direction of Judith's outstretched hand and pointed finger. George and Annie were walking directly towards them, their son David tagging along, slightly behind.

Before Jeannette could do a thing to stop her, Judith had wriggled free and was walking ahead shouting, 'Daddy, Daddy,' waving her little hand frantically.

It was Annie that spotted Judith first, her relaxed expression quickly turning tense as she linked her arm into George's and turned him in the direction of the kerb. George looked to his wife, puzzled. They came to a stop. Judith shouted loudly again, 'Daddy!' He spotted his little girl in an instant, the colour draining from his face. Annie was talking frantically into his ear, pulling at his arm. He turned to his wife and when he looked back at Judith, Jeannette could see the pain in his eyes. He smiled weakly and raised his hand in a half wave, before allowing Annie to lead him across the road. She called to her son, who followed them both, oblivious to the occurrence, and Jeannette caught hold of her daughter's hand and could do nothing but stand, fixed to the spot, and stare as the other shoppers kept moving around them, jostling past, aggrieved at the obstruction. It all happened with such swiftness, but he made no attempt to stop, glancing back only one more time, to mouth the word *sorry* to Jeannette.

Jeannette looked down at her daughter's sad face and felt something shift. A light inside her flickered and faltered, irreversibly dimming. She soothed Judith and bribed her to walk towards home with the promise of a stop at the sweet shop on Broughton Street. She wiped the tears from her little girl's face and realised that, at that moment, she herself wasn't crying, that perhaps she should be, but there just didn't seem to be any tears left.

Sunday had been awful. They hadn't left the flat at all, Jeannette's thoughts being overrun by the event on Princes Street the previous day. How could George have let that happen? The minute he looked back at her, as Annie led him across the road, away from his daughter, she had caught sight of a weakness in him that had turned her stomach. She had known where his priorities lay, but to have these demonstrated so openly, to watch him choose between his two existences, had torn at her pride as well as her love for him.

On Monday morning, Jeannette knew she would barely get the chance to take off her coat before Annie was summoning her into the office. Annie had made a special trip to be there, her role at the office having been mostly taken over by an eager young woman called Eileen who had styled herself on Annie and taken a dislike to Jeannette in an act of comradery with her idol.

There was a pot of tea already on the mahogany desk, which Annie poured without asking whether Jeannette would like a cup or not.

'Milk?' Annie asked. Jeannette nodded and sat down in the familiar chair. It was the same chair she had sat in when Annie had confronted her about the pregnancy, all those years ago. She felt, once again, that she was a schoolgirl visiting the headmistress.

Annie passed Jeannette a teacup and saucer and perched on the edge of the desk.

'Firstly, I want to apologise,' she began, 'I panicked. You know my son has no idea that Judith exists, and I couldn't stand for him to find out so publicly.'

Jeannette took a sip of tea, shuddering at the lack of sugar.

'The thing is,' Annie continued, 'and I'm not sure how much George has spoken to you about this, but we've been having something of a reconciliation over the last few months. A rekindling, I suppose you might call it,' she paused and smiled slightly, 'of our marriage.'

Jeannette held the saucer tightly to stop the cup from rattling. She chose not to speak; not trusting which words would emerge. George had been distant for a while, she supposed this was the reason why. It seemed at odds with what she knew of him, of what she knew of their feelings for one another, but who was she to argue with Annie? She was his wife after all, and he had never, in all the years they had been in each other's lives, made any kind of move, taken any kind of action, to suggest that he would ever leave her. *Fool*, Jeannette told herself. What a fool to believe this day wouldn't come. She felt completely exhausted all of a sudden.

Jeannette knew her role was to be subservient in all of this, she was, after all, responsible for her own shame. She should be grateful that Annie had ever helped her. Anyone who knew how generous Annie had been when faced with the choice of helping her husband's lover or casting her out would say, 'Isn't she a marvellous woman? So forgiving, so accepting.' At that moment however, Jeannette felt unable to feel grateful, although she knew she should.

Annie leaned back in her chair, her expression pained. 'I know this is difficult for you, Jean. Heaven knows, the last five years have been difficult for all of us. I've been thinking about things though, and I wonder if I might pass an idea by you. Just a suggestion.'

Jeannette listened. She supposed, under the circumstances, it was the least she could do.

It was the following Saturday before she could get down to the farm. Jeannette had spent the week in a slightly stunned state after her meeting with Annie on Monday morning. She had been desperate to talk to her best friend but wanted to have the conversation with her face-to-face, and as a result had spent the week going through a variety of emotions and responses to the offer she'd been made.

Morag collected them from the train station in the old green Land Rover, her hair tied up in a scarf, wearing khaki trousers and wellington boots that were caked in mud.

'Very Land Army,' commented Jeannette as she kissed her friend on the cheek.

'It's the latest from the catwalks of Paris. You know how glamorous Tom likes me to be.' Morag laughed. 'Now where's my cuddle from my favourite wee girl?' she asked, stretching out her arms. Judith stepped forward to be folded into a cushiony hug.

Morag filled the interior of the car with chatter for the ten minutes it took to get from the station to the farm. Her children were all keeping her busy, one of their pigs had won first prize at an agricultural show and Philip, a new addition to the farmhands, had taken ill and been admitted to hospital in Edinburgh.

'I suggested to Tom that he got someone else to help out. There's plenty of young lads looking for work around here, but he's determined Philip will be back in no time, and we can't afford to have two extra hands. Between you and I though, I'm not sure Philip will be coming out of hospital any time soon. Fiona went to visit him on Wednesday and says he's turned a very odd colour.'

Fiona was Morag's youngest sister. She was still single and beginning to get so desperate to meet a man, she would even volunteer to visit a stranger in hospital, in the hope that he might be 'the one'.

Jeannette listened to Morag's news, enjoying the respite from her own thoughts. She had forgotten how easy it was to get caught up in one's own problems and reminded herself that she must talk to people more often when she was becoming too introspective; an easy thing to do, living alone with only a four-year-old for company in the evening.

As they pulled up in front of the farmhouse, Morag's three very excited daughters rushed out of the front door, quickly claiming Judith for themselves, and disappeared back inside, arguing about which games they were going to play and who was in charge.

'Patricia's learned to do something called a French plait,' Morag told Jeannette. 'I'll apologise in advance for any damage done.' She smiled, grabbing Jeannette's overnight bag and slamming the driver's door shut with an almighty bang.

Morag moved around the kitchen, boiling the huge iron kettle on the range, fussing over the mess the children had left and laying out her usual selection of baked goods. 'These ones are cheese scones,' she indicated a plate in the centre of the table. 'Tom made the mistake of putting jam on one the other day,' she warned. 'Although he ate it and said it was actually rather good.'

Jeannette helped herself to a large slice of Victoria sponge and thought momentarily how lovely it was that being in Morag's house always made her feel as though she had come home.

'So, come on,' Morag pulled out a chair and sat opposite Jeannette. 'What's the latest from the Forrest dynasty?'

Jeannette laughed. Ten minutes with her best friend was all it ever took for her to begin to see her own situation in a far more humorous light than she was ever able to see it by herself.

'Goodness. Dynasty is pretty spot on.' Jeannette took a sip of tea, burning her tongue a little on the hot liquid. 'George and Annie. It seems they're back together. I mean, they were always together, but now they're a proper couple. Again.' Jeannette didn't think she would ever see the humorous side to the thought of that.

'Oh, Jeannie,' Morag reached across the table and took her friend's hand, her brow furrowed. 'The man is a complete idiot. He will never be happy. You deserve happiness, you and Judith both do.'

'Yes but . . .' Jeannette swallowed over the tight lump in her throat. 'I'm still in love with the complete idiot and I feel like such a fool myself.' Jeannette sniffed and blew her nose into the large white hanky Morag handed her. 'I think I've known all along that he would never be with us, not properly. He's got his big fancy house and his rich wife, and I was just some stupid girl who had never been in love before. I'll bet they have a good old laugh at me, sitting in that flat alone at night, waiting for him to throw me a scrap of affection.' Jeannette threw the hanky down on the table and clenched her fists.

'At last!' Morag clapped her hands together. 'You're angry! You don't know how long I've waited to see you get cross with that man. Please don't take this the wrong way, but all these years he's kept you dangling on a string – keeping his own options open, no doubt, in case Annie saw sense and had enough. It's not that I don't understand why you've been waiting for him, Jeannie, I honestly do understand that.'

Jeannette felt a spark of defensiveness within. She didn't like the insinuation that she had been too much of a pushover but knew her friend, her very best friend, was only telling her the truth.

'That's not the end of it.'

Morag raised an eyebrow. 'Go on.'

'Annie's father has an office in London. There's a position vacant, and it's mine if I want it.'

'Wait.' Morag looked confused. 'London? Why would you go to London?'

'I don't know. A fresh start maybe. No chance of bumping into them and Judith shouting at her daddy in the middle of Princes Street.'

'She didn't?' Morag put her hand to her mouth but didn't manage to hide her smile.

Jeannette nodded.

'I like London. It would be an adventure.'

'But it's just Annie telling you what to do again. They never seem to stop having a bit of control over you. Telling you where to live, where to work. You don't have to do any of it. Come and live here with us, you know I want you to.'

The offer for Jeannette and Judith to go and live on the farm had been extended on numerous occasions. It wasn't one Jeannette ever took seriously though, despite the warmth it gave her to think of her friend's generosity. It would only ever be temporary though, and she needed something more permanent for herself, and for Judith. She needed to at least try to find that, by herself this time.

'It might just be the new beginning I need. Life after George.'

'Have you spoken to him about it?'

'No, not yet. He's not been in touch. Annie says he's away on business, but I think that was a lie.'

'Well, if you do decide to go to London, I'm sure Douglas will help you settle in.' Douglas was Morag's brother, as well as the boy Jeannette had once shared an experimental passionless kiss with in their teenage years.

A rumble above their heads indicated the girls thundering down the stairs. They burst into the kitchen, a gaggle of giggling and entwined arms. 'We're hungry,' Patricia announced. The others were already swarming down on the cakes and scones like locusts. Jeannette watched Judith who was smiling, happy to be part of this group. If Jeannette took her little girl to London, she would undoubtedly miss this as much she herself would miss Morag.

'We can always visit you in London,' Morag said, as though reading her friend's mind. 'The children need to see their Uncle Douglas occasionally. And you'll come up in the holidays, I'm sure?'

Jeannette smiled and gave a small nod, unable to talk over the lump in her throat. Morag came to stand behind her friend, leaning down she wrapped her arms around Jeannette's shoulders and landed a firm kiss on her cheek. 'And if it doesn't work out, you can always come home.'

*

London. She wasn't going because Annie told her to. Or at least that's what Jeannette had convinced herself of in the days and weeks after making the decision to sell the flat and start a new life there. Annie had merely planted the seed, an idea that blossomed into a whole new world of possibilities for herself and her daughter. London was vibrant and exciting, full of people from all walks of life. A single mother was unlikely to draw as much attention in the capital city, where diversity was visible throughout. Jeannette had visited London a few times in her twenties. One of her mother's sisters lived there, and she had a cousin, Rosamunde, who was a year younger than Jeannette and fairly mischievous. She had taken her to a secret club one night where they had witnessed a man kissing another man as they drank vodka in tiny sips from thick glass tumblers. The scene had shocked her at the time but now it gave her a feeling of strength. Surely London was the perfect place to go unnoticed, if that was the way you wanted things to be.

She had waited for George to get in touch following Annie's revelation regarding their marital reunion. Although she wanted to speak to him, wanted his side of the story, it would be unseemly to chase him now and she was still carrying the anger towards him she'd felt rising within her at Morag's. Despite this, Jeannette couldn't help thinking that Annie's version of events didn't quite ring true, that, regardless of his reluctance to leave his home, for reasons she completely understood, loving Annie in the way he loved her didn't seem plausible. Perhaps she was being delusional though, perhaps that had been her problem throughout the whole sorry affair.

A postcard arrived at the flat one morning a few days later; only a date and a time written on the back. She knew he meant for them to meet at their usual café in their usual booth. He had signed the note with a simple 'G'. No kiss. Jeannette's stomach turned at this glaring omission, but she stopped herself from spiralling, she must keep her resolve. The decision had been made; she was taking control and she would tell him so when they met.

Jeannette traced her finger along a scratch on the melamine tabletop. He was late. The tea she had ordered half an hour ago had stewed in the pot for too long and was now luke-warm and bitter. She glanced again at the clock above the door at the far end of the room. The second hand ticked lethargically, as though it couldn't quite be bothered to mark the passage of time. It was so unlike him to be late. They had met in this café on so many previous occasions. This was their table, the booth at the back with the frosted glass panel that the occupants could choose to hide behind if necessary. The booth practically vibrated with all the memories, all of their conversations, all of the promises made there; promises which were now as empty as the seat opposite her.

Jeannette was considering leaving when the door swung open and George walked straight in, nodding at the waitress to confirm that yes, he would have his usual coffee, before striding towards their table and sliding into the seat without taking off his coat. He removed his hat and reached across the table to touch her hand. Jeannette pulled back. She had decided that he mustn't touch her, if he did, she knew there was a chance that she would falter in her resolve.

'Jeannette, I'm so sorry,' he pleaded. 'It's been a tough couple of weeks. Annie did not react well to seeing Judith on the street.'

'I know. She came into the office specifically to talk to me. She told me that the two of you are – how did she put it? – reconciled.'

She had hoped that he would look shocked, would instantly deny the accusation, but to her dismay, he leant forward and put his head in his hands and closed his eyes. He stayed that way for a moment before letting out a long slow sigh. He rubbed his eyes with his fists. Jeannette felt her heart pull towards him. He looked exhausted. She wanted so much to hold him and be held by him. How had they reached this stage, she wondered, where it was so obviously hopeless and yet she felt so much love for him, even now?

'It's complicated. I can't really say why, but Annie is making it impossible. I don't want to lose you but if I leave Annie, I'll lose everything. She's putting so much pressure on me not to see you, not to see Judith. Someone in her Women's Guild heard rumours and was asking loaded questions at their last meeting. Annie was embarrassed. She laughed it off in public, of course, but I think that's what started this whole thing. That and Judith waving at me.' He rubbed his eyes again. 'I'm so sorry about that day. I can never apologise enough, I suspect. How is Judith, does she need anything?'

'She needs her father,' Jeannette snapped. George flinched. 'But as that seems to be a diminishing possibility, then she needs something else. I need something else too.' Jeannette took a deep breath. 'I've taken the decision to sell the flat and we're moving to London.' There, she had said it. Now the words were out she felt as though it was really happening.

George's face crumpled in confusion. 'Don't be ridiculous, why would you move to London?'

'There's nothing ridiculous about it. It was Annie's idea at first. She clearly wants us away from Edinburgh. She offered me a job at her father's firm in the city. Didn't you know?'

George remained silent.

'I've decided to reject her offer though. I'm a bit tired of being dictated to by your wife. She has obviously been labouring under the idea that her acceptance of this whole situation somehow gives her control over me. I need that to end now, I've lived with it for too long.'

'What on earth are you going to do in London? What about Judith?'

'My cousin Rosamunde has organised an interview for me in a factory office. They make blinds. For windows,' Jeannette confirmed. 'Not that it matters. It's a job. She's also set us up with a flat to rent for a while and helped me organise a place at school for Judith.'

'You're taking my daughter away from me.'

'I'm not saying you can't visit her.'

George shook his head. 'I have a right to see her. She's my child too. You can't just take her away.'

'That's the thing though, isn't it?' Jeannette felt bitterness rising; years of sleepless nights, lying awake, wishing he was beside her, of feeling like second best, bubbling to the surface. 'You don't have any right to her. You're not even legally named as her father. Because of you, she has that awful word attached to her name. Anyone who ever sees her birth certificate will know she's a . . .' Jeannette couldn't bring herself to say the word. This was an argument they'd had once before. The last time, it had ended in George promising to look into changing the birth certificate. Another empty promise.

He tried once more to touch her. Jeannette brushed his hand away, their fingers grazing. She slid out of the booth, grabbing her coat and gloves.

'I never wanted it to be like this, George. But it's obvious where we're heading, it's been obvious for years and I'm tired of living like this.'

'Jeannette, come on now, sit back down,' George pleaded. 'Let's talk more about this. You mustn't do anything rash.' He stood up, blocking her path to the door, placing his hands on the tops of her arms.

'Rash? This isn't rash. I've been waiting patiently for you for years. There is nothing rash about this decision, George, I can assure you.'

'You can't do this, I love you. I love Judith.'

'If you don't let me go right away, I will scream,' she stared hard at him, daring him to test her will. He dropped his hands down by his sides.

'I wish you would just . . .' he began, but she was already walking towards the café door, not turning to look back at him. She hadn't even said goodbye, but she knew that this time it truly was the end.

Jeannette had hoped to leave the city sooner, but selling the flat was a more complicated matter than she had imagined. It wasn't something she had any experience of doing before. In the end, she accepted an offer of a little under one thousand pounds, which she eventually took possession of in the form of crisp paper notes, each one bound together neatly with nine others and wrapped in a strip of white paper. For the first time in her life, she was in possession of wealth and, she soon realised, choices. They could go anywhere with the money, do anything. But it also felt unearned, illicit, as though she had stolen it from Annie and George. It was as equally liberating as it was constrictive. She purchased a brand-new leather suitcase with shiny brass locks and tucked the notes neatly inside: blue and green soldiers sleeping in rows, then placed an old blanket on top and clicked the locks shut.

They stayed with Morag for a week before leaving.

'One last holiday on the farm,' Morag had said. Jeannette had wavered then; could she really imagine not being in Edinburgh, near her friends and everything she knew as familiar?

The suitcase with its valuable contents, which she had stored under the bed in the guest room, was a constant source of worry for her. It was all they had now, and they would need every penny of it for their new life. Morag had laughed when she'd showed her the contents.

'But why won't you put it in the bank, Jeannie, it'd be far safer than lugging it all the way to London. What if you're robbed?'

'Anyone that tries to get near this case will have to prise it out of my cold, dead hands,' Jeannette had replied. 'And besides, I don't trust banks. They're in the habit of losing people's money too often.'

She didn't like to admit it, but Jeannette had gained some pleasure from selling the furniture from the flat to add to their funds. The green velvet sofa was worn in spots but had fetched a decent price, along with the polished round table. Two men arrived to lug the items downstairs, Judith standing in the stairwell watching them with fascination through the railings as they manoeuvred the heavy pieces awkwardly down. She wasn't able to sell the rocking horse though. It spent most of its occupancy where George, or whoever had originally furnished the flat, had put it; staring out of the big bay window at the top of Calton Hill. Tom came and picked it up and took it to the farmhouse, where the children positioned it in one of the upstairs windows so it could have a view of real horses galloping in the distance through the fields.

Eventually it was time for them to say goodbye. The bus to London left from the station in St Andrew Square where Morag stood waving, a huge smile on her face as she dabbed at her eyes with a white handkerchief.

Jeannette watched her city go by, as they trundled through the streets towards the outskirts of town and said a silent goodbye to all the familiar places they passed. She had managed to pack their belongings into only four suitcases, one of which contained the funds from the house and furniture sale. This one she kept beside them for the entire trip; squeezing it in front of their seats so Jeannette had to travel with her legs out in the aisle most of the way. It was a long journey with only three stops for refreshments and to use the toilets at dubiously sanitised service stations. The other passengers looked oddly at her as she alighted the bus each time grasping the suitcase tightly in one hand and holding on firmly to Judith with the other.

By the time they reached London, Judith was fast asleep, slumped over her mother's lap. When she tried to wake her, she cried until eventually Jeannette managed to coax her onto her feet so they could walk to the taxi rank with the suitcases piled on a luggage cart. It was early morning and the London rush hour appeared to be in full swing already. There was a condensed heat about the city, even at that hour, which she found immensely comforting as it wrapped its warmth around her. You would never experience such a thing in Edinburgh, where the North Sea wind whistled in off the Firth of Forth, bringing the temperature down even on a sunny day.

Judith hugged her favourite bunny rabbit to her chest as they waited in the taxi rank queue. It was the one George had bought for her second birthday. Jeannette's heart gave a small squeeze of sadness at the thought of him. She had managed to read part of a book on the bus and had been so preoccupied with getting the suitcases and Judith off safely that, for a few hours, she hadn't given him a thought; an unusual experience for her.

The taxi driver mumbled as he helped them and their luggage into his cab.

'Scotch, are ya?' he asked in a rich cockney accent.

'Scottish,' Jeannette corrected him.

'Same difference, innit?'

He drove them to the address Rosamunde had given Jeannette, asking questions all the way and telling her about the bits of London she was to avoid at night unless she was with her husband, of course.

'Where is your old man, luv? Is he already 'ere?'

'Yes. He'll be waiting for us at the accommodation.' She twisted her mother's weddings ring. She had been asked questions so many times about her 'husband' that she had almost begun to conjure a picture of him in her head to accompany the lies. Strangely, he was nothing like George.

When the driver pulled the suitcases onto the pavement, he gave her a clumsily affectionate slap on the arm and wished her good luck.

'I'll leave the suitcases to 'im indoors,' he said, indicating the building.

Jeannette and Judith stood on the pavement staring up at the building with its dark brickwork and white painted sills. She knew that the flat they were renting was on the very top floor, the old servants' rooms, no doubt. She stared up at the windows high above the pavement and then down at the four large suitcases containing their worldly possessions. She supposed she would be carrying them up there all by herself.

22

London, 1962

They had only been in London for a few days when Jeannette had realised she'd relaxed for the first time in years. She could never have imagined the difference a few hundred miles would make. In fact, she hadn't realised quite how much she had been suffering; living in Edinburgh in the flat bought by the Forrests, working for Annie's family firm. Jeannette had spent the last five years in shameful acceptance of her own wrongdoing, trying desperately to work out a way to atone. If it weren't for George and Annie's generosity, it would have been difficult to afford to live in Edinburgh, impossible to own a home. They'd allowed her to look after her daughter, to keep her baby from adoption. It wasn't a thought worth contemplating. But now, the burden of being in their debt, under their control, had lifted. There was no more sitting in the flat of an evening, waiting for George just in case he had time to drop by, watching the embers of the fire die in the grate as the chances of him arriving diminished with them. She no longer had to sit three desks away from Annie's old office door each day, behind which were the memories of being confronted, being shamed.

Not being able to jump on the train at the weekend to visit Morag was the only snag; that and the growing worry that her father really wasn't coping. She'd written to him the day they'd arrived, but he was yet to respond. Morag had sent Tom to knock on his door, but there had been no answer and Tom reported that one of the panes of glass in the front window had been smashed, mended only with a tattered square of brown cardboard.

It was Morag's brother, Douglas, who really helped them settle into life in London. He was a kind man, gentle and open. He confided in Jeannette that, like her, he was in London to gain some level of anonymity that seemed less achievable in Edinburgh. He was a bachelor and shared an apartment in South Kensington with another single man, Arthur. There were two bedrooms in the apartment, both with double beds, one of which had the distinctly untouched appearance of a guest room.

It was Douglas that arranged for Jeannette to be introduced to Alexander; a work colleague who had recently gone through a divorce when his wife ran off with a musician. As Douglas put it, Alexander was back 'on the dating scene'. Jeannette laughed. 'There's a scene, is there?' But she reluctantly agreed to meet Alexander one Saturday evening, despite her reservations.

'Don't worry about a thing, we'll have a marvellous time. Arthur has brought costumes back from the theatre, I think he's planning on doing a full-scale production in the lounge. Just go and have a drink with the man, enjoy yourself.' It was an unfamiliar concept that she could enjoy herself with a man, other than George. She wondered how he would feel if he knew she was considering joining the dating scene. Would he be jealous?

Douglas and Arthur had agreed to entertain Judith for the evening. Arthur was something quite senior in one of the theatres, a director of some sorts. He had given her tickets to take Judith to see *Carnival* at the Lyric Theatre, the story completely lost on the four-year-old who was more fascinated with the colours and bright lights of the stage. Jeannette had always favoured the cinema over the theatre, but she could admit to being transfixed that day; it was more like being in a movie than watching one.

By the time Jeannette had taken Judith on two buses and walked the rest of the way to South Kensington, Alexander was already sitting in one of the velvet winged armchairs by the fireplace, waiting for her to arrive. He stood when she entered the room and held out his hand. It was slightly clammy, and Jeannette was quick to take her own hand back, subtly wiping it on her woollen coat. *Don't judge too early*, she thought, *perhaps he's nervous*. She certainly was. Arthur came into the room wearing a brightly coloured oversized turban and began dancing and singing a song from a musical that Jeannette failed to recognise. Judith giggled and was swept away to the kitchen – or backstage, as Arthur called it. They were going to dress up and discuss which performance to put on for Douglas later.

It was just after 5 p.m. and as she watched her little girl disappear from the room, Jeannette felt a sudden urge to cancel the whole thing and stay to watch the show. Alexander had other ideas though and made a move towards the front door.

'Shall we get going then? I know a super place over in Belgravia where the barman shouts insults at some of the richest clientele and the cocktails are divine.'

Jeannette forced an image of George laughing at the idea of a cocktail out of her mind. It was silly to compare, she knew that, but it was difficult all the same not to notice the decided lack of any kind of attraction she was feeling towards this man.

They walked from the flat to the bar in the twenty-two

minutes Alexander had predicted it would take. The small talk flowed quite naturally and by the time they reached their destination, Jeannette had decided that she had been too quick to judge and that Alexander was a decent enough sort.

He ordered them both a Tom Collins and laughed when Jeannette tasted it; her mouth puckering at the bitterness. She was used to the syrupy sweetness of sherry and after attempting, out of politeness, to drink the cocktail, she had to admit defeat halfway through.

'That's fine,' Alexander remarked, 'some tastes are just a little more sophisticated. I'm sure they can rustle you up something more *pedestrian.*'

'You don't think I have sophisticated enough tastes?' Jeannette teased.

Alexander blustered. 'I didn't mean . . . I just meant that some things are designed for a more developed palette. I didn't mean to cause offence.'

'You didn't. I was just . . .' Jeannette looked at Alexander again and felt herself falter. 'Never mind.'

She didn't really have much to say after that, which didn't seem to deter Alexander. He ordered more drinks and talked endlessly about the places he'd been in the world and how knowledgeable he was when it came to geography as a result.

'My parents loved to travel with us in the school holidays. The more adventurous, the better. By the time I was fifteen, they used to joke that I was more well-travelled than Marco Polo.' Alexander laughed loudly, snorting at the same time. Jeannette believed the cocktails had gone to his head already. She had an overwhelming urge to stand up and leave. Politeness prevented her.

'So, Jeannie. How about we go and get something to eat?'

'It's Jeannette,' she said. There was only one person allowed to call her Jeannie and the thought of her friend at that moment made her feel very far away from home.

Jeannette looked down to check the time on the gold watch George had given her for Christmas one year. How long ago had that been now – three, maybe four years? She couldn't quite remember.

'I'm so sorry, Alexander. I think I'd better be getting back for Judith and I do have a bit of a head coming on. I suppose you were right about me not being sophisticated enough for these cocktails.'

Alexander appeared instantly aggrieved; a child informed that it was time to leave the playpark.

'Well if that's how you feel. I suppose I should walk you home.'

They traced their steps back to Douglas's apartment mostly in silence. Jeannette commented on how busy London was compared to Edinburgh and tried fruitlessly to make the same small talk they had made on the walk there, but Alexander was festering in some kind of alcohol-induced sulk.

When they reached their destination, Jeannette turned towards him.

'Thank you for an interesting evening, Alexander. I had a lovely time,' she lied.

He seemed to rally from this statement but was swaying a little on the spot, his eyes swimming with the strong liquor from the bar. 'Shall we do it again?' he asked.

'Thank you, but I don't think so. I did have a lovely time though.'

'Wait a minute,' Alexander sneered, his face transforming into something much less attractive than when he smiled. 'You don't want to go out with me again?'

'I'm sorry, I just . . .'

He laughed another loud laugh again and slapped his thighs, shaking his head theatrically.

'I was only doing Douglas a favour. I didn't really want to go out with you again. I mean, you've got an awful lot of baggage, haven't you?' Jeannette stepped backwards but Alexander was on a roll. She watched him flail his arms out and continue. 'You'll be lucky you know, finding someone. Even in London. Who wants to take on another man's child? Not me, that's who.'

Jeannette turned and walked up the stairs. She put the spare key Douglas had given her in the lock and pushed the door open. Before she closed it she looked back at Alexander one last time.

'Oh, come on, Jean, I was only joking. Sorry. Let me have another chance?'

Without a word she clicked the door shut. If this was the dating scene, she thought, she wanted nothing more to do with it.

23

London, 1963

The news arrived on a Saturday morning. Mrs Reeves, the landlady, called up the stairs just before 10 a.m. to let Jeannette know there was a telegram boy waiting to receive her signed acceptance of the note. *It must be from Morag*, she thought, telling Judith to sit nicely and keep doing the jigsaw they had started while she slipped quickly down the three flights of stairs. Morag was the only person she knew who still favoured a telegram over a letter delivered by the Royal Mail.

Mrs Reeves was standing tapping the bannister at the bottom, wearing the brown headscarf and tabard that she always wore – her landlady uniform of choice. She slung her thumb over her shoulder to indicate the messenger and then disappeared into her own flat, to stand and look through the spyhole, no doubt.

Jeannette smiled at the boy; he could only be around fifteen years old, if that. Perhaps he knew the content of the carefully sealed piece of paper as he didn't meet her eye and ran off as soon as the telegram left his hands.

She thought nothing of tearing it open immediately; didn't for a moment foresee the great sledgehammer that was poised, suspended on a loose thread over her life, over her heart.

She had to read the typed capital letters three times before she could make any sense of it.

WITH REGRET COMMA GEORGE PASSED AWAY SUDDENLY
STOP HEART ATTACK STOP FUNERAL LAST WEEK STOP
MRS A FORREST STOP

Jeannette tried to put her foot on the bottom step, but her leg wouldn't hold her weight and she crumpled, catching her shoulder on the thin wooden rail that ran along the wall. She took a sharp intake of breath at the stabbing pain. Mrs Reeves, hawk-like in her observations from behind her own front door appeared, hovering. 'What is it?' Her voice was clipped; she was not a woman in possession of much sympathy for others, least of all her tenants. Jeannette couldn't speak for fear that it wouldn't be words that came out of her mouth. She shook her head, holding her sore shoulder with one hand and pulled herself up the bannister with the other.

Judith was standing at the top of the stairs. 'I told you to stay inside,' she whispered to her daughter, ushering the little girl back through the door. The sensation of floating out of her own body overtook all her other senses. She could see Judith looked upset and apologised for snapping. 'Cinema,' she said next and dumbly put on shoes and coats and hats and led Judith down the stairs and along the road, holding her hand tightly, onto the main thoroughfare where there was a cinema showing a morning matinee for children. Even though they had missed the beginning, Jeannette insisted to the ticket clerk this was fine and bundled Judith into a seat.

The screen flickered for the following hour, the moving images dancing on her retina but not quite filtering through. They went next to a hotel and had afternoon tea and Jeannette brought a crisp one-pound note out from her purse and laid it on the table at the end to pay, forgetting to wait for her change. The kind waiter ran down the street after them to hand over the money. It was an act of thoughtfulness and honesty that threatened to tip her over the edge, yet she managed to give the man a small smile and a tip from the change. When they were safely back under the sloping ceiling of the tiny attic flat, Jeannette boiled some water and made as deep a bath as she could in the round tin basin for Judith, where the little girl splashed and made bubbles from a bar of Pears soap for what seemed like hours.

It was only 6 p.m. by the time Judith was in her nightclothes and Jeannette had wrapped her up warmly in bed, telling her it was time for sleep. It was February and the nights were still drawing in early so there was no need for convincing that it was indeed bedtime. When Jeannette was certain that Judith had dozed off, she picked up a pillow from her own bed and took it into the tiny kitchenette off the even smaller corridor. She shut the concertina door, though she knew its flimsy material would provide little privacy, and pushed her face into the pillow so she could let out the howl that had been trapped deep inside her since the moment she had read those very final words that morning.

The next day, Judith woke early, having slept for almost twelve hours. It was only 6 a.m. and the darkness was yet to lift from beyond the curtains. She climbed into bed next to her mother and Jeannette groaned and wondered fleetingly if it was possible to die of tiredness as she pulled her little girl in towards her and they snuggled for a while longer. It was Sunday after all, she could pull the duvet around them tightly and pretend that the waking nightmare she'd experienced yesterday was only a dream.

The days and weeks that followed became a blur. Jeannette carried on: she went to work in the small office above the factory floor, where, despite the best efforts to insulate the walls, the clack-clack of the machinery below could be heard and felt all day long. She picked up Judith at five thirty from the childminder, stopping at the grocers on the corner of their street to buy something she could quickly make for dinner: a tin of corned beef and a couple of potatoes to fry some chips, perhaps a tomato to slice if they had one in the shop. She didn't taste what she ate, only concerned for Judith, who was growing into such a long, thin girl, spindly legs, no meat on her bones, no matter how much she ate.

Since hearing the news of George, it was all Jeannette could do to let her girl go in the morning. With him no longer on the earth, Judith was the only connection she would ever have to him and the thought that she could lose this too terrified her. But they had to keep going. Her mother's voice spoke clearly in her mind: *get up and get on, it's no use sitting around wallowing in your own self-pity.*

It didn't help that sleep was elusive. A few glasses of sherry helped send her off, but she would wake, usually around 3 a.m., and the finality of the news would sit like a giant rock on her chest, crushing her ability to see any hope in the world.

In those sleepless hours between dusk and dawn, Jeannette began to construct a theory; that George was in fact still alive and that Annie had sent the telegram to give her even less of a reason to return to Edinburgh. The thought planted a seed, which sprouted rapidly and soon its branches had wound around every part of her thoughts. In the end it was inevitable. She handed her notice to Mrs Reeves and the girl that Rosamunde knew from the factory office and booked the bus tickets in advance. They were going home.

24

Edinburgh, 2018

Sasha arrived at the flat that evening like something from *Made in Chelsea*, brandishing two bottles of champagne and declaring herself 'utterly fucked' after a stressful week at work. Amy smiled inwardly. She was pretty sure her stepsister's 'job' entailed swanning into her mother's interior design business around lunchtime, gossiping with the salesgirls for an hour, before heading back out again to a 'client meeting'.

Amy and Jeannette had talked earlier in the week about who to tell next.

'It might be a good idea for you to get in touch with the boy's father. Find out what he thinks about all of this?'

Amy had winced at the thought. 'How do you tell someone six years too late that they're a dad? Eh, hello Magnus, just wanted to say – congratulations, it's a boy!' They had managed a laugh at that, albeit a strained one. Jeannette suggested it might be easier to start with Sasha.

'She's been your friend for a long time, as well as your big sister. She'll maybe know how to approach Magnus.' Neither of them had given Sasha's reaction too much thought.

Sasha popped her head round the living-room door to say hello to Brodie who was lying on the floor, forcing Jeannette to watch a repeat of *You've Been Framed*, pausing and rewinding it regularly so he could make sure they hadn't missed anything.

'You OK squirt?' Sasha asked, ducking into the room to give Jeannette a quick kiss on the cheek. Brodie gave her the thumbs up without taking his eyes from the screen.

In the kitchen she shrugged off her elaborate leather and fur coat and threw it over one of the dining chairs, then pulled Amy into a brief hug before beginning to rummage in her huge handbag.

'What's going on? You were acting like a proper weirdo on the phone.' Sasha had adopted her authoritative demeanour and Amy suddenly felt like the ten-year-old girl she'd been when they'd first met.

'Will I open one of these?' Without waiting for an answer, Amy tore off the gold wrapper and eased the cork out with a satisfying pop.

Sasha frowned at her mobile phone, raising it towards the ceiling then moving towards the back doors.

'Your house is the fucking Bermuda Triangle of phone reception.'

'It's because of the walls. Didn't you save the Wi-Fi password?'

Her stepsister tutted, throwing her phone back into her handbag and taking a seat at the table. 'Doesn't matter. So come on, spit it out – you said you had something to tell me. I'm assuming you're pregnant again.'

An unnaturally high-pitched laugh escaped before Amy could prevent it. 'No, no, thank goodness. I'm not pregnant.' She handed Sasha a glass of champagne and sat down next to her. 'I do have something I need to tell you though.' She took a sip of the alcohol, praying for it to provide her with some instantaneous courage. 'It's about Brodie's father.'

'Nick?'

'Well, that's the thing . . .' Amy stopped. She hadn't quite planned on what words she would use.

Sasha was growing impatient. 'What about Nick?'

Amy placed her glass down on the table. 'It's not Nick I need to talk to you about. It's Magnus.'

'What about Magnus? What are you going on about Amy, you're being a complete ditherer you know?'

Amy took a deep breath. 'Brodie's father . . .'

Sasha nodded, encouraging her to go on.

'Brodie's father is Magnus.'

The statement hung in the air between them, the process of osmosis almost visible.

'My Magnus?' Sasha's features twisted almost inwardly in an attempt to understand the revelation. '*My* Magnus?' she said again, pointing her finger at her own chest, 'is your Brodie's *father*?' She hissed the last word as though the power behind her voice had cut out.

Amy nodded. Her eyes ached at the effort to hold back the tears. Why hadn't she done this years ago?

'I'm so sorry I didn't tell you before,' she reached for Sasha's hand. Her stepsister pulled away.

'How?'

'It was the night of your birthday party, when you were in hospital. Magnus drove me back to my flat and we sat on the sofa, drinking and talking.'

Sasha was shaking her head slowly. 'But he's my brother . . .' Her eyes widened. 'For fuck's sake, Amy, he's *your* brother.'

'That's not fair, Sasha.' But she'd known the argument would arise. Perhaps that was why she'd never told anyone. 'He's not my brother though, you know that. We hardly saw each other growing up, not like you and me. I know what

you mean, but please don't paint it like some kind of . . .'
She couldn't say it out loud.

'*Incest*.' The word sprayed like venom across the space between them. 'That's exactly what it is. Our parents were married. He was your stepbrother.' The chair scraped noisily against the floor as Sasha stood up. 'Not to mention the fact that you've been lying to me for all these years.' She snatched her jacket from the chair, shoving her arms roughly into the sleeves.

'I haven't lied . . .' Amy began.

'Oh no! Not you as well. You're like every fucking man I've ever been out with. You haven't lied? Not directly maybe, but you haven't been honest either, have you?' Sasha's voice was raised as she jabbed a pointed finger in Amy's direction. 'How many times have I talked with you about Nick, about how he was behaving and how I could have helped you and you never once managed to admit that he wasn't Brodie's father?'

The room reverberated with her stepsister's anger.

'I'm so sorry.' Amy went to stand. 'Please sit down and we can talk about it?'

'What? So you can convince me to be OK with this news? So you can feel better about being a slutty, lying little whore with my brother?'

The words landed like knives in Amy's chest. For a second she thought she saw regret pass over Sasha's face, but then she was gone; her heels clacking loudly on the wooden floor of the hallway before the front door slammed.

Amy followed Sasha's footsteps. Fortunately, the living room was closed tightly. She hoped Brodie hadn't heard Sasha shouting. What an idiot she'd been; how could she have thought that her news wouldn't cause upset? She'd hoped it would all be explainable, that she could talk her way through to them all being one big happy family. For years she'd watched Sasha with Brodie and thought that Sasha knew deep down that she was related to him in some way. Apparently not. Amy wiped her face with the sleeve of her jumper. She'd been wrong not to tell everyone the truth when Brodie was born. Sasha felt betrayed, of course she did. It was exactly how Amy would feel.

Brodie was still lying on his stomach in front of the television, laughing at a man flying over the handlebars of his bike on the screen. Jeannette turned towards her.

'Did I hear the front door? Where's Sasha?' she asked.

'Something came up. She had to go home. Can I get you anything?'

Jeannette requested a cup of tea and Amy was glad of the excuse to go back to the kitchen. She poured the glasses of champagne down the sink and watched the bubbles fizz in protest then quickly evaporate. The black crow was back, stretching its wings and getting ready to flap. She thought for a moment she might be sick but then rallied, swallowing down the temptation to try and purge herself of the anxiety. Sasha would calm down. Once she had a chance to think about it, they could talk and sort things out. She'd been hoping Sasha would help her to work out what to do about Magnus, having miraculously managed to avoid him for years now. He lived in London with his wife Felicity; she knew that much through Sasha and Ben's occasional updates. It didn't bear thinking about that now though; her focus had to be on getting Sasha to talk to her again. She flicked the switch on the kettle and rested against the worktop. The problem was, she had no idea how she was going to do that.

Amy spent the rest of the evening on the sofa with Brodie curled into her side. At nine o'clock, she declared bedtime and managed to coax him through getting his pyjamas on and brushing his teeth, despite protestations.

The television was off when she came back into the living room and Jeannette was squinting at one of her puzzle magazines.

'They make the letters so bloody small in these things,' she said, putting it down on her lap. 'So, come on then, missy. What happened? I take it she wasn't best pleased?'

Amy slumped down onto the sofa. 'Oh God, it's all so awful, Grandma.' She closed her eyes. 'I thought she knew, deep down at least. I thought I would tell her and she'd be happy. She loves Brodie.'

'It's just the shock. She'll come around, once she's had a chance to think about it.'

'She called me a whore.' Despite themselves, they laughed.

'She's just hurt. Probably a wee bit embarrassed too. It's pretty obvious to anyone looking that Brodie's related to that family. But, of course, people don't always see what's right in front of their noses.'

'I shouldn't have waited this long. When I think about it now, it seems ridiculous that I thought it would be something I would never have to face up to.'

'You always were quite good at keeping secrets, dear.'

Amy thought of Ken; another conversation she should probably have, he was Brodie's grandfather after all.

'I just kept thinking that it would all work out somehow. Or if I ignored it, it would just go away. Stupid really.'

'You'll get through it, Amy. You're strong enough for this. You just needed to face up to it. The hardest bit is done.'

Amy groaned. 'What's Mum going to say?'

'I don't think you need to worry about what your mum has to say. She's not one who can stand in judgement of others. And anyway, she's too wrapped up in herself as usual. You'll be lucky if she even pays it any attention.'

'I still can't believe she actually left you alone that Sunday. She's been putting off seeing me ever since, just keeps saying she's too busy.'

'She's just wrapped up in this art thing. Your mother's always been like that. When she decides she's doing something, it's the only thing she can think about. I used to call it determination when she was small.'

'Seems more like selfishness to me.'

'Now, now, don't be too hard on her – that's my job.' Jeannette smiled, a smile that transformed seamlessly into a deep yawn.

'Bedtime?'

Jeannette nodded. Amy helped her through to the bathroom. She'd noticed lately that her grandmother was finding it more and more difficult to move around. Once again in Brodie's single bed, Amy tucked the quilt in around her and sat on the edge.

'Do you remember doing this for me when I was a wee girl and we lived at Morag's?'

'I do indeed.' Amy could see the memory of her friend flash behind Jeannette's eyes. Morag had passed away just after Brodie was born. Amy was always glad that Morag had been able to hold Brodie once; she'd been like another grandmother to her when she was little after all.

'It's a shame she won't be there at your birthday party.'

'Oh, she'll be there dear. In here.' Jeannette slowly reached her hand up from beneath the covers and touched the side of her head. Her eyes were closed.

'Night night, Grandma.' Amy bent down and kissed Jeannette's forehead. She was already fast asleep.

Brodie let out a small sigh in his sleep and stretched his arms above his head. The bed wasn't big enough for them both and he began every night tucked into one side, only to squirm his way into the middle during the night, pushing Amy to the very edge of the mattress. She hadn't been able to fall asleep. The conversation with Sasha kept replaying in her mind, its unexpected outcome making her wonder if she could have revealed the truth differently, in a way that would have caused less upset. The digital alarm clock lay face down on the bedside table in an attempt to put an end to its constant mockery of her insomnia. She lifted it now to check the time: only 1.34 a.m.

Amy turned over restlessly, trying to adjust the duvet without waking her son, and watched the light flicker off Brodie's eyelids. The familiar rush of love swept through her; a love she hadn't been prepared for when her son was born. It was as though he was still connected to her through an invisible thread that tugged each time she saw him or thought of him.

The wind outside the bedroom window picked up again, rustling the thin branches and leaves of the silver birch tree in the back garden. The small piece of private outside space had been one of the main reasons for buying the flat in the first place. It was only Ben who'd been dubious about her choice.

'It's not a basement, it's a garden flat,' Amy had argued.

'That just makes it sound posher than what it is. It's a flat in the lower-ground floor of a tenement; it's a basement.

Also, it's a bit dark in here, isn't it?' he'd said when the estate agent was showing them around. 'Basement flats are notoriously damp too, you know.'

But he hadn't been able to put her off the property. She'd loved the long galley kitchen with the tall thin double doors at the end, leading out to the small patch of garden. All the other flats they'd looked at had shared drying greens or nothing at all. She rolled her eyes when Ben started talking about security but let him buy her new industrial padlocks for all the iron gates that flanked the windows and doors at the back of the flat.

She turned over in the bed again. It was no use. If she was ever going to get back to sleep, she would need to get up for a bit. She slipped her feet out from under the covers and onto the familiar soft rug Brodie had insisted she buy from IKEA, scrunching her toes in among the long white fluff. The heating, which even in August was necessary for an hour or so in the evening, had gone off at half ten and the old stone walls lost heat quickly. Amy wrapped her dressing gown around her with a shiver.

Padding through to the kitchen, she flinched as her feet touched the cold floor tiles. The lights underneath the cabinets cast a warm glow across the lower half of the room and made mirrors of the inky-black squares of glass in the back doors. As the kettle boiled, she avoided looking at them and instead concentrated on the mug, the Ovaltine, stirring the spoon. When she had relaxed a little, the warm liquid settling in her stomach, she glanced up at the doors. The iron gates on the outside that provided a second layer of security weren't shut. It wasn't like her not to make sure they were locked in her ritual pre-bed shutdown of the flat: TV off, windows locked, front door double-locked. If she didn't close them now, she wouldn't be able to sleep.

Amy turned the key and reached forward to pull the gates towards her. The padlock wasn't hanging on one of the bars as it usually was. She cursed. It must have fallen onto the ground. Stepping out, her eyes scanned the ground in the near darkness, eventually locating it a few feet in front of her. She bent down to pick it up. When she straightened, she almost jumped out of her skin.

'What on earth are you doing?'

Nick was slumped on one of her garden chairs on the edge of the grass, holding an empty glass bottle. He was wearing one of his typical dark suits, but his white shirt was wide open halfway down his chest. Amy put her hands on her heart and tried to steady her breathing. Nick stayed silent. 'You gave me a fright.' She looked around. 'How did you get in here?'

He glanced up then, his eyes bloodshot and glassy. 'The gate was open.' Nick flapped a hand in the general direction of the back wall. Amy was sure it had been locked. She never unlocked it because it went onto a lane that some of the teenagers in the area would use for secret drinking sessions. She hadn't wanted them stumbling into her garden for a pee.

She stood for a moment, unsure what to do. Nick broke the silence.

'She left me,' he said.

The black crow began unfurling its wings for the second time that day.

'Vanessa?' She started to feel bile rising, swallowed it down. Nick was making to stand, struggling to push his unsteady body from the chair.

'Yep. My lovely Vanessa. And,' he coughed, then spat on the grass, 'she has killed my baby.'

Amy closed her eyes. Vanessa had gone through with it. Nick dropped the bottle, which landed with a thud on the grass. He took a few steps towards her. The strength of alcohol on his breath was overwhelming. She tried to move away but he reached forward and grabbed onto her upper arm tightly. Her body froze, rigid.

'You spoke to her, didn't you?' he slurred. His face was only an inch or so from hers. She was transported suddenly back to when Brodie was a baby.

'She contacted me, Nick.' Amy tried to stand her ground firmly, tried to keep her voice from quivering. The crow was in full flight inside her.

'It's your fault. It's all your fault.' He jabbed his finger into her chest. 'I've lost everything because of you, you fucking *bitch*.' His saliva landed on her cheek. Amy tried to pull her arm free, but he held on tighter. 'I've lost Vanessa, my baby, I've lost Brodie.'

Amy tensed. 'He was never yours to lose,' she said quietly and without thinking. Memories were flooding back; Nick down on his knees, begging for forgiveness when he'd thrown the bedside lamp across the room at her, the glass base shattering at her feet as she tried to protect Brodie from the impact; locking the bathroom door, singing to her son who was in the bath, as Nick beat his fists against it, screaming obscenities. She had been wrong to believe that he'd changed; he was still the same old Nick: still Jekyll and Hyde. She knew she had to get away from him, had to lock the doors and keep him out of their lives.

She tried again to prise his fingers from around her arm. 'Just let me go, Nick, please.'

A chair scraped on the floor in the kitchen. Amy twisted her head and saw Jeannette standing in her nightdress in the doorway, her frail figure almost bent double.

'You get your hands off my granddaughter, young man.'

Nick threw his head back and laughed. 'Oh look, Granny's come to save you.' He gave another shallow laugh but dropped his hand from Amy's arm and took a step back. 'Amy and I were just chatting.' He raised his arms in surrender. 'I'm going now, don't worry,' he said, sobering up momentarily; the television Nick making an appearance. Amy rubbed at her arm; feeling the spots where the bruises would appear.

Nick leant back towards her, his voice a whisper. 'I'm going to take everything away from you too,' he promised calmly. Amy watched him stagger away across the garden and pull the wooden door in the back wall of the garden open. When he closed it behind him, she ran forward and slid the bolt across the top. The big iron key that permanently stuck out of the lock was missing.

Jeannette had taken a seat on one of the kitchen chairs and was bent over, holding her chest. 'I don't think I'd have been much use if he'd tried anything there, dear,' she said.

'Are you OK, Grandma? I'm so sorry.' Amy was pulling the gates shut, securing them, the padlock rattling against the iron as her fingers fumbled.

'Not your fault, dear. You might want to think about reporting him to the police though. What if Brodie had woken up.'

'I will. I'll report it tomorrow. Let's get you back into bed for now.'

Amy helped Jeannette back through the flat, glancing in at a slumbering Brodie on her way past her bedroom door. He was completely unconscious. Her grandma was right though, what if he had woken up? She wasn't going to be Nick's victim again. This time she would go to the police, tell them what he'd done.

25

The end of the school summer holidays came with a huge sigh of relief from all the parents, and an even bigger one of disappointment from all the children, who were now overly familiar with spending mornings in their pyjamas arguing for extra screen time. Brodie was going into Primary 3, a fact which Amy was struggling to come to terms with. It seemed like only a few months ago he'd been making the transition from nursery to school.

The whole school thing hadn't started as well as she'd hoped. She had been nervous about it in a way she hadn't been nervous for any other stage in Brodie's short life so far. Arriving at the parent induction, she'd picked up the folder marked *Brodie Aitken* and sat down next to a woman who tried immediately to convince her that joining the PTA was imperative to Brodie's future. After promising to give it serious consideration, the woman turned to her husband to discuss something about their older child's dilemma between playing the cello or the piano (there simply wasn't time to do both), which gave Amy a chance to look around at the other parents. It was a small school in a good area, better than the one near the flat where the children casually used expletives to punctuate their sentences. Amy loved their home but it was outside the catchment area for the better schools, a fact she hadn't considered when buying the property because Brodie was still so little and school seemed like a lifetime away. So when the time had come, rather than move from their home, she wrote letters to the council, begging ones, and someone, somewhere, had been looking down on them because she eventually received the news that he'd been awarded a place in one of the nicer schools closer to her work.

When she arrived at the parent induction evening, she'd been hoping for at least one other child in Brodie's class to have a variation on the old-fashioned parenting model. Where were all the two dads or two mums that they read about in Brodie's *Families Come in all Shapes and Sizes* book? There had been a man sitting alone for around ten minutes whom she'd pegged as another potential single parent, until his wife ran in, heels clacking quickly over the wooden flooring as the head teacher almost deafened everyone by switching on the microphone and clearing her throat simultaneously.

It had been a long day and the air in the school hall seemed to be thickening with each click of a new PowerPoint slide. Amy hadn't realised there was so much to consider about going to school; her own education hadn't appeared as administratively intensive as Brodie's was about to be. She was wondering where she was going to find the time to manage Brodie's academic career along with everything else and must have zoned out when the instruction was given for the summer-holiday homework. Her error didn't become apparent until four weeks after Brodie had started school, when the parents were invited to the classroom one afternoon. The children were meant to have collected things from their summer holidays – tickets to attractions, photographs of days out so that each child could make a poster, a summer-holiday collage, to be displayed on the classroom wall. She'd almost cried at the sight of Brodie's poster. He'd had help from his Primary 7 buddy to draw some stick figures and a swimming pool. There was a crude sketch of Muriel's caravan too. Amidst the bright photos of grinning families and tickets to Alton Towers, however, it looked as though they either hadn't done anything throughout the summer holidays or she just hadn't bothered to provide her son with his homework. Either way Amy could barely take the feeling of guilt at the thought of her little boy sitting in a class full of children glue-sticking their cherished holiday memories onto bits of coloured card while he scribbled away with a grey pencil. Brodie, of course, didn't have a clue what she was talking about when she brought it up with him at dinner that evening. If he had felt left out or anything on the day of the poster making, he certainly didn't seem affected by it now. He was much more interested in whether he could download a new game on her phone or get an extra half-hour of cartoons after dinner. It was that incident, however, that made Amy feel acutely aware of her single-parenthood status and she wanted to prove at every possible opportunity to his teachers and to the other parents that she did care about her son, that she could do all this parenting stuff just as well as anyone, despite the fact she was doing it alone.

Brodie's school uniform was laid out on the chair in her room, his schoolbag packed with the obligatory new pencil case, pencils, etc.

'We'll fill your water bottle in the morning,' she told him when he insisted he absolutely needed to remember water or he would get into really big trouble.

'Miss Robertson said it keeps us healthy. Water's a need you see, Mum. You need it to live. I would die without it.'

They'd been talking about needs and wants over the weekend, Brodie desperately trying to categorise his want for an iPad into a need. Amy glanced guiltily at the box on top of the wardrobe. Since Nick's visit on Friday night, she'd been going over and over everything in her mind. A bunch of flowers had arrived on the Saturday evening. The note read simply, *Going away for a few weeks, will talk when I'm back. Sorry.* She hadn't reported the incident to the police by then and the flowers made her doubt herself more. Perhaps it had just been a drunken mistake. He'd been upset about the whole Vanessa thing and would leave them alone now, wouldn't he? He had nothing to gain from making their lives a misery.

Sasha still hadn't replied to any of her messages and so Amy was preoccupied with how she could make things up to her stepsister. She was also concerned with the thought of going back to work the following day. Despite the current ongoing drama in her life, two weeks away from the oppressiveness of Christine's watchful eye had been blissful. Amy thought, as she always did the night before going back to work, about looking for a new job. She'd been unhappy at work for a long time, but the hours were perfect to fit around Brodie's schooling and the money wasn't too bad either. Perhaps she'd have a look after her grandmother's party. It was only four weeks away and she hadn't organised anything apart from the venue and the invites so far. Grabbing a Post-it notepad, she scribbled various tasks on each one and stuck them to the dressing-table mirror in her bedroom. There was still a lot of organising to do.

Ben, who had been on nightshift all weekend and looked as though he could fall asleep standing up, came to visit them that evening, surprising Amy by also turning up with their mother in tow. Amy hadn't seen Judith in weeks and when she mentioned this, her mother wafted away the suggestion with a hand and told Amy to pour her a glass of wine. Natalie was at home with baby Etta, who was suffering from colic and, according to Ben, making noises that resembled some manner of hell beast.

'It's horrendous to watch, and that's saying something given all the things I've witnessed in A&E.' Ben took a sip of his beer. They were sitting in Amy's back garden, enjoying a spell of sunshine; it had been raining all week, which it tended to do in Edinburgh in August, mainly to spite the numerous visitors to the festivals that were taking place in the city that month.

'I'm assuming you've tried all the obvious remedies?' Judith was stretched back on one of the deckchairs, face tilted towards the sun.

'Yes, Mother.' Ben gave Amy a look. 'Should I go and see if Grandma wants to come out in the garden? Brodie, do you want to help me get Gee-Gee out here?' Brodie, who had been digging a hole in the muddy border with a trowel looked up. 'She's sleeping,' he said, wiping a hand across his face, which left a long smear of mud on his cheek.

'She's been sleeping a lot recently. Could you maybe give her another check-over? I've tried to get her to go to an appointment at the GP but she keeps saying she's fine.' Amy's concern for Jeannette had been growing steadily over the last couple of weeks. Being at home all day, she could see her grandmother was struggling to do simple things, things she'd had no trouble with before the fall.

'No problem, I'll have a look over her before I go. So anyway, you said on the phone you had something to tell me.'

Amy hadn't banked on her mother being there too, but she supposed it killed two birds with one stone. 'Brodie, would you do me a favour and go inside to check on Gee-Gee, please?' Brodie began to protest. 'You can watch some cartoons if you like.' Her little boy dropped the trowel and shot off into the house.

Amy stole herself for a moment and took a deep breath before letting the truth tumble out.

Neither Ben or Judith said anything at first, although Judith looked towards her and raised her sunglasses before dropping them again and turning her face back towards the sun.

'Maggie is Brodie's father?' There was a smile playing on the corners of Ben's mouth. Ben and Magnus had spent more time together growing up, and as adults too. They'd drifted apart when Ben started working in Edinburgh and Magnus had settled in London, but Amy knew they still counted one another as friends.

Amy nodded. 'I'm sorry I didn't tell you both before. To be fair, when Brodie was born, I wasn't entirely sure if he was Nick's or Magnus', but I sent off for one of those tests when Brodie was a few weeks old and found out Nick wasn't his biological father. Then I buried my head in the sand.'

Ben whistled then laughed. 'Jeezo, Amy, you're a bit of a sly one keeping that to yourself for so long. I'm not sure I trust you anymore.' He punched her playfully on the arm.

'Mum? What do you think? Are you angry with me?'

Judith didn't move position but sighed. 'It's all a bit Jeremy Kyle isn't it, darling? "My brother and I have a baby", that kind of thing.'

Ben snorted; Amy returned his punch, not quite as gently. 'He's not my brother really. And you'd been divorced from Ken for a while when it happened. Sasha's not talking to me because of it.'

At this, Judith sat up. 'You told Sasha before you told us?'

'Only because she was coming round one night and I wanted to get it over with. I thought she could help me talk to Magnus too.'

Ben's eyes widened. 'You mean Magnus doesn't know?'
Amy shook her head.

'He probably has a few kids dotted around to be fair. He was a bit of a shagger back in the day. Probably still is.'

'Thanks for that lovely image of the father of my child.' Amy shook her head. 'I don't want anything from him. I just think he has a right to know. Then he can decide if he wants to have anything to do with Brodie.'

'Does Brodie know?'

'I haven't said anything to him about any of this yet. I know he's going to ask more as he gets older though, so I just want to sort it out as far as I can first.'

'What about Nick?' Amy knew her brother wouldn't have forgotten about him. 'How did he take the news?'

'He was fine. I don't think we'll see much more of him around here again.' She tried to push the image of his face in hers out of her head.

'Good riddance. Seriously though, I'm just glad that he isn't Brodie's dad. I never got what you saw in him or why you kept making excuses and covering up for him.' Ben drained his beer. 'OK if I get another one?'

'Help yourself.'

Ben wandered into the kitchen. Amy sat in silence with her mother. A cloud passed over the sun, causing the temperature to drop suddenly.

'You know you won't get any money from Ken,' Judith said, unprompted. 'He's lost a whole lot. Not quite penniless, I've heard, but a damn sight poorer than he was. His latest squeeze left him when she found out he wasn't going to be lavishing her in diamonds and exotic holidays.'

It was news to Amy. She couldn't quite picture Ken being poor somehow.

'I don't want Ken's money, Mum.' It was just like Judith

to think of the mercenary aspect of a situation. 'Anyway, how do you know all that about him?'

Judith didn't answer straight away.

'Mum, how do you know about Ken?'

'Oh, he dropped by the gallery. Apparently he knows the owner, Steve. I didn't know that before, of course.' Judith pulled her cardigan more tightly around her shoulders. 'He took me out for dinner, if you must know,' she continued. 'Told me he misses me and regrets our divorce.'

Amy couldn't quite believe what she was hearing. 'Does he want you back?'

Judith laughed. 'My darling, even if he did, do you really think I would be desperate enough to go back to a man who spent the entirety of our marriage being unfaithful?'

'You knew?' Amy's mouth dropped open, she sat forward in her chair.

'About the other women?' Judith slid her glasses onto the top of her head and turned to look at her daughter. 'Of course I knew. He was a terrible liar, completely rubbish at hiding it. I just enjoyed the life we had, enjoyed that you were getting everything that your father couldn't provide.' Judith tapped her sunglasses back down and resumed her position on the deckchair. The sun came out from behind the cloud.

Amy was speechless.

26

After five minutes of sitting back down behind her work desk, Amy felt as though she had never been away. There were one hundred and forty-eight emails to go through and Christine had given her a lunchtime deadline on an educational brochure that was already late for the printers. It wasn't until after she'd managed to finalise the proof and get it sent off that she noticed the reply from the solicitors she'd contacted about George Forrest's son, David. Unbelievably, there was someone at the office who had worked with David and still kept in contact with him. The reply contained a personal email address for him and said he had agreed to be contacted. Amy considered her grandmother's response to the news. The fact that she had even tried to look David up had riled Jeannette. The niggling feeling that she wanted to pursue this further wouldn't leave her alone though, and she reasoned that if she did receive a response, she wouldn't necessarily have to tell Jeannette; it wasn't as though he would know where they lived . . . she felt herself slipping into another secret and despite her grandmother's insistence not to meddle, she wrote quickly, hitting send on an email to her mother's half-brother before she had time to talk herself out of it.

On Thursday morning, Amy arrived home to find an official-looking letter propped up against the toaster.

'Shona said she didn't get a good feeling from it.' Jeannette's home help fancied herself as a bit of a psychic.

'Oh, did she now? I hope you two didn't steam it open for a nosy.' Amy smiled. She tore at the envelope. Shona had been right. The letter was from a solicitor representing Nick. Amy's face drained of any colour.

'What is it dear?'

'Nick says he's going for joint custody of Brodie. This letter says I've deliberately stopped him seeing his son.' Amy's mind was racing. Why on earth would he be doing this?

'But he can't get custody of Brodie. He's not his father, he's no rights to him.'

Amy sat down heavily on one of the kitchen chairs and put her head in her hands. 'Unfortunately, he does have rights,' she said, her voice muffled.

'How?'

'He's on Brodie's birth certificate. I put him on it because I didn't want to leave it blank. I thought if Nick was on the birth certificate then that would prove to him, and maybe me, that he was the father.' Looking back, Amy remembered her rationale at the time. It seemed absolutely bonkers now, but she hadn't wanted Brodie to be fatherless.

'But surely you'd have to be married or something for him to have rights. And anyway, why does he want custody when he knows darn well he's not Brodie's father.'

'He doesn't really want custody of Brodie, Grandma.' Amy smoothed the letter out on the kitchen table. 'He's just trying to play a game, show he's still got some power over me.'

'What are you going to do?'

'I'm going to ignore it for now. I'm sure he'll only take it so far before he realises he would have to prove he's Brodie's father.'

She folded the letter, hiding the contents from view. The problem was, she wasn't sure at all.

By the following Tuesday, Amy had received another two letters from Nick's lawyer, each one with more allegations of her own behaviour. He was accusing her of the lies he'd fed Vanessa: that she was jealous and possessive and violent. She began to worry about who would see these letters; what if his allegations were taken seriously by someone, perhaps even social services?

One of the girls at work recommended a lawyer who had apparently done wonders for her sister during a messy divorce.

'Her husband, Scott, was a real pig. Controlling, violent, the lot.' Paula sat at the desk next to Amy's. They often shared packets of biscuits among titbits of their own and other people's lives. 'This lawyer wiped the floor with him. The kids don't have to see him anymore unless it's supervised, which is just as well 'cause he had started to take his hand to my oldest nephew Jake.'

Amy thought Paula's sister's situation sounded horrendous. 'Oh well, thankfully it's not that bad. Nick's not really wanting to be part of Brodie's life, he's just trying to get at me.' Even as she said it, Amy could feel herself downplaying the seriousness of the situation. The letters had been vile. She'd thrown up after reading the second one.

She called the number Paula gave her from inside one of the locked toilet cubicles. The lawyer could fit her in on Thursday morning while Brodie was at school. Amy made the appointment and crossed her fingers that he would be able to help her.

On Wednesday afternoon, as Amy was finishing up a couple of emails, one appeared in her inbox that caused an instant rush of nerves to run through her whole body, goosepimples causing the hairs on her arms to stand to attention. It was a reply from David Forrest, his name bold and clear in the sender column. She hesitated before clicking it open. What if he was annoyed that she had been looking for him, or worse still, what if he knew nothing about Jeannette and Judith? She glanced across at Christine's office. Her boss was entertaining the marketing manager from one of the local colleges they produced brochures for; she would be in there for at least another hour.

Amy opened the email, holding her breath. She read it through once before she allowed herself to exhale. A second reading was needed for her to believe that she had not made a mistake by contacting David; in fact, he was delighted to hear from her.

> *I must apologise, I have known about your mother's existence since my father passed away. Although my mother tried to conceal the affair, there was a reference made to Judith in his will and after a bit of persistence, I managed to uncover the truth. Despite the knowledge of my half-sister, I'm afraid I was at a loss as to what I should, or indeed could, do. When my mother passed away fifteen years ago, I found a box when clearing possessions from her home; it contains some documents and photos that I believe rightfully belong to your grandmother. I wonder if you could provide a forwarding address for them, and perhaps pass my regards to Judith also, and let them both know I would be very willing to meet or talk on the telephone, should they wish. I look forward to hearing your thoughts.*
> *Very best,*
> *David Forrest*

Amy stared at the screen until she heard the click of Christine's office door open. It was almost 5 p.m. She had to leave to collect Brodie from after-school club. She hurried to close down her computer and scuttled past Christine, who was leading her client out through the foyer. She'd decided not to ask Christine for time off the next morning to visit Paula's sister's lawyer, planning instead to fake a minor medical emergency for herself, something to do with her periods should stop Christine asking too many questions.

Some of the children from the after-school club were in the playground when Amy arrived to collect Brodie. A slightly weary playworker gave Amy a half-smile and told her Brodie was inside. The woman inside, however, looked confused and said she was sure Brodie had gone outside to play.

'Let me check the register. We mark down who's inside and who goes out.'

Amy felt her nerves begin to jangle. She'd had a similar feeling when Brodie escaped her at a supermarket when he was three.

'He's definitely marked down as being outside. Here, I'll come out with you.'

The woman in the playground panicked immediately, feeding Amy's own nervousness.

'He said he was going in, I promise.'

'It's OK, Brenda, as long as he's not gone out the school gates, he'll be around here somewhere. You keep an eye on these ones and we'll have a look around.' Brenda appeared to be on the verge of tears. Amy had a sudden urge to shake her.

They found Brodie quickly enough; sitting on a set of steps that led into the infant school around the side of the building. Hugging his knees, his petted lip was firmly in place. Amy bent down in front of him, unsure whether to scold him for leaving the group or hug him because of the enormous rush of relief she'd experienced on spotting his familiar figure as they rounded the corner.

'They're always somewhere on the grounds,' the manager of the club reasoned. 'You know you're not meant to come to this bit by yourself though, Brodie.' She waggled a finger at him.

'It's fine, I've got him now. We'll come and get his bag in a minute.' Amy sat down next to her son on the step. 'What's up, kiddo? Is everything OK? Why were you hiding?' She put her arm around his shoulders and pulled him gently towards herself.

'I'm going to be in trouble,' he said.

Amy laughed. 'What, for hiding here?'

'No,' Brodie shook his head. 'I'm sorry, Mummy. I talked to a stranger.'

Amy felt the nerves resurface; the black crow in her stomach waking.

'Which stranger did you talk to?' She was trying to keep a level of calmness in her voice.

'It was a man. He was at the gate. He knew my name.' Brodie reached into the pocket of his school shorts. 'He said he was your friend and he told me to give you this.' Brodie thrust a folded piece of white paper into her hand.

Amy unfolded it and stared. Her hand began to shake. His journalistic scrawl was so familiar, mainly from all the cards he had given her when they were together; love notes at first, slowly becoming apologies as time went on. She crumpled up the paper and pushed it into her coat pocket.

'Brodie,' she said sternly. 'I'm not angry with you but I want you to listen very carefully. You should never talk to anyone you don't know. And if anyone tries to talk to you like that again, you should tell one of our trusted grown-ups straight away. OK?'

'I know that, Mummy. I'm sorry. I just got a surprise. I was going to tell Brenda but then she was giving Dennis and Michael a telling-off for being naughty and we're not supposed to interrupt.' He looked up at her, eyes wide.

Amy hugged Brodie again, squeezing him tight. 'Come on, let's get your stuff and go home.' She kissed the top of his head and ruffled his hair.

She was going to have to do something about this now.

The crumpled piece of paper lay on the kitchen table. Jeannette and Amy sat opposite one another, two mugs of untouched tea whispering steam into the air between them.

'Please tell me that you're going to the police now, dear?' Jeannette peered over the top of her glasses at her grand-daughter and then back down at the note.

see how easy it is to get close to something special. Imagine that was taken away. How would you feel?

'Of course I am. I'll go straight after I've been to see the lawyer. I just want to ask his advice on something first.'

'Well make sure you do. I don't like the thought of that man being anywhere near Brodie. He reminded me of your father the other night, out there in the garden.'

'Was my dad really that bad?'

Jeannette thought for a moment. 'It's the anger I suppose I'm comparing. It's what happens to men, when they don't face up to things and can't talk about how they feel. Every bit of negative emotion in them builds up and makes them a bubbling ball of angry rage. Either that or they crumple into themselves with sadness.'

'I think that's why my dad got better; he talked to Muriel about things from his past. I'm not sure Nick would ever be that brave.' Amy folded the letter and placed it in an envelope along with everything else she was taking to the lawyer the next day. 'You know, when we were together, he told me stuff, some really horrible stuff that had happened to him when he was little. But when I tried to talk to him about it later he'd brush it off and say he could handle it.'

'Most people probably believe they can, dear.'

'He certainly couldn't. He'd be fine for a while and then it would all build up in him again and he'd explode at the tiniest thing. It was the bits in between that I loved about Nick at the time. I was always worried no one would understand why I stayed with him because they couldn't see how brilliant he could be. It's amazing how often you can make yourself believe that someone won't do something again, especially when you think you see something in them that no one else does. I really thought that each time was the last time. Until it was the very last time and I just knew.'

Jeannette smiled sadly. 'We all want to believe we're being told the truth, dear, you're no different from anyone else there. Especially when it's someone we love making us promises. Look at how long I believed George for. I was completely under his spell for a lot longer than you put up with Nick. I truly believed he would find a way to leave Annie and be with me and your mother.'

Amy thought momentarily of the email she'd received from David. Perhaps now wasn't the right time to admit to her grandmother that she'd gone against her wishes.

Jeannette went on, 'It takes a lot of strength to stop believing, so don't chastise yourself for being someone who trusts what you're being told – being trusting makes you the good person.'

'I feel like a fool.'

'Oh, my dear, you're no more a fool than I'm Lady Gaga. He was, and still is, the fool. My concern now though is that once again he's a dangerous fool and all this nonsense won't stop at lawyers' letters and threats. What if he hurts Brodie, or you?'

Amy closed her eyes. 'I know, Grandma. I know I have to do something, and I will go to the police tomorrow, I promise.'

27

Duncan Walker's office was situated on a main road above the Renegade Lounge, the slightly worn lower exterior of which was scribed with an interesting array of spray-painted expletives. Amy found the door to the left of the pub entrance, pressed the button on the intercom and waited.

'Yes?' a voice crackled through the speaker.

'I've an appointment with Mr Walker,' Amy said as loudly as she deemed reasonable, conscious of the two men standing smoking behind her, outside the entrance to the bar.

'Hello?' the voice said again. Amy coughed.

'I've an appointment with Mr Walker,' she said more loudly this time.

The door buzzed and Amy pushed her way in.

'Give my regards,' one of the men outside the pub shouted after her.

The edges of the stairs were covered in a deep-burgundy carpet, the middle of each step worn threadbare where the main traffic had traipsed up and down throughout the years. The woodchip wallpaper above the bannister had been painted numerous times and now wore a thick layer of dark-orange paint. It wasn't quite what Amy had expected, although at that moment she was unsure exactly what her expectations had been.

The office had clearly once been residential accommodation and she followed the sign for reception into one of the rooms that would have served as a bedroom. A tiny woman with long dark hair was tapping away on a keyboard. She looked up at Amy over her glasses.

'Take a seat, sweetheart. He'll be with you in a minute.' She pointed a long, fuchsia pink fingernail at two dining chairs against the wall opposite her desk. Amy sat down and tried to keep her gaze from wandering back towards the woman and her luridly bright floral blouse, fixing her gaze instead on a poster informing her that she could *Still Get Legal Aid*. She certainly hoped so.

After a few minutes, the phone on the desk rang. 'Right you are, Duncan,' the receptionist said into the handset before placing it down with a loud clunk. 'He'll see you now, sweetheart. Through to the left.' She smiled, revealing a set of well-spaced teeth.

The door to Duncan Walker's office was slightly ajar. Amy pushed it open to be greeted by a man whose exterior appearance contradicted his setting immediately. His grey hair was combed over smartly to one side and he wore a full three-piece suit in dark-navy wool with a wide pinstripe. From his jacket pocket, a pale-blue silk handkerchief peeked out, which matched perfectly with the colour of his tie.

'Miss Aitken,' he smiled widely, indicating her to take the seat opposite. 'You're well I hope, other than for the reason you've come to see me today?'

Amy was slightly taken aback. 'Yes, I suppose I am.'

'And what is that reason may I ask?' He squinted at a scribbled note on a piece of lined paper in front of him. 'Barbara says you're having some kind of problem with your ex-partner.'

He looked up expectantly. Amy cleared her throat.

'That's right. He's been sending me letters, or his lawyers have rather, saying he wants custody of my son.'

'And do you have copies of these letters, Miss Aitken?'

Amy produced the envelope and took out the three sheets of headed notepaper filled with accusations and passed them over the desk. Duncan Walker spent the next minute or so skim-reading through each one.

'Can I ask, and please don't be offended by my question, if any of these allegations are true?'

Amy shook her head. 'Absolutely not. It was Nick that left, when Brodie was a baby. He was violent, you see. I never actively stopped him seeing Brodie, but that's the thing. He's not actually Brodie's father.'

'But it says here he's named on the birth certificate.'

'He is. But he isn't his biological father. I made a mistake at the time.' Amy felt the blush rising. She knew exactly how it would sound to this stranger when she admitted that she hadn't known who the father actually was.

'Miss Aitken, did you knowingly make a false entry on your son's birth certificate?'

'I wasn't sure at the time. I didn't know what to do, but Nick was living with us and I wanted to believe he was the father.'

'The correct answer to my question is "No, I believed Nick was the father of my child at the registration of his birth." It is an offence to lie to the registrar, Miss Aitken, so we'll just forget you ever alluded to having any doubt about your child's paternity and crack on with the matter in hand. The fact is, he is currently on the birth certificate and we must respond to his requests for access to "his" son. We can deal with the mistaken paternity issue too, but that will take time.'

Amy tried to process the information. 'So are you saying Nick might be able to have access to Brodie?'

'If it's what he pursues, then, yes. I doubt very much any court in the land would grant an absent father full custody on request, in fact it's impossible, but the law is very much in favour of the child's rights to a relationship with both parents, and the processes and decisions tend to reflect this.'

'But he's violent. He has an explosive temper on him. I've seen it. We were in danger from it.'

'And did you ever report this violent behaviour to the police, Miss Aitken?' Duncan Walker was looking down at his desk, scribbling notes again.

Amy sighed, shaking her head. 'No, never. Although I'm going to the police after this. He turned up in my garden in the middle of the night threatening me. And then he passed this note through the railings to my son at school.' Amy gave Duncan Walker the crumpled paper.

He studied it for a moment.

'As my client, I am bound to act in your best interest, and it would seem from what you're telling me that this Nick character isn't a very nice man. We can respond to these requests with an offer of supervised contact at first. But please assure me, Miss Aitken, if I pursue the notion that this man is violent, I will not be made to look like a liar?'

'Absolutely not. I mean, I'm not sure if he's still violent, he hasn't done anything physical yet, except . . .' Amy paused, then took off her jacket and lifted the sleeve of her T-shirt. Nick's fingermarks bruised the skin on the top of her arm. 'He did that, when he was in the garden.'

Duncan Walker removed his glasses, looking from her arm to her face and then back again. 'I can only reiterate what I'm sure you already know. If someone is being physically violent towards you, you must report it to the police.' He put his glasses back on, pushing them up the bridge of his nose with his index finger.

Amy let her sleeve drop and slid her arms back into her jacket. 'I know. I just . . . I promise you . . . he can be violent.'

'Very well then, Miss Aitken, we'll respond as such. The matter of his removal from the birth certificate is a more complicated issue, I'm afraid. We will be required to petition for a paternity test, which takes time and there are all sorts of legal loopholes they can use to delay this. Bear with me on that one and we'll arrange another meeting to discuss the way forward. I assume you're aware that there will be fees attached to all of this?' He waved his heavy gold fountain pen across the desk.

'I was hoping there may be a possibility of some legal aid to help with that. I suppose I have to apply for it or something though?'

Duncan Walker looked unperturbed by the question. He was scribbling on another lined piece of notepaper. She wondered briefly if most of his clients needed legal aid.

'Speak to Barbara about that on your way out. She has a form or something, I think.'

Taking this as her cue to leave, Amy stood. Duncan Walker looked up from his notes.

'Thanks for your time, Mr Walker,' she said.

'Not at all, Miss Aitken, my pleasure.' He stretched back in his chair and removed his glasses again, rubbing his eyes with his free hand. 'Can I ask you one more thing?'

Amy nodded.

'What would you really like the outcome to be?'

She was unsure what he meant.

'I suppose as long as we respond and if any contact was supervised until we can get him removed from the birth certificate that would be the best I could hope for.'

Duncan Walker laughed lightly and leant forward, placing his elbows on the desk.

'But, Miss Aitken,' he continued, 'in complete confidence, I am asking – what would you *really* like the outcome to be?'

It struck her that this might be a trap, but for some reason she trusted him.

'I would really like,' she paused for a moment, noticing the framed picture of his children on the bookcase, 'for him to be completely gone from our lives.'

Duncan Walker smiled and nodded. 'Have a good day, Miss Aitken, I'll be in touch.'

As she walked over the road to get the bus back into town, Amy wasn't sure what had just happened. It felt as though she had employed the services of a hitman, but, of course, she knew that all Duncan Walker would be able to do was fight Nick's lawyers with any legal position he could. The thought of Brodie having to have contact with Nick, even if it was supervised, turned her stomach. Her happy, secure little boy would be thrown into a situation that was all completely of her own making. What an idiot she'd been.

Amy walked into work having completely forgotten to go to the police station to report Nick for . . . She stopped to think for a moment. What had he actually done? He'd been in her garden, which had been scary, but he'd gone as soon as Jeannette had appeared. She couldn't prove he'd given her the bruises on her arm. The thing at the school gates was more sinister but she also had no proof that it had been him. From a police perspective, she doubted there was very much they could do about it. He hadn't texted or phoned her; he wasn't harassing her in the traditional sense. They would think it was all just a domestic spat.

Christine was standing at Amy's desk before she had a chance to sit down.

'My office, now,' she instructed.

Amy sat down on the plastic chair reserved for talking to her staff members. There was a soft leather chair pushed into the corner of the room.

'I am assuming you have an incredibly good reason for not turning up at work until' – she made a show of studying her watch – 'forty-eight minutes past eleven.'

Christine folded her arms and stared hard. 'I'm waiting,' she said, when an immediate response wasn't forthcoming.

'I was having my smear test,' Amy lied.

Christine began to look as though she had tasted something disgusting.

'I'm so sorry I didn't let you know, but I get so anxious about going along for my *smear test*,' she said the words again to see if they would have the desired impact, which they did, 'and I completely forgot to book in the time for the medical appointment. We are allowed medical appointments, aren't we?'

Christine smiled bitterly. 'Of course you are, Amy. Preferably they would be booked in on the system so as not to inconvenience other members of staff that have to pick up your workload, but I'll let you off this time, seeing as you were so *anxious.*' She smiled another insincere smile that resembled more of a grimace. 'The thing is,' she went on, 'that isn't the only reason I wanted to talk to you.'

Amy felt the hairs on the back of her neck stand up.

'I had a visit last night, after you left the office, from a man named Nick. I think you know Nick, Amy, don't you? He's your son's father, I believe.'

The conversation had taken such an unexpected turn that Amy felt as though she was listening to it from somewhere outside her own body. She didn't respond. Christine continued.

'What a lovely man. I'm quite surprised you managed to bag him in the first place, to be honest. But listen, he came to talk to me because he's worried about you. He says you've been harassing him and begging him to get back with you. He says you won't let him see his son if he doesn't agree to be your partner again and move back in with you.'

Amy couldn't speak. Christine went on.

'He was very apologetic for involving your workplace, but he's just so keen to sort things out amicably and he wondered if I could have a word with you, try to make you see some sense.'

There was no point in saying anything. What could she say? It would just look as though she was lying, particularly to Christine who had clearly been charmed by Nick's television persona. There was no reason for her to have to defend herself here, Nick had crossed another line but again, he wasn't doing anything other than painting himself as the victim. It had always been his most convincing role. Amy pushed the chair back and stood.

'Are we finished now?'

She turned without waiting for an answer, her disbelief, anger, frustration, everything growing with each step she took towards her desk. She sat down and stared at her screen.

'You OK?' whispered Paula.

'I will be,' Amy replied, opening her work email and forwarding the one from David to her personal address. The rest of her inbox she selected and pressed delete. It asked her to confirm she wanted to delete every email. She clicked yes. Then she went into her sent items and did the same. The entire contents of her computer was deleted within three minutes. None of the files she'd been working on, or correspondence she'd had with the printers or any clients existed anymore. She logged herself out so that Christine would need IT's help to make the discovery. She hoped it happened in front of a room full of people.

Amy stood up and put on her jacket. She felt lighter than she had in months.

'What are you doing?' hissed Paula.

Amy turned to her colleague. 'I'm leaving.' She slung her bag over her shoulder.

'What? You can't leave!' Paula's voice had risen. A few other people in the office looked up. Christine appeared, strutting towards Amy's desk.

'And where do you think you're going?'

Amy smiled at Paula. 'I'll text you,' she said, before walking towards the door.

Christine called after her, 'You can't walk out like this you know, Legal will have you in breach of contract. They'll, they'll . . .' she stuttered, 'they'll sue you!'

Amy turned at the door and looked at her boss, unable to believe she had spent the last few years putting up with her shit.

'Fuck you, Christine,' she said. Then she turned and walked out of the office for the very last time.

She was Jerry Maguire; she was Bridget Jones! Amy bounced along the pavement, savouring in her memory the vision of Christine's face at her last statement. *Fuck you, Christine.* My God she had wanted to say it so many times over the years. It had felt amazing.

She kept walking, purposefully but with no aim for the next ten minutes until she spotted a row of shops ahead, one of which was a bank. She faltered. She was free of Christine. But it didn't give her quite the same rush as it had ten minutes before. She wouldn't have to go back and put up with her bullshit ever again. It was great. A little voice in the back of her head was calling out for attention. *But you don't have a job! You won't have any money* it was saying. She pushed back. She could get another job. She had loads of experience, plenty of contacts. *But you won't have a reference* shouted the annoying little voice. She knew the voice had a point, but there was some money in her flat. If she got desperate, she could get some of it out. She could temp for a while, work out what she wanted to do, maybe she could get some freelance work.

Amy picked up her step again and headed to where her car was parked. She would go home and do some more organising for her grandmother's ninetieth birthday party and then pick up Brodie from school and take him out for tea wherever he wanted to go. Perhaps it was all the stuff with Nick; she was on the verge of that place he'd led her to all those years ago, where she doubted herself and believed that she wasn't good enough for anything or anyone else. Not this time though. She wouldn't let it happen again. This time, she would be in control.

28

Duncan Walker appeared to have granted her wish and delivered the perfect outcome. Amy received a letter exactly a week after they met, explaining that Nick's lawyers had been instructed to drop any pursuit of custody and, in the meantime, any form of contact, in lieu of their client considering his options.

'It can't be this easy,' she said, showing Jeannette the letter.

'Maybe he's just run out of steam, or perhaps the police paid him a visit after you reported all the things he'd done.'

Amy swallowed. She'd been vague when her grandmother had asked how it went with the police. 'Not much they can do I don't think,' she'd said, her back turned as she chopped an onion on the kitchen counter.

'Hopefully he's just come to his senses, like last time. He'll disappear and this time he won't have a reason to come back.' Amy couldn't quite understand herself why she was so reticent to go to the police. She had tried to walk up the steps to the station one day last week but it was as though an invisible wall existed, stopping her from stepping through the automatic doors. If it had been someone else's story, she would've thought they were an idiot not to report him, but Nick's voice still played in her mind even all these years later: *you're overreacting, it wasn't that bad, no one will believe you.*

'And that lawyer fellow, he's going to sort out the birth certificate stuff?'

'It's a bit more complicated than I thought. I have to involve Magnus if I want Brodie to have his real father on there. It'd take paternity tests if Magnus doesn't want to. Not that he has any idea yet.'

'You haven't contacted him? I thought you were going to send an email. What if Sasha's already spoken to him?'

'Well Sasha hasn't been back in touch since she walked out that night, so if she has, then I don't know anything about it and Magnus clearly doesn't want anything to do with Brodie because he's not been in touch either.'

'It's only been a few weeks, dear. Why don't you try Sasha one more time? I've a feeling she'll be ready to hear from you now.'

Amy looked at her Grandma and could instantly tell she knew something. 'What have you done?'

Jeannette smiled. 'I might have given her a wee ring and had a chat with her about a few things. My, she's a stubborn one that girl, almost as bad as your mother. But she came around in the end.'

'You're saying you meddled in my business?' Amy kept a straight face.

'I wouldn't call it meddling, dear . . .'

Amy smiled widely. 'I'm just teasing, I'm glad you did.' Amy had been dying to tell Jeannette about the correspondence she'd had with David and felt as though she now had a legitimate counterargument for being interfering.

'Oh, and why would that be?'

'I know you told me not to, but I got in touch with David Forrest.' Amy waited for the news to land, expecting the same response as last time.

Her grandmother sighed. 'Go on,' she said.

'Oh, I'm so glad you're not angry.'

'I haven't decided on that yet. As I said, go on.'

'He was really pleased to hear from me, Grandma. He says he's known about you and mum for years but he was a bit like you and didn't really know what to do about it. He thought if you wanted to know him, you would've got in touch.'

Jeannette remained unreadable. Amy continued.

'He has some documents that he thinks belong to you. They were left in his father's things after he died but he didn't find them until Annie passed away. He apologised for not getting them to you before now but again, he didn't know what the best thing was to do.'

'Is he sending them here?' Jeannette appeared wary.

'Well that's the thing. He said he was going to send them by courier but he was worried about them going missing and then he mentioned that his son was coming to Edinburgh in September and he could give them to him to deliver and then I said, well, why didn't he come too and he could meet you and Mum and . . .' Amy was running out of breath; she was so pleased to be finally telling her grandmother about David.

'Wait, he's coming to Edinburgh?'

'Yes! That's what I've been wanting to tell you. He's coming up on the weekend of your party.'

Amy had considered waiting until the day of the party and surprising her with the visit. But the idea that she may react badly or get such a shock she had a heart attack had meant she'd planned to break the news beforehand.

'Are you OK? Grandma?'

Jeannette was staring straight ahead. The news that George's son was planning on visiting still sinking in. It was as though the past had just plonked itself right on the table in front of her.

'Grandma? Are you angry with me?'

Jeannette came to, noticing her granddaughter's perplexed expression. She shook her head. She was tired again, too tired to worry anymore about the past, or what that past might bring into the present for her. 'No dear, I'm not angry with you. I'm probably a wee bit shocked is all. But it's fine. I'm glad he wants to see us, glad he wants to meet Judith.'

'Phew! That's a relief. I've been on the edge of telling you for days now, I don't think I realised how tense it was making me feel.' Amy laughed lightly. 'And you say you think I should get in touch with Sasha? That she's ready?'

Jeannette nodded. 'You should give her a call.' She reached out towards Amy. 'Now give me a hand dear, I'd like to watch some television if that's all right?'

Jeannette sat in front of the television, the screen flickering as her mind whirled with thoughts of David and George and of course Annie. What would it be like to see George's son after all this time? The last time she remembered was when he followed his parents across Princes Street the day Judith had shouted for her daddy. He had been a teenager then, which meant he would be in his seventies now; a man like his father. It was eleven days until the party, only ten until she turned ninety years old. She had never imagined living this long; it sometimes felt as though she had been around forever. Some days she would wake feeling so tired that it didn't seem like such a terrible alternative to just keep on sleeping, to never get up again. But of course, she didn't want to leave Amy and Brodie, or anyone else for that matter. And now she would meet David and see what these possessions were that he thought belonged to her. Jeannette's heart twisted a little. Yes, she hadn't realised it, but she needed to meet David, needed there to be some kind of ending to her own story. And perhaps, she thought, it would give Judith a new beginning to hers.

29

It was the end of the first week of September when Judith arrived at the flat for a Sunday lunch Amy had fully expected her to decline. She had assumed her mother would say she was too busy getting ready for the gallery opening in two weeks, but Judith had surprised her by accepting straight away.

'How is she?' Judith had asked.

'Grandma? She's doing alright I suppose. Ben's a bit worried about her weight. We're trying to get her to eat more, but her appetite's small and she gets full quickly. She's still sharp as a tack though, as always, so doing OK in that respect.'

'Good, good . . . Amy?' Judith had paused.

'Yes?'

'Thank you.'

Amy almost dropped her mobile. 'What for?'

'For looking after Mum . . . Grandma. I've not been . . . it's been . . .' Amy had never heard Judith struggle for words or sound as unsure. 'Just, thank you.'

Amy had hung up the call completely bewildered. There was obviously something going on with Judith, but for the first time ever, Amy's stomach hadn't lurched and the feeling of dread she usually experienced when her mother was going through a transformation was notably absent.

When Amy opened the door to Judith that Sunday, she noticed the change in her immediately. The bright lipstick and oversized jewellery were gone, and she was wearing some of her clothes from before the 'arty' transformation.

'Grandma's in the garden. Why don't you go through and sit with her there?'

Judith nodded. 'Ben called me. He says he doesn't think Grandma has very long left.' There was a haunted look in Judith's eyes. It was news to Amy; Ben hadn't quite framed his observations in that way to her.

'She's certainly becoming more and more frail each week that goes by, but I don't think it's immediate or anything. Go on through and see her for yourself. She has something to tell you anyway.' Judith raised a questioning eyebrow. 'Go on,' Amy insisted, 'you're not getting anything out of me. It's Grandma's story to tell.'

Amy watched her mother and grandmother sitting side by side in the garden from the kitchen. She was sitting at the table peeling potatoes when Brodie came in.

'Can I go out in the garden to see Nana?' he asked.

'In a wee minute, kiddo.' Amy pulled her son onto her lap and buried her nose into the top of his messy blonde hair.

'What are they doing?'

'They're having a very long overdue chat about something.'

'What about?'

Amy hesitated. It was a conversation she would need to have with him someday soon too.

'Oh, just about things that happened a long time ago. About Nana's daddy.'

Brodie was quiet for a moment. He picked up one of the potato peelings, turning it in his fingers.

'Where's my daddy, Mum?'

Amy realised she was about to have the conversation sooner than she had imagined. She took a deep breath.

'Your daddy lives in London. Do you know where London is?'

He pondered the question, his tongue poking out the corner of his mouth as it always did when he concentrated. 'Is it in Scotland?'

Amy laughed softly. 'No, it's not in Scotland. It's in England. About three hundred miles from here, and then a bit more, which is quite far away.' She turned her son on her lap to face her. 'Do you remember we talked about the man who gave me a seed to make you?'

'Yes,' nodded Brodie, 'but Archie Smith says that's a load of old rubbish and that seeds only make plants, not babies.'

Amy felt a prickle of annoyance towards Archie Smith.

'Well he's wrong. You need an egg from a woman and a kind of seed from a man to make a baby. And when they get together, they multiply millions and millions of times, like pop, pop, pop,' she tickled Brodie under his arms until he laughed, 'until eventually you get this wonderful squishy little baby who pops out into the world from their mum's tummy, just like you did.'

Brodie looked thoughtful for a moment. 'Did I pop out of your belly button?'

'Kind of. Anyway, the thing is, I got the seed from a man called Magnus, but then by the time the seed and the egg had got together, Magnus had to go off and live in London and I was here in Edinburgh and so I thought, "I'm just going to look after this wee baby and we're going to have a great life here in Edinburgh with Nana and Uncle Ben and Gee-Gee." And now we've got Natalie and Etta and we've always had Sasha too, of course.'

Amy glanced out to the garden and was surprised to see her mother reach across between the garden chairs to hold Jeannette's hand.

'Where is Sasha?' Brodie had obviously noticed the lack of Sasha's normally regular presence in their lives.

'She's been on holiday, but she's coming back soon.' Amy hoped this was true. Sasha had agreed to come to Judith's art gallery opening when they'd spoken on the phone the day before.

'Look I'm really sorry for deserting you, Amy,' she'd said. 'It was all just a bit of a shock. And then Clemmie called me and said she had a spare room in a villa in Sorrento and I thought that getting away would help me get my head around all this. Did you get the flowers?'

Amy thought back. 'I did, yes, but I thought they were from Nick.'

'What's happening with him? Your grandma said he's been causing trouble?'

'He was, but I went to see a lawyer and it all seems to have died down now. I haven't heard anything from him since he decided to drop custody proceedings so hopefully he's just given up.'

She didn't want to mention that she thought she saw him a few days before, sitting in a car at the end of their street. She hadn't been able to get close enough before the driver sped away and after that she managed to convince herself she was just being paranoid.

'He wanted *custody*? Why on earth, he's not even his father? Oh, talking of which, I hope you don't mind but I told Magnus.'

The revelation had left Amy speechless for a moment, although she wasn't surprised. If she was totally honest with herself, she probably knew deep down that Sasha would have difficulty keeping her mouth shut.

'What did he say?'

'Fuck, mainly. A lot of fucks, actually. He's thinking

about it. I told him not to talk to you until he's decided what he wants to do and that he should talk to me first. I hope that's OK.' Sasha becoming her secretary in this matter hadn't occurred to Amy, but she supposed it was better than having to face Magnus directly herself after all these years.

'It's fine. Let me know when he comes back to you though.'

The phone call with Sasha had left Amy feeling slightly detached. She wasn't sure what she'd imagined Magnus would say but wondered now if she was disappointed that he hadn't immediately arrived at her door, begging to see his son. But, she guessed, everyone needed to take the news in their own time and adjust in whatever way they needed to. Her focus was on keeping Brodie happy.

Judith was helping Jeannette in from the garden.

'Nana, guess what, I've got a daddy and his name's Magpie!' Brodie announced.

They both looked at Amy quizzically. 'It's Magnus, kiddo,' she corrected her son.

'Mummy, can my daddy visit us?'

Amy's heart did a little flip. She hadn't thought that far ahead in the current conversation. She hoped Magnus would want to have some kind of contact, but she had no idea if he actually would.

'I hope so, kiddo. We'll have to see about that later, OK?' Brodie nodded and jumped down from her lap, racing out into the garden to see the neighbour's cat which had just sprung over the wall.

'You OK, Grandma?' Amy asked.

'Oh, your mother's just helping me into bed for a bit, dear. I need a wee rest before dinner.' Her grandmother looked worn out from just sitting in the garden.

'It's been quite a time of family revelations after all,' Judith was holding onto Jeannette's arm. Her tone wasn't nearly as clipped as it usually was in her mother's company. She looked at Amy. 'I have a half-brother,' she blurted, shock still clear in her eyes.

'You do,' Amy touched her mum on the arm lightly as she went by.

It seemed to Amy that the secrets they'd kept in order to keep their family together, had actually been keeping them all apart in one way or another. As she continued to prepare Sunday lunch for her family, Brodie helping by laboriously peeling carrots one tiny strip of skin at a time, a feeling like something close to contentment settled over her. The crow appeared to have gone to sleep for now, its sharp beak tucked neatly into its glossy black feathers.

Without having to go to work, Amy had found herself at a loose end during the week of her mother's art show and her grandmother's ninetieth party. They had all become slightly curious as to the type of paintings Judith was going to display but she had closed down on them at their requests to visit the studio.

'You can bloody well wait and criticise me on the night like everyone else,' she had apparently told Ben. Amy had mused with her brother on the phone that their mum was at last showing a vulnerable side and she hoped the paintings were reasonably good, otherwise it might spiral her into some kind of breakdown.

'You know they're talking properly again, Mum and Grandma,' she'd said to him.

'About time,' her brother had replied. 'Shame it took until Grandma was pushing ninety and practically on her deathbed.'

'Ben!' Amy scolded. 'Don't say things like that.'

'Sorry, I didn't mean to be so blunt about it, but you know she's not well though Amy. She's probably going to need to be hospitalised at some point over the next few months.'

'We can't do that. Why can't she stay here?'

'Because she'll need proper care and drugs and, at some point, you'll need to get a job again.'

Amy had managed to organise a bit of freelance proof-reading and was playing with the idea that she might be able to avoid ever having to go back to a regular job. She knew of a few other mums from school that managed to work from home and seemed to do all right for themselves. Although admittedly they probably had husbands earning a steady income to fall back on. Still, it didn't mean she couldn't try to make a go of it herself, why shouldn't she.

'I know, but can't we work something out that's better than putting her in a horrible hospital. She'll be devastated. There's also absolutely nothing wrong with her mind, Ben. She'd be completely aware of everything going on around her. I can't imagine putting her through that.'

'Don't get carried away just now. We'll have a think and make the best decisions when the time's right. Hopefully Mum will be involved now too. I'm sure between us all we can work out what's best.'

30

On the Tuesday before the show, with Brodie at school, Amy found herself at the gallery, helping the organisers get ready. The gallery owner, Steve, wasn't as Amy had expected at all. Less businessman and more overgrown puppy, with his long wispy hair and even longer limbs which he didn't seem to be fully in control of. When Amy was introduced to him as Judith's daughter he said, 'Oh yeah, man, Robbie mentioned you,' and it had piqued Amy's curiosity as to why Robbie would mention her. She hadn't seen him since he'd picked up her mum from outside Ben's house the day they all went to meet Etta. Even then, he had only given them a half-smile and wave through the windscreen as Judith jumped in the car.

When she'd arrived at the gallery, a quietly mannered girl wearing round spectacles handed Amy a sheet of measurements and a spirit level and asked if she wouldn't mind helping to put up the hanging brackets.

'If you've any questions, I'll be around somewhere,' the girl said, flapping her hands.

Amy was curious. 'Where are the actual paintings?' She had thought she would be in for a sneak preview of her mother's work.

'Oh, they're being kept top secret. Steve and the artists are going to be hanging the work themselves over the next couple of days.'

'Oh well, I guess I'll have to just wait to see them.'

The girl smiled at Amy and left her in a section of the gallery that would be dedicated to Judith's paintings.

Amy worked away, following the guidelines on the bright white wall as to where the pencil marks should be made, and the brackets hammered in. When she'd checked off most of the items on the sheet, she wandered off to try and find the girl again to see if she could help with another task when she found herself in the room that contained all of the artwork that would be on display. Ignoring Judith's voice in her head, she began looking through the crates for her mother's name. In the fourth one, she found four paintings carefully wrapped in material and, before thinking, lifted the first one and gently removed the covering.

The moment the painting was revealed to her she wished she hadn't been so impatient. Her mother had been right, she should have waited. The painting was so personal, so obviously belonging to her mother, that she felt as though she'd stolen and read Judith's diary. Amy quickly wrapped it up in the material and placed it back in the crate. One thing was for sure; Jeannette was going to know on the evening of the opening that, despite the conflict over the years, her daughter loved her very much.

Brodie was staying over with Natalie and Etta at Ben's house on the night of the show.

'Are you sure you don't want to come?' Amy had asked her sister-in-law. 'We could share a babysitter for them both.'

Natalie had smiled but declined politely. 'I would love a night out, Amy, especially with you and Ben and everyone, but I'm so exhausted I reckon I'd be asleep in the canapés after twenty minutes. I've resigned myself to one event a month until Etta is at least two and Jeannette's party will be enough of a social life for me tomorrow.'

'Well thank you for having Brodie, I really appreciate it.'

'Don't be silly. I love looking after him, it's no trouble at all.'

Ben agreed to be the sensible one that night and drive Amy and Jeannette to the opening. 'I don't think Grandma will last the distance, so I'll just take her home when she's done. We don't want her too exhausted for tomorrow,' he'd reasoned. 'You stay out though if you want. Brodie will be fine with Natalie and you never get a night off. If Grandma needs me to stay with her for a bit I will, but if she's happy just to go to sleep I might come back.'

'I'm sure I'll be coming back with you guys after an hour,' Amy had said.

'Oh my, it's quite bright, dear.' Ben pushed Jeannette in her wheelchair into the gallery. Judith, who had been waiting near the entrance for them to arrive came rushing forward.

'You're here, *finally*,' she said, pushing Ben away from the handlebars. 'None of the artwork has been revealed yet, thankfully. It was Steve's idea to cover them all in paper and have a fun reveal for each artist.'

Amy glanced at Ben; she hadn't told him about the piece she'd looked at earlier in the week.

'Let's get a drink first though, Mum,' Judith was saying. 'I asked Steve to get you in some Croft's especially . . .' Judith wheeled Jeannette over to the bar.

'I'm not sure alcohol is the best thing for Grandma,' Ben tried to call after them.

Amy made a face at her brother. 'Why not? Will it kill her? She'd probably be better off if it did, given the alternative of going into hospital for her last . . . you know.'

'Look, I know you don't want to hear it, Amy, but she's only going to become more physically frail as time goes on. She'll need care,' Ben shook his head suddenly. 'Look, tonight isn't really the night to be talking about all of this. Let's both get a glass of something fizzy, obviously a Diet Coke for me, and have a look at what our mother's been up to for a year.'

'You do know she's decided against going on to the art college though?' Judith had made the announcement at the Sunday dinner when Amy mentioned she'd noticed a bit of freshers' week activity advertised around town.

'It's not like I need it,' she'd reasoned. 'I've already got a gallery show.' When she didn't expand further, Amy became suspicious.

'What else have you got planned?' Judith had swirled a piece of roast chicken around on her fork for a while before answering.

'Steve and I might be considering a bit of travelling in the spring. It wouldn't make sense for me to do a four-year degree when I can be off painting wonderful landscapes in Italy, France . . . It's not like I can't already paint.'

Amy knew now that her mother had been right. She could paint. The evidence had been in the fourth crate of the stockroom during the week. She was intrigued to see what else her mother had managed to create.

Ben and Amy found Judith and Jeannette near the bar.

'It's quite genius,' Judith was telling Jeannette, 'they designed little tabs that you pull, and it rips the paper so you don't damage the painting . . . Oh hello, you two.'

Ben put his arm around his mum. 'Can't wait to see what's under all of them,' he said. 'Really proud of you for doing all of this you know.'

'We all are,' joined in Jeannette. She raised her sherry glass. 'Here's to my Judith,' she glanced at Amy, 'determined as always.' They clinked glasses.

'Wait for me,' Amy heard the familiar plummy voice she loved, before she turned and saw Sasha, her face glowing with Italian sun and perhaps a glass or two of fizz already.

'Cheers everyone.' They all clinked glasses again and Sasha gave Judith a couple of kisses that threatened to actually touch her cheeks.

'Well done for telling my dad to bugger off by the way, Jude, glad to see he's finally realising what an arse he is.'

Judith smiled at her ex-stepdaughter. 'Never a fool twice, darling,' she replied.

They waited for another twenty minutes before a glass was clinked and Steve, in all his long-limbed, wispy-haired glory, stood on an upturned crate and addressed the crowd.

'I'd like to thank you all for coming along tonight. Those of you who know me know how much I love art. Art and people. They are my two greatest loves.' Some people cheered and a spattering of applause rippled throughout the room. He continued. 'So when I was given the opportunity to take over this old shell of a building and turn it into whatever I wanted, I couldn't think of anything else I would rather have than a space to display people's art. And I mean *people's* art.' Steve took a breath and swept his gaze over the whole room. 'There's a snobbery, as you all probably know, about art.' A ripple of agreement swept through the crowd. 'And I am a hater of any type of snobbery.'

Listening to Steve, Amy began to wonder how big a part he had played in the changes she'd witnessed in her mother over the last few weeks. 'So when I thought about having a gallery, I didn't want it to be crammed with the work of the artists that are used to displaying and selling their paintings for thousands of pounds. I also didn't want it to be a mausoleum of work from artists who can no longer profit from their own work. I wanted this gallery to be about people who are living in the here and now, who don't consider themselves a cut above everyone else but who have real art within them that they would like the community, their friends and family to see.' Some more applause ensued.

Amy decided she liked Steve.

'I don't want to go on about it all night, and we've got four very talented artists' work to start revealing, but I want you all to know now, to spread the word throughout your networks, that if anyone you know has struggled to find someone or somewhere to believe in them because they've not been to the right school, or the right university, because they don't come from a background that supports them expressing themselves, I want you to let them know that this is the place for them. That we love art here, but more than that, we love people.' A huge applause went up and Amy felt as though she was being carried along on some kind of evangelical wave. Steve's passion was effervescent. He raised his hands to quieten the crowd.

'So we have some of that art, by real people, to unveil tonight. My brilliantly creative friend Robbie,' Steve stretched his hand in the direction of his friend and more clapping resulted. Amy could only see the top of Robbie's brown hair from where she was standing. 'My friend Robbie, who is also now my business partner in this venture,' Steve continued, 'introduced me to a wonderful, fabulously complex and undeniably beautiful woman, who I can promise you all, does not only have a place in the gallery due to the fact that I now have the privilege of calling her my girlfriend.' The crowd rewarded him with light laughter and a few cheers. 'She is an utterly talented artist, who hadn't picked up a brush since high school until a year ago, and I can assure you, it is a good job she decided to do just that. We're going to start with revealing Judith Aitken's artwork tonight, because her mother is here and quite frankly she's had one too many sherrys already and might need to go home soon.' The crowd provided more laughter and Jeannette tutted. 'I'm joking, of course. The real reason,' he smiled at Judith, 'is because my wonderful girlfriend's mother, Jeannette, has turned ninety years old today!' Everyone turned towards Jeannette in her wheelchair and someone initiated singing 'Happy Birthday' and before Amy knew what was happening, the room was hip-hip-hooraying her grandmother. The crowd settled down again. Steve went on. 'So, without further ado, let's bloody well get on with it!'

Steve stood in front of Judith's ten paintings, all concealed by off-white recycled paper, and asked for ten volunteers to come and rip the tabs off at the same time.

'Do you want us to volunteer?' Amy whispered to Judith. Her mother shook her head. 'You lot just watch.' She had her hand placed on Jeannette's shoulder who had been positioned at the front of the group so she could witness the reveal.

'On three then,' Steve shouted after he'd positioned all the volunteers. He encouraged the crowd to join in. 'One, two . . . three!'

The tabs were pulled and the paper ripped open to reveal the paintings that Judith had been working on all year. People made oohing and ahhing noises and another round of applause broke out.

Amy's eyes had been fixed on the reveal of the painting that she had looked at during the week. She was more interested in watching her grandmother's reaction to that piece of work than to look at any of the others. She looked up again as the paper covering tore off. It was a painting that Amy knew was based on a photograph, which lived in one of Jeannette's albums. As children, they had all been allowed to look at the black-and-white photos of Judith growing up: her trips to Morag's farm, her first day at school. They were familiar with them all. The picture Judith had chosen to recreate, in her rediscovered deftly skilled artistry, was a photo of herself aged around four, sitting on Jeannette's knee, both of their faces open with laughter at whatever was going on between them or behind the camera. The most beautiful and poignant aspect of the whole picture being that mother and daughter's eyes were locked, lovingly, in the moment they were sharing.

Amy watched her grandmother raise her hand and place it on Judith's, who bent down and whispered something in her mother's ear.

Ben tapped Amy on the shoulder. 'Look,' he said, indicating the other paintings.

Amy swept her eyes over the rest of the work. They were all replicas of family photos from throughout the years but painted with such feeling that they were a hundred times better than the photos had ever been. Judith had included everyone that she'd called family at some point in her life. There was a recreation of a young Judith and Tony, standing at the bottom of the Eiffel Tower in the seventies, bell-bottom jeans and carefree smiles on their faces. One painting was of a three-year-old Ben leaning over a baby that she recognised as herself in an old-fashioned pram. He was grinning and holding a huge ice cream. She had even included Ken and painted, in her own style, one of the Christmas photos taken at the big house. Ken and Judith, Amy and Ben, and Sasha and Magnus; all posing around the elaborate mantelpiece with stockings hung. Amy was considering this painting when she heard a voice behind her. 'Looks like I missed the grand unveiling.'

She recognised it immediately, knowing the moment she turned around, it would be his face she would see. There was nothing else to do. She turned.

'Hello, Magnus,' Amy smiled.

'Hello, little one,' he replied.

He wasn't annoyed. She was relieved at that. He had every right to be after all; she'd concealed his son from him for almost seven years. They'd taken their drinks out onto the balcony at the back of the building that was suspended above the water of Leith. The river rushed by below.

'I completely understand why you didn't tell me.' Magnus leant his forearms on the edge of the railings and looked over at the water. 'To be honest, I'd have run a mile back then anyway.' He laughed. 'I almost ran a mile the day Sash phoned me to tell me. It was a bit of a shock.'

'Does Felicity know?' Amy couldn't help wondering if Magnus had been brave enough to tell his wife.

'She does, yes. I thought perhaps I could hide it, I'm not going to lie, but then Sash pointed out that it wouldn't be fair on Brodie if he was a secret, and I thought about it for a bit and I guess my dappy little sister had a pretty good point.'

'How did she take it?'

Magnus breathed in through his teeth and grimaced slightly.

'I've had better dates with my wife than that one, I can tell you. She flipped out at first. Mainly because she quickly put the dates together and realised we were engaged when Brodie was conceived. I think that was the main thing she had to get over.'

'And she got over it?' Amy could imagine what Felicity had gone through on discovering the betrayal and felt her heart squeeze with the pain they'd caused.

'She did. In fact, she's become a little overexcited by the whole thing. You know we don't have any children?'

Amy nodded.

'We were going to adopt but that whole process became incredibly disheartening. I think Flick has an idea that perhaps Brodie will fill the child-shaped hole in our lives.'

'So you want to be involved in his life? I mean, Felicity obviously does for her own reasons, but do *you* want to be Brodie's father?'

Magnus turned, a look of confusion on his face.

'Of course I do. He's my son.'

Amy smiled. That was all she had needed to know.

'I'll start supporting him financially as well, naturally.' Amy felt uncomfortable at the conversation, yet knew it was one that all parents had. She was just so used to doing it alone.

'You don't have to, we've always managed.' She thought of the parallels between her own situation and Jeannette's in the past; she didn't want Magnus and Felicity to have any control over her, as unlikely as that was.

'I can just give you whatever you need. Whatever the standard amount is.' He smiled apologetically. Amy had no idea how much an absent father paid for their children's upkeep.

'We can work it out later. Come on, let's get back inside and have a look at these other paintings.' She linked her arm through his. He didn't walk with her immediately.

'One more thing, Amy. I just wanted to say, I'm not really sure what happened that night, why we . . . but . . . I feel like I owe you an apology.'

She knew he was talking about how it had gone too far, and they'd been too drunk and, as the man, he probably felt like he should have stopped things. But she also knew she hadn't asked him to stop at any point and she knew if she had, he would have, straight away.

'Water under the bridge,' she said, leading Magnus inside as the river below rushed onwards.

31

When she woke the following morning, Amy had to piece together getting home and getting into bed. At first, she panicked when Brodie wasn't next to her but then remembered he was at Ben's with Natalie; probably just as well he wasn't at home, witnessing her waking up like this.

She padded through to the bathroom and sat on the toilet for longer than was necessary. Her head wasn't sore exactly, just foggy, and her mouth was scratchy and dry. Looking in the mirror, she grabbed at some cotton wool and started wiping off the black eye-make-up that had smudged all over her face. How had she got home?

Her grandmother was still sleeping when she checked on her, so Amy crawled back into bed and pulled the covers up to her chin. It was over; or just beginning perhaps. Magnus was accepting Brodie as his son. She'd invited him to the birthday party tonight. She groaned. Whose idea was it to have two big family events over one weekend? Hers, she remembered. At least her grandma's party was an early-evening thing. They were allowed into the venue at 4 p.m. to start decorating and were to vacate by 11 p.m., so, unlike last night, it wouldn't go on into the wee small hours. Amy chastised herself for not being more sensible. Today was about her grandmother turning ninety years old and she would be riding on a wave of nausea for most of it if she didn't sort herself out.

There was some Alka-Seltzer in the medicine box, which she took before going to lie down on the sofa in the living room, a Saturday-morning cookery show playing on the television to try and give her some kind of sense of normality. She was having flashbacks to the night before; small clips of scenes that she wasn't sure were real or not. Had she spoken to Robbie? Had she tried to kiss him, and he had backed away. She dialled Ben's number.

'What happened?'

'What do you mean, what happened?' Her brother was laughing on the other end of the line.

'I mean, what did I do, did I make an arse of myself?'

Ben had taken Jeannette home and made sure she was OK before coming back to the party and joining Amy, Sasha and Magnus in getting stuck into the free Prosecco and beer.

'You always make an arse of yourself, Amy,' he joked.

'Ben! Stop it, I really want to know, what did I do?'

'Nothing that bad. We were all pissed. You were talking to that Steve guy's friend for quite a bit though. What's his name?'

'Robbie. Did I kiss him, or try to kiss him? I have a horrible half-memory of his face quite close to mine.'

Another loud burst of laughter filtered down her phone.

'I don't know! I don't think so. Maybe. Who cares anyway? It was a great night. What about Mum's paintings? She's really good.'

Through her fug, Amy remembered her son. 'Is Brodie OK? Shit, sorry, I should've asked that first.'

'He's totally fine. Natalie had him helping her change Etta's nappy this morning. He says he's never having babies when he grows up.'

Amy smiled. She was looking forward to being at the party tonight with her boy.

303

'You know Magnus is going to come and meet Brodie?'
She couldn't remember if they'd talked about it last night.

'Yeah, and I think it's great. Maggie's a good guy, Amy
– Brodie could do far worse in the father stakes.'

They hung up after making the arrangements for later
and Amy began to think about Magnus and Brodie. Part of
her felt a little threatened, she had to admit that to herself.
It had just been the two of them for so long, the idea of
another family being involved was slightly scary, to say the
least. She knew she wouldn't lose him completely, but she
was on the edge of having to share him, something she
hadn't really thought about before. Ben was right though;
Magnus was a good man and he would give Brodie life
experiences that she couldn't give him. She thought back
to her own childhood, about the times they had very little
compared to the times they had far too much. Brodie would
have something in between, she hoped.

Amy had completely forgotten about her arrangement with
David and it was only by sheer chance that she had showered
and dressed when he rang the doorbell at midday.

Jeannette was in the garden, wrapped in a big woollen
coat and picking at a plate of oatcakes and cheese when
Amy led the tall stranger out through the kitchen doors.

'Grandma,' she said. 'You have a visitor.'

Jeannette tried to stand. David moved forward, reaching
his hands out towards her. 'Please, it's fine, stay sitting.' He
bent down in front of Jeannette's chair. He was an old man
himself but next to Jeannette he looked positively sprightly.

Jeannette took a sudden intake of breath. She reached
out her frail hand and touched the side of David's face.
'My goodness, you look so like your father,' she said, tears
gathering in her eyes.

304

David smiled. 'I've brought you some things.' He laid a parcel in her lap and helped her untie the string holding it together.

Amy could see some black-and-white photographs on top of the pile of papers. She immediately felt as though she was intruding on a very private moment.

'I'll go and make some tea,' she said, excusing herself. 'I'm sure you two have some catching up to do.'

32

Amy arrived at the venue at four as instructed by Janice and began hanging the pictures she'd had blown up and printed all around the room. She'd stolen the idea from her mum earlier in the week when she'd sneaked a look at the painting. The photos weren't as good as Judith's paintings, but they showed Jeannette's life, almost from the beginning, until now.

Ben turned up with Natalie and Brodie and baby Etta soon after and the grown-ups inflated balloons and hung lanterns and extra fairy lights until the room had taken on a magical atmosphere and Amy felt as though everything might just be perfect. The caterers arrived and moaned about the facilities and the band arrived to set up. They were technically a jazz band but had promised Amy they could play all sorts from the Frank Sinatra era too. Her grandmother loved all of that.

Judith was in charge of Jeannette's arrival, a job they'd entrusted to their mother earlier, as long as Steve was involved too; they had all agreed last night that Steve was a good influence on Judith.

Before the guests arrived, Amy took Brodie over to one of the tables in the corner of the room. She pulled him up onto her knee.

'You look really smart, kiddo,' she told him.

Brodie tugged at the shirt collar, buttoned right up to his neck. Amy didn't doubt he would have it undone before the party had even started.

'So, I wanted to tell you that I've got a bit of a surprise for you tonight.' Brodie perked up; she was certain that the idea it might be an iPad was crossing his mind. 'It's not an iPad.'

He confirmed her theory by slumping his shoulders down and letting out a little *Oh*.

'You remember we talked about the man that gave me the seed to help make you?'

'Magarus?'

Amy laughed. 'Magnus, that's right. Well, Magnus has decided to visit from London, and if it's OK with you, he'd like to meet you tonight?'

Brodie's eyes widened and he grinned at his mother. 'You mean my daddy is coming to Gee-Gee's party?'

She nodded.

'Yes!' He pulled his fists in towards him in a kind of victory display.

'Are you happy you're going to meet your dad then?' Amy asked.

Brodie looked at her, his eyes sparkling. 'Yeah, that'll be good. But I can't wait to tell Archie Smith that seeds don't just make plants. I'm going to ask my daddy to give me some of his seeds so I can show him.'

The guests began arriving as the band kicked off with some background swing music. Her dad and Muriel were one of the first couples to arrive. Tony kissed Amy on the cheek and she reached up to give Muriel a hug.

'Thanks for coming – Grandma will really appreciate you being here.'

Her dad raised an eyebrow and smiled. 'Where is the guest of honour?' he asked.

'Mum's bringing her in a bit, once most folk have arrived.

She has to conserve her energy into small bursts at the moment.'

The caterers interrupted them to have a word with Amy about the hot food.

'I'll see you in a bit, Dad. Ben's over there, he'll sort you out with a drink.'

Half an hour later, Amy's mobile phone started buzzing in her hand. It was her mum.

'We're almost there, darling, Steve's just ahead of me, wheeling her up the path.'

The band wound down their number and Amy took over the microphone to let everyone know that Jeannette was about to arrive. The guests gathered round the entrance in a semicircle and waited.

When Judith opened the door and Steve pushed Jeannette through, Amy and Ben were standing ready to welcome them in and all of the guests broke into a round of applause. The band started up a low-key version of 'Happy Birthday'.

From where she sat in her wheelchair, Jeannette's eyes swept over all the people Amy had invited. There were girls she'd kept in touch with from the office job she'd held until retirement. They were twenty years younger and so now retired themselves too, but as Jeannette smiled at them and gave them a wave, she saw them as the young things they were when she'd been their manager and they'd kept her up to date with what was fashionable.

There were the women she had played bowls with at the leisure centre, most of whom were in their early eighties now too. Her home help, Shona, was there with her husband and her two teenage children. There were some neighbours from her old street, who, until she'd moved in with Amy, had been a big part of her life for the previous thirty years.

Jeannette gave Muriel and Tony a wave and noticed Sasha and Magnus among the crowd. She tugged on Amy's hand. 'Did you invite Ken?' she asked her granddaughter. Amy shook her head and laughed. 'I think Mum made sure his invitation got lost in the post.'

Judith pointed out all the decorations to her mother, including the photos on the walls from Jeannette's life. Amy had arranged them in date order; from the first picture of Jeannette she'd found in her photo album of her as a baby, to a couple of pictures they'd taken of them all in Amy's garden that summer. Judith stopped at a picture of Jeannette with Morag when they were down at the farm.

'Can you see that one, Mum? Look at you and Morag – you were always thick as thieves, you pair. Nobody got a look-in.' Jeannette gazed up at the photo.

'We were indeed. She got me through it all. Made everything seem better when it was tough. Got you through a fair bit too, remember?' Judith nodded; she had never forgotten her mother's friend's kindness.

Amy spotted Magnus standing at the bar looking in her direction. She realised he was politely waiting for her to introduce him to his son. She cornered Brodie who was trying to prove to Natalie that he could do ten laps of the room in under three minutes and walked him over to where Magnus was standing.

'Brodie, I'd like you to meet someone. This is Magnus.'

Brodie stared straight up at the man in front of him, his eyes unblinking. Magnus bent down to come to eye level with her boy.

'Hi there, Brodie,' he said. 'It's really nice to meet you.'

'You're the seed man.'

Magnus looked questioningly at Amy. 'It's nothing,' she brushed it off. 'Brodie knows that you're his dad.'

'And what do you think about that?' Magnus looked at his little boy. The strings inside her that still attached her to Brodie tugged a little.

Brodie thought for a moment. 'I don't know. Maybe it's OK. Do you have an iPad?'

Magnus laughed. 'I do have an iPad somewhere, I think. But not with me. We could go for a walk out in the gardens if you like. I brought you this.' Magnus went into a bag at his feet and produced a mini-rugby ball. 'I could teach you how to throw it if you like?' He glanced at Amy. 'If that's OK with your mum, of course?'

Amy nodded. 'I think that would be a great idea.' She watched her son and his father walk hand in hand towards the gardens, already chatting, getting to know each other.

Sasha bumped into her side. 'All right, liar?' she teased.

Amy pulled a face at her stepsister. 'I thought we were over that?'

Sasha put her arm around Amy's shoulders. 'We are.' They looked around the room together for a moment. The band had started playing some Frank Sinatra tunes and one of Jeannette's old neighbours had coaxed her out of the wheelchair for a shuffle around a spot on the dancefloor. Judith was close by, dancing with David, Steve hovering around them with a camera, trying to get a shot of the newly reunited half-siblings.

'Could you imagine if your mum had stayed with my dad?' Sasha asked.

Amy thought for a moment, then shook her head. 'I'm glad she's met Steve though, and I didn't ever think I would say that about my mum and another man. You know I thought it was his friend Robbie she was dating?'

'What? The guy you tried to kiss at the gallery?'

'I thought I did! Oh shit, what happened, was he completely repulsed?'

'Absolutely.' Sasha turned to her stepsister. 'But don't worry, it wasn't because of the way you look. It's because you're a woman.'

It took a moment for the realisation to dawn. 'Oh. I see.' Amy slapped a hand to her forehead. 'Still pretty embarrassing, flinging myself at him, though.'

'Go and apologise then, he's just over there.' Sasha pointed at Robbie who was on the opposite side of the room, talking to Shona, the home help.

'I couldn't.'

'You could,' Sasha was already walking her over towards him. In an instant they were by Robbie's side. 'Listen, Shona,' she said, quickly turning after depositing her stepsister. 'I've been meaning to ask you . . .' Sasha linked arms with Jeannette's home help and led her away.

Robbie gave Amy one of his half-smiles. Amy's blush began to rise.

'I just wanted to say, I'm so sorry about last night. I don't get out very often.'

'Don't worry about it. I could just tell you were a bit . . .'

'Pissed?'

They laughed. 'Well, you'd had a few, and I'm never one to take advantage of that type of thing.'

'Or this type of thing,' Amy indicated herself and laughed.

Robbie frowned; a look of uncertainty flashed across his features. Oh God, she was making him feel uncomfortable again.

'Sorry, you probably don't want to be standing here chatting to me. I better find Brodie. I think he went outside with Magnus,' Amy was backing away as she spoke. 'Catch you later,' she blurted before turning and practically running out into the gardens.

Amy walked a few steps away from the building before realising darkness had almost fallen. The path towards Inverleith Row and the exit was lit by lanterns, but most of the garden was sleeping under the dusty blue cloak of nightfall. She squinted and tried to see if Magnus and Brodie were ahead, but there was no sign. They'd probably gone back inside when it started to get dark anyway, she thought.

One of her Grandma's old neighbours was having a cheeky cigarette at the side of the door back into the building. The smell reminded Amy of the nights in the student union in Glasgow, when smoking was still allowed indoors and she would inhale just enough of a cigarette to make it look like she was smoking and then blow it out quickly in a long thin stream of smoke, in the way she'd watched Judith do over the years.

Amy smiled as she walked past the man who gave her a small wink. It was cool outside and she was glad of a break from the noise and the music and chatter. Her hangover had abated but left her feeling in need of a good night's sleep. When she got to the end window on the front of the building, she looked in on the party and saw Magnus on the dance floor with Brodie on his shoulders. She smiled at the sight of them together and a feeling that everything was going to be OK settled over her.

Leaning against the end wall of the building, Amy closed her eyes. What a year it had been. She was still trying to work out what to do about a job, but she knew there were a thousand possibilities and it made her excited for the first time in years about earning money. She wished her grandmother hadn't had to have her fall for them to become even closer than they already had been, but she was grateful for the time they'd spent together. Then there was Nick. A dark cloud cast over her mind as she thought about him and in just the same moment she felt a hand grasp round her neck, squeezing tightly, dragging her along the wall and around the side of the building.

Amy opened her eyes, fighting for breath. Nick's face was only an inch or so from her own, his breath rancid as he panted in her face.

She tried to speak but couldn't.

'I told you you'd lose everything,' he was slurring, squeezing his hand more and more tightly around her throat. 'You think you're so fucking fancy, with your family,' he was spitting through his teeth now, 'and your fucking friends . . . and parties . . .'

Amy's eyes were wide. She knew he was completely uncontrolled, seeing red. This was what she had feared when she'd lived with him: that he could snap, do something he would ultimately regret. She tried to pull his hand from her throat, but it was useless, she wasn't strong enough. She couldn't breathe. Her mind started to float. She thought of Brodie and how she couldn't leave him. Nick was about to take her away from him. She tried to struggle again but he pressed harder and she felt herself fall deeper. At least he had Magnus now. Magnus and Felicity would look after him. And Sasha too. Her instinct was fighting against it; she didn't want that, didn't want other people bringing up Brodie but there was no strength in her left to fight. She stared Nick straight in the eye, hoping that he would see her, see something that would make him stop.

Tony landed the punch perfectly. Nick stumbled sideways then back, holding onto his face and then lost his footing. He landed on the gravel with a crunch.

'What the fuck!' Nick shouted. 'You've broken my face.' Blood was gushing down the side of his head.

'I'll break more than that if you ever lay another finger on my daughter, ya fucking bastard.'

Amy gasped for air, holding on to her throat. Tony was more animated than she'd seen him in years. He stomped towards Nick and swung his leg back, booting him in the ribcage with a sickening whack.

'Dad,' Amy croaked. Tony turned and came back towards his daughter. 'Are you OK, love?' His eyes were full of concern as he put his arm around her. They both watched Nick lying on the ground, writhing from the pain in his face and ribs.

'Let's get you inside,' he said to Amy. 'I'll phone the police for that fucker.'

Amy let her dad take her back to the party where she managed to clean herself up without too many people noticing. A curious part of her wanted to keep watching Nick suffer on the ground, but, of course, she wouldn't do that. If she had, she would've seen Nick push himself up, spitting blood onto the gravel and stand, holding his ribs as he stumbled towards the exit of the gardens and up the road for the next five minutes, heading towards the top of Inverleith Row. She would've seen him spot a shop on the other side of the road where he had an idea he could buy a bottle of water and rinse the blood off his face and maybe buy a bottle of something stronger to numb the pain; his face was throbbing and there was a deep hollow emptiness in his gut. What she didn't see, because she didn't stay watching him suffer, was that Fraser Harker, a retired detective inspector who had failed to let the DVLA know of his recent eye test, was driving up Inverleith Row, having spent the night with his old friends at the club, celebrating the retirement of another of his colleagues. Fraser Harker hadn't been drinking; he would never be so reckless, and he had tested himself before getting in the car that afternoon and found he could still see a number plate if he squinted from ten metres away.

He was sure all these eye tests were a bit too rigorous anyway. He'd only meant to go to the retirement do for an hour and should've been driving back when it was still light, but Bernie McConville had turned up and bought him another Diet Coke and they'd reminisced about the old days in the force when things were simpler and young people had respect for the police. He was finding the beams from the other cars blinding and although he was driving slowly for most of the way, he saw the traffic lights were changing from green to amber and he pressed a little harder on the accelerator so he could make it through because his wife, Kate, would already be annoyed at him for being so late. That's when he felt the slight bump on the passenger side of his car, something under the tyre, and thought he'd gone over some rubbish lying at the side of the road; people were always fly-tipping on the streets when their grey bins were overflowing: the council really needed to get a handle on this whole waste and recycling thing. Fraser Harker continued on his way, making it through the amber light and home in time for *Match of the Day*.

If Amy had followed Nick out of the Botanical Gardens and watched him stumble up Inverleith Row, watched him spot the shop across the road and step his foot off the kerb between two parked cars, she would have known that what Fraser Harker hit certainly wasn't the type of rubbish he thought it was.

33

'I think I'll invite everyone round once a month on a Sunday for lunch, what do you think?'

A week had passed since Jeannette's ninetieth birthday party and Amy was helping her grandmother out of her clothes and into her nightie.

The police had arrived at the party to take a statement from Amy and said they would be in touch. It wasn't until Wednesday that she'd received a phone call from them to let her know that Nick had been in some kind of hit-and-run accident.

'He's in intensive care but it's not looking good I'm afraid.' The police officer had sounded as though he delivered this type of news too often.

'Has anyone . . . is there anyone that's been in to visit him? Does he have anyone?' Despite what he'd done, Amy had felt a huge sadness at the image of him lying alone in a hospital bed.

'I believe his parents have come up to Edinburgh to be with him.'

Amy had paused, confused. 'But he doesn't have any parents,' she said. 'They died years ago.'

The police officer had given a small laugh. 'Well, there's definitely a man and a woman sitting by his bedside. Maybe they're just pretending to be his parents though. Although to come all the way from Portsmouth for someone who isn't actually your son would be a bit daft.' He laughed again.

Amy had finished the call and spent the rest of the day with more of Nick's untruths spinning around her mind. Who would lie about their parents being dead?

Jeannette hadn't answered Amy's question, she was miles away in her mind, walking through a part of her life from long ago.

'Grandma?'

'Sorry, dear. I'm tired,' she sighed. 'It's been a long ninety years.'

'Hey, enough of that! You've got to make it to one hundred now.'

'Wouldn't that be something? A card from the Queen.'

Amy tucked the blankets around her grandmother's ever-decreasing tiny frame.

'Can you pass me that letter?' Jeannette asked. 'The one on the top of the pile.' Amy did as she was asked. The envelope was open, and she could see a handwritten letter inside.

'Who's it from?'

Jeannette smiled as she clutched the letter tightly against her chest. 'It's from him.' Amy knew who she meant, of course.

'Is it a love letter? What does it say?'

'Never you mind, nosey parker,' her eyes were closed but the smile stayed playing on her lips.

'He must've meant a lot to you – I'm glad you've got something to remember him with.' Amy smoothed down the covers one more time and went to leave the room.

'Amy, wait.' Jeannette opened her eyes and turned her head slowly. 'Don't let Nick, or anyone for that matter, put you off finding someone you truly deserve. Because you do deserve happiness.'

'Oh, I'm OK, Grandma, don't worry about me. I've got Brodie, he makes me happy.'

'Yes, but there are different kinds of happiness, Amy, different kinds of love. All I'm saying is, don't let it pass you by if it comes your way. You deserve those butterflies.'

'Is that what you had with George, butterflies?'

Jeannette nodded slowly, clutching the letter more tightly. 'I've got them now, just thinking about him,'

Amy smiled. 'Maybe one day I'll have them too.'

'Fingers crossed.'

'Night night, Grandma, love you.'

'Love you too, dear.'

34

They couldn't wake her in the morning. Jeannette lay on Brodie's bed, alive but unconscious, the letter still resting on top of the quilt. Amy phoned an ambulance and then called Ben, who said he would meet them at the hospital, but that he wasn't surprised.

Brodie stood in the doorway to his bedroom, clutching his toy giraffe to his chest.

'What's wrong with Gee-Gee?' he asked quietly.

'She's just a bit under the weather. She needs to go to hospital so they can make her better again.' As Amy said it, she knew she wasn't being completely honest, but she couldn't even bring herself to acknowledge the truth.

Later that night, it was only Amy and her mother, sitting either side of the hospital bed when Jeannette finally let go of this world. They each held one of her hands, Judith talking quietly, her face bathed in the glow from the nightlight above the bed, remembering stories from her childhood, places they'd been together, people they'd known, through tears that fell silently and constantly. Amy held her grandmother's hand in both of her own against her cheek and tried to swallow down the pain that was pushing upwards. It felt as though her heart was trying to escape.

The letter from George lay on Jeannette's chest, and as she passed away, Amy imagined him striding into the room, just as her grandmother had described, when he'd come to collect her and their baby from the hospital all those years ago. This time, though, he would stay with her, holding her hand, and he wouldn't let go.

Brodie had taken the news in his usual contemplative manner at first, although he did ask Amy a couple of times if it was the party that had killed his Gee-Gee. He seemed to have accepted it until one day, a few weeks later, the information had percolated and an encounter in a café flicked the switch on a little lightbulb of realisation in his mind. The waitress put his plate down in front of him and said, 'Here you go, wee man, one scone and jam,' and Brodie burst into big fat blobby tears, his shoulders giving small shrugs as he hung his head down onto his chest. The waitress looked at Amy, alarmed, before backing slowly away from the table.

Amy leant across towards her son, taking his hand and rubbing her thumb in a circle around his palm. 'What's wrong? Did you not fancy a scone today?'

'That's what Gee-Gee calls me,' he sobbed.

'What does she call you, kiddo?'

'She calls me her wee scone,' he said, pointing at the innocent lump on his plate. 'She's not going to call me that ever again, is she?' Brodie looked up at her then, his eyes wide and wet with tears.

Amy shook her head slowly. 'No, I suppose not. But can you still hear her saying it in your head? Can you remember what she sounded like the last time she said it to you?'

Brodie looked thoughtful, his eyes travelling from the table to the ceiling then back to his mother.

'She said it to me at the party, "You'll need your bed soon, you're a tired wee scone."'

Amy laughed at the impression. Jeannette would've laughed too, she thought, and at that moment it struck

320

her that her lovely grandmother wouldn't get to see her boy grow into a man and another huge wave of sadness crashed over her.

She swallowed the lump in her throat and squeezed Brodie's hand. 'Well, you just keep that memory locked safely away,' she tapped the side of his head lightly, 'and any time you need her, she'll be there.'

Brodie nodded, wiping his nose with his napkin. He took a large bite of his scone.

Amy watched him from across the table, this boy that may never have been if she hadn't taken a chance, if she hadn't believed that because Jeannette could do it alone, so could she, and she thought how lucky she was to be able to call him her son. Some people think they give their children life, but she was absolutely certain, right then, that it was the other way around: Brodie had given Amy her life, and she would never be able to thank him enough.

Epilogue

Amy counted the bottles of Prosecco in the fridge, thinking she should perhaps nip to the shop and pick up some extra, just in case. It was the first time she'd organised an opening night at the gallery by herself and she was keen to prove to Steve that she could manage it: she really wanted the job.

She was thinking about putting up some more lights around the entrance, perhaps another few lanterns to illuminate the path, it would be dark later, when Robbie appeared, his hands stuffed into his pockets and one of his half-smiles playing on his lips.

'Hello,' he said, stopping a few feet away.

'Hello,' Amy replied, smiling.

'The place looks great.' Robbie looked around the room, stepping further inside and nodding his approval. 'What time do the guests start to arrive?'

'Around seven, although I'm sure there'll be some early ones in search of the free booze.'

Robbie gave a small laugh, digging deeper into his pockets. 'Where's Brodie?'

Since Steve had employed Amy to do some work for him, setting up events, researching potential new artists, Brodie had been hanging around with her at the gallery on the occasional afternoon. She'd had to cancel after-school club for a while to save some money. But Robbie was always happy to entertain her son for an hour or so if he was there too.

'He's staying with Magnus and Felicity tonight, they're visiting from London, booked into a suite in the Balmoral apparently. I spoke to Brodie earlier and he's overly excited about the fact there's a swimming pool in the hotel. Apparently we're going to need to buy a house with one now.' Amy laughed at the thought. She hadn't ever told Brodie about the swimming pool at Ken's house. Perhaps she never would now. 'Have you heard from Steve?'

Robbie shook his head. 'Your mum?'

'Nope, they must be having too good a time to bother with us.'

Judith and Steve had flown off to the Canary Islands two days previously on what they were calling *the first of many adventures*.

'Is there anything I can do to help get set up?' Robbie was taking off his jacket and rolling up the sleeves of his crisp white shirt.

Amy felt something close to a fluttering of nerves in her stomach and busied herself setting the Prosecco glasses in rows on the table at the entrance. 'There's some leaflets and brochures that need setting out on that stand over there, if you don't mind.' She didn't look up.

'No problem.' His shoes tapped lightly on the wooden floor as he made his way across the room.

She still felt a little bit awkward around him, even though it had been months ago she'd drunkenly tried to kiss him. When they'd spoken after her grandmother's funeral, there had been more confusion until eventually he'd said, 'I get the feeling you think I'm gay.' And Amy had blushed furiously, insisting that she was cool with it until he embarrassed her further by confirming that he wouldn't mind being gay, but that he absolutely wasn't.

When she'd asked Sasha why on earth she'd thought he was, she'd shrugged and said that she could usually tell, but that sometimes she got it wrong. Amy had vowed to remember how unreliable her stepsister could be.

'I think that's all the leaflets out now,' Robbie was standing next to her again. 'Anything else?'

Amy tried to think but she was finding it difficult with him standing so close. She looked around for inspiration.

'Actually, do you know what, I think we're all good now. You can get off if you want.' Her voice was slightly higher than normal, as though her vocal cords were being stretched taut. She could feel the heat of a blush rising. What was wrong with her?

Robbie stepped back. 'I was thinking about staying for the opening actually. Steve wanted me to chat to a few of the guests, folks he thinks might be able to invest. There's some people coming from the art college too I think.'

'Oh, great, sounds . . . great.' Amy poured herself a glass of water from a jug on the table and drank thirstily. She was suddenly boiling hot.

Robbie was looking at her, smiling. 'You OK?' he asked.

'Yep, totally fine, just a bit nervous about this evening going well I think.'

He stepped towards her again, touching the side of her arm. His eyes searched for hers and when she finally managed to look at him he said in a quiet voice, 'It'll all go brilliantly. You're really good at all this.' He waved his free hand around the room. 'Seriously, it all looks fantastic.'

Amy felt herself relax a little. He was right, the evening would all go to plan. She had been on top of every tiny detail for weeks now. But something else was bothering her.

'I was wondering,' Robbie went on, 'if maybe after we finish up here tonight, we could go for a drink – or something to eat, depending on how late it is?'

'Like a date?' The words tumbled out before she had a chance to bite them back. 'Sorry, I'm sure you don't mean it as a date, just friends, of course you just mean as friends, I'm so sorry I . . .' She was babbling. She closed her mouth before it could do any more damage.

Robbie laughed, his face lighting up. 'I'm not sure what we should call it. If a date is too much then it's just a drink, whatever feels most comfortable. I just know I'd like to spend some time with you, that's all.'

Amy noticed he hadn't taken his hand away from her arm. She could feel his fingers gently resting against her skin. She looked back up at him, waiting expectantly for her answer and she felt them begin then, fluttering gently at first, opening their delicate wings, bright and beautiful.

She thought of Jeannette and the last words her grandmother had said to her. She thought of Brodie and how happy he was to be spending time with his dad, and how she could still be everything he needed her to be, even if she was having a little bit of some other kind of happiness herself.

'I think a drink would be a great idea, I'd really like that,' Amy said finally.

And after all, she thought secretly, glancing upwards in the hope that Jeannette was looking down, spurring her on, *what's life without a few butterflies?*

Acknowledgements

Writing a book as a single working mum would have been impossible without the support I have from my wonderful family and network of friends, who so often feel like family too. In this sense it's been a collaborative project in more ways than one. So, here goes with the thanks . . .

Firstly, to single parent charity Gingerbread and Trapeze for running such a brilliant competition, highlighting that One in Four families in the UK are headed by a single parent and that there are so many positive stories to share. The opportunity the competition has given me is the stuff of dreams.

To Katie Brown and colleagues at Trapeze for guiding me through writing my debut novel, for being so supportive and encouraging and keeping me going even when I thought I might not be able to do it.

To my agent Rowan Lawton, for the opportunity to be represented and for being another fabulous advocate for the positivity of single parenting.

To Emma Rogers for the most beautiful cover design.

To my lovely mum Janessa, for being nothing like Judith and for keeping your mother's memory alive through stories. I never met my grandmother but have always felt she was somewhere nearby because of this.

To Mum, Sam, Dougie, Calum and Lindsay, for all your support and for providing Archie and me with a family full of love and laughter.

To Hannah, for the eagle-eyed spotting of the competition in the newspaper and unwavering belief that I could do it.

To Kate, for your constant encouragement, story ideas and one last sweep of the manuscript to hopefully mitigate any embarrassing blunders.

To all the mums who have taken Archie for playdates to allow me to write for a few hours uninterrupted – you know who you are and I'm very much indebted to you – return playdate invites coming soon.

To my colleagues at the University of Edinburgh who have been so supportive and made allowances for my incessant wittering on about the book, and to my friends for also listening, for sharing the odd bottle of wine and for making single parenting a whole lot less lonely.

To Moniack Mhor for the most peaceful week of concentrated writing and to Ailsa Crum for organising the writing week at Cambo House – despite the fact I couldn't join in with 4 p.m. bloody Mary's on the lawn.

And finally, to Archie, for understanding how important writing is to his mum and for being the best boy ever. Love you, kiddo.

Gingerbread
Single parents, equal families

About Gingerbread

Gingerbread is the leading national charity for single parent families. Our mission is to champion and enable single parent families to live secure, happy and fulfilling lives. Since 1918, Gingerbread has been supporting, advising and campaigning with single parents to help them meet the needs of their families and achieve their goals. Our vision is a world where diverse families can thrive. Whatever success means for a single parent – a healthy family, a flexible job, stable finances or a chance to study – Gingerbread works with them to make it happen.

www.gingerbread.org.uk